ON THE ICE

A STICK SIDE NOVEL

AMY AISLIN

TITLES BY
AMY AISLIN

ISBN-10: 1980807302
ISBN-13: 978-1980807308

Beta read by LesCourt Author Services
First draft content editing by Meroda UK Editing
Edited by Brenda Chin
Proofread by Kiki Clark (LesCourt Author Services)
Cover design by Lee Hyatt
Interior design and formatting by Champagne Book Design

For Reya, the light of my life.
May you grow up in a world free of prejudice and
injustice.

AUTHOR'S NOTE I: TIMELINE

Mitch and Alex were first introduced as side characters in my novella, *The Play of His Life*, which takes place during Christmas 2017. In *The Play of His Life*, Mitch and Alex have already been married for six years. They were never intended to be more than side characters in that novella, but they wouldn't leave me alone and begged to have their story told. In order to do that, I had to go back in time and start at the beginning, to 2008 when they first met. Thus, *On the Ice* takes place in 2008/2009.

ONE

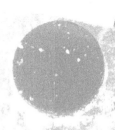

OCTOBER 2008

IT WAS STANDING ROOM ONLY IN THE TWO HUNDRED-person capacity lecture hall. Had Mitch Greyson known how popular this evening's kinesiology lecture-slash-panel discussion would be, he would've shown up early instead of arriving at the last possible second.

There was one last empty seat in the back row sandwiched between a blonde munching on a granola bar and a slim dude who smelled like pot even from all the way over here. Fuck. No wonder no one was sitting there. Well, beggars couldn't be choosers and all that jazz.

A shouted "Yo, Grey!" followed by an ear-splitting whistle had Mitch scanning the audience. About midway down, Chuck Yano, his teammate and closest friend on the college's hockey team, waved at him and gestured to the empty seat beside him.

Mitch pointed at his own chest. *For me?* he mouthed.

Yano gave him the finger.

Taking that as a yes, Mitch wove his way around people propping up the walls and sitting in the stairs. More than one person gave him the stink-eye when he settled into what looked like the second to last seat. He dropped his cafeteria smoothie—dinner of champions—in the cup holder attached to his chair's armrest.

"I thought you weren't coming," he said to Yano. He

nodded a hello to their friend Marco Terlizzese sitting in the row behind them.

"Changed my mind," Yano said. "What are you doing?"

"Huh?"

Yano flicked a finger against the notebook Mitch had taken out of his backpack. "What's this? You taking notes? This is an *optional* lecture series. We're not being tested on it."

Mitch dug into his backpack and found a pen at the bottom. "It's just in case someone says something useful. Possible career paths, helpful resources, post-grad degree or certificate programs that might be beneficial. Things like that."

Yano squinted at him. "This from the guy who's determined to get drafted into the NHL."

"Well, yeah." Mitch shrugged. "But just because I want to be a pro hockey player, that doesn't mean I will be. I'm good, but somebody better than me could come along. Or I might get injured and have to quit."

"Seems smart to me," Marco said from behind them.

Yano shook his head at them. "Seems like you're over-thinking things to me."

"Doesn't hurt to be prepared," Mitch said.

He inhaled half his smoothie, and took in the panelists seated behind a large table at the bottom of the lecture hall. The table was draped with a pine green tablecloth depicting the school's coat of arms, and each panelist had a microphone in front of them, as if this was a press conference. Who knew Glen Hill College had anything so fancy?

Glen Hill College—or GH as the locals called it—was a small school in the college town of Glen Hill, Vermont, so named for the hill behind the school called, you guessed it, Glen Hill. Or maybe the hill was named after the town,

Mitch wasn't sure. Either way Glen Hill (the actual hill) wasn't even really a hill. It was more of a hump, or a knoll.

"Do you think Glen Hill is a knoll?" he asked Yano.

Yano looked up from his phone. "The fuck is a knoll?"

"It's definitely not a hill," said Marco.

Mitch held his fist over his head. Marco fist-bumped it.

"The fuck is a knoll?" Yano asked again.

"Like a small hill," Mitch said.

Yano stared at him as if nothing Mitch had said made sense, his dark eyes all small and confused. He brought up the browser on his phone and started typing.

"It starts with a 'k,'" Marco said, peering over Yano's shoulder.

Mitch snickered.

"Grey, dude, check this out." Marco handed him a brochure. *Kinesiology Lecture Series*, it read, with a breakdown of the guest panelists speaking at each of the monthly talks. Marco pointed at one name in particular, Dr. Harry Hoare.

Mitch's surprised burst of laughter had heads turning their way.

"Brutal," Yano said. "I'd change my name as soon as I was legal."

"I don't know. There's a lot you can do with it." Mitch lowered his voice to a husky drawl. "Hey there. I'm Harry, Harry Hoare. Do you want to Hoare your way into my pants and lick my Harry balls?"

Yano and Marco cracked up. Even the guy sitting next to him tried to stifle a laugh. The girl in front of them, however, shot him a disgusted frown over her shoulder. Mitch waggled his fingers in her direction in a silent hello. She rolled her eyes and turned back around.

Well shit, what did she expect out of immature, horny sophomores?

"Dude," Yano said through gasps of laughter. "You got no game."

"Please," Mitch scoffed. He had game. His game just didn't involve women. Not that he'd ever tell his teammates that.

Only one empty seat remained at the table at the front of the room. He read the name tags in front of each panelist, double-checking them against the brochure he'd yet to surrender back to Marco.

Dr. Harry Hoare—*don't laugh, don't laugh*—expert in treating athletes with diabetes was a surprisingly good-looking guy in his early thirties. Then there was a specialist in drug prevention among athletes, a sports nutritionist, a massage therapist, and the ever-elusive fifth panel member, the guy Mitch was here to see: Chris Blair, director of sports science and rehabilitation for Tampa Bay's NHL hockey team. But where the fuck was he? The lecture should've started five minutes ago. The crowd was getting restless and Mitch was sure the panelists who'd arrived on time were about to lose some of their audience.

As if he'd conjured the missing Chris Blair, the door at the bottom of the lecture hall opened and in walked someone who was decidedly *not* Chris Blair. According to the picture in the brochure, Blair was a fifty-something gentleman with salt and pepper hair and a goatee. Good-looking in an older-dude way, if Mitch was the type to go after a guy three decades older than him. But the guy who walked in was—

Holy jumping hockey sticks! The tall, jacked guy who'd just come in was none other than Alex Dean, a Tampa Bay defenseman who'd recently been put on the injured reserve list due to a broken arm. He was huge and muscled, his almost-black hair in disarray, khakis and checkered shirt wrinkled, as if he'd gotten dressed in the dark or in a hurry.

Mitch might've drooled. Just a little.

"Is that who I think it is?" Marco whispered in his ear.

The crowd half-hushed as recognition of the newcomer set in, and dozens of hockey fans surreptitiously dug out their phones. Or not so surreptitiously, in the case of Yano, who stood to get a better angle.

Marco kicked his seat. "Dude, have some decorum."

Yano made a face at him and sat.

"It means—"

"I know what decorum fucking means, douchebag."

Mitch ignored them both. He only had eyes for Dean. The man wasn't handsome in the traditional sense. Rugged features, big eyes, thick eyebrows arrowing across his face, a nose that had been broken a time or two or six. Added to his pink lips, stubbled jaw, and the sheer commanding presence he entered the room with, it made for a highly attractive combination.

In the looks department, Alex Dean was leaps and bounds beyond anyone Mitch had ever met, and that included the guys on Mitch's hockey team, the GH Mountaineers, many of whom were certainly nothing to sneeze at. Take Yano and Marco. Yano, with his tawny-gold skin tone, sharp cheekbones, high forehead, and hooded, wide set eyes could've modeled for a men's fashion magazine. And big, burly Marco, who babied his shoulder length hair to a glossy shine and somehow fit his man bun under his goalie mask, had a dark, sexy smolder that mesmerized women. Had Marco been gay—and more importantly, had they not been friends or on the same team—Mitch would've tapped that. As it was, they *were* friends, on the same team and Marco *wasn't* gay. So the point was moot.

Mitch didn't sleep with friends. Anonymous hookups were just fine, thanks. No muss, no fuss, and above all—no emotions.

Dean had a brief conversation with John Halley, director of the kinesiology department at GH, then took the vacant seat at the end of the panelists' table. Halley stood behind the podium and raised his hands to quiet the rest of the crowd.

"Good evening, everyone," he said. "Thank you for coming and apologies for the late start."

"My fault," Dean said into the microphone in front of him, his deep voice resonating through the lecture hall. The half-grin on his lips practically oozed charm and confidence.

The crowd tittered. No lie, they fucking giggled, as if even the non-hockey fans knew they had a celebrity in their midst.

Halley introduced the lecture series, then the individual panelists. "And finally, we have Mr. Alex Dean, NHL defenseman with Tampa Bay."

The crowd applauded loudly. Mitch felt for the other panelists, who'd gotten only mild claps, but, well, they weren't celebrities.

"Unfortunately," Halley continued, "Chris Blair, Tampa's director of sports science and rehabilitation, was unable to make his flight due to unforeseen circumstances. However, as Mr. Dean was already in the area, he kindly agreed to take Mr. Blair's place at the last minute."

What the hell was Dean doing all the way in Vermont? It was a long way from Tampa.

"As some of you may know," Halley continued, "Mr. Dean is a GH alumnus and he'll be speaking this evening about his experience from the perspective of a patient."

More applauding from the crowd. Dean shifted in his seat, embarrassed.

"Without further ado, I pass the microphone over to this evening's highly qualified panelists."

Finally, each person spoke about his or her field of expertise. Mitch jotted down relevant notes every now and then, but his gaze kept moving down the line of experts to focus on Alex Dean.

Dean had once been the Golden Boy of the GH Mountaineers. During his four-year tenure at GH, he'd helped raise the Mountaineers' standing from a so-so NCAA Division I team, to a standout one that even went to the Frozen Four in Dean's senior year. They lost, but it was the first and only time in GH's forty-nine-year history that any of its sports teams had made it to the championship games.

Dean was a legend among the Mountaineers. Hell, Dean was one of the reasons why Mitch had chosen GH. Not because Dean was his hockey hero—though he wasn't ashamed to admit that Dean was his hockey crush—but because if GH's hockey coaches could take a small-town kid like Dean and turn him into a first round draft pick by his senior year, what could they do with Mitch, who'd taken figure skating and gymnastics as well as hockey while growing up, in order to improve his skating and flexibility? Mitch could be first round draft material too, and GH could help get him there.

Mitch had a plan for the next ten years. He may not have all the minute details figured out—like which team he'd be drafted by or what post-grad courses he'd need for his post-hockey career—but the steps were clearly laid out in his head.

Step One: Get good grades to keep his partial scholarship.

Step Two: Play good hockey.

Step Three: Help the Mountaineers make it to the Frozen Four. (As a sophomore, he still had three years to make this happen.)

Step Four: Lay the groundwork for a post-hockey career in sports science and rehabilitation.

Step Five: Get drafted.

Mitch was fully aware that the latter steps were all contingent on Step One. If he lost his scholarship, he wouldn't be able to afford GH and he'd have to drop out, which would have a ripple effect on his dreams (AKA Steps Two through Five), knocking them over like dominoes.

Step Four, however, was why he was attending this evening's optional lecture-slash-panel-discussion: Chris Blair. But Chris Blair wasn't here to discuss sports science and rehabilitation, which was a bitter letdown. It wasn't that Mitch didn't like looking and listening to Dean, but he wasn't the reason he'd come tonight. He didn't care about injury rehabilitation from the perspective of a patient. He needed to know what courses he should take, what postgrad certificates he should consider, who he should talk to, or even shadow, in order to get to the same kind of position Chris Blair currently held. Because that was what Mitch wanted once his career in hockey was over. Mitch had a list of questions for Chris Blair as long as his arm and he didn't think Dean—who'd majored in creative writing, if Mitch remembered correctly—would be able to answer them. Hockey, like most sports, was a young person's game. However, when Mitch graduated with a Bachelor of Science with a speciality in kinesiology, he'd be set to work with athletes, keeping him in the sport long after he'd retired from active play.

Hockey had been part of his life ever since he could skate, and it would continue to be a part of it until he died. He fucking loved this sport, everything about it. The skill, grace, strength, and athleticism that was part of every game… The friendship and camaraderie with teammates…

The power of a slap shot hitting the back of the net… The violence of a check that sends someone flying into the boards… The exhilaration that tickled his belly before every game, right before he stepped onto the ice… The scramble of players in front of a net, desperately trying to score or prevent the other team from doing so… Hell, he even loved playoff beards.

This was his sport. And if he didn't get drafted, he wanted something that would give him a foot in the door and allow him to work behind the scenes.

Dean opened his speech by echoing Halley's apology on behalf of the missing Chris Blair before launching into a short but impassioned talk about how an athlete is always connected to many people who can help them recover from an injury.

As soon as Dean sat back down and Halley opened up the evening to a question-and-answer period, Mitch's hand shot up. Next to him, Yano groaned.

Mitch saw—he *saw*—Halley's eyes land on him before he called on somebody else. Huffing, Mitch lowered his hand.

"My question is for Mr. Dean," a girl near the front said. "Will you be staying in Vermont while you recuperate from your broken arm?"

Mitch rolled his eyes.

"Um…" said Dean.

"Let's keep the questions pertinent to the lecture, please," Halley said, an edge to his voice. "Is there anybody with a relevant question?"

Again, Mitch's hand shot up. Again, Halley called on someone else. On and on it went until finally, *finally*, Halley pointed at him three minutes before the lecture was to end.

"Go ahead, Mr. Greyson, since you've been so patient,"

Halley said. Mitch was sure that by *patient*, Halley actually meant *annoyingly persistent*, but whatever.

"Don't get yourself thrown out this time," Yano muttered to him under his breath.

Mitch ignored him. "I have a question for Alex Dean. Mr. Dean, given that you've been with the NHL for the past two-plus years, and knowing what you know now about the organization, is it what you expected? And if you had to do it over again, would you make the same decisions?"

"Mr. Greyson, if you can't keep your question relevant to the lecture, I—"

"But it is relevant," Mitch argued.

"How so?"

"Well, in another life, had Mr. Dean decided not to join the NHL after graduating from GH, he likely wouldn't have a broken arm right now. But he did, and he does, which is how he ended up here today, talking to us about injury recovery from the perspective of an injured athlete." Mitch shrugged. "So it's relevant in a non-linear way."

Halley didn't seem to understand. His mouth kept opening and closing, probably searching for words.

From his seat at the table, Dean smiled at Mitch. Mitch enjoyed the flare of attraction that rose when Dean's eyes met his. The chances of Dean being gay were needle-in-a-haystack small. Hell, the media had linked him to a woman a few months ago. But that didn't mean Mitch couldn't try.

"The answer to your first question," Dean said into his mic, "is yes, but also no. The answer to your second question is a definite yes."

Before Mitch could ask him to elaborate, Halley said, "That's all the time we have this evening, folks. Thank you for coming and please join me in thanking tonight's guest speakers."

Mitch was already halfway down the auditorium stairs, making a beeline for Dean, by the time the applause died down.

Pushing himself off the chair to stretch his legs, and ignoring the phone that had started buzzing in his pocket ten minutes ago, Alex Dean wasn't surprised to find a tenacious Greyson standing on the other side of the table. What did surprise him was the tangle of nerves that knotted his belly when he got a better look at how attractive the other man was.

Greyson was lean and wiry and several inches shorter than Alex's own six-feet-four, putting the top of his head level with Alex's chin. His eyes were the color of chocolate, which matched his evening scruff and his messy, curly hair. Curls fell over his ears and his forehead. Alex wasn't sure if he wanted to run his fingers through them or pull on a lock to see if it would spring back into its curly place. A backpack slumped off one shoulder, he had a notebook tucked under one arm, a smoothie in his hand, and an impish spark in his eyes.

The man was hot. He knew it too, if the way his smirk widened while Alex took his time checking him out was any indication. Attraction, however, meant nothing to Alex without emotions, so a person's physical appearance didn't usually elicit a response reminiscent of a teenage girl with a crush.

Nonetheless, he shook Greyson's proffered hand. Greyson was twenty years old at most, and his flannel shirt didn't suit him at all. He looked like a kid playing farmer in his older brother's clothes.

"Mitch Greyson," Greyson said, setting his notebook and smoothie on the table. His backpack thunked onto the floor at his feet. "Nice to meet you. Can I ask a follow-up question? Or five?"

Five?

Without waiting for Alex to answer, Mitch continued. "Can you elaborate on how the NHL is and isn't what you expected?" He opened his notebook to a page with a list of questions that was way more than *five*. "I also had some questions for Chris Blair that you might be able to answer? What kind of hands-on experience do I need for a career in sport rehabilitation? Also, should I be getting involved in any kind of formal or informal research? Are there any courses that you know of that would help me get better prepared for a career in sport rehabilitation? If you were looking for an athletic therapist, what qualifications would you—?"

"Whoa, whoa," Alex said, chuckling, holding his hands up to ward off more questions. "Hold it, hotshot. You're asking the wrong person. Isn't there anyone here you could interview, like Halley?"

"I've already talked to them all," Mitch replied. "But they're all academics now, or they work in fields I'm not interested in. I wanted to talk to someone specifically about sports science and rehabilitation."

"You must've been disappointed when I showed up instead of Chris."

"Do you think he'd talk to me?" Mitch asked, eager as a puppy. "We could set up a phone call. Or I could email him my questions. Do you have his card?"

Alex tilted his head sideways and tried to read the questions in Mitch's notebook. There had to be at least two dozen, and he got the feeling Mitch was the kind of person who would have follow-up questions to his follow-up questions.

"Let me talk to Chris," Alex offered. "See if I can't set something up between you." It wasn't an offer Alex would usually make, but he felt bad that Mitch hadn't gotten to hear Chris speak when it was clearly something the kid had prepared for.

Mitch's whole face—which was expressive to begin with—lit up. "Yeah? Let me give you my info." He jotted his name, email, and phone number on a blank page of his notebook, ripped the page out, and slid it across the table to Alex.

"And, you know," Mitch said, tapping the paper right above his phone number. "If you want to use this for something else too, I'd be okay with that." Then he winked.

Wait. Was Alex being hit on?

He was mentally backtracking through their conversation when something must've caught Halley's attention. He made his way over to them with clipped strides, his mouth in a tight line.

"Mr. Greyson," he said. "You are not the only one wishing to speak with Mr. Dean."

Mitch glanced around and his eyes went big at the line of students behind him waiting to talk to Alex. Alex bit back a sigh. His line was longer than the other panelists'. He sent a mental apology to his friends waiting for him at the pizza place in town, even as the phone in his pocket buzzed again.

"Should you wish for an autograph from Mr. Dean," Halley continued, "the request needs to be made on your own time."

"Autograph?" Mitch repeated. "Why would I want his autograph?"

Alex choked back a laugh. It was refreshing to talk to someone who didn't give a shit about his pseudo-celebrity status.

"We were discussing career paths, actually," Alex said, coming to Mitch's defense. It was becoming clear that Halley had it in for Mitch for some reason.

"Is that so?"

"Yes, sir."

Mitch stood silently, his arms crossed, an annoyed gaze on Halley.

"Don't take up too much of Mr. Dean's time please, Mr. Greyson." Halley gestured at the cluster of students behind Mitch. "There are others waiting to speak with him."

As Halley walked away, Mitch eyed the line over his shoulder before turning back to Alex.

"Bet *they're* all wanting an autograph," he muttered.

In line were three women—one of whom was holding a tiny mirror up to her face and applying lip gloss—a man wearing a blue and white Tampa Bay jersey, and another who was unashamedly filming Alex's conversation with Mitch.

"You never answered my question," Mitch said to him.

"Which one?"

"Why the NHL is and isn't what you expected." Mitch tucked his pen into the notebook and slid both into his backpack.

"You follow hockey?" Alex leaned a hip against the table.

"Of course."

Alex tried to think of a response that wouldn't sound wishy-washy, but also wouldn't give anything too personal away. He didn't know this guy from Adam. What if he was with the school newspaper and was angling for a sound-bite?

Except as he was wracking his brain for an appropriate answer, it hit Alex all at once that Mitch Greyson was blatantly checking him out. Okay, not so blatantly that someone not looking directly at his face and body language could tell, but blatantly enough that Alex—who never got hit on by men—finally clued in. He was, in fact, being hit on.

It completely threw him and whatever Mitch's question had been? Yeah, it was gone. Not that Mitch seemed to care anymore whether or not Alex answered.

Was Alex giving off some kind of gay vibe or something? He'd promised himself a long time ago that if he ever made it to the NHL, he wouldn't divulge his sexual preferences for anyone. He didn't want to make a Thing out of it, wasn't going to give the media something other than his skills to talk about. Not that he was worried—at twenty-four years old, he could count on one finger the number of times he'd been sexually attracted to someone. At this point, he was pretty sure the whole dating-romance-marriage-babies thing wasn't in the cards for him. Not only did it take him forever to figure out if he was attracted to someone, but the way dating was going nowadays, nobody wanted to be friends first and wait for romantic feelings to develop, if they developed at all. There just wasn't an app for that. Instead, people were too busy jumping into bed with random strangers and having casual friends-with-benefits hookups.

No, thank you.

Hell, he didn't even like kissing. He'd kissed all of two people in his life and it hadn't done anything for him either time. It was wet and gross and unpleasant. The way things were going in his nonexistent love life, he'd be a virgin for the rest of his life. Others might bemoan their virgin status at twenty-four years old, but frankly, Alex didn't care. What was the big deal about sex anyway?

In today's sexually-charged culture, Alex often felt like an alien.

That didn't, however, prevent him from acknowledging the attractiveness of another person. Like Mitch, for example. Alex's extremely limited sexual experience was the reason the butterflies had come out when faced with such an outwardly beautiful person.

Mitch's gaze swept him up and down, a half smirk on his face, his thumbs tucked into the waistband of his jeans and drawing attention to his crotch. The man really was attractive in an I-know-I'm-the-shit kind of way. It was the kind of personality type Alex usually avoided. It was disingenuous and he didn't have time for fake people in his life. Alex's bullshit meter clanged and any butterflies that'd appeared at Mitch's good looks disappeared in the face of Mitch's in-your-face personality.

Mitch's gaze landed on Alex's mouth for one, two, three seconds. Then he took his time cataloguing Alex's face. When Mitch's eyes met his again, the man's smile turned lewd.

It was possible Mitch was the type of person who hit on anything that moved.

Eyes hooded, he leaned in across the table and whispered, "Maybe I'll see you around sometime."

Well, it was blatantly obvious what *that* meant.

With one last parting glance at Alex's mouth, Mitch turned and left.

Forty-five minutes later, Alex finally walked into the pizza joint in tiny downtown Glen Hill, Vermont. He was still faintly horrified that Mitch had hit on him while in full view of the other speakers and lingering students, but as he started to realize that no one had been paying them any attention, except for the guy who'd been filming them from far enough away not to get any sound, horror gave way to mild amusement.

It was also a nice ego boost, even though he wasn't interested.

Mama Jean's was two-thirds packed at almost ten o'clock. College kids having a bite before they hit the bar down the street, most likely. Alex took a moment to fondly remember his own college days.

His friends were sitting in a booth against the front window. JP and Jay were both Jonathans with unpronounceable last names, so on their first day of practice with the GH Mountaineers in their freshman year, Coach Bedley had given them nicknames. Yet people still got them confused even though they looked nothing alike.

Six-foot tall JP had light brown skin, dark eyes, and dark hair cut short that matched the perpetual scruff on his face. He had the whitest teeth Alex had ever seen and the friendliest smile. Jay, on the other hand, often joked that he was the palest guy in America. He was only about five-foot-six and he'd let any muscle from their college hockey days run to fat now that he wasn't playing anymore.

Alex slipped into the booth next to Jay and grinned at his friends. He might've spent the past two-plus years since graduation playing for Tampa, and he'd made great friends on the team, but JP and Jay were family.

"We ordered for you," JP said by way of greeting, taking a pull from his beer bottle. "Your usual. Told Mama Jean to hold the order until you arrived, since we didn't know how long you'd be."

"God, I miss Mama Jean's pizza." Alex missed Vermont food in general. He snagged a half-eaten slice from the mostly empty tray in the middle of the table.

"Is it weird being here while your team is still going on as if nothing happened?" Jay asked.

"Yes. Thanks for pointing it out, jackass."

"It's what I'm here for, man."

"How'd your lecture talk thing go?" JP asked, taking a bite of pizza crust.

Alex shrugged. "It was a lecture talk thing."

It was too bad that Chris had missed his flight. The kinesiology students would've gotten more out of his talk than Alex's boring last-minute speech. It was just Alex's bad luck that he'd been visiting his grandpa in Montpelier when Chris had called. Alex hadn't had the heart to say no to the man.

"How's your grandpa doing?" JP asked, as if he'd known where Alex's thoughts had gone.

Heaving out a long sigh, Alex rubbed a hand over his face.

"That good, huh?"

"Sorry, man." Jay patted his arm.

"He's not getting any better," Alex said. Suddenly not so hungry, he set the rest of his slice back onto the tray. JP nabbed it.

"People don't usually get better from Alzheimer's, do they?" Jay asked.

From what Alex could tell, based on an extremely thorough and in-depth internet search combined with in-terviews with as many neurologists as he could find who would give him the time of day, sometimes Alzheimer's pa-tients did get better, or at least stabilize, for periods of time.

But not Grandpa Forest.

It killed Alex to see the man he remembered as being upbeat, fun, outgoing, and wicked smart reduced to a shell of who he used to be. And it was compounded by the fact that Grandpa Forest kept mistaking Alex for his own son—better known as Alex's good-for-nothing dad.

All Alex wanted was five damn minutes where his grandpa would look at him with familiarity, smile his bright, toothy grin, and say, "Alex, my boy!" the way he used to, then envelope him in his trademark bear hug.

Five minutes for Grandpa Forest—Alex's biggest supporter—to see him play in the NHL.

"Let us know next time you head to Montpelier for a visit," JP said. "We'll come with you."

"That's… No—"

"Yes," JP interrupted him. "You've always been there for us. When my mom died, when Jay's grandma had a heart attack. You're going to let us be there for you, whether you like it or not."

Jay pointed at JP with his beer. "What he said."

"Fine," Alex grumbled, though he had no intention of taking them up on their offer. Still, his heart warmed at the support from his friends, even as he found himself annoyed that they wouldn't let him sulk in peace.

"How long have we got you for?" JP asked as a server deposited Alex's pizza onto the table. "A few more days?"

Alex took a bite, grunted around the food in his mouth, and swallowed before answering. "I'll be here until end of November probably. Just need to get back to Tampa for a charity gig at the end of this month, and I might spend a couple weekends with my mom in Toronto. Other than that, I'm here."

"You don't need to be near your doctors for…" JP waved at Alex's arm.

"There's nothing they can do until the cast comes off. There might be some rehab after that, but we won't know until my arm's healed."

"What will you do with yourself while you're here?"

"Oh, shit!" Alex slammed a hand onto the table, startling his two friends. "I didn't tell you guys. Do you remember Kate Harvey?"

"Nope," Jay muttered.

JP straightened and his eyes went big. "From our creative writing classes?"

"Wait, the one who wouldn't give you the time of day?" Jay asked JP.

"That's her," Alex confirmed. "She works for a publisher in New York and approached me about writing a book about hockey."

"Shut the fuck up. Dude!" Jay raised his glass in a toast. "That's awesome."

"What's the book about?" JP asked.

"That's the thing." Alex wiped his hand on a napkin. "I don't think the idea she pitched is going to work. She wants it to be autobiographical, chronicling my career. But truthfully, my story's not that interesting. I've been trying to find another angle."

"What about a highlights book?" Jay suggested.

"It's been done to death. I was hoping to dive into the sport, get into the nitty gritty. I just have to figure out what direction to take it. Anyway." He finished off his slice. "Tell me what's going on here."

They spent two hours talking about nothing and everything. Eventually, the crowd at Mama Jean's thinned, then it got busy again as semi-drunk college kids came over from the bar for food before heading back to the dorms for the night.

It wasn't until they were getting ready to leave that Alex discovered a giant purple drawing on his cast.

He glared at Jay. "Dude, seriously? Did you not hear me say that I still have a charity event to attend?"

"You can educate them while you're at it," Jay said, smirking.

"Pretty sure the only thing he'd be educating them on," JP said, peering closely at Alex's cast, "is that you're anatomically deluded."

There, drawn with a purple Sharpie on Alex's cast, was a giant cock and balls.

TWO

THE NEXT MORNING DAWNED GRAY AND MISERABLE, which pretty well summed up how Mitch felt. Sleep continued to tug at him, but he firmly told his body that it had gotten all the sleep it was going to get for now. He couldn't even bring himself to be glad that it was Friday, not with the full day ahead of him, and the full weekend, and the upcoming full week. He wasn't likely to get a full night's sleep until next summer.

It might only be 6:37 in the morning, but his roommate and best friend, Cody, was already mid-yoga routine in the living room attached to the kitchen in the townhouse they shared off-campus when Mitch dragged his feet downstairs. The lamplight reflected off the sun catcher in the window, casting multicolored hues against the walls.

Cody was just about the most beautiful person Mitch had ever seen. It had nothing to do with his tall and lithe frame, flawless fair skin, wispy dark blond hair, pale blue eyes, or perfect Cupid's bow lips, and everything to do with the fact that Cody had had his back since they met in first grade on their elementary school playground in the Hamptons. Mitch trusted him more than just about anybody on the planet, except for his dad. Once upon a time, he'd also trusted his brother the same way, but five years ago Dan had cut Mitch out of his life for reasons Mitch still didn't understand. Cody had stuck by him while Mitch cried on his shoulder and hypothesized about what he possibly could've done wrong that was so bad it had made his older brother hate him. Mitch and Cody had been joined at the hip since they were six years old, so Cody had felt just as betrayed by Dan's one-eighty as Mitch had.

Mitch knew Cody better than anyone, just like Cody knew every part of Mitch, even the parts Mitch wished no one knew. Like all the crap that had gone down with his mother.

"Hey," his best friend said, distracting Mitch from his thoughts. Cody's lean runner's body made a reverse V on his yoga mat, his feet and hands planted on the ground, butt in the air.

"Hey, Codes. You got in late last night."

"Yeah." Cody straightened out into plank. "You were asleep on your bed with your laptop next to you and an open textbook on your chest, light still on."

Mitch grunted. He plugged the blender in and found strawberries, raspberries, and blackberries in the fridge. They went into the blender. He peeled a banana and added it to the rest of the fruit.

"How was last night's lecture?" Cody asked. He'd moved onto his back. His head and shoulders were on the mat and he was folded in half with his feet behind his head. "Did you get kicked out again?"

Fuck, really? Why couldn't everyone forget about that? *Once.* It'd happened *one time* during last year's lecture series. One of the panelists spoke about the importance of tailoring exercise regimes to suit client needs, and Halley hadn't appreciated Mitch's question, even though Mitch still insisted that "Is sex considered an exercise?" was a valid question. Wasn't his fault Halley didn't have a sense of humor.

"No, I didn't get kicked out, thank you very much. I kept my questions strictly PG."

Cody snorted.

"Dude, you won't believe who was there." Mitch paused for dramatic effect. "Alex Dean!"

"Should I know who that is?"

Mitch rolled his eyes. He added orange juice to the blender, then got ice cubes out of the freezer.

"Alex Dean," he repeated, dumping the ice into the blender. "Defenseman for Tampa Bay."

"Defenseman? What's that, football?"

"Hockey, you moron," he said before Cody's snickers reached his ears. Cody was messing with him, the jerk, his body twitching with laughter.

Mitch threw a stray raspberry at him. It bounced off Cody's hip and landed on his mat soundlessly. Cody popped it into his mouth.

Ew.

"What was he like?" Cody asked.

"Really fucking hot," Mitch said, hunting for the peanut butter. It wasn't in its usual spot in the cupboard above the toaster.

Cody groaned. "Tell me you didn't hit on him."

"Only a little." If broadcasting his interest by checking Alex out and winking at him could be considered *only a little*.

"Is he even gay?" Cody brought his legs down, sat up, and bent forward into a lunge.

"Is anybody gay in pro sports?" Mitch countered. The short answer was *no*. Or, more accurately, yes but not many. Not yet. People who came out in pro sports lost sponsors, lost playing time, lost fans. Mitch wasn't going to let his queerness affect his future career, which was why the only people who knew he was gay were Dan, their dad, and Cody. If he had to keep his sexuality a secret until he retired, so be it.

"But what if you find somebody you want to spend the rest of your life with?" Cody had once asked.

Mitch had laughed and laughed. After Dan had turned his back on him, and his mother had cut him off financially when he'd declared his disinterest in the family business and his intent to pursue hockey as a career, Mitch wasn't letting anyone get near his heart ever again.

Besides, Mitch was so closed off with everyone but his dad and Cody that simply the idea of someone getting far enough past his defenses to discover who he really was, was laughable.

His search for the peanut butter brought him to the empty container in the recycling bin. Fuck, he was supposed to buy some yesterday and forgot.

"Did he hit on you back?" Cody asked.

"No." Mitch found a container of yogurt in the fridge and added half to the blender. It'd do for now as a peanut butter replacement. Then he added some protein powder. "He did check me out, but it was more curious than sexual."

Yeah, Alex hadn't seemed to know what to do with Mitch's shameless come-on. Mitch had seen it on Alex's face, when the man had realized he was being hit on. Alex's eyes narrowed and he got a little furrow between his eyebrows. The confusion had been adorable.

"Probably because he's not gay, dummy."

Unfortunately, that was most likely true.

Cody's laptop, which sat open on the island, beeped with an incoming message. Mitch opened the email, which turned out to be a Google Alert set for "Greta Westlake."

"Why are you keeping tabs on my mom?"

"I want to make sure she's not talking shit about you to anyone she shouldn't be," Cody said, falling into forward splits.

Aww. That was his Codes. Always having his back.

"Please." Mitch clicked on the link. "She doesn't give me a second thought, unless we lose a game."

The link took him to a job posting for an executive assistant to the CEO of Westlake Waterless Printing, Greta Westlake. Which meant that his mother had lost yet another EA. That made, what?—three?—in the past year, if the information he got from his dad was correct. It wasn't at all surprising that nobody wanted to work for his mother. She was a difficult, unforgiving, ruthless woman who took no excuses and expected two hundred and fifty percent. She'd once fired an account manager who'd asked for a day off to grieve her recently deceased dog. And she'd fired a guy in accounting because he'd had the gall to ask for a week's vacation that coincided with the company's busy fall season. She got away with it because she had an excellent team of lawyers at her back.

And she wondered why Mitch didn't want to work for the family business. *Yes, please. Sign me up for that bullshit.*

Not in this lifetime.

Mitch poured maple syrup into the blender, secured the lid, and turned the machine on. The obnoxious whirring broke the quiet morning and made Mitch wince. While his smoothie blended, he stuck a couple slices of bread into the toaster. By the time he was finished pouring the smoothie into two to-go cups, the toast was done. He spread Cheese Whiz on each slice, slid one onto a plate, and set it and a smoothie on the living room table for Cody.

"Thanks," Cody said, on his back with his legs tucked into his chest.

"Welcome."

As per their usual morning routine, Mitch rinsed the

blender so the dregs of their smoothie wouldn't crust and left it in the sink for Cody to wash.

With eleven minutes left to make the four-minute drive to the rink for practice, Mitch finished off his own toast and Cheese Whiz in three bites, then collected his equipment bag from the dining room they never used. He found the keys to the car they shared on a side table, secured the spill-proof lid on his to-go cup, and slipped into his hoodie and running shoes.

"See you after practice?" Cody asked.

"Yup."

He was out the door thirty seconds later.

Alex had no idea what he was doing at the GH hockey rink at seven thirty in the morning, sitting anonymously in dark jeans and a black hoodie in the stands, hidden in the shadows. Reliving his college hockey days? Regretting the broken arm that prevented him from playing for the next six to eight weeks?

Occupying his mind until his visit with Grandpa Forest this afternoon?

It wasn't uncommon for players on the injured reserve list to continue to travel with their team and even participate in practice sessions. Alex's broken arm, however, made it impossible for him to hold a hockey stick, which meant his attendance at practice would be limited to cardio conditioning and strength training, exercises he could do on his own anyway. And, as much as he would've liked to travel with his team, Alex had been given a temporary leave of absence because of Grandpa Forest's deteriorating condition.

A whistle blew, dragging Alex's eyes from where he'd

been staring into space and onto the ice, where his old coaches were putting their players through a power play drill. Alex couldn't see player names on the back of jerseys from where he sat, but he'd been sitting here since practice started at seven and he was starting to recognize skating patterns and body language.

The Mountaineers had won their first two games of the season. The third was an away game tomorrow against Colgate that Alex suspected they'd win.

Were any of the players on the team guys he'd played with when he'd been at GH? Probably. Maybe? It was possible some of the seniors had been freshmen when he'd been a senior himself. He was attempting to do the math when a shadow fell over him.

"Thought that was you," Coach Bedley said. He took the seat next to Alex. Alex secured his sleeve over his cast, hiding the giant purple cock and balls. Fucking Jay.

Bedley was a big guy, rough around the edges, but he was a stellar coach. Alex never would've been drafted without him. Bedley had spent almost twenty years coaching in the AHL before making the move to college hockey. He claimed it was less pressure but Alex couldn't see how that could be true.

"Hey, Coach." Alex offered his right hand, remembered it was broken, then offered his left.

Bedley snorted and they shook left hands.

"How's it going, Dean?"

Alex wiggled the fingers sticking out of his cast. "It's going."

"Yeah, I heard about that. You'll be out for a while, it seems. I'm surprised you're here instead of with your team. Sticking around long?"

"A few weeks."

"Miss us that much?"

Alex didn't deny it. Playing for the NHL was a dream come true. But playing for the GH Mountaineers had been...well, for lack of a better, non-cheesy phrase, the time of his life.

Bedley nodded at the ice. "Let me know if you want to get on the ice with my guys while you're here. If you're not going to practice in Tampa, might as well practice here. Give my guys some real competition."

"You don't think Colgate is real competition?"

Bedley scoffed. "Please."

Alex considered Bedley's offer for a second. "I don't know. We'll see."

"If you want to get back in the game in full-form once that cast comes off, you need to spend time on the ice. Shoulda stayed in Tampa, practiced with your team."

Alex didn't take offense. Bedley was all about the game, first and last.

"I have some stuff to take care of here," Alex said.

Bedley grunted. He nodded at the players again and said, "Tell me what you see."

"What do you mean?"

"You notice everything, Dean. That's why I always said you should be a goalie. I saw you arrive when practice started, which means you've been here a while. So tell me what you see."

To Alex's utter surprise, Bedley took a small notepad and pencil out of the pocket of his GH-branded windbreaker.

"What?" Alex huffed a laugh of disbelief. "Are you serious?"

Bedley waited for him, pencil poised above his notepad.

"Okay." Alex leaned forward in his chair, elbows on

his knees. "That guy—" He pointed at a tall dude who punched the Plexiglass. "—gets angry too easily. It costs him the puck. Your backup goalie doesn't interact with the other players enough on the ice. Shorty over there, number twelve? Nerves get the better of him." A freshman, if Alex had to guess.

"Do you have anything nice to say?" Coach asked, the *scratch scratch* of his pencil flying over paper.

"I'm getting to that."

A whistle blew. One of the assistant coaches said something Alex couldn't hear, and the players set their hockey sticks aside and started cool-down laps.

"Your D-men play together as if they've been doing so since they could skate," Alex said. "Your forwards are really fucking fast. And that guy, the left-winger, number nineteen." Alex pointed to a player who was chatting with the guy next to him, hands gesturing as he spoke. "He's agile. Got great footwork and speed. Incredibly flexible. He's smart, looks for openings. He's got a lot of talent."

"He's also a math genius."

Alex looked at Bedley.

"Seriously. I swear he does math during games, like he's calculating the perfect angle at which to shoot the puck at the boards so that it ricochets into the net."

"You're kidding."

"He does it in a split second," Bedley added. "I wouldn't have noticed it if I didn't know the kid like I do. It means he's overthinking things on the ice, and I don't know yet if that's a hindrance or a gift."

"Only time will tell," Alex said.

"You were right when you said he was smart. He's also the most dedicated player—and student—I've seen in a long time. He's doing a kinesiology degree, so most of his classes have labs once a week on top of lectures. He has a key to this place and comes in to skate and shoot the puck on mornings we don't have practice." Bedley crossed his arms over his chest. "And I get the feeling he doesn't get a lot of support at home. The kid kills himself working two jobs on top of classes, practice, and games, never mind the amount of homework that comes with a science degree."

Two jobs? Holy shit. Alex had never known a Division I player who'd had time for one job during the school year, let alone two.

"But Jesus, he's also the biggest shit I've ever worked with."

A laugh burst out of Alex. "Really? *Ever*? In your twenty-plus years of coaching, *that* guy's the biggest shit you've ever coached?"

"He's arrogant, and loud. Thinks he's God's gift to the world. And don't ever put him in front of a reporter. The stuff that flies out of his mouth…"

Alex made a mental note to peruse the online archives of the student newspaper later. He was about to ask Bedley for the player's name when yet another whistle blew, and the players trudged off the ice.

"Come on." Bedley stood. "Coaches Hannon and Spinney will want to see you."

Alex followed Bedley to the offices where he spent a few minutes catching up with his old coaches. By the time he said his goodbyes and stepped back into the hallway with Bedley, twenty minutes had passed.

Two men carrying equipment bags exited the locker room, one a tall Asian guy and the other… The other was lean and wiry and had curly brown hair.

"Here's the little shit," Bedley said under his breath, nodding at the guy on the left. At Mitch.

Wait. Mitch Greyson, the shit with the in-your-face attitude Alex had met yesterday, was a math genius and super talented hockey player? Something wasn't adding up. Mitch's personality on-ice—he had great stick-handling skills, uncanny vision as to where his teammates would be and didn't hog the puck, even though there had been a couple of instances during practice when he should've—didn't mesh with his personality off-ice. Although, there were hints that Mitch was equally as smart both on and off the ice. Alex had seen them last night when Mitch had come to the lecture prepared with questions. Mitch was clearly serious about two things—school and hockey.

Who the hell was this guy?

Alex wasn't in the mood to be hit on again and he briefly considered slinking away. Mitch spotted him before Alex could decide and he lost his chance to escape unseen.

Mitch's mouth kicked up into a half smile.

"Greyson, Yano," Bedley said. "Meet Alex Dean, defenseman for Tampa. He was a Mountaineer before your time."

"We've met," Mitch said, smirking, mischief alight in his eyes. "Come to see me play?"

Alex raised an eyebrow. Yano rolled his eyes.

Bedley sighed and stepped aside. "Get out of here, Greyson."

"Yes, sir, Coach." Mitch stepped forward into the space recently made by Bedley. He kept his eyes on Alex and that infuriating smirk on his lips never faltered.

If Alex had to guess, he'd say the brush of Mitch's bicep against his as Mitch slid past him wasn't an accident.

"There's a party tonight at Mama Jean's," Mitch said, full of smug defiance. "You should come."

Well, Alex knew where he *wasn't* going to be tonight.

But seriously, the kid was going to a party the evening

before he had to get on a bus for a five-hour drive to Hamilton, New York, where his team would play a mid-afternoon game against Colgate? For real, who *was* this guy?

Yano rolled his eyes again. "Ignore him." He pushed Mitch to get him walking. "It was nice to meet you, Dean. See you in the morning, Coach."

Mitch and Yano headed down the hallway and as Alex and Bedley watched, Mitch threw Alex a wicked grin over his shoulder.

Bedley sighed again. "See what I mean?"

Mitch hated parties. So much, in fact, that he'd rather work at a bee farm surrounded by hundreds of bees plotting his death, one bee sting at a time.

A headache pulsed at his temples. He hid in a bathroom stall at Mama Jean's and massaged his temples with the thumb and middle finger of one hand. The other hand held a beer he didn't want, bought for him by someone older. Mama Jean's was packed for tonight's party, whoever it was for.

He had to be on a bus tomorrow morning at seven. Mitch checked his watch: nine-fifteen. He had a biomechanics lab on Tuesday and a musculoskeletal tutorial on Wednesday he needed to do the readings for. His weekly written assignment for his human growth, motor development, and physical activity class was due Thursday, not to mention all the reading he still needed to do for his electives. Tomorrow was a write-off unless he could get some reading done on the bus ride to and from Hamilton. On Sunday, he had a full shift at his part-time job at the long-term care facility in Montpelier, then a two-hour session tutoring a couple of freshmen in college Algebra 101. It was brainless work for Mitch that provided him with some much-needed cash. His partial scholarship helped, but it covered only about sixty percent of his expenses. He still needed to pay his bills, and for gas, food, rent, and a portion of next semester's tuition and textbooks. He had some cash left over from his full-time job at a café in Montpelier last summer, but if an emergency came up—like the car broke down or he needed to replace lost or broken hockey equipment—he was fucked.

It would probably be another sleepless weekend as he did his damnedest to get everything done. If Mitch wasn't completely in love with his school and his program and his hockey team, he'd throw his arms up in defeat and call it a day. But he *did* love his school and his program and his hockey team and he'd earned them all on his own. Fuck if he was going to quit and prove his mother right.

So not happening.

She believed, in her own Greta Westlake way, that sports were "an enormous waste of time. It's not a real career, Mitch. It'll make you irresponsible and immature and if it's really what you want, then you'll have to do it without my help. When you come to your senses and realize that you need to pursue a business degree, like your brother, then I'll give you your tuition money back."

He shook his head, remembering. Even if, for some reason, he decided to drop both hockey and kinesiology and transfer to a business program, there was no way in hell that he'd *ever* ask for her help. She'd made it perfectly clear that she didn't respect his choices. He'd make it on his own, thanks. He didn't need her help. He didn't need anybody's help.

Determination was all well and good. However, if he

wanted to stay past this year, he had to keep his grades up so the school would renew his partial scholarship. And keeping his grades up meant putting in the work, which was what he should've been doing tonight instead of waiting around for Alex to show up.

Mitch might've told Alex this party was for a friend, but the truth was that he had no damn clue whose party this was. He'd heard about it somewhere and it had seemed like the perfect opportunity to hang out with Alex. Mitch wanted to go home, but he also wanted to stay in case Alex showed up, though the chances of that were laughably small. As in somewhere around negative twenty. He hadn't had any trouble reading the clear "Hell no" on Alex's face when Mitch had invited him. Alex either wasn't gay or wasn't interested. But for some reason, Mitch couldn't leave it alone. The way Alex looked at him… He wasn't checking Mitch out. It was more like he was trying to figure Mitch out.

That alone meant Mitch should steer clear of him. He didn't need another person in his life he was bound to disappoint.

Fuck, he wanted to go home. Because seriously, that bee farm was looking better and better.

His phone vibrated against his thigh and he fished it out of his pocket to find a text from Cody.

Need a rescue yet?

Cody always seemed to have a sixth sense for when Mitch was ready to commit murder. Or kill himself, whatever got him out of this miserable party faster. Cody wasn't even here and he knew Mitch was slowly dying of forced cheer and gregariousness.

I'm about to sneak out the back door, Mitch texted back.

I'll come pick you up. Give me 5.

The door to the restrooms crashed open, bringing with it the sound of voices and music that were once again muffled when the door closed.

"I'm not having sex in a bathroom stall, you jerk," a giggling female voice said.

"But it's Mama Jean's." An amused male voice this time. "You know it's clean."

"Not happening, Eddie. My brother's here and I don't want him walking in on us."

"Your brother loves me."

"Not if he finds you macking on his sister in the restroom. Besides, I have a perfectly good dorm room with a roommate who's away for the weekend."

A gusty sigh. "Fine. I must love you if I'm willing to wait an extra fifteen minutes."

The woman's laugh was throaty, and then she too sighed, but hers was tinged with desire. Gasps, moans, and the sound of wet sucking reached Mitch's ears.

Great. He was stuck as the unwanted third wheel as his two uninvited guests settled in for a make-out session. It made him realize that he hadn't had a make-out session of his own in a few months. Not since he and Cody had headed back to the Hamptons to visit for a couple of weeks over the summer holiday, and he'd found a hot guy in a gay bar in Manhattan who'd been just as willing and eager for a one-night stand as Mitch.

There was a clang, then, "Ow, crap!" Sounded like she bumped into the exposed piping next to the sink.

"Sorry, baby." The guy's voice was low, gruff.

"It's okay." A fast kiss, a second, a third. "Come on, let's get out of here."

They left.

Mitch rubbed a hand over his chest and leaned his head

back against the stall wall. Sometimes he wished he had an Eddie. Someone to come home to. Someone whose family would welcome him. Someone to soothe his hurts. He was usually too busy to acknowledge the loneliness inside him, but listening to Eddie and his girlfriend kiss not only with affection but with tenderness? The loneliness hit him suddenly, like a check into the boards he hadn't seen coming.

He might've promised himself that he wouldn't let anybody close again—he had to protect himself somehow, so he wouldn't be hurt when the world found him lacking—but that didn't mean he didn't miss the connection with another human being. Not necessarily a sexual one, but an intimate one, like the one he used to have with Dan. It was because of Dan, and because of his mother's callousness, that Mitch had come to GH in the first place, determined to start fresh. No one knew him here except for Cody, so he could be whoever he wanted to be with everyone else, hide behind a brash exterior.

But that meant that nobody really knew him. Sometimes, he felt the pressure of hiding who he was wearing him down, but he'd gotten into the habit and he didn't know how to make himself vulnerable, how to let anyone in. How could he, when he didn't really know who he was anymore? Had he turned into the person he'd been pretending to be for over a year, the one that was only meant to keep his heart safe? Or was he still the same person he'd always been, the one Cody knew?

The pulsing in his temples had turned into a throb. Mitch lowered the toilet seat, sat, and waited for his best friend to come rescue him.

THREE

MITCH HAD WANTED TO TAKE A FULL COURSE load of kinesiology courses this year, but his academic advisor had strongly hinted that it would benefit him to take a few courses outside his major. Apparently, it would make Mitch seem like a more well-rounded person. Plus, he still needed to fulfill his general electives. So instead, he found himself with two non-kinesiology courses: geography—which was hella interesting—and creative writing—which was not. Creative writing was, in fact, kicking his ass.

That was why he found himself trudging into his creative writing tutorial with trepidation on the Thursday after the Colgate game—which they'd won handily, 6-1. He'd gotten a lousy grade on his previous assignment and he wasn't expecting much better on the one he'd handed in two weeks ago. They were supposed to get their grades today, but Mitch wasn't sure he wanted his.

It was just his luck that he'd ended up with the TA who was rumored to be a hardass. A rumor that had proved true when the TA had called Mitch's previous assignment amateurish.

"It lacks substance," he'd said.

Substance. How was Mitch supposed to inject *substance* into a short story of five hundred words or less?

When class started, the TA, John, handed him back his assignment. As Mitch had suspected, it was marked with red pen. Everywhere. Instead of a grade, he had a note written in all-caps at the top—again in red pen: SEE ME DURING OFFICE HOURS.

Fuck.

Mitch read through John's comments, which spanned everything from grammar and sentence structure to character development and setting. He should've ignored his academic advisor and gotten a head start on next year's kinesiology classes, at least the ones that didn't have a second-year prerequisite. Math and science were way easier than this writing shit.

If he failed this assignment, would that bring his GPA down enough to affect his scholarship? Heart pounding, he ignored the TA droning on at the front of the room and flipped his assignment over. He drew two columns on the back with shaking hands. The number of credits for each course went into one column; his anticipated grade on a 4.0 scale went into the next. Assuming he'd ace his kinesiology and geography courses—they were no-brainers compared to this—and failed creative writing, or did poorly enough that his grade hovered just above passing… He did some quick math, and…

Shit. It would bring his GPA down just enough that he'd be below the cut-off GPA for the scholarship.

When the TA turned his back, Mitch got his phone out.

I'M GONNA FAIL OUT OF SCHOOL! He texted Cody. Fail out of school and prove to his mother that he really was irresponsible and immature.

Losing the scholarship, despite it being a partial, meant he wouldn't be able to pay his tuition. No tuition money meant no school, no hockey, no eventual Frozen Four, no draft, no Bachelor of Science with a major in kinesiology, no job as a sports science and rehabilitation specialist.

Okay, wait. No need to panic. *Don't panic. Not yet.*

He was panicking. So much that he didn't realize the forty-five-minute tutorial had ended until the screech of chair legs on tile floor and the mass exodus of a dozen students brought him back to the present from a future where he really did work on a bee farm.

"Mitch?" John said. "My office hours start in fifteen minutes. Drop by if you'd like to go over your assignment." He smiled and it was a friendly smile, not one that said *I can't wait to fail you, plebeian!*

Mitch nodded, but he had no intention of going, not today. The TA packed up his bag and left, leaving Mitch sitting alone in an empty classroom.

Eventually, he had to get up and go when students started pouring in for the next class. He met Cody at the car, convinced he'd never listen to his academic advisor ever again. Not that he'd have to, seeing as he was about to fail out of school.

Cody took one look at him and said, "Tell me what happened."

So Mitch did, and got no sympathy from his best friend.

"Literally nobody fails creative writing," Cody said, navigating out of the student parking lot. "Don't you think you're being overly dramatic?"

"I'm allowed to be, since I'm going to *fail out of school.*"

"Why don't you just drop the class?"

"Can't. The drop deadline's passed. I wouldn't get a refund and it's too late in the semester to join a different class, which means I'd be down a credit that I'd have to make up next semester or next year, but I don't have time for an extra class and—"

"Okay, breathe." Cody squeezed Mitch's knee. "Breathe, Mitch."

Doing as ordered, Mitch took a deep breath in, then let

it out slowly. He waved a hand at the Green Day song on the radio. "This is going to be me any day now. Walking on the boulevard of my broken dreams."

Cody laughed and couldn't seem to stop. "You're ridiculous. And you're not going to fail. When you stop being all princess-y over it, you'll realize that it's early in the year and that there's still plenty of time to make up your grade."

Mitch didn't know what *being all princess-y* meant, so he ignored Cody and stared out the window at the rolling Vermont hills they passed on the way home. At this time of the year, the colors were vibrant reds and golden oranges and sunny yellows. It was fall tourist season in Vermont, but he rarely bumped into visitors unless he ventured into Montpelier. Glen Hill wasn't a big enough town to warrant a visit, and it wasn't on the way to anywhere that was. Mitch liked it that way.

"Did you talk to your TA?" Cody asked.

Mitch sighed and rested his head back against the seat. "No, I just…couldn't. He has office hours on Monday. I'll go then."

"It's probably a good thing that he wants to talk to you," Cody said. "And you said he didn't actually grade your assignment, right? Maybe he's willing to give you a chance to revise and resubmit."

Good point. In which case, he could do more research on what *substance* was. And if the TA wasn't willing to let him resubmit, Mitch could ask for an extra credit assignment and/or work harder on the next two assignments to get a better grade. He did some quick math in his head. If he brought his mark up in the class by a few points, it should bring his GPA back up to where it needed to be for the scholarship. He'd work extra, extra hard and put some serious mojo into the next assignments, since they weighed more in the final grade calculations. If he failed those too, he'd really be in the sin bin.

"Maybe I overreacted," he said.

Cody laughed. "Nah, you just needed to have a meltdown before logic kicked back in. Trust me, you're not going to end up working at a bee farm for the rest of your life. If such a thing even exists."

"They must. Isn't that where honey comes from?"

Cody pulled into their driveway. "I guess?"

"Speaking of honey, do we have any food?"

"Besides Cheese Whiz?" Cody made a dubious face. "Fruit. Bread. Mama Jean's?"

"Can we afford it?"

"If we split a pie."

"Let's do it."

"Dude, it won't work."

"Oh, I'll *make* it work."

Alex sighed and let JP attempt to use correction tape on the purple cock and balls on his cast.

"It didn't work when I tried it earlier," Alex said. He nabbed a slice of pizza with his free hand.

Like during their college days, Alex and JP found themselves at Mama Jean's for dinner on yet another Thursday evening. Also like their college days, they were trying to deal with another sample of Jay's crude artwork.

They were tucked into a booth in the back corner, where the lighting was dim and the smells coming from the kitchen made him crave a second pizza.

"Looks like it works okay to me," JP said.

"It'll flake off in an hour." And now, instead of a purple

cock and balls, he had a stark white cock and balls that stood out like a sign on his cream colored cast. Truthfully, he wasn't sure which was worse. Fucking Jay.

JP ran his thumbnail along the edge of the correction tape. It flaked right off.

He huffed and sat back against the booth. "Well, that sucks. What if we expand on the drawing and turn it into, I don't know, balloons?"

"Like party balloons?" Alex tilted his head and peered at the drawing on his cast. "That might work. But I wonder if it'll only make things worse."

JP got a spiral bound notebook and pencil out of his bag. He replicated the drawing from Alex's cast onto the paper, added a third circle in between the two balls, colored in the cock head and added two triangles attached to its sides, forming a bow.

"Now it looks like a cock with three balls being offered as a present," Alex said.

"Think it's possible for a dude to have three balls?"

"Yeah. It's called polyorchidism."

"You would know that." JP paused. "*Why* do you know that?"

"I don't know. Probably research for something I was writing."

JP drew another replica of Alex's cock and balls on his paper and added…a tail?

"What the fuck is that?" Alex asked.

JP added two small triangles on top of the cock head. "We might be able to turn it into a cat."

"I don't want a cat on my cast."

"Do you want a cock and balls?"

"Well, no. But I don't want your creepy cat wannabe either."

JP drew a big X on the cock and balls turned cat and snapped his notebook closed.

Alex kicked JP's foot with his under the table. "What's going on with you today? You've been in a mood since we got here."

JP stole the crust out of Alex's hands and took a bite.

"Hey!"

"I have a student," JP said around his mouthful, "who's *this* close to failing out of my class. Pretty sure he knows it too, but does he come see me during my office hours today? No. I don't want to fucking fail this kid, but if he doesn't show up to talk to me about it, what am I supposed to do?"

"Who the hell fails creative writing?"

"Right?"

"He's not turning in his assignments?" Alex guessed.

"No, he is. They're just not any good."

"So, he's half-assing them?"

JP dropped the rest of the crust on the tray and wiped his hands on a napkin. "Thing is, I don't think he is. I think he's putting as much effort as he can into them, but he's just… not a writer. He doesn't understand the structure of a story. I think he's a science major. His writing reads more like a lab report than a story." JP sighed. "Fuck, I need another beer."

Alex got up and headed for the order counter where he got them each a beer, giving his friend a moment to stew. Grabbing the bottles by the neck with his good hand, he made his way back to JP, set the beers down, and said, "Is there a tutor who could help him?"

"The English department has a few on the roster," JP said. "But they tutor in English lit, not creative writing."

"You'll think of something."

"I think the reason he didn't come see me—" JP winced. "—is because I called his last assignment amateurish."

"John Patrick!"

"I know." JP buried his face in his hands. "I know, okay? So unprofessional. But he walked into my office after class, waving his assignment at me, demanding to know who the hell I thought I was to give him a D-minus, and it caught me off-guard. I said his writing had no substance."

"That's not the worst feedback," Alex said in an attempt to make his friend feel better.

JP sighed and slumped in his seat. "Can we go back to talking about your cock and balls? That was much less stressful."

"For you, maybe. I have to go to a charity event at the end of the month with this thing."

"Wear long sleeves."

"It's a street hockey game with underprivileged kids. In Tampa." It was fucking hot during the day in Tampa, even in October. He'd sweat his balls off in a long-sleeved T-shirt.

"Oh, shit." JP grinned wide. "Can I come?"

"Hell no."

"Aww, have some love for your black brother."

"I have a lot of love for my black brother. Just not enough to put him in front of impressionable kids."

"Hey, I'm not the one who drew a cock and balls on your cast."

That was true. "Did I tell you that I think I figured out an angle for the book?"

"No shit? Tell me."

"Coach Bedley gave me the idea." Alex took a sip of water. "There's a kid on his team who's basically killing himself for the game. He's got a key to the rink so he can practice every morning that there isn't already a scheduled practice. He's in a science program, so he's busy as fuck and yet he still works two jobs to make ends meet since he doesn't see much support from his parents. According to Bedley, anyway. But it gave me the idea to dig deeper into the psyche of a hockey player. What will they do in the name of the game? What will they sacrifice? What's the cost of a hockey career?"

"Hmm." JP drummed his fingers on the table. "So, it's like the darker side of sports."

"Exactly."

"I like it. Did Kate go for it?"

"She did." Thank God. He didn't want to think about going back to the drawing board. Luckily, his editor had loved the idea.

"Cool." JP leaned forward, his gaze earnest. "Don't suppose you'll give me her number?"

"So you can be shot down yet again?"

Buffing his nails on his T-shirt, JP said, "Hey, I have slicker moves now."

That was highly doubtful.

Alex's phone buzzed in his pocket. He checked the caller ID, then waved the phone at JP. "Mind if I take this? It's my mom."

"Still a mama's boy," JP teased, a glint in his dark eyes.

"Still a jackass," Alex replied.

Alex headed for the hallway that led to the washrooms, where it was quieter, ignoring JP's laughter trailing after him.

When Mitch spotted Yano, Marco, and a few other friends entering Mama Jean's, he ducked down in the booth he was sharing with Cody. He wanted a quiet night with his best friend, not an evening of forced cheer and crude jokes.

That was the problem with a small school and a small town—everywhere he went he inevitably ran into someone he knew.

He slid all the way to the end of the bench seat and turned his face into the wall.

"Subtle," Cody said.

"Fuck you," Mitch said, chuckling.

A few seconds later, Cody said, "They're out of sight."

Sure enough, when Mitch looked up, his friends were gone, likely occupying a booth on the other side of the restaurant.

"This isn't the best place to be if you don't want to run into them," Cody said, pointing out the obvious.

Mitch eyeballed him, unimpressed.

Cody shrugged. "What? I'm just saying." He took some change out of his pocket and left it on the table for the tip. "Ready to go?"

"I need to use the restroom first."

Mitch took the long way around to avoid being seen by his friends. He wasn't in the mood to be social. He wanted to go home with Cody, do some course reading, and sulk about his creative writing class.

His plans took a backseat when he found Alex Dean getting off his phone in the hallway that led to the restrooms. Alex noticed him and his head jerked back, his hand clenched on his phone, and his entire body language said *Brace for impact!*

Not exactly flattering, but Mitch didn't let that stop him. He tilted his head and smiled at Alex in a way that often had guys falling at his feet.

Unfortunately, Alex appeared to be immune.

Mitch pressed on anyway, despite the small part of him that told him to quit while he was ahead. Alex obviously wasn't interested, but this was Mitch's hockey crush and Alex was *right there.* Yet still, Mitch couldn't get him to give him the time of day.

What did a guy have to do for five minutes of Alex Dean's time? He'd even take non-sexy time. Five minutes to talk about Alex's journey from small-town Canadian hockey player, to the Ontario major juniors, to being recruited by GH, to the freakin' NHL *draft.* Five minutes to find out what, if anything, Alex would've done differently, knowing what he knew now. Five minutes of conversation to learn something from him, maybe have him autograph a napkin.

Instead of going the getting-to-know-you route, Mitch fell back on an old standard: sex. Sex was easy. In and out, no games, and better—no expectations.

He normally wouldn't hit on a guy without first knowing A) whether the object of his lust was gay, and B) whether they recognized him as the GH Mountaineers left winger with aspirations of playing in the NHL. Because there was undoubtedly some asshole out there who would delight in outing Mitch publicly, thus fucking up his career prospects.

That being said, there was something about Alex that screamed "I'm trustworthy!" So where Mitch would hesitate with almost anybody else, he found Alex's confidence and calm made him feel...surprisingly safe. Not safe enough to show the man who he really was, but certainly safe enough that flaunting his gayness in Alex's face didn't make him feel threatened.

Slinking up to Alex, Mitch laid a hand on Alex's unbroken arm, opened his mouth and—

"Good game against Colgate," Alex said, pocketing his phone.

The mask slipped off Mitch's face. "You were there?"

Alex shook his head. "Watched it on TV."

Holy crap! An NHL player—Mitch's hockey crush, no less—had watched his game. At a loss for words, Mitch stood there blinking at Alex like a putz.

"You've got impressive foot work," Alex said.

Mitch continued to blink at him.

"You skated circles around Colgate and that goal in the third?" Alex smiled wide. "You broke Colgate's end as if the defensemen were pylons. It was beautiful."

"I—" Mitch cleared his throat. "Well, McCall passed me the puck at just the right time, so… I mean, I did figure skating for years and…" He had no idea what he was trying to say.

"Huh. I know a couple of guys who did some figure skating after their game slipped and it helped them re-bound. It's something I've been considering to improve my foot speed." Alex leaned a shoulder against the wall and crossed his arms, but his cast got in the way so he ended up shoving one hand in his pocket and letting the casted one dangle. "Your training shows in your footwork. How else has it helped your game?"

In total disbelief that an *NHL player* was asking him for advice, Mitch said, "Figure skating is about using edges and your body to change direction on the ice. It's about learning to cut a corner or to pivot the right way while maintaining your speed. It made me a better skater."

"It shows."

God, the compliments were going to go to Mitch's head.

"What made you decide to stick with hockey instead of figure skating?"

Mitch shrugged and told the truth. "I liked hockey better."

"Could you do a triple axel in full hockey gear?" Alex asked, a teasing grin on his face.

Mitch had to laugh. "I've never tried." But now he was itching to.

"No? What about a—" Alex held his index finger up and moved it in small circles, "—with the leg out in front?"

"A sit spin?" Mitch scratched his head. "I actually think that one might be harder than the triple axel in full hockey gear."

They stood there smiling at each other for a moment, Alex's eyes the color of the Green Mountains in summer. The man was too gorgeous for words and he was *nice* to boot. Mitch couldn't help staring at Alex's mouth, red and surprisingly soft in an otherwise rugged face.

Alex cleared his throat and edged around Mitch. "I've got to get back to my friend."

"Wait, I—" The hallway was empty so Mitch plastered his sex smile back on his face, walked right into Alex's personal space, and put a hand on Alex's hip. "Why don't you come over tonight and we'll—"

Alex palmed Mitch's shoulders and pushed him away. "Look, kid—"

"I'm not a kid."

"*Mitch.*" Alex held him at arm's length. "Whatever it is you're trying to do here, it's not going to happen. I don't even know you."

"What difference does that make?"

Alex dropped his arms. "I don't jump into bed with people I don't know. Hell, I don't even jump into bed with people I *do* know."

Alex wasn't saying *I'm not gay*, but it did sound like he was saying *I'm asexual* or something similar, which left Mitch exactly nowhere.

"Mitch, this person that you pretend to be?" Alex said quietly, like he was trying to tame a wild cat. "He has no substance."

Pretend. No substance. The words hit Mitch like a physical punch and he took an instinctive step back.

"In the three times we've bumped into each other, the three-minute conversation we just had is the most real you've been," Alex continued. "I like that guy. I like the guy who talks to me without ulterior motives or any pretense. The guy who showed up to last week's lecture full of questions for Chris. The guy who plays wicked hockey and is dedicated to his team and serious about school and who, I'm told, is a math genius."

Damn Coach's big mouth.

Alex shrugged. "I'd like to get to know that guy. He's the type of guy I could be friends with."

Friends? The only friend Mitch had who truly knew him was Cody, and they'd known each other since first grade. Yano, Marco, the other guys on the team… They saw what Mitch wanted them to see.

"This flirty and impetuous person you pretend to be?" Alex said. "Honestly, I don't really care for that guy, but I don't think that's who you are inside."

How had Alex figured him out so correctly, so fast?

"Look." Alex rubbed Mitch's upper arm. Mitch flinched and stepped back, bumping into the wall behind him. Alex sighed. "I don't want to keep fending off your come-ons. But if you want to get together for a coffee or a pizza and have a conversation about hockey or whatever, I'd love to sit down with the guy I spent the last few minutes talking to about figure skating. Good luck against Denver tomorrow." He walked away, leaving Mitch alone in the hallway outside the restrooms.

Nobody, *nobody*, had ever figured out the game Mitch played to keep the world at bay, the one that kept his true self hidden behind twenty-foot high walls so that the world couldn't hurt him anymore. How had Alex figured it out in three short, less-than-stellar encounters?

Alex wasn't interested in him. Alex didn't even *like* him, at least not the facade he presented for everyone except Cody. But Alex was willing to give him the time of day if only Mitch could be himself.

Problem was, he wasn't sure who that was anymore.

Cody found him a few minutes later, leaning against the wall, staring at nothing. He ran his eyes over Mitch's face, which Mitch was sure was tomato-red with something akin to bewildered hurt.

"What happened?"

The sympathy in Cody's voice tugged something loose in Mitch. He shook his head and blinked the burn out of his eyes.

"Mitch?"

I have no substance. I'm worthless.

FOUR

LUCK, AS IT TURNED OUT, WAS NOT ON THEIR SIDE during Friday evening's game against Denver. Mitch wasn't the only one playing badly, but he was, admittedly, playing the worst out of everyone on the team. He missed passes, he couldn't find the back of the net with a basketball never mind a small, round disc, and, once, he whiffed the puck like an amateur wielding a hockey stick for the first time. He'd been so shocked, he'd stood there in mortified confusion while Denver stole the puck and proceeded to score.

The one saving grace was that they were playing in Denver, so at least they hadn't embarrassed themselves in front of a home crowd.

Assistant Coach Spinney pulled Mitch aside during the second intermission, when the Mountaineers were down 4-0. From the tiny office attached to the visitors' locker rooms, Mitch could hear Coach Bedley giving the rest of the team an angry pep talk.

Coach Spinney parked his ass against the office desk. Mitch propped his stick against the wall, threw his helmet and gloves onto a chair, and ran his hands through his sweaty hair. Frustration thrumming through his veins, he kicked the chair with his skate.

Spinney raised an eyebrow. "Your head's not in the game."

No shit. Mitch almost said it, but he wasn't in the habit of giving lip to this particular coach. Spinney, unlike

Coach Bedley, wasn't all hockey, hockey, hockey. He actually gave a shit about the players' well-being outside of the sport. Bedley cared inasmuch as it affected a player's game. Spinney cared because he was a good guy.

"Talk to me, Greyson."

Mitch guzzled water from his water bottle and considered what to say. "I'm just having a shit week."

"School or personal?"

Huffing an unamused laugh, Mitch drank down another third of his water. "Both."

"Anything I can help with?"

Not unless Spinney knew a way to lighten Mitch's course load so he could get a decent night's sleep. Not unless Spinney could turn back time so Mitch could tell his academic advisor to stuff her creative writing course up her ass. Not unless he knew of a way for Mitch to avoid starving to death, and to be able to pay bills, gas, and next semester's tuition without having to work two part-time jobs.

Not unless he could make Alex Dean like him.

Why that last one was important, Mitch was having trouble understanding. It wasn't like Alex was the first person to not like him. Hell, Mitch's own mother and brother didn't like him. What was one more person, a relative stranger at that?

Whether it was their shared love of the sport, last night's easy conversation, or something else, Mitch had no clue what made him want to spend time with Alex. On top of desperately wanting to jump Alex's bones, he also wanted to be Alex's friend. Alex, however, didn't like Mitch when he was "on", but Mitch wasn't sure if he could let down his guard enough to be himself with Alex.

He should cut his losses.

But he didn't know how to do that either.

"No thanks, Coach. It's just stuff I need to figure out."

"Is it a girl problem?"

"No," Mitch said, scoffing.

"Boy problem?"

Mitch kept his face expressionless.

"Wouldn't matter if it was," Spinney said with a shrug. "Not to your coaches, and not to them—" He nodded toward the locker room. "—either."

Yeah, right. People didn't come out in sports. It just wasn't done. There was a rule about it somewhere, Mitch was sure.

"Doesn't matter, Coach. I'll be fine. Just need to get my head on straight."

Spinney sighed at Mitch's evasive answer. "Okay. You know where to find me if you need to talk." Spinney paused, then said, "Think you could maybe skate better during the third?"

Mitch actually huffed a real laugh at that. "I'll do my best."

Turned out his best was mediocre, but it was enough so that the Mountaineers at least got a few shots on goal during the third period. Compared to how well his team had played last week against Colgate, tonight Mitch felt like a bumbling toddler learning to skate.

Was Alex watching this game on TV? Fuck, Mitch hoped not. But he also kind of hoped Alex was, which meant Mitch was all kinds of fucked up in the head.

It was on the tails of that thought that Yano passed him the puck and, without thinking, without evaluating where the other players were, without calculating the best angle, Mitch shot...and scored.

Well, shit. That shouldn't have worked.

The team took a few moments to celebrate, but

considering it was their first goal against Denver's four and there were only three minutes left in the period, their celebration was lackluster at best.

With that, the Mountaineers lost their first game of the season. It wasn't the end of the world and it was only one game. But still, seeing as they had to play Denver again tomorrow night, morale was predictably low as the team trudged back into the locker room.

Mitch wanted to apologize to his teammates for his shit playing on the ice, but as he'd heard from every coach he'd ever had, there was no *i* in *team*. He hadn't lost this game by himself. Besides, he was sure their goalie, Marco Terlizzese, was feeling just as bad, if not worse.

The Mountaineers' equipment manager stuck his head in the room and said, "Bus leaves for the hotel in thirty minutes," then left as quickly as he'd arrived.

It was quiet in the locker room, as it usually was after they lost a game. Everyone would shower and change as fast as they could so they could get back to the hotel and get shitfaced on the cheapest beer available.

Mitch took his time removing his equipment, then dawdled some more by checking his phone. He could see Yano eyeing him, but Mitch wasn't in the mood to talk. If he could time it so that everyone was already on the bus when he exited the showers, he might be able to avoid the "What's going on with you?" conversation he knew Yano wanted to have.

There were three texts and a voicemail on his phone. The voicemail was from his mom. Apparently, he was a sucker for punishment, because he gave it a listen, when usually, he deleted them unheard.

"Mitch, it's your mother." Her smooth, cultured voice made him grit his teeth. "I've just been informed that your college hockey team lost tonight's game against…" A pause as she no doubt double checked who they'd played against. "Denver. As I've told you time and time again, hockey is not a real career. If you were any good, you wouldn't have lost tonight's game."

Mitch growled low in his throat.

"I do think it's time you invested your time and energy into something else. Now, I spoke with the dean at Columbia. Transferring to another college usually takes several months, but Ms. Aberdeen is willing to expedite yours so that you can start your business degree in January, in time for the new semester, provided that you make up any missing courses you need to catch up over the summer. Here's what I'll need from you to make the transfer happen: your transcript—"

He hung up, then leaned his forehead against the metal divider between his locker and the one to his right, taking a deep breath.

He wanted to cry.

Instead, he checked his texts. Neither of them were from his brother, who, once upon a time, had been Mitch's biggest supporter.

The first text was from his dad. *Tough loss, kiddo. Don't take it too hard. Every team has off days. Good luck tomorrow!*

The second text was also from his dad. *By the way, I'll be in Burlington for a meeting Friday. Flying back to NY Saturday morning. Early dinner Friday before your game?*

Mitch quickly typed out a message. *Yeah! Let me know what time you'll be here.*

The last text was from Cody. It wasn't as encouraging as Mitch's dad's, but it made Mitch laugh:

You forget how to skate?

Think you could do better? Mitch texted back.

He was digging his towel out of his bag when Cody replied. *Better than you did tonight? Uh YEAH.*

Rolling his eyes, Mitch texted, *Why am I friends with you again?*

Because I give it to you straight.

Mitch was mid smart-ass reply, something along the lines of "I'll find someone to give it to me not-straight" when Cody messaged, *DO NOT MAKE A SEX JOKE.*

Grinning, Mitch left the phone on the shelf in his locker and went to take a shower in much better spirits.

He wasn't grinning fifteen minutes later when he emerged to find Yano waiting for him. Everyone else was gone.

"Going to stand there and watch me get changed?"

Yano grunted. "As if I haven't seen your bare, gay ass before."

Mitch froze with his underwear half on at the word "gay", then forced himself to move, to finish getting dressed. He had no idea if Yano was joking or not and didn't ask, but he must've had a look on his face, because Yano asked, "Were you trying to keep it a secret?"

Mitch completed his outfit of jeans and a blue T-shirt with his favorite Vermont Flannel and turned slowly to face Yano. "Who else knows?"

"I don't know," Yano said, shrugging. "It's not like we sit around talking about it."

"How did you figure it out?"

"Dude, my best friend from high school's gay. You look at guys the same way he does. I might not know how to spell *knoll*, but I'm not stupid."

No, he certainly wasn't. Mitch had underestimated his friend's perceptiveness. "So, the rest of the guys…?"

Yano shrugged again. "Oblivious idiots. Not that they'd care, even if they knew."

Mitch wasn't so sure about that.

"Most of them, anyway, but—" Yano waved his hand as if physically tossing aside their previous topic. "—that's not what I wanted to talk about. I wanted to ask about that." He jerked his thumb over his shoulder, indicating the rink, the game, and everything that had gone wrong. "What happened out there? It was like you couldn't see the other players, never mind the puck."

Mitch sat to put on his shoes and carefully avoided Yano's much-too-observant gaze. "Just got a lot on my mind."

"Dude troubles?"

"Why does everybody keep asking me that?" Mitch grumbled under his breath. "No, there's no dude." It wasn't quite a lie.

"Trouble in BFF land with Cody?"

"No, Cody and I are solid."

Leaving his equipment bag since they'd be back for game two tomorrow, Mitch grabbed his overnight one and headed for the door, Yano behind him. Out in the hallway, Yano bumped his shoulder against Mitch's as they headed for the parking lot with three minutes to spare. "So, what's up?"

While he appreciated Yano's concern, all Mitch wanted to do was to crawl into bed and hope to wake up tomorrow with a clearer head on his shoulders.

"School stuff mostly," he told Yano. It was only half the truth, but Mitch didn't want to tell Yano that he was also feeling lousy over the fact that Alex didn't like him. He hadn't even told Cody yet, and the man had been pestering Mitch to tell him what was wrong since last night's dinner at Mama Jean's.

"Classes giving you trouble?" Yano asked. "My socio-logical theory course is whooping my ass. Don't ask me why I took a stupid *theory* course. What good is theory in real life anyway?"

Appreciating Yano's attempt to make him feel better, Mitch said, "For me, it's creative writing. Apparently, my writing has no substance." And neither did he, according to Alex. But he wasn't going to think about that right now. It made his heart hurt.

"You're not a writer," Yano said.

"No shit."

"So, why'd you take a writing class?"

"Fucking academic advisor."

Yano made a sound of disgust. "Hate those guys. How do you think I ended up with fucking theory? Know any-thing about sociological theory?" He turned hopeful eyes on Mitch as Mitch pushed the exit door open. Coach Bedley was waiting in the dark parking lot under a lamp post, holding a clipboard. When he spotted them, he tapped his watch, a scowl on his face, and pointed at the bus.

"Nope," Mitch answered Yano. "Know anything about writing?"

"Enough to know that *knoll* starts with a *k*?"

Laughing, ignoring Bedley's I'm-annoyed-with-you face, they joined their teammates on the bus.

Weekends at Grandpa Forest's long-term care facility in Montpelier were always busy, but not quite as much on a Saturday night after dinnertime. Alex usually kept his visits to the afternoon, but he wanted to watch the GH vs Denver game with his grandpa and, because of the time difference, it didn't start until nine EST. He didn't usually watch college hockey, but now that he essentially had nothing to keep him busy while he recuperated, he tried to catch his alma mater's games.

Alex and Grandpa Forest had talked hockey for as long as Alex could remember. Back when Grandpa Forest still knew how to use a computer, they'd email each other after NHL games and speak on the phone after Alex's, back when he was in the major juniors. Grandpa Forest had always had time for Alex and his mom, even making a point to visit them several times a year.

It would be nice if Grandpa Forest remembered those times, or even who Alex was.

"Judd, come on in!" Grandpa Forest said when Alex knocked on his open door.

Alex swallowed a disappointed sigh and stepped into his grandpa's room.

Grandpa Forest picked a shirt off the couch and nudged a pair of dirty socks under the couch. "I wasn't expecting company today."

No, he never was.

"I brought munchies," Alex said, holding up a bag of ketchup chips he'd brought back from his last trip home. "I thought we could watch the hockey game together."

Grandpa Forest laughed. "Little Alex used to love those. Remember, Judd?"

"I remember," Alex said, dropping the bag onto the coffee table.

Judd was Alex's piece-of-shit father—Grandpa Forest's son—who'd left Alex and his mom when Alex was nine. Judd had cut off all ties not only with his wife and son, but with his father as well. As much as Alex wished every day that his grandpa would remember who Alex was, even if only for five minutes, he was glad Grandpa Forest couldn't remember how devastated he'd been when his only child had effectively disowned him and disappeared.

That Alex looked uncannily like Judd was a constant source of annoyance for Alex.

Grandpa Forest stood in sweats and a hoodie, contemplating the table next to the window as if he didn't know what it was. Which could possibly be the case. Alex had learned over the past couple of years not to ask open-ended questions and since he had no clue what Grandpa Forest was trying to remember, he didn't ask what was wrong.

"Is Alex joining us?" Grandpa Forest asked.

Alex swallowed hard. "No, not today."

"That's too bad. How's my boy doing? He must be, what, nine now?"

"Yeah," Alex said past the lump in his throat. To Grandpa Forest, Alex would be nine forever.

Grandpa Forest stopped trying to figure out what was wrong with the table and sat on the couch next to Alex. "He still playing hockey?"

"Yeah." Desperate for a distraction, Alex found one in the bag of ketchup chips on the coffee table. He opened it and offered it to Grandpa Forest. "Do you have a drink, Grand—um, Forest?" The nurses had told him that it was better to address Alzheimer's patients by their names, but in two years, Alex still hadn't gotten into the habit.

Grandpa Forest snapped his fingers. "Drinks. I knew I forgot something. I'll be right back."

The kitchen was at the end of the hall. Grandpa Forest was liable to forget where he was going before he got halfway there and there was a high probability that Alex would find him aimlessly wandering the halls, so he said, "I'll go. Maybe put the hockey game on?"

"Good idea."

When Alex got back from the kitchen a few minutes later, it was to find Grandpa Forest engrossed in a game show.

"Look at these guys." Grandpa Forest waved a hand at the TV. "They're never going to win the money."

Alex placed their water glasses on the coffee table and sat next to his grandpa.

On the TV, the game show host repeated the question for the next family member. "Top five answers are on the board. One more strike and play goes to the other team. If a witch wasn't paying attention to where she was flying, what might she crash into?"

"The CN Tower!" the game show contestant yelled.

Next to Alex, Grandpa Forest muttered, "That's too specific. Buildings. The word you're looking for is *buildings*. Or trees. Or planes."

"Think a witch can fly as high as an airplane?" Alex asked.

Grandpa Forest shot him a baleful grin. "Don't see why not."

Alex chuckled and stole the chips.

They watched the rest of the game show, then Grandpa Forest flipped through channels until he happened to land on the GH vs Denver game.

"Want to watch the game, Judd?"

Alex forced a smile on his face. "Sure."

Tonight's game was much more exciting than last night's, which had been about as interesting as watching paint dry. The entire team was playing much better tonight, as if someone had lit a fire under their collective asses. Mitch played like he was a force of nature, his determination evident even through a TV screen.

Last night, while watching the game in his rental cottage, Alex hadn't been able to keep himself from wondering if what he'd said to Mitch on Thursday at Mama Jean's had affected him so deeply that it had hindered his play. Then he'd called himself all sorts of stupid—he and Mitch were barely acquaintances. There was no way something said by a relative stranger would affect Mitch that way.

Yet Alex couldn't help remembering the crushed look on Mitch's face when Alex had walked away from him. For the second day in a row, Alex called himself all sorts of stupid, this time for treating Mitch as badly as he had. He just hadn't known how to get the other man to back off.

"Uh, a simple 'I'm not interested' probably would've worked just as well," JP had said when Alex returned to their table and told him what happened.

Alex winced. Yeah, he'd been unnecessarily mean. Hell, he'd told the kid he had no substance. Alex had no excuse for what he'd said. He was a writer. He understood the power of words.

On screen, the game was tied 3-3 in the third period. Both teams played ferociously, each of them wanting the win. The Mountaineers probably wanted it more, though, after yesterday's blowout.

However, it was not to be. With forty-eight seconds left in the game, Denver sent a backhand shot into the net. After that, it was game over, although GH put up a fight until the final buzzer sounded.

"You know, Judd," Grandpa Forest said, "you might not have made it past midget hockey, but Alex, he's got the heart of a hockey player. He'll make it big one day, you'll see."

Alex's breath faltered and the wetness behind his eyes appeared instantly. Three years ago, he and Grandpa Forest had sat on the outdoor patio of a tiny café in Montpelier at the beginning of Alex's senior year. It was the day Grandpa Forest had told Alex how bad his Alzheimer's was getting, although he hadn't stopped recognizing Alex until almost a year later. He'd never gotten to see Alex play in the NHL.

"Alex, my boy," Grandpa Forest had said on that late summer morning, the sun reflecting off his bald head, "this disease, it's going to kill a part of me, a part of me I fear might include you." He'd clasped one of Alex's hands in both of his aged ones. "I want you to know that no matter what you decide to do with your life, if you choose horse ranching, or dentistry, or teaching, or something else entirely instead of hockey, know that I will always be proud of you. Keep being the generous and kind person I know you are and you'll go places, my boy."

Grandpa Forest would be ashamed of Alex for what he'd said to Mitch yesterday.

Turning his face away, Alex discreetly knuckled the tears out of his eyes, his heart aching for that lost part of Grandpa Forest that had taken Alex with it.

"Judd!"

Alex jolted at the shout and shot out of his seat. "What? What's wrong? Do you need the nurse?"

"Your arm's broken, son."

"Oh." The fight went out of Alex and he dropped back onto the couch. "Yeah. I fell."

Grandpa Forest lifted Alex's casted arm and brought it up to his nose. "Why is there a purple penis on it?"

Snorting in amusement, Alex said, "Because my friends are stupid?"

"Ah. Boys will be boys in every generation, it seems."

Wasn't that the truth?

FIVE

MITCH STOOD OUTSIDE HIS CREATIVE WRITING TA's open office door fifteen minutes before the end of office hours late Monday morning, assignment in hand. There was a student already in there with John, so Mitch waited in the hallway and perused the piece of paper taped to the wall that listed the office hours for this particular postage stamp-sized office.

A small school meant there wasn't enough room for the TAs, so many of them shared office space. The next TA would be taking over John's office five minutes after John was done. A tiny part of Mitch hoped the student in there now took the rest of John's scheduled time, leaving Mitch another few days to freak out over his impending expulsion from GH. But then he'd have to face his TA's disapproving frown during Thursday's tutorial, and that wouldn't be much fun.

Luck wasn't with him today. The student came out of John's office, leaving Mitch exactly twelve minutes to find out if John was going to fail him.

Mitch doubted it would take that long. He knocked on the doorjamb.

John looked up from his laptop. "Mitch." He waved Mitch in. "Have a seat. I'm glad you came."

Mitch perched on the edge of a folding chair and held up his assignment. "I noticed there's no grade on this." Maybe not the way he should've started this meeting, but if John was going to fail him, he might as well cut to the chase, right? "Is it because it's worse than an F?"

John let out a gust of laughter. "No, not at all. The reason I didn't grade it is because your short story didn't follow the assignment guidelines. Technically, yes, I should've failed you, especially since your assignment didn't have any of the short story elements that we talked about in class, but…" John tapped his pen against his desk, appeared to think something through, then said, "Mitch, why did you take this class?"

"My academic advisor recommended it. And I still need my general electives, so…"

"What's your major?"

"Kinesiology with a specialty in sports science."

"I thought you might be a science major," John said. "Your story reads more like a lab report than fiction."

Mitch winced.

"Listen." John came around his desk and sat in the chair next to Mitch. "I really hate to fail my students, which is why I wanted to give you the chance to revise and resubmit."

"I appreciate that," Mitch said. "Really. But if it was a piece of crap the first time, I don't think writing it a second time is going to make it any better."

John took Mitch's assignment out of his hand. "We'll go through my comments, one by one. Hopefully that'll help you see the areas you can improve on."

"Which is everything, right?" Mitch slumped in his seat with a huff. "I know I'm no writer."

"You don't need to be. Seriously," John added when Mitch threw him a skeptical glance. "I'm not looking for flowery prose, but what I do need to see is basic story structure along with short story elements. Do that within the given two thousand-word limit and you should be fine."

"When you told me my last assignment had no substance, you meant that it lacked the elements of a short story?"

John grimaced. "I'm sorry I ever said that. It was completely unprofessional. But yes, that's what I meant."

Mitch's writing had no substance. He himself had no substance. At least John was going to show him how to fix his writing. Mitch had no idea how to fix months of pretending to be someone he wasn't.

Minutes later, after going through John's notes on how to use these supposed "elements," Mitch threw his arms up in defeat and swore. "I thought I was already doing that."

John pursed his lips. "Have you considered getting a tutor?"

Mitch bristled. "I don't need help."

John pointed at the assignment in Mitch's hands. Fuck, a tutor? As if he wasn't broke enough already? And working something else into his already busy schedule? He groaned and sagged in his chair. If it would help him get his GPA up so he could stay at GH, so be it. "Is there one who can work around hockey practices and games and my part-time jobs?"

John tilted his head, regarding Mitch with renewed interest. "You're a Mountaineer?"

"Uh-huh. I'm also a broke college student."

"What if I could find a tutor who would do it for free?"

Alex had been finishing up a draft outline for his book when JP had called and offered him a potential interviewee.

"You remember the guy in my tutorial? The one I told you about, who's almost failing?" JP said, his voice hitting higher calibers in his excitement. "Turns out he's a

Mountaineer who works two jobs. I don't know his story, but I thought you might want to talk to him for your book. Oh, and I also need you to tutor him and basically hold his hand while he takes my course."

Sure, Alex could tutor in exchange for some fresh perspective for his book. Hell, at this stage, he'd take anything he could get.

Which was how he found himself strolling into the library on Monday afternoon.

He took the corridor to the right of the library entrance, the one that led to the study rooms, and found number eight, where he was meeting his student. The person already sitting at the small table, impatiently tapping a pen against his thigh and swivelling his chair from side to side, was not at all who Alex was expecting.

He froze in the doorway, double checked the number on the door…and looked at Mitch Greyson. "Are you JP's—John's—student?"

Mitch, wide-eyed and equally frozen in his chair, asked, "*You're* my free tutor?"

Guess that answered that, then.

Setting his messenger bag on the floor, he took a seat across from Mitch and waited for the kid to decide how he was going to play this.

It took another few seconds, where they sat eyeballing each other in what was no doubt shock on both sides. Mitch took a sip of his smoothie, his cheeks hollowing around the straw, a blatant come-on if Alex'd ever seen one. He swallowed and shot Alex a flirty smile. "Miss me that much?"

Disappointed, but not surprised, Alex held a hand out for Mitch's assignment. Mitch's smile dimmed and he hesitated. Alex understood—sharing your work with someone else was scary.

But then Mitch squared his shoulders and slid his assignment across the table before slumping in his chair, arms crossed.

Mitch's story was titled *The Hockey Player*. Not exactly original, but he'd give Mitch the benefit of the doubt until he gave it a read.

Two paragraphs into a story that wasn't as awful as he'd feared it would be, Alex could feel the weight of Mitch's stare.

"What?" Alex asked.

"Just wondering what you're doing here."

"What do you mean?"

"For someone who claims not to like me, you agreed to tutor me awfully quick."

"I didn't know you were the one I'd be tutoring…" Alex broke off and stifled a wince when Mitch didn't quite manage to keep the hurt off his face before replacing it with a smirk that didn't reach his eyes.

"Well, surprise!" Mitch said, throwing his arms out. Then he rubbed his eyes with a thumb and forefinger and released a heartfelt sigh. Reaching across the table, he snatched his assignment from Alex's hands and stuffed it in his backpack.

"Thanks anyway." Mitch stood, gaze on the door at Alex's back. "But I've got it from here."

Alex, however, was faster. He was standing in front of the door by the time Mitch made it around the table.

Mitch fisted his hands on his hips. "Move."

Alex said the first thing that popped into his head: "Make me."

The regret was immediate when a challenging light entered Mitch's eyes. Even so, Alex stood his ground, his body blocking the door. He was here to help and help he would, whether the kid liked it or not.

Mitch plastered what Alex was sure was meant to be a sexy smile on his face and sauntered up to Alex, resting a hand on Alex's hip exactly the way he had at Mama Jean's the other night. Lifting up onto his toes, Mitch brought his mouth to within an inch of Alex's.

Mitch's breath was warm against Alex's lips and his eyes were brazen as they locked on Alex's. It would've been hot, had Alex been the type to get turned on by people he barely knew.

"Going to let me kiss you, hot stuff?" Mitch murmured.

Alex leaned forward a touch. Mitch's eyes flared with surprise. "You're going to have to do better than that if you want me to move."

Huffing, Mitch rolled his eyes and dropped onto his heels. "This is ridiculous. You don't even want to help me."

"Actually, I do."

"Why? You don't even like me."

"That's not what I said."

Mitch's laugh was incredulous. "Really? Should I replay the conversation for you?"

No need. Alex remembered it clearly. "I didn't mean to imply that I don't like you. That's not what I was trying to say."

"Could've fooled me with your whole 'you have no substance' thing." Mitch noisily sucked the last of his smoothie through his straw, then chucked the cup in the room's garbage can.

Yeah, that had been a wrong choice of words. Alex had known it as soon as they'd come out of his mouth, and he knew it now. He'd been searching for the right thing to say and JP's words about telling his student—*this* student, as it turned out—that his story had no substance had been front and center in Alex's brain and he'd spoken without thinking.

"I don't care anymore, anyway," Mitch declared. "Move. I have shit to do and you're in my way."

Again, Alex refused to move, and again, he spoke without thinking. "What's the magic word?"

Instead of rolling his eyes and huffing like an angry cat as Alex expected, Mitch cracked up. His laugh was unguarded and carefree and he was still chuckling when he retook his chair and dug his assignment out of his backpack.

"Fine, let's do this thing if you want to help so bad," he said. "Come tell me how much my story sucks."

But Alex wanted more of this Mitch, this open and real and honest one who spoke to Alex like he was a human being instead of a sex object.

Rather than sit back down, Alex picked up his messenger bag. "Want to get out of here?"

Alex didn't mention the book. And he didn't ask Mitch for his story. Free tutoring in exchange for some background on his tutoree was a great idea in theory, until he found out his student was Mitch Greyson, whose walls were sky-high and made of Kevlar. Alex had a feeling Mitch wouldn't appreciate him digging into his personal life. Instead they passed the five-minute drive in Alex's rental car from campus to Mama Jean's in awkward silence.

The change in circumstance meant Alex would be left tutoring in exchange for nothing, but he didn't mind. He was happy to help out JP, even if Mitch wasn't too receptive to the idea.

Only a few tables were occupied at Mama Jean's, so they snagged a private booth at the back of the restaurant.

Smells of tomato sauce and baking dough reached Alex's nose, making his stomach rumble.

Alex dropped his bag on the bench seat and removed his wallet from the inside pocket. "I'll go order," he said to Mitch. "What can I get you?"

"A beer and a personal-sized Meat Eaters." Mitch fished a twenty out of his wallet and held it out to Alex.

Alex waved it away. "It's on me."

"Why?"

"Why not?"

Mitch continued to eye him with suspicion.

"My treat, okay? An apology for what I said to you the other day."

Without waiting for an answer, Alex turned and headed for the order counter. He returned to the table minutes later with a beer for himself and a soft drink for Mitch.

Mitch poked at his glass. "This isn't beer."

"How observant of you," Alex teased.

Mitch was unimpressed.

"Sophomore, right?" Alex said. "Which makes you, what, nineteen? Twenty?"

"Nineteen. Twenty in January."

"I'll buy you a beer when you're legal."

"I'm legal in Canada."

Alex chuckled. "We're not in Canada, smart-ass." He pushed Mitch's glass closer to him. "Stop being a brat and drink your pop."

"My pop." Mitch took a sip as instructed. "We call it soda, here in the great state of Vermont."

"I'm Canadian," Alex told Mitch. "Some habits are hard to break."

"What other Canadianisms have you held onto?"

"All of them, I think. I still write in Canadian too."

Mitch shook his head. "For shame. And this is after how many years of living in the U.S.?"

"Six," Alex said, enjoying this side of easygoing Mitch. "I got dinged for it quite a bit when I first started at GH. Eventually I got with the program, but as soon as I wasn't being graded on it anymore, I reverted right back. 'Color' looks wrong without the 'u.'"

Mitch was smiling the kind of unreserved smile Alex hadn't ever seen on his face. It made him look boyish and charming, but with a hint of vulnerability that didn't surprise Alex at all. When Mitch noticed Alex watching him, he glanced away and stirred his drink with his straw, making the ice cubes clink against the glass.

"Mitch, I wanted to apologize for—"

"It's fine."

"No, it's not. What I *meant* to say last week is that you don't have to pretend with me, don't have to put up a wall. I'd like to get to know you, the real you. I'm sorry if what I said hurt you. That wasn't my intention at all."

"You didn't. I mean, how could you? We barely know each other." Mitch scoffed and stirred his straw again. "Besides, how do you know that the person you say I'm pretending to be, isn't actually who I am?"

Alex nodded slowly. "Good point. I guess I don't. Truth is, I don't know you well enough to say that with certainty, but I've always had good instincts about people."

"Really?" Mitch crossed his arms, the smirk on his face telling Alex without words that Mitch thought he was full of shit. "And what are your instincts telling you about me?"

"That you're scared."

Mitch's eyes widened and the smile slipped off his face, even as he made a sound of disbelief. "What is it you think I'm scared of?"

"I don't know." Alex suspected it had something to do with the reason Mitch was always "on." "And you seem reluctant to let me get to know you, so I might never know."

Their pizzas arrived, interrupting their stare-down. The size of Mitch's pizza distracted him from their conversation.

"I thought you were getting me a personal-sized one." He eyed his large pizza as if it were about to bite him. "I can't eat all this by myself."

"I figured you could take the leftovers home."

"How come you didn't get a big one?"

Alex inhaled the delicious aroma of his own personal-sized pizza. "I'm not supposed to be eating pizza, so it's better if I don't have any at home tempting me over to the dark side."

Mitch laughed, and it made Alex smile.

"The NHL has you on a strict diet?" Mitch asked, before taking a huge bite.

"I wouldn't say it's strict, per se, but pizza four times a week definitely isn't on it."

"Why is there green stuff on your pizza?"

"It's avocado."

Mitch shot him a look. "I know what it is. Why is it on your pizza?"

"I like avocado on my pizza."

"Oh no. Tell me you're not one of the few patrons of Mama Jean's who orders the cauliflower crust?"

Alex took a bite of his pizza and groaned theatrically.

"First of all," Mitch said, laughing, "that was mean. Second, *ew.*"

"Don't knock it 'til you try it. Here." Alex tore off a small piece of his pizza using a fork and the tips of his fingers sticking out of his cast and dropped it on Mitch's plate. "Try it before you '*ew*' it."

Mitch poked at it dubiously, but finally popped it in his mouth. He wiggled his hand in the universal so-so gesture and said, "It doesn't suck."

"High praise indeed."

Mitch laughed again.

There you are. There was the guy Alex wanted to get to know. No masks or pretense, just a laid-back guy who was easy to talk to.

"You never answered my question, you know," Mitch said after he'd inhaled his first slice.

"What question is that?"

"About how the NHL is and isn't what you expected."

"You're not going to let go, are you?"

"Nope."

Alex finished his second slice and chased it down with a sip of beer. "Are you hoping to get drafted?" he asked Mitch, curious about why Mitch wouldn't let this go. "Or is hockey simply a way for you to attend school? The partial scholarship," he added when Mitch shot him a questioning look. That same partial scholarship had been the only reason Alex had been able to attend GH at all.

"The scholarship is one of the reasons I chose GH," Mitch said. He didn't elaborate on his other reasons, and Alex didn't ask. "But hockey's not just a hobby. I *am* going to get drafted."

He said it with so much conviction, Alex found himself believing him. Besides, Alex had seen Mitch play, so he knew how good the kid was. If he could keep that up over the next two-plus years and remain injury-free, he'd be a shoe-in.

"And your kinesiology degree?" Alex asked. "That's for when you retire from hockey?"

"Yeah, I want to work with injured athletes. It's why I wanted to talk to Chris Blair."

"I'm sorry you didn't get the chance."

Mitch shrugged. "Not your fault." He pushed his plate away, most of his pizza still uneaten, and averted his gaze. "Did you, um, ask Mr. Blair about talking with me? Setting up a phone call or something?" He must've seen the answer on Alex's face, because he shrugged as if it was no big deal. "It's fine, no sweat."

"Shit, I'm sorry, Mitch. Let me email him now."

Mitch's eyes went big with something like awe as Alex retrieved his phone from his bag and brought up the email app. "You can just…" Mitch waved a hand at Alex's phone. "Email him out of the blue like that?"

"Sure. Why not? Chris has been emailing me every morning since I got here anyway. See?" Alex turned the phone toward Mitch, where this morning's email from Chris was displayed. It was basically the same as every email he'd sent, ever since Alex had arrived in Vermont almost two weeks ago, asking "How's the arm?"

Alex tapped out a quick email, slightly hobbled by his broken arm, as Mitch watched from across the table.

"What are you writing?" Mitch asked, leaning over to get a look at Alex's screen. "What'd you say about me? Maybe don't tell him I have a lot of questions, okay? I don't want to scare him away."

"He's not likely to be scared away by an ambitious sophomore," Alex said, completely charmed by this side of Mitch. Once done typing, Alex handed the phone to Mitch. "How's this?"

Hi Chris. I have a friend at Glen Hill College in VT in his second year of a kinesiology degree. He wants to work with injured athletes, like you. Would you have an hour or so to spare in the next few weeks to chat with him?

Mitch was quiet when he handed Alex the phone back,

but he nodded, which Alex assumed meant that he was fine with the way the email was written. Alex hit "send."

"You called me your friend," Mitch said quietly.

Confused, Alex blinked at him. "What else would I call you?" He slipped his phone into his bag and turned back to Mitch, who was watching Alex with a tiny smile. If Alex didn't know better, he'd say a few more of Mitch's walls had come down, though Alex had no idea what he'd said or done to cause them to fall. "Should we go over your assignment?"

"Oh." Mitch blinked and shook his head forcefully, curls bouncing every which way. "Right." He pulled his assignment out of his backpack and set it between them on the table.

An hour, two more soft drinks, and a whole lot of explanation later, Mitch's eyes were starting to cross, so Alex called it a day. He picked Mitch's pen up off the table and handed it to him, then dictated his own email address and phone number for Mitch to jot down. With his broken right arm, Alex was left without a writing hand.

"Once you've made the revisions we talked about," he said to Mitch, "send it to me and I'll look it over before you submit it to JP, okay?"

"JP?"

"Sorry. John, your TA."

Mitch put his assignment away. "How come you call him JP?"

"His name's John Patrick, but he's been JP to me since we met in first year hockey practice."

"He played for the Mountaineers too?"

Alex nodded. He motioned to Mitch's leftover pizza. "Let me get you a box for that."

He got a box from the order counter and waited for Mitch to pack up his food before placing his bag over his shoulder and leading Mitch out of Mama Jean's. They fell into step on the sidewalk, the early evening air cooling Alex's skin, overheated from the restaurant.

Mitch shot him a cheeky grin. "So, when are we going on date number two?"

Alex couldn't help but laugh. "Excuse me? When was date number one?"

Mitch jerked his head in the direction of the restaurant. "We just had it. You invited me, you paid. Ergo, we had a date."

Alex wasn't sure about that logic, but he let the kid have his point.

"So," Mitch continued, "when's date number two? Unless, um…" He scratched his head and paused on the sidewalk. "Do asexuals date? I'm afraid I'm embarrassingly ignorant about that."

"What makes you think I'm asexual?"

Mitch regarded him with unsure eyes. "Um, you? You said you don't jump into bed with people you don't know, or even people you do."

"Well, I imagine all asexuals are different, but I'm not ace. I'm demi."

"Demi…"

"Demisexual. It means—"

"No, I know what it means. That one I'm familiar with." Mitch looked away, but he didn't appear to see the small bookstore on the other side of the street, or the students sitting on the small patio of the coffee shop, or the dog walker who maneuvered around them. Finally, he nodded. "My question stands. When's date number two?"

"Mitch—"

"Demis only feel sexual attraction for someone they have an emotional connection to, right?"

Alex nodded.

"And you said we were friends."

Alex nodded again.

Mitch's eyes lit with triumph. "If we're friends, it means you already have an emotional connection to me. So, if we keep seeing each other, maybe sexual attraction will develop."

Had this conversation happened even just a few days ago, Alex would've accused Mitch of wanting in his pants simply because of who he was—a pro hockey player. However, things appeared to have changed between them in the past few hours. Alex suspected that Mitch putting himself out there by asking Alex out on a date—or assuming there was going to be a second date, as the case was—was really fucking hard for him.

"It might," Alex acknowledged. "But it also might not, Mitch. It isn't that black and white and I don't want to set you up to be disappointed."

Mitch inhaled deeply and let his breath out slowly, pizza box held in front of him. "Even if you never feel anything for me beyond friendship, we'll still be friends, right?"

"Right."

"Okay. So date number two? Friday?"

"You're persistent, I'll give you that," Alex said, chuckling. He got them moving toward the parking lot again. "Also, you have a game on Friday."

"Shit, yeah. On Saturday, too. Wait." Mitch stopped in the middle of the parking lot. "I'm going the wrong way. Home's that way."

Taking Mitch's arm, Alex guided him to his rental car. "I'll take you home."

"I can walk. It's only twenty minutes."

Jesus, the guy didn't like to accept help, did he?

Alex opened the passenger door. "Just get in."

Mitch did as told without further argument.

Once they were on their way with Mitch navigating, Alex kept his eyes on the road but he could feel Mitch's stare piercing the side of his head. When Alex chanced a glance at him, Mitch looked away and bit his lip.

"How about next Monday for date number two?" Alex asked.

Mitch smiled at him, happy and sincere, and Alex made himself a mental promise to tread carefully where Mitch was concerned. The kid came across as invincible and confident, but Alex suspected there was a very fragile soul underneath the layer of impenetrability Mitch had created around himself.

SIX

"**D**UDE, PAY ATTENTION," CODY SAID, scratching Mitch's head where it lay in Cody's lap.

Mitch placed his cell phone on their living room table. "I am."

He'd had good intentions and had started off multitasking: a textbook in front of him as he and Cody watched an NHL game on TV. Then Alex had texted him and Mitch had abandoned his textbook. Now he sprawled on the couch with his head in Cody's lap, not paying much attention to the game.

"This was your idea, you know," Cody said.

"Yeah, yeah."

His idea had been for him and Cody to bring the homework they'd been working on in their rooms down to the living room so they could hang out after days of hardly seeing each other. But the game had proved to be a distraction, and Alex an even bigger one.

"Who were you talking to?" Cody asked.

"Alex." Mitch had emailed him his revised short story yesterday and Alex wanted to see one more small revision before it was "good to go," according to his text.

"Aww." Cody pulled Mitch's hair. "Monday can't come soon enough?"

Mitch sighed and scratched an itch on his belly. Thinking of his pending date with Alex made his stomach flip, even though it was still four days away.

"What's wrong?" Cody asked.

"I don't know if asking him out was a good idea."

"Why not?"

"He doesn't even like me. I kind of forced it on him." Mitch didn't think Alex would've given in if he hadn't wanted to, but he still felt like he'd steamrolled right over Alex.

"He said yes, didn't he?" Cody said. "Means he must like you, to some degree."

"He also said I have no substance."

Cody scoffed. "He said the person you pretend to be, the person you are when your walls are up, has no substance." Cody paused for a second. "He's not wrong."

"You're an asshole," he told Cody without any heat. "He wants me to be myself with him." That was the scariest part of all this, never mind the fact that Mitch had never been on a date in his life and didn't know what to expect. Or wear. Or how to behave.

"And you don't think you can do that," Cody intuited.

"I don't know if I know who that is anymore."

"Sure you do. It's the same person you are with me."

"Yeah, but I trust you." There wasn't anyone Mitch trusted more, except his dad.

"Nothing says you shouldn't trust Alex. Maybe give him the benefit of the doubt?"

"What if he's just being nice to humor me and he turns into a giant douchebag?"

Cody pulled Mitch's hair again. "Not everyone is your brother."

Sometimes it was really annoying to be around someone who knew him so well, when all Mitch wanted was for Cody to agree with him that the rest of the world wasn't to be trusted.

When he told Cody that, his best friend held Mitch's head in both hands and leaned over to peer at him upside down. "You're a better judge of character than you give yourself credit for."

Mitch snorted. "Yeah, right."

"I'm serious. Yano's your best friend on the team and he's got your back about the gay thing. Marco would too, and you know that. Your TA's trying to help you pass his class, even though he probably should've failed you on that assignment. Alex is tutoring you out of the goodness of his heart. You knew, from your first practice, that Coach Spinney was the one to talk to about personal problems, just like you knew that Coach Bedley would be the one who'd improve your game. And hell, you knew I was awesome right away."

Mitch sat up and rearranged himself, flopping onto the opposite end of the couch and tucking his bare feet under Cody's thighs. "You punched a bully for me."

"I'd do it again too. That kid was a fucker." Cody slouched in his corner of the couch and kicked a textbook aside so he could put his feet up on the coffee table. "So, tell me. What is it about Alex?"

"He's…" Mitch broke off and rolled his eyes at himself. "He's real. What you see is what you get."

Cody made a "hmm" sound. "Then he's probably looking for someone who's his equal, who'll be just as real with him."

Mitch debated not saying anything, seeing as it was none of Cody's business, but Cody might actually have some useful advice. "He's also demi."

Cody cracked up. Okay, that wasn't what Mitch expected.

"What the fuck is so funny?" Mitch poked Cody

in the thigh with his foot. "Don't laugh at him, you hypocrite."

"I'm not laughing at him," Cody finally calmed enough to say. "I'm laughing at you."

Mitch threw a pillow at his so-called best friend. "Why?"

"Alex is demi." Cody grinned and placed the pillow behind his head. "That's fucking perfect. Means you can't be anything *but* real with him, otherwise he won't give you the time of day. It's so completely opposite to your usual screw 'em and leave 'em routine. Man, he's going to be so good for you. He's going to turn you inside out and upside down. I can't wait to see it."

"First, you're mean. Second, he already has. I asked him out, didn't I? I've never done that before."

"I wish I could record this."

"Fuck you. Seriously." Mitch reached for his phone. "Forget it, I'm cancelling."

"Oh, hell no." Cody ripped the phone out of Mitch's hands and tossed it onto the loveseat. Then he grabbed Mitch by the arm and hauled him up. When they were sitting face-to-face on the couch, Cody said, "Tell me honestly. Do you like him?"

Sighing in misery, Mitch nodded. "At first, I just wanted to do him. Now I want to do him *and* be his friend."

"Aww, you're smitten."

Groaning, Mitch flopped backward. "Nobody uses that word, except old-fashioned moms."

"Mitch, do me a favor, okay?"

Mitch locked eyes with him.

"Give Alex a chance. Hell, give yourself a chance. Do you want to wonder 'what if' for the rest of your life?"

"No, but what if he never feels anything more than friendship for me?"

"Then you'll have gained a new friend. One who knows you the way I do and who likes you for you."

If Mitch couldn't get a nice guy like Alex to fall for him, what did that say about him? He rubbed his face and, hidden behind his hands, mumbled, "What if I disappoint him?"

"Like I said." Cody rubbed Mitch's knee. "Give him the benefit of the doubt. Maybe you shouldn't go into this with the expectation that Alex *will* develop feelings for you. That way if he doesn't, you're not too disappointed. And don't call it a date. Just call it hanging out and pretend you're getting to know a new friend, which is basically what you're doing anyway."

"You're not going to tell me that if Alex can't see how great I am, he's a jerk who doesn't deserve me?" Mitch teased.

"Nope. For a demisexual, an emotional connection doesn't automatically equal sexual attraction. I'm emotionally connected to you, but I've never been sexually attracted to you."

"Really?" Mildly insulted, Mitch glared at Cody. "Not once in the thirteen years we've known each other?"

Cody shook his head in mock sadness, his pale blue eyes lit with laughter.

"Stomp all over my pride, why don't you?"

"You've never been attracted to me, either."

"That's not true," Mitch protested.

Cody's eyes went wide.

"I was attracted to you for, like, five minutes." Mitch said. "Before I realized you could eat me for breakfast."

"Damn right. So could Alex."

Yeah, Mitch knew it.

"You'll probably find yourself liking it," Cody predicted.

Mitch threw another pillow at him.

Mitch strolled into The Green Onion the next afternoon at four thirty on the dot. It smelled like frying onions and grilling meat, and Mitch's empty stomach made itself heard. His dad, Geoff Greyson, was easy to spot in the tiny six-table restaurant.

"Hey, kiddo." His dad's smile was huge as he stood and engulfed Mitch in a hug.

Mitch dropped his equipment bag next to their table and hung on to his dad for an extra few seconds. The feeling of being in the arms of one of only two people who actually loved him was overwhelming and comforting at the same time.

"What's wrong?" his dad asked.

"Nothing." Mitch shook his head and sat. "It's just good to see you, that's all."

His dad had that expression on his face—his lips pressed in a tight line, brow furrowed—the one that said "my son is hiding something." Mitch knew that face well.

His dad crossed his arms over his chest and peered at him from narrowed eyes. "Want to try again?"

Chuckling wryly, Mitch played with his napkin. "I'm just tired. Overworked and…" He traced a scratch on the table.

"You always did push yourself harder than anybody I've ever known."

How else was he supposed to prove that he was worth it? To his mother, his brother, his coaches, and NHL scouts.

"How are your classes?"

"Good." Mitch nodded absently. "Really good, actually. Except creative writing, which I apparently suck at."

His dad laughed. "That doesn't surprise me, to be honest. Good for you, though, for getting out of your comfort zone."

"My academic advisor bullied me into it. Should've taken physics or something."

"Only you would think physics is an easy elective."

Their server arrived, delivered two ice waters and a bread basket, and took their orders. The Green Onion was their standard dinner spot whenever Mitch's dad was in town. It was quieter than Mama Jean's and Mitch unashamedly took advantage of his dad's attempt at feeding him something other than pizza and cafeteria smoothies.

"Your mom says hello," his dad said when the server left.

Like hell she did.

His dad shrugged when Mitch did nothing but stare at him. "Fine, that's a lie."

"She left me a wonderfully uplifting voicemail after we lost to Denver last week," Mitch said.

His dad's raised eyebrow told Mitch he didn't miss the sarcasm.

Mitch played with the straw in his glass. "What's her problem with hockey, anyway?"

"Kiddo, that's a complicated answer." His dad leaned his forearms on the table. "Did you know that your grandfather, your mother's father, was a professional athlete?"

Mitch straightened. "He was?" He'd never met his grandfather, Edward Westlake, and his mother never talked about him. He'd died in a skiing accident before Mitch was born.

"Skier," his dad said. Well, that made sense. "Went to the Olympics in…shoot, I forget the year. Your mother was a teenager. Anyway, he wasn't home often, and was always away training. It essentially left your grandmother a single parent and, Mitch, your grandmother was a *hard* woman. Strict. Unemotional. Took no excuses. Abusive, verbally and physically." He took a sip of his water. "She raised your mother to be the same way."

So, what do you see in her? What made you marry her? Why are you still married to her?

Before Mitch could ask his questions, his dad continued. "I think sports scare your mother. Her father was so obsessed with being the best, with winning the next competition, that he neglected his responsibilities at home and she never got to know him. I think she partly, if not mostly, blamed him for her harsh living conditions. I think she's afraid you're going to turn into him. That you're going to forget about everyone who loves you in your journey to the NHL."

Mitch shook his head at the hypothesis, though not to argue. He understood where his dad was coming from and, for the first time, his mother felt more relatable than she'd ever been. But Mitch was his own person and he wasn't walking in anybody's footsteps but his own. "So Mom turned into her mother when she had her own kids?"

"No," his dad insisted. "No, your grandmother was much, *much* worse. Constantly belittling your mother, finding fault with every little thing she did." He sighed and scratched his chin. "Your mother wasn't always the way she is now. When I first met her, she was bright and ambitious, with a zeal to succeed. But when your grandmother passed away and running the business fell onto her shoulders, I think the weight of it made her determination that much stronger, but it made her harder too. It was almost as if she was trying to make her mother proud from beyond the grave, so she took on a part of her personality."

A part? Or all of it? Well, his mom wasn't physically abusive, so he'd give her that.

"Mom's never talked about any of this."

"No," his dad agreed. "She plays things close to the vest."

"Except when she disapproves, in which case everybody knows about it."

His dad shot him a look. Mitch grinned and waggled his eyebrows, making his dad laugh and dispelling the tension that had come along with the discussion.

"How's Dan?" Mitch asked. Just because his brother didn't want anything to do with him anymore didn't mean the opposite was true.

"Your brother's doing well. He moved into a new apartment in Manhattan last week. He's seeing a new girl. Can't remember her name."

Didn't matter. She'd last as long as the others, which was about how long it took to walk from one end of Glen Hill to the other.

So, seven minutes.

"That's not nice," his dad reprimanded when Mitch voiced his thoughts.

Mitch shrugged. "But it's true."

His dad sighed, a faraway look in his eyes. "I'm sorry you two still aren't getting along."

"Not your fault."

"Not yours either, I suspect."

The hard edge to his dad's voice had Mitch eyeing him closely. "What do you mean? I always thought it was something I did that made him hate me."

"Dan doesn't hate you."

Mitch scoffed.

"It's true. He asks me about you all the time."

Mitch actually laughed at that.

"Hey." His dad reached across the table and tapped Mitch's cheek. "I'm serious."

"Okay, so if he doesn't hate me, he's put this distance between us for the past five years for, what? Shits and giggles?"

"No, I suspect…"

"What?"

His dad shook his head.

Mitch kicked his foot under the table. "What?"

The expression on his dad's face this time said, "behave or I won't pay for your meal."

Huffing, Mitch sat back. "I emailed him, you know. Yeah." He nodded at his dad's raised eyebrows. "During the summer. The week before Cody and I went back to the Hamptons to visit. I wanted to let him know I was going to be there if he wanted to get a coffee or something. His return email said 'you shouldn't email me.'"

His dad winced. "I'll talk to him."

"Don't bother. I'm done with it."

Liar, liar, pants on fire!

Shut it, brain.

Mitch selected a roll from the bread basket and tore it in half. "Anyway, what are you doing in Vermont? A meeting or something?"

"Yeah. Client in Burlington wasn't happy, so I thought I'd make a personal appearance. Smooth some ruffled feathers."

That was his dad, constantly trying to put out fires.

The server returned with their meals. Mitch's medium rare steak in peppercorn sauce and loaded baked potato smelled fucking awesome. Seriously, smoothies and pizza were good and all, but a growing hockey player needed his meat and potatoes. Too bad he only ate this well when his dad was in town, which was only once every couple of months or so.

They chatted through dinner, Mitch keeping an eye on the time. Coach Bedley would bench him if Mitch arrived late at the rink, but Mitch had mastered the art of sneaking in right under the wire.

"I got a ticket to your game tonight," his dad said after he'd ordered dessert.

"Yeah?" Mitch grinned wide. "Cody's coming too. I promise not to suck today."

"I won't hold it against you if you do. Like I've said since you were a kid—"

"Hockey isn't everything," Mitch interrupted. "Yeah, I know."

"Speaking of… Did you ever get to talk to that guy? The sports guy from the NHL team you were telling me about?"

"Chris Blair. No, he missed his flight and didn't make the lecture. Someone else from the team showed up, though, and he's going to try and set something up between me and Chris."

His dad chased an ice cube with his spoon and popped it in his mouth. "That's nice of him," he said, crunching. "Or her. Who did they send in Chris Blair's place? Another trainer?"

"Alex Dean."

His dad almost choked on his ice cube. "The defenseman? Damn, why didn't you lead with that as soon as you got here? Did you get an autograph? A picture?"

Mitch laughed at his dad, who was acting like a pre-teen who'd bumped into Miley Cyrus on the street. "No, I wasn't there for an autograph. I was there to talk to him, get information."

His dad shook his head. "Kid, I worry about you sometimes." The server returned with his brownie sundae, and he promptly cut himself a huge bite. "What's he like? He as big in person?"

"Bigger." Six-four, broad shoulders, huge thighs, biceps Mitch probably couldn't wrap a hand around. Deep set green eyes, perpetual dark stubble, kissable lips.

"You're blushing."

"What?" Mitch blinked and the restaurant came back into focus. "No, I… No. I don't blush. Geez."

His dad grinned at him, an unholy gleam in his eyes. "You are. Question is why. Is it Alex Dean, or someone else you're thinking about?"

"I—I wasn't…" Mitch groaned and rubbed his hands over his face.

His dad continued to laugh. Mitch balled up a napkin and threw it at him.

Giving up his protests, Mitch chuckled along with him. "Yeah, it's Alex."

His dad moved his dessert plate to the center of the table and offered Mitch a fork. "What's going on? You seeing each other?"

"No? He's my creative writing tutor."

"Well, that's not where I saw this going."

Mitch forked a tiny piece of brownie and ice cream. "When I said I sucked at writing," he said around his bite, "I meant it. Alex's been helping me out."

"That's nice of him, but…why?"

"He's benched for the next few weeks. Broken arm."

His dad grunted. "Right. Heard about that."

"And he's here because… Actually, I don't know why.

Forgot to ask. Anyway, he's a GH alumnus and one of his friends is my creative writing TA. He asked Alex to tutor me, so…" Mitch shrugged. "That's pretty much it."

"Huh." His dad eyed Mitch closely. "And there's nothing else going on?"

Mitch cut himself another bite of brownie and avoided his dad's knowing look. "No."

Silence.

"Maybe?"

More silence.

"I don't know, okay?" Mitch dropped his fork, then ran a hand through his hair, and yanked. "I don't know. I mean, he doesn't even—" *like me.* Fuck, he did not want to admit to his dad how pathetic that was, and how hurt he still was by it, even though things had changed between him and Alex after Monday's impromptu pizza date-slash-tutoring session.

"Doesn't what?"

"He's not like me, or you, I guess. He's demisexual." Mitch shouldn't have blurted it out like that. Alex no doubt wouldn't appreciate Mitch telling a second person about his sexuality, but this was his *dad.* He wasn't going to advertise it to the world.

His dad blinked, brow furrowed. "So, he likes sex only half as much as other people? How do you measure something like that?"

Mitch snorted a laugh. "No. It means he doesn't experience sexual attraction unless he's formed a strong emotional bond with the other person."

"Ah. He falls with his heart first. Like Cody."

It was Mitch's turn to blink at his dad. "How do you know that?"

"Please," his dad said. "I'm not stupid. I've noticed how

he is. Which means, I've also noticed how my own son is. Is it the fact that you have feelings for Alex but he doesn't have any for you that has you twisted up in knots?"

Laid out so plainly, Mitch's unrequited crush made him seem pitifully immature.

"Sorry, kiddo."

"He said he could have feelings for me. At least, I think that's what he said?" Mitch scratched his head and blew out a breath. "He needs me to be real with him, but I don't know how to do that."

"Take your time," his dad said. "Nobody said it's now or never. You have a fragile heart—"

"What? I do *not*."

"—and you're very protective of it. If you explain to Alex that it's going to take you some time to become comfortable with him, I'm sure he'll understand. Especially since as a… What did you call him?"

"Demisexual."

"Right. Since he's demisexual, it's going to take him some time to develop feelings for you. If he does at all."

Mitch buried his face in his hands. "Thanks, Dad."

"I mean, of course he will." His dad patted Mitch on the head. "All I'm saying is, you're both going to be taking your time with each other for different reasons. Use that time. Get to know each other. And if nothing comes of it, then you'll have probably made a new friend for life."

"That's what Cody said."

"Because he's smart. He was always good for you. Anyway, shouldn't you be going?"

Jesus, two hours had flown by and Mitch needed to be at the rink in the next fifteen minutes if he didn't want to be benched.

Mitch waited outside in the setting sun, equipment bag

over his shoulder, while his dad paid the bill. When his dad came out of The Green Onion, he handed Mitch a wad of twenties.

"Here," he said. "Get some food in you. You've lost weight."

Mitch looked down at himself. "Have not."

His dad stuffed the money in the front pocket of Mitch's jeans. "I'll transfer some money into your account when I get back in front of my computer."

"Dad, you don't have to do that. Cody and I get by fine."

His dad put a hand on Mitch's back and steered him toward a rental car parked on the street. "By 'fine', I assume you mean living from paycheck to paycheck?"

Cheeks flushing, Mitch bumped his shoulder against his dad's. "Thanks."

"Don't mention it. Where are you parked?"

"I'm not. Cody dropped me off."

His dad grunted. "Why didn't he come in? You both know I wouldn't have minded if he joined us."

"You know Cody. He didn't want to intrude."

Another grunt from his dad. "Come on, I'll give you a ride to the rink."

Mitch put his seatbelt on and waited for his dad to pull out into the minimal traffic before asking, "Will I see you after the game?"

"I don't know, will you? Don't you guys party after games? This is college, right? Where everybody is always drunk."

"Sure, but if I tell my friends that I'm visiting with my dad since he's only in town for the day, then I don't have to go."

"Oh, I see. I'm your beard."

"Uh, I don't think that's how that word is supposed to be used."

"No?" His dad shrugged. "Huh. Regardless, why don't I come over after the game? I'll bring beer."

"Yeah? Alex wouldn't buy me beer the other day. Said I wasn't legal drinking age."

His dad pulled into Glen Hill College's athletic center parking lot and shot Mitch a wink. "I like him already."

It smelled like popcorn, sweat, and ice inside the Glen Hill College ice rink. Fuck, Alex loved this smell. Nothing smelled quite like a hockey rink, and damn he missed hockey.

His friends had dragged him to the GH vs Sacred Heart game after he'd spent the past four days ignoring them. The words were flowing, which meant his social life got put on the back burner in favor of writing. He'd spoken with a guy on his team earlier this week who was happy to share his story with Alex for his book. He and his wife had waited to have kids until after he retired from hockey, which was likely to be in the next couple of years. But they'd recently discovered that due to a pre-existing medical condition, she was past the age where she could safely bring a child to full term without endangering herself or the baby.

Dark side of sports, indeed. He'd written over ten thousand words in the past four days in between short breaks to visit Grandpa Forest. It was slow going, given he couldn't move the fingers sticking out of his cast much, but he was making it work.

"No pressure," his editor and former classmate, Kate Harvey, had said over the phone when he'd pitched his idea to her last week. "But we'd love to release this book in August or September next year, in time for the NHL preseason. So the sooner we have it, the better."

It left him until the end of February to get her a first draft.

Yeah, right. No pressure.

The crowd jumped to its feet, jerking Alex from his wandering thoughts. Fuck, his team had scored and he'd missed it.

On his right, Jay stuck two fingers in his mouth and let out a piercing whistle. When he sat back down, Alex asked, "What'd I miss?"

"Seriously?" Incredulousness dripped from his voice. "Where've you been?"

"Just…" He shook his head. "Lost in thoughts."

"Your grandpa?" Jay bumped his shoulder. "Sorry, man. So, who's the guy you're tutoring?"

The topic change wasn't exactly subtle, but Alex jumped on it anyway. "That guy." He pointed. "Number nineteen."

"That's the guy who just scored."

Alex had to laugh. Of course it had been Mitch who'd scored. Alex had learned via archived GH newspaper articles and Youtube videos that Mitch was the Mountaineers' top scorer, even last year when he'd been a green freshman.

Coach Bedley had told Alex that they tried not to put Mitch in front of reporters, and now Alex knew why. His favorite Mitch Greyson quote was from an article last year, when the reporter had asked Mitch how he felt about winning the game.

Mitch's response? "Why do reporters ask such stupid questions? How do you think I feel? We fucking won. Jesus."

Alex had stumbled on the articles accidentally when he'd been searching for some background on Mitch for his book. He still hadn't asked Mitch for his help, sure that the kid would close down and retreat behind his walls if he did. Mitch no doubt wouldn't appreciate Alex going behind his back and digging for information online, but really, there was nothing to find. Only numerous articles and a seldom used social media account.

"Man, that guy is on fire!" Jay yelled when Mitch scored yet again in the third.

"He might suck at writing," JP said from Jay's other side. "But he's one hell of a hockey player."

No argument, there. Mitch was wicked on the ice, playing with a renewed fire that had been missing from last week's games against Denver. His speed was incredible. He did some kind of fancy footwork that allowed him to turn on a dime and then turn the other way again, all while weaving between players and shooting a cross-ice pass to his right winger. Mitch moved so fast, the other players seemed to be standing still. It was amazing to watch.

Alex pictured himself attempting Mitch's fancy foot-work, then imagined himself promptly falling on his ass. Maybe he'd ask Mitch for some pointers.

The game ended with a shutout for the Mountaineers. Embarrassingly, Alex had missed most of it, lost in thoughts about Grandpa Forest and his book and Mitch's latest revisions to his short story for JP's class.

Mitch's story was incredibly sad. It was about a kid who had one last chance at joining a hockey team. Despite being a talented player, no other team wanted him because they didn't like him. This was his last shot. He didn't make it, and he ended up working a job he hated—on a bee farm—for the rest of his life, where he eventually died from one too many bee stings.

Was that how Mitch felt? Like the entire world was against him? Was he worried that he'd end up alone, in a job he despised, where he'd work himself into having a heart attack at an early age?

Alex wouldn't normally read so much into a person's story, but since Mitch wasn't a writer and thus unschooled on creating characters and conflict, he'd most likely unconsciously written a character and situation that mirrored his own. It gave Alex a whole new perspective on who Mitch was.

Mitch's character was lonely and sad because he'd been hurt by people who were supposed to love him, and he'd built a wall to keep everyone at arm's length.

Had Mitch created a character who was basically... him?

Midway across the parking lot on his way to JP's car, Alex stopped. Jay almost bumped into him.

"Dude," Jay said. "Don't stop in the middle of the road."

Up ahead, JP paused to wait for them.

"I'll meet you guys there." Alex reversed course and headed back the way he'd come. "There's something I need to do first."

He found a freshly showered Mitch in the hallway outside the locker room talking to a tall blond guy who looked about Mitch's age, and an even taller guy with a shaved head who looked like a boxer. Shit, Alex didn't want to interrupt. Wait or go, wait or go.

Mitch's shouted "Alex!" took the decision out of his hands.

Alex joined the little group and was promptly introduced to Mitch's best friend, Cody, and his dad, Geoff.

"I hear you're tutoring Mitch in his writing course," Geoff said.

"Yes, sir."

"He needs it."

"I know it."

"Hey!"

Alex laughed. "I'm kidding," he said to Mitch. "Actually, the last revisions you sent me this morning were spot on. You can go ahead and submit it now."

"Oh, okay. Thanks." Mitch bit his lip and blinked at Alex blankly. "Is that what you came to tell me?"

Alex jerked a thumb over his shoulder. "Some friends and I are headed to the Bean Bag for an hour or so. I was going to ask if you wanted to join us, but, uh…" He waved at Geoff and Cody.

"You were?" Mitch's voice rose. He cleared his throat and fidgeted on his feet. "Thanks, but…" He looked at Geoff. "My dad's only here for the day."

"You should go out with your friends, kiddo."

"What? No, I—"

"It's okay," Alex said. The image of Mitch as sad and lonely because he thought nobody liked him made Alex's chest hurt. If he needed friends, Alex was going to god-damn give them to him. JP and Jay accepted anyone, as long as they were decent. And Mitch was that, once he relaxed enough to drop his walls. But the indecision on Mitch's face was obvious and Alex didn't want to put him in a tough spot. "Next time?"

Mitch beamed at him. "Definitely."

Alex backed away. "It was nice to meet you," he said to Geoff. He nodded at Cody, who'd stood mutely watching the interplay with interest. "Nice game tonight, Mitch."

"Thanks. See you Monday?"

Alex nodded once, turned, and started the short walk to the coffee shop to join his friends.

SEVEN

THE NINE-TO-FIVE STINT ON SUNDAYS WAS MITCH'S only shift at the long-term care facility in Montpelier, and since it was about as interesting as reading the phone book, he inevitably left the place every weekend tired and grumpy. Combined with the head-banging math tutoring session with his freshmen this morning, he was ready for dinner and a nap—not necessarily in that order—before hunkering down with the reading for tomorrow's biomechanics lecture.

Finding a dejected pro hockey player in the facility's parking lot wasn't part of his evening plans, but Mitch didn't mind, especially when that hockey player was Alex Dean. Mitch's heart leapt, and then crashed when Alex's slumped shoulders registered.

Alex sat on the trunk of his car, his feet on the bumper, elbows on his knees, with one hand buried in his hair. He stared at the ground and was so lost in thought, he didn't react when Mitch stopped in front of him and cleared his throat. Mitch shifted on his feet and cleared his throat again. He wanted to reach out and run his fingers through Alex's beard, but resisted the urge. Alex would probably slap his hands away.

Bending at the knees, Mitch peered up at Alex's face until he caught Alex's eyes.

"Jesus!" Alex jerked up, hand on his chest. "Where the fuck did you come from?"

A witty reply was on the tip of Mitch's tongue, but he

resisted that urge too. He jerked a thumb over his shoulder. "I work here."

"You…" Alex's brow furrowed. "Doing what?"

"Office stuff. Filing, returning phone calls, inventory, ordering supplies, restocking, that sort of thing."

"Sounds…fun?"

"It's about as much fun as my creative writing class."

Alex laughed, and Mitch mentally patted himself on the back for putting a little bit of light back into his friend's dark eyes.

"What are you doing here?" Mitch said.

Alex lost his smile, and his shoulders slumped further, if that was possible. "I was here to visit someone, but the nurses said he's not having a good day and I should come back tomorrow."

Questions raced through Mitch's head. *Who are you visiting? How long've they been here? What does 'not a good day' mean? How long have you been sitting here?*

Can I touch your beard?

Stop that!

Mitch shook his head to scatter his wayward thoughts. Dropping his backpack next to the car, he hopped up to sit on the trunk next to Alex. "What are you up to now, then?"

Alex shrugged those massive shoulders and squinted against the setting sun. "Dunno. I was going to go home, but…"

Mitch waited, but Alex never finished his sentence. Instead, he stared off into space, unmoving, looking so hopeless that Mitch had to bank the desire to reach out and put his arm around him.

They sat quietly for a few minutes, breathing in the chilly evening air. Mitch shivered in his long-sleeved T-shirt, but didn't get up to fish the hoodie out of his backpack, afraid any sudden movements would ruin the comfortable silence they'd settled into.

The facility was built on the outskirts of Montpelier, nestled between a hill with trees that were slowly losing their leaves to winter, and a stretch of flat land that led downtown. Away from the relative hustle and bustle of State and Main Streets, it was peaceful and still, and it smelled like wet grass. Mitch felt the stress that was a constant weight on his shoulders release.

Alex turned to him with narrowed eyes. After a few seconds of yet more silence, Mitch looked down at himself, but didn't note any stains. Was Alex looking at something behind him? Mitch turned to check, making Alex laugh.

"What?"

Alex shook his head, lips quirked. "Nothing. I'm hungry. Let's get dinner in town." He hopped off the trunk, making Mitch bounce in place as the car adjusted to the sudden loss of over two hundred pounds, and headed for the driver's side door.

"Actually," Mitch said. "I have a better idea."

An hour later, their bellies full of drive-thru burgers and fries they'd picked up on their way back to Glen Hill, Mitch was in his skates and drawing figure eights on the ice. A few feet away, wearing borrowed skates Mitch had pilfered from Marco's locker, Alex grinned and pulled his sleeves up, exposing a strong forearm dusted with almost-black hair. A thick cast encased the other forearm. There was some kind of drawing on it, but Mitch couldn't tell what it was from this distance.

Alex waved his hand at him. "Show me what you just did."

Mitch came to a stop. "What did I just do?"

"That thing with your feet."

Confused, Mitch scratched his head.

Alex pointed at the figure eight on the otherwise pristine ice. "Do what you just did."

Mitch skated to the middle of the eight, where the top and bottom circles connected, and pushed off on his right outside edge. He completed the figure eight, slowing his moves so that Alex could follow along, speaking them aloud as he did them.

"I want to learn that," Alex said.

It was one of the earliest moves Mitch had been taught in the figure skating lessons he'd taken as a kid and he'd mastered it almost instantly. Alex, on the other hand, fell on his ass attempting the first turn.

Mitch hovered over him. "Don't break your head as well as your arm."

"Fuck you." Alex pushed himself up, groaning.

"Anytime, big guy."

"I'm not *big*."

Mitch tilted his head and zeroed in on Alex's crotch. Even through underwear and jeans, Mitch could tell the man was hung.

Alex let out a laugh, stood, and brushed the ice from his ass. "You don't give up, do you?"

"Nope. Again?"

Half an hour later, Alex admitted defeat. "Teach me how to skate backwards."

"Uh, I'm pretty sure you already know how. You're a hockey player."

"I mean like you. With the—" He made a move with

his arms, crossing one hand over the other. "The crossover. But backwards."

"That's not any easier than the figure eights. It takes time to become comfortable skating backwards."

"Yeah." Alex skated right up to him. Mitch sucked in a breath at his proximity. Goose pimples broke out over his neck and his stomach quivered. "But as you've oh-so-helpfully pointed out," Alex said, "I already know how to skate backwards. Just not as fast as you. Show me."

"Okay, come on." Mitch led Alex to the boards, where he had Alex place his hands on the barrier in front of the GH Mountaineers' bench. "Feet shoulder width apart. Knees slightly bent. You want to make sure your weight is on the balls of your feet."

Alex's eyebrows went up. "You know I've been skating longer than you, right?

Mitch threw his hands up. "I just want to make sure you're not going to tumble onto your ass. Again."

"We'll see who's falling on his ass."

"That an invitation?" Mitch asked, even though he knew it wasn't.

"No, it isn't, you horn dog."

Chuckling, Mitch told Alex to take the position and then had him push off.

"What's the point of this?" Alex asked as he slowly coasted backwards.

"I just wanted to make sure your athletic stance was good. Which it is."

Alex scowled at him. "Of course it is. You just wanted to ogle my ass."

"That too."

"You're impossible."

"I prefer incorrigible."

"Okay, smart-ass. Show me what's next." Alex pointed a finger at him. "For real, this time."

It took Alex no time at all to get the hang of it. By the time he was confident doing backwards crossovers, Mitch had convinced himself he was hallucinating.

Here was a professional hockey player asking Mitch for tips. It was fucking surreal. Alex was a strong skater, even without extra tools in his wheelhouse, and Mitch was dying to play either with him or against him, he didn't particularly care. He just wanted to be wielding a stick during a game at the same time as Alex.

"You should join us for practice sometime," he said to Alex once they'd retired to the Mountaineers' bench.

Alex held up his broken right hand. "I can't hold a hockey stick."

"You don't need one for some of the drills we do."

"True." Alex took a pull from his water bottle. "I'll think about it. Coach Bedley did say I was welcome."

"Then you should totally come. We practice Monday, Wednesday, and Friday mornings. Friday practice gets moved to Thursday if we have a Friday evening game."

"The schedule hasn't changed, I see."

Mitch untied his laces. "Is it weird being back here?"

Alex's lips pursed. He took a minute to answer. "Yes and no. This was home for four years. I haven't skated in this rink in over two years, but it's still familiar. Yet at the same time, it feels foreign. I don't know if that makes any sense."

"It does." Mitch slipped out of his skates and into his running shoes. "It's like when I go home for a visit. It always feels like I've been gone for years, but also like I was just there two days before."

"Yes." Alex turned his gaze on Mitch, and he studied

him with what Mitch liked to think was appreciation, or maybe affection. "That's it exactly. That's what it feels like to be back here."

Mitch smiled back at Alex. *Don't look at the beard!* The beard made him think sexy thoughts. Namely what it'd feel like against his jaw when they kissed.

Fuck. Mitch's cheeks heated despite the coldness of the rink. He pressed his water bottle to his forehead and took a deep breath. "Do you miss your team?"

"I miss some of them," Alex said. "The guys who are good friends. I'll see them in a couple of days, though."

The water bottle slipped out of Mitch's hand, bounced away, and rolled to a stop against the boards. Shit, was Alex going back to Tampa already?

Alex reached forward and rescued the bottle. "We're playing a game of street hockey with some kids from a shelter on Thursday," he said, handing Mitch his water.

"Oh. So you're not leaving yet?"

"No, I'll only be gone a few days. I don't head back for good for another month or so."

A month. A month was all Mitch had to get Alex to like him. Was that enough time? Considering his mother had had almost twenty years to warm up to him, the answer was most likely a resounding "hell no."

Alex bumped his shoulder against Mitch's. Warmth pooled in Mitch's chest at the friendly gesture. "Thanks for this," Alex said. "How did you know I miss skating?"

Mitch shrugged. "I didn't. Just figured it'd probably been a while since you'd been on the ice. I'd miss it, if it was me."

The expression on Alex's face confused Mitch. Furrowed brow with a slight smile. He looked like a pleasantly surprised bear.

"What?"

Alex shook his head. "You surprise me."

"In a good way, right? 'Cause I'm awesome."

Alex laughed.

Mitch bit his lip to contain a grin and sat on his hands to warm them. "Do you want to talk about it? Whatever was bothering you earlier?"

Alex's sigh held an ounce of resignation, but none of the dejection from earlier. "My grandpa has Alzheimer's."

Mitch winced. "I'm sorry. I shouldn't have asked."

"No, it's fine. I don't mind." Alex took a breath before continuing. "He doesn't know who I am. Hasn't in two years."

Mitch shifted closer to Alex, offering what support he could.

"I got this for him." Alex held up his left arm.

On the inside of his wrist, "Hockey" was written in script. The last vertical line in the "H" and the bottom of the "Y" met underneath the word in an "X" formed by two hockey sticks. Before he could think better of it, Mitch reached out and palmed Alex's wrist, running his thumb over the tattoo.

Alex froze.

"Sorry." Mitch snatched his hand back. Shit. If Alex was anything like Cody, he didn't like to be touched except by people he considered his. For Cody, that amounted to his mom, Mitch, and Mitch's dad. For Alex, the list, however long it was, most certainly did not include Mitch.

Yet. Mitch was working his way there.

"It's okay." Alex lowered his sleeve, covering the tattoo. He blinked, and whatever confusion Mitch might've seen in his eyes was gone before Mitch could be sure it'd been there to begin with. "Anyway, he wasn't having a good day today apparently, so I couldn't visit him."

"I don't know what 'not having a good day' means. Sorry, I don't know much about Alzheimer's."

"I hope you never have to," Alex said. "It means he's angry and confused and doesn't know what's going on. It usually happens when he's overly tired or stressed, so he must not've been sleeping well lately."

"I'm sorry." Mitch didn't know what else to say. "Do you visit him often?"

Alex scratched an itch on his hand. "When I'm in Tampa, no. Not as much as I'd like. But while I'm here, I've been going every day."

"Wow. That…" *must be so fucking hard.* "That's dedicated."

"He doesn't have a lot of time left." Alex's smile was sad and it pulled at Mitch's heart. "He was a constant in my life growing up. My biggest supporter, along with my mom, when it came to hockey. And he never got to see me play in the NHL." Alex's voice was raspy, and his heartache so palpable, Mitch felt like he'd been whacked in the stomach with a hockey stick. He could only imagine what Alex was going through.

"I don't know what to say, Alex. Except, that fucking sucks."

Alex huffed a breathy laugh that sounded anything but amused.

"I was wondering why you came here while you're out of the game."

"To see my grandpa mostly," Alex confirmed. "And I get to visit some old friends too. I'm also using my down-time to write a book. I doubt I'll get it all written, but I'm hoping to get a decent head start, since I'll have less free time once this cast comes off."

"You're writing a book? What kind? Wait, can I guess?

Science fiction," Mitch said without waiting for a response. "No, fantasy. A kid's book?"

Alex chuckled, crinkling his eyes at the corners. "None of the above, although I do hope to write a romance one day. I'm actually writing a nonfiction about hockey. Coach Bedley gave me the idea, but you inspired me."

"Me?"

"Coach Bedley mentioned how hard you work for your team and for your degree. He said he'd never seen a more dedicated player or student, and it got me thinking—what's the cost of a hockey career? Physically, mentally, emotionally, even personally. What do people sacrifice in the name of the game?"

Mitch gazed at the rink, the ice smooth except on the half they'd skated on. "I don't feel like I've sacrificed anything."

What had he given up, exactly? His mother's respect and acceptance? He wouldn't have had that, even if he had gone into the family business. His social life? He had Cody and he had the camaraderie with his teammates. What else did he need?

"Nothing?" Alex asked. "There's not a single thing you've given up in order to play that you wish you hadn't had to?"

His personal life. The freedom to be who he was without fear of reprisal. It was something that hadn't mattered as recently as a few weeks ago, until he met Alex. Not that he was under the delusion that Alex had feelings for him yet—if ever. But the possibility had him suddenly longing for a world where being something other than heterosexual wasn't a big deal.

"You don't have to answer," Alex said when Mitch remained silent. "I'm not trying to dig into your life, just show you the angle I'm using for the book. Professional sports isn't all money and fame. There's a darker side to it too."

"Like what?"

Alex leaned forward, elbows on his knees. "One guy I interviewed plays for an NHL team in Canada. He got divorced because his wife couldn't handle all of his travelling. He gave her up instead of the game. Another guy's mother passed away just before he joined an ECHL team and he'd inherited her credit card debts. There were a lot. He couldn't afford to pay them *and* rent, so he lived in his car so he wouldn't have to give up playing the game he loved in order to get a better paying job in an office or something."

Man. Mitch couldn't imagine living out of a car. How would he eat? Shower? Go to the bathroom? But then again, he couldn't imagine giving up hockey either. Would he make the same decision under those circumstances?

Yes. Definitely yes.

"Anyway." Alex shook his head and smiled sheepishly at Mitch. "Thanks for bringing me here today." He squeezed Mitch's knee. "I really needed it."

"You're welcome." Mitch ignored the tingle in his leg. "Ready to head out?"

"Can we stay a little while longer?"

"Sure."

"Unless… Do you have somewhere to be? Sorry, we can go." Alex bent to untie his skates.

"No, Alex, it's fine. I don't have anywhere to be." Nowhere that was more important than helping a friend who needed it.

"Yeah?" Alex shot Mitch a grateful smile that had Mitch's inside doing weird things. "Thanks. Come on, let's get back on the ice."

"Hang on, I've got to put my skates back on."

They didn't try any fancy moves, simply skated leisurely laps side by side. Alex was a tall guy without his skates, several inches over six feet. On skates, he was a fucking giant. Add his broad shoulders and muscles and unfairly gorgeous face and the man was just...

Mitch wanted to climb him like a tree, right there and then. Of course, he couldn't. Not until Alex gave him the okay, if that ever happened. He'd just have to keep jerking off to a lonely shower.

"Hey, Alex?"

"Hmm?"

"You know you have an anatomically incorrect cock and balls on your cast, right?"

Alex swore and covered his cast with his sleeve. "I was hoping you wouldn't notice."

"It's purple. Not exactly inconspicuous."

Alex grumbled something under his breath that sounded like "Fucking Jay."

EIGHT

"HA!" MITCH THREW HIS CONTROLLER ASIDE and leapt off the couch, arms in the air. "Told you I'd win. Suck it, Dean."

"You won the first race." Alex navigated through Mario Kart's menu. "One race does not a championship trophy win you."

"Thank you, Master Yoda."

"I could be Yoda."

Mitch cracked up.

Instead of finding himself sitting across from Mitch at a restaurant enduring stilted getting-to-know-you conversation, Alex sat on Mitch's loveseat engrossed in a fierce Mario Kart battle on this, his second date with Mitch. Not that he was under the delusion that their pizza dinner-slash-tutoring session at Mama Jean's last week had been anything but just that. But letting Mitch call it a date had seemed like a saner idea than arguing with him.

Except this "date" was more of a hangout than a date, which was fine with Alex. Less pressure, more fun. Mitch was on his best behavior too. No come-ons, no innuendos. Nothing except a crack about how pizza was his favorite after-sex food. It was a little freaky sitting here, attempting to anticipate when Mitch's flirty half would make an appearance.

But maybe it wouldn't. Maybe that guy, the I'm-the-shit-and-I-know-it guy, was finally taking a backseat, allowing the real Mitch, the video game playing, hockey loving, hard-working one, to take over.

Alex was kicking ass in the next race despite the hindered mobility in his right hand and enjoying the hell out of it, especially when he took a detour and Mitch lost his mind.

"What the fuck?" Mitch said, incredulous. "Where the hell are you? There's no shortcuts in this race."

"That's what you think."

"What? No. I Googled."

Alex let out an evil cackle. "Not hard enough."

"You're going to show me where that is."

"Not in this century, I won't."

"I'll blow you for it," Mitch offered.

"I'm sure you would." Alex won the race with Mitch still a lap behind. "Who's crowing now, brat?"

"This is so not how I saw this going." On screen, Mitch's poor, sad player finally completed her final lap. "Ugh." Mitch picked a cold broccoli floret off the pizza they'd ordered from Mama Jean's and chucked it at Alex. It bounced off Alex's shoulder, landed on the loveseat, then rolled onto the floor. "For a laid-back dude, you're way more competitive than I expected you to be."

"I'm an athlete." Alex pointed out the obvious and picked up the wayward broccoli. He popped it in his mouth.

"Ew." Mitch's face scrunched. "That's disgusting. What if I'd, I don't know, peed on the floor or something?"

"Man, you had me fooled. Here I thought you were civilized."

Mitch gave him the finger.

Hungry again, Alex nabbed one of the last slices of pizza out of the box on the coffee table and ate it cold.

"I can warm that up for you," Mitch said. He cued up the next race, but didn't start it.

"No need." Alex bit into the cold pizza, still stunned

that Mitch had ordered the cauliflower crust. It was unexpectedly thoughtful.

Mitch's townhouse was warm and cozy, done in simple earth tones. There wasn't much in the way of decoration except for a few table lamps, a couple of dusty cookbooks on the kitchen counter, a bookshelf in the corner of the living room filled with DVDs, and a crescent-shaped wooden sun catcher in the window. As the townhouse was boxed in on both sides, there wasn't much natural light, but the bright indoor lighting created a sense of peacefulness, a quiet space to just be.

There was a small pile of dirty dishes in the sink and a clean pile in the dish rack. A laptop, a couple of anatomy textbooks, and a thick binder sat atop the island. There was a hoodie draped over the back of one of the island barstools, a haphazard pile of DVDs underneath the coffee table, and a discarded pair of socks next to the TV.

"Do you have any roommates?" Alex asked.

"Just one." Mitch removed his ever-present flannel shirt, leaving him in jeans and a blue T-shirt. He stretched out on the couch, one arm behind his head, making his T-shirt ride up to expose his toned stomach as if he was modeling for a magazine. The smirk on his face told Alex it was intentional. "Cody."

"Where is he?"

"Work. He has a job at the campus library. Should be back soon, I think."

"How'd you guys meet?"

Mitch's smile turned genuine and he let out a small laugh. "First day of first grade. Some older kid was picking on me. Cody punched him in the 'nads."

Alex laughed, even as he cringed and fought the urge to protect his sensitive bits.

"We got in so much trouble. It was awesome."

"Only you would think so." Alex polished off his slice and wiped his hands on a napkin.

"How's your grandpa today?" The laughter disappeared from Mitch's face. "Any better?"

Alex ran a hand through his hair and avoided Mitch's sympathetic gaze. "He was still a bit agitated." It was hard to imagine that Grandpa Forest had once been Alex's staunchest supporter, his sounding board. A man who never judged, who always had time for people in need, and made Alex feel safe when his dad had walked out. Grandpa Forest had put his own life on hold to spend four months in Toronto with Alex and his mom right after Judd left, spending hours with Alex, eating ketchup chips, as they dissected the previous evening's hockey game. That his disease had turned him into someone who sometimes got so confused, he suspected people of poisoning him was often impossible to grasp. It left Alex feeling like he was swimming in mud.

"So he remembered who you were?" Mitch asked.

Alex's belly clenched. "No. He hasn't recognized me in over two years. He thinks I'm my dad."

"Oh." Mitch sat up. "Shit, Alex. That blows. Who does he think your dad is, then?"

Alex shrugged. "My dad doesn't visit. He left my mom and me when I was nine. Cut off all contact with us and with Grandpa Forest."

Mitch's eyebrows pulled together and he opened his mouth.

Alex grabbed his controller. "Let's play the next race."

"Alex, I—"

The front door opened, cutting Mitch off and saving Alex from what was, in all likelihood, pity Alex didn't want or need.

"Dude!" Cody—presumably—called as he trudged down the hallway toward them. "My eyes are broken."

"What the fuck does that even mean?" Mitch asked.

"It means there was a—oh, uh, hi."

"Cody, you remember Alex?" Mitch muted the television. "Alex, my BFF-slash-roommate, Cody."

"Hey." Alex stood and offered his left hand. "Good to see you again."

"Uh-huh." Cody shook Alex's hand, eyeing Alex, then Mitch, then Alex again. "What'cha guys up to?"

Twin spots of color appeared on Mitch's cheeks for no reason Alex could figure out. "Just playing Mario Kart. Why are your eyes broken?"

Cody pilfered the second to last slice of pizza and took a seat on one of the barstools. "There was a fucking used condom in the men's room at the library. First, it's a fucking restroom. Why couldn't you find the goddamn garbage? Second, who the fuck does it in the library?"

"People who like books?" Mitch offered.

"You're such a brat." Cody spoke around the pizza in his mouth.

Alex grinned and threw his hands in the air, as though he'd just scored the game winning goal.

"Shit." Mitch flopped back on the couch and covered his face with a pillow.

"That's what I've been calling him," Alex told Cody.

"I never should've introduced you," came Mitch's muffled voice through the pillow.

Cody beamed at Alex. "We're going to be such good friends."

"Just shoot me," Mitch mumbled.

"What was that you were saying the other day about Alex and I being able to eat you for breakfast?" Cody asked him.

"I have no idea what that means," Alex said.

"Nothing." Mitch popped up and found a third controller. "It's nothing. Codes, want to play?"

They spent an hour and a half playing round after round of Mario Kart. Cody, it turned out, wasn't very good but he didn't seem to care that he lost every race.

Eventually, Mitch paused the game. "Gotta piss," he said, and disappeared down the hallway.

Alex got up to refill his glass. Other than the water jug, the fridge also held butter, assorted condiments, three jars of Cheese Whiz, a plethora of fruit, celery, and about four gallons of maple syrup. What the hell Mitch and Cody were making with those ingredients was anybody's guess.

"Mitch invited you over tonight?" Cody asked when Alex had retaken his position on the loveseat.

"How else would I be here?"

"It's just…" Cody lowered his voice. "Nobody has ever set foot in this house since we moved in last year except me and him, his dad, and my mom."

"Okay?" Alex squinted at him. "Sorry, I'm not understanding."

Cody peered down the hallway, keeping an eye out for Mitch, most likely. "It was Mitch's suggestion. That this should be our space. I think he sees it as his safe space, where he can let his guard down and be himself, not have to be 'on' or pretend. None of his friends have ever been here. I don't think they even know where he lives. Yet, here you are."

"Here I am," Alex repeated, baffled. "What does that mean?" Did it mean that Mitch felt safe with him? Safe enough that he didn't feel like he had to pretend to be somebody else? Safe enough to let down his guard and his walls? Mitch was certainly less "on" with Alex than he had been, but Alex wasn't dense enough not to notice that for every piece of personal information he gave Mitch, Mitch held one back. Mitch had revealed virtually nothing personal about himself in the few times they'd hung out. Everything Alex knew about him was surface stuff anybody could've learned by spending a few hours with him. The one thing Alex did know—that Mitch didn't invite people into his home—hadn't even come from the man himself.

"Honestly, I have no fucking clue." Cody moved the empty pizza box to the floor and propped his feet on the table. "Make of it what you will."

Unhelpful. Okay, that was fine. Alex could wing it, which is what he'd been doing since meeting Mitch anyway.

"What was that thing about eating Mitch for breakfast?" Alex asked.

Cody's smile was sly. "You'll have to figure that one out for yourself."

Fucker.

Mitch slid back into the room, slipping and sliding on socked feet on the wooden floor. He grabbed his controller from the table. Instead of retaking his seat on the other couch next to Cody, he plopped himself next to Alex. "What'd I miss?"

"We talked about you the whole time," Cody said.

"All good things, obviously." Mitch brought up the next race. "'Cause I'm the bomb diggety."

Cody called Mitch a nerd, Alex chuckled, and they played Mario Kart until well after midnight.

Three days later, Alex pulled into the parking lot next to Amalie Arena. Exiting the car, he squinted against the

Florida sun, even with his sunglasses on. The heat was so oppressive, it was hard to breathe and his T-shirt stuck to him almost instantly.

He fucking hated Florida.

Alex was Canadian, born and bred. He wanted snowy winter landscapes, spring rains, summer kayaking, and fall colors. Instead, he was stuck in Satan's armpit. He loved playing hockey for Tampa, but Florida could kiss his ass.

Inside the arena, it was blissfully cool. Almost too cool, compared to the heat outside, like most indoor establishments in Florida. A happy medium did not exist. You either sweated your balls off outside or froze your nipples inside.

He missed Vermont already.

Chris Blair was exactly where Alex expected: in his tiny office attached to his treatment room.

"Knock, knock," Alex said as he approached the door.

"Alex." Chris stood and shook Alex's left hand. "It's good to see you. Come in, have a seat. You won't bump into any of your teammates, I'm afraid. There's no practice today."

"I saw them this morning." Alex took the chair across from Chris's desk. "For the game of street hockey with the kids from the shelter?"

"Right. I forgot that was today. How'd it go?"

Alex shrugged. "You know what it's like, trying to get Southern kids interested in hockey. I think most of them were just happy for an excuse not to be in school."

"Any of them mention the dick on your cast?" Chris tilted his head, ostensibly to get a better look at it.

Alex groaned. The comments from the kids had ranged from "Did you draw that?" to "I hope you're not fucking anyone with that thing."

Seriously. The vocabulary on some of these ten year olds.

"Didn't you see the doctor this afternoon about your arm?" Chris leaned back in his chair. "Could've asked him for a new cast."

"I thought about it," Alex admitted. "Seemed like a waste of time and resources, when this one's still perfectly fine. Barring the purple penis, that is."

Chris chuckled. "What'd the doc say about your arm? Rehab?"

"He thinks no. Just regular exercise to strengthen it back up. I'm sure my arm looks like a shrivelled melon under here." It was also itchy as hell. "He'll know more once the cast comes off, but everything looks good for now."

"When does it come off?"

"Five weeks from now."

Chris grunted and rubbed his chin. "First week of December. Add in a couple of weeks for strength training and drills… You talk to Coach yet?"

"Yeah, I called him on the way here. He's thinking PT and drills once the cast comes off, then putting me back in the game after Christmas."

"Makes sense."

It meant another two months on the IR list, which, in turn, meant more time with Grandpa Forest. Rather than anticipating all that extra time, Alex felt the weight of his grandfather's disease press on his shoulders. It was becoming clearer and clearer that his grandpa would never see him play in the NHL. JP and Jay kept giving him shit for visiting alone, insistent that moral support would make things easier.

Alex was certain nothing could make Alzheimer's easier. At least he had the book he was writing as a distraction.

"I talked to your friend today," Chris said, interrupting his thoughts. "Mitch Greyson."

"You did?" Alex had been texting with Mitch since he landed in Tampa on Tuesday morning and Mitch hadn't mentioned a thing. "How'd it go?"

"I like him. He's intense, but he's got a good head on his shoulders. Determined. Ambitious. Asked a lot of questions—the *right* questions. Smart. Knows what he wants. Hell, if he was graduating this year, I'd offer him an internship if he didn't get drafted."

Mitch's ability to get people to like him was off-the-charts. He was personable and friendly, and when he wasn't trying too hard or hiding behind his walls, he was…actually very sweet and considerate. That Mitch had stayed with him on Sunday when Alex hadn't been allowed in to see Grandpa Forest had meant a lot to Alex. Mitch could've wished him better luck next time and went on his way. Instead, he'd sat quietly with Alex and then taken him ice skating to get his mind off things and make him feel better.

Yeah. Sweet. It was hidden under Mitch's hard surface, but it was there. It was there in how he hadn't felt it necessary to fill empty silence with words. It was there in how he'd so optimistically insisted that if they could just become friends, Alex might become attracted to him. It was there in how he'd adorably and firmly declared that their tutoring session had been a date. It was there in how he'd ordered the pizza with the cauliflower crust, just because it was the one Alex liked.

Alex leaned forward, his elbows on his knees, and refocused on the conversation. "Did you tell him that?"

"Yup. He told me to keep him in mind in two and a half years if things don't go his way with the draft."

"That sounds like him. I'm pretty sure he'll be drafted, though."

"I'm with you on that." Chris turned his laptop toward Alex, where a video was paused. "I was watching YouTube videos when you arrived. I think he might be better than you were at his age."

"There's no 'might' about it." Mitch was in a league of his own. Whoever drafted him would, however, need to spend some time schooling him on what not to say to the press. *Why do reporters ask such stupid questions?* wouldn't fly in the NHL.

Alex nodded at the laptop. "There's a video of his highlights from last season on there."

"Where? Show me."

"Actually, before we get to that," Alex said, "there's something I wanted to ask. A favor."

"Shoot."

"So, I'm writing this book…" He gave Chris the same explanation he'd given Mitch, about the dark side of professional sports, and finished with, "Do you think I could interview you for the book, get your perspective? You've probably got tons of stories about athletes playing through injuries or against doctor's orders. Is there anything you can share? And if this goes against client confidentiality, just say the word and I'll pretend I never asked."

Chris nodded slowly. "It does, but I also think this is a good thing you're doing. Lots of people only see the glamor of professional sports, but you're getting into the nitty gritty, into what a player's willing to sacrifice for the game. There are a couple of people whose stories would be good for you to hear. Let me talk to them, see if they're okay with me talking to you." He snapped his fingers. "Have you seen Theresa? Or Todd or Barb?" The team's nutritionist, psychologist, and head physician.

"Not yet. I plan to before I leave."

"Good, good." Chris grinned. "Now that that's out of the way, show me Mitch's highlights."

Mama Jean's was always packed on a Friday night, but what Alex walked into the next day, after the GH Mountaineers won against Northeastern with a shutout, was chaos multiplied by a thousand. It was loud, and standing room only. Also, because it was Halloween, there was orange beer and orange pizza and fake spiderwebs on the walls. And, of course, costumes.

"Jesus," JP said from behind him. "I forgot how crazy people get after we win."

Crazy didn't even cut it.

They found Jay and his girlfriend, Leah, at the order counter, which was the only area of the restaurant where there was still a tiny bit of space. Alex had to shout his drink order over Katy Perry's "I Kissed A Girl" to the vampire behind the counter.

In the middle of the restaurant, Mitch, dressed as Tom Cruise in *Risky Business*, dragged a taller, broader guy—the Mountaineers' goalie, if Alex wasn't mistaken—onto a tabletop. Mitch raised the goalie's hand into the air. "Who kicked ass tonight?" he yelled into the insanity that was Mama Jean's.

A collective "Marco, Marco, Marco!" went up from the crowd, the cheer so loud Alex's ears hurt.

Mitch was in his element as he hopped off the table and traipsed from group to group, chatting and laughing. For once, his affability in a crowd didn't look fake. Rather, he looked like he was having fun and letting loose and enjoying his win. And he damn well should—he'd scored two of the four goals.

Parties had never been, and still weren't, Alex's scene, but being here after a win brought back all sorts of memories of his four years at Glen Hill College. Good ones—like playing hockey, meeting friends who would become family, and making it to the Frozen Four his senior year. And some not so good ones—like the team choking at the Frozen Four, and Grandpa Forest's diagnosis.

"Buy me a beer, hot stuff?"

Alex turned at the voice near his ear. Mitch stood next to him, flushed, curly hair completely disheveled, oversized shirt hanging limp, white socks dirty from the restaurant's floor.

Genuinely happy to see him, Alex smiled and leaned closer so he wouldn't have to shout. "Did we fast-forward two years without my knowledge?"

Mitch shivered. He was probably cooling off now that he wasn't running around. He stole Alex's beer from his hand and took a sip. Alex let him. Truth was, if they weren't in such a public spot, Alex would buy him a beer, no question.

A stool freed up. Mitch dragged it over and perched on the edge. "How was Florida?"

"Hot."

"Hot like you?" Mitch asked, smug smile on his face.

Alex took his beer back from Mitch as "I Kissed A Girl" started over again for at least the third time since he'd walked in the door. "I'm too hot to handle."

Mitch's snorted laugh turned into a genuine belly laugh.

Alex smiled back at him. "Get it? 'Cause Florida has a pan*handle*."

"That was so lame," Mitch said through chuckles. "Tampa's not even on the panhandle."

"No?" Alex shrugged. "Okay."

"How'd it go with the kids?"

Alex raised his broken arm. "They were focused too much on my purple penis, and not enough on hockey and teamwork."

Mitch grinned and stole Alex's beer again. "Purple penis," he said after a sip. "Sounds like a cocktail at a gay bar."

Alex laughed and didn't bother reclaiming his drink. Over on the other side of the restaurant, a group made of Yano, Marco, and a few other guys sang along to the music.

Fuck, why was this song on repeat? Was Satan torturing him for leaving Florida?

Leah sidled up behind him. "Why does Mama Jean hate us?" She clutched his arm and pleaded with big eyes. "Make it stop!"

"Hey, now," Mitch cut in. "This is our victory song."

"But why?"

Mitch shrugged. "Apparently a team of college dudes equates to a team of perverts who think two girls kissing is hot." He raised a hand. "Present company included, even though I'm firmly dudes-only." He choked out a cough and his eyes went huge in his face. "That's not... I mean, I'm not..."

Shit. Mitch had outed himself to someone he didn't know and was panicking. Alex could see the fear written all over his face.

Concerned, Alex reached for him. "Mitch—"

"Yo, Grey!" someone called from somewhere behind them. Mitch hopped off his stool, threw a "Be right back," over his shoulder, and disappeared into the crowd with Alex's beer.

"Dean, tell me something." JP slung an arm around

Alex's shoulders and came in close, as though about to impart important knowledge. "How long have you been flirting with my student?"

"What?" Alex frowned and shrugged off JP's arm. "We were just talking. Friends do that."

"Do they do that while standing too close and gazing into each other's eyes, or while sharing a beer through the same metaphorical straw?"

"I—What?" Alex glanced at Jay, standing behind JP, for support. "He's crazy."

"He's also right," Jay said. "You were making googly eyes at each other. Like this." Jay pursed his lips, widened his eyes, and batted his eyelashes.

"You look like a demented cartoon horse," Leah told her boyfriend.

Jay pointed at Alex. "Googly eyes."

Alex threw his hands up. "I've never made googly eyes at anyone in my life."

"Yeah, we know," JP said. "That's why it's so weird that you're doing it now."

"Except, I wasn't."

JP patted him on the cheek. "You're so cute in your obliviousness."

"You like him," Jay said in a singsong voice.

Of course Alex liked Mitch. If he didn't, he wouldn't be spending so much time with him. Alex liked tutoring him and hanging out with him and talking to him. He even got excited when he checked his text messages and found one from Mitch. Mitch made him feel special in ways he hadn't anticipated. The way Mitch focused all of his attention on Alex when they were together made Alex feel like he was the center of Mitch's universe. Mitch had a way of making the world seem brighter, less intense.

But he didn't *like* like Mitch. Did he?

God, when had he reverted to teenager status?

"You liiiiiiike him," Jay kept singing.

Annoyed, Alex left and went to find Mitch.

Mitch left Yano and Marco behind and, ignoring calls of "Grey!" from somewhere on the other side of the room, headed to the back of Mama Jean's where he was sure he'd find Cody.

It was quieter back here, the music not quite as loud, and the noise from the crowd muted. Cody was sitting in a booth across from a couple of people Mitch didn't know. Mitch ignored them both and squeezed in next to his best friend.

"Where'd you get the beer?" Cody asked. "And how come you didn't get me one?"

"It's Alex's. I stole it. Here." Mitch held his glass out to Cody with a shaking hand.

Cody ignored it and narrowed his eyes on Mitch. "What's wrong?"

"What? Nothing."

"Don't lie to me. Your eyes are bigger than your face. What happened?"

Mitch took a fortifying sip or three. Swallowing roughly, he leaned toward Cody. "I just came out to a complete stranger. In the middle of a crowded restaurant."

"Excuse us," Cody said to his friends. He pushed Mitch out of the booth and followed him to the hallway that led to the restrooms, where they tucked themselves into a tiny out-of-the-way alcove. "Tell me."

"I don't even—" Mitch reclined against the wall and rubbed his chest. "I just blurted it out."

"To who?"

"I think she's a friend of Alex's."

"Oh." Cody rubbed Mitch's shoulders. "Then I'm sure you're fine. Alex doesn't strike me as the type to be friends with people who are dickheads."

"Right." Mitch's hammering heart slowed. "Right, of course. You're right." He fell forward onto Cody and rested his forehead on Cody's shoulder. "I was careless. Then I tried to backpedal and tell them I'm not gay, but I couldn't lie. Not with Alex right there."

"You were being yourself." Cody ran his nails through Mitch's hair. "That's a good thing."

"Anybody could've heard. What if there'd been a recruiter nearby? Or worse, a reporter? Fuck." Straightening, Mitch downed the rest of the beer, then set the glass on the floor.

Cody's eyebrows pulled down and he rubbed Mitch's arm. "Because you can't be gay in sports."

"No. At least not yet." Mitch had been having so much fun tonight after their win. Then he'd gone and fucked it up by opening his big mouth. What if Alex's friend, whoever she was, told someone who told someone else who told a reporter who splashed it in the newspapers?

NHL scouts would never look twice at him and he could kiss a pro hockey career goodbye.

"Want to go home?" Cody asked.

Mitch bit his lip. "Alex is here."

"How did I know you were going to say that?"

They ran into the man himself right outside the hallway. "Hey, there you are," said Alex. His presence took over the room and his broad shoulders were so perfectly outlined in his long-sleeved T-shirt, Mitch wanted to jump him, audience be damned. "Hey, Cody."

"Hey, man."

"You okay?" Alex asked Mitch, eyes soft.

Mitch nodded once. "Peachy."

Cody cleared his throat. "I'm heading home. Alex, you mind giving Mitch a ride back when he's ready?"

"No problem."

Cody said his goodbyes and left.

"Uh, sorry." Mitch scratched his arm, feeling exposed for the first time all night. "I can get a ride from someone else."

Alex tilted his head. "Why?"

"Because my best friend just foisted me on you?" There were so many jokes Mitch could make with that. That he couldn't think of a single one was a testament to how out-of-sorts he was feeling. Accidentally outing himself to a stranger, plus being in Alex's presence, made for a jittery, nervous Mitch.

Yeah, he was a total badass.

"I don't mind," Alex said. "It's not like you live very far and it's a little too cold to walk. Especially with no pants."

"I have pants. Somewhere."

"It somehow doesn't surprise me that you don't know where they are."

Mitch dropped his gaze to Alex's long legs. "You could shed yours and join me à la *Risky Business*."

Alex grinned wide. "Not going to happen. Do you want to maybe go find them and come with me?"

"Where?" Mitch asked. Not that it mattered. He'd go anywhere with Alex. "To get more beer?"

"Not quite. I have something for you, but it's in my car."

Mitch went to find his pants.

He joined Alex outside five minutes later in jeans and a hoodie, because Alex was right—it wasn't exactly warm.

Fall had truly hit earlier this week. Goosebumps broke out over the back of his neck as he hopped up onto the trunk of Alex's rental car.

"What'd you get me? Is it dirty? Wait, can I guess?"

Alex got something out of the car before joining Mitch on the trunk. "Sure."

"Hmm." Mitch drummed his fingers against his lip. "A prostate massager?"

Throwing his head back, Alex laughed long and loud, the sound reaching into Mitch and settling in the vicinity of his heart. He, Mitch, had done that—made Alex laugh so hard he almost fell off the car. Mitch couldn't do anything but chuckle along with him. In the bright glow of the streetlamps and glare of headlights from passing cars, Alex's hair was more cinnamon than dark brown, the laugh lines around his eyes more pronounced.

"No," Alex said. "It's not a prostate massager."

"Am I warm?"

"You're very, very cold. It's just a little something from Florida."

Mitch had never been to Florida, so… "Sunscreen?"

"Not quite. Though you'll definitely want to bring some when you come visit me."

Mitch stilled. "You…want me to come visit you?"

"Yeah, why not? My friends, the ones I'm here with tonight, they come at least twice a year. You could tag along with them."

Mitch scrunched his nose.

"Yeah," Alex said. "Didn't think you'd go for that. For someone who appears to have a lot of friends, you're really more of a loner."

It shouldn't come as a surprise that Alex was more observant than Mitch was used to. Every time Alex noticed

something about him that Mitch had so successfully managed to keep hidden for years, it was like another part of his
soul got exposed, leaving him naked and floundering.

"Anyway." Alex handed Mitch a small, generic plastic
bag. "Here. It's nothing big. But it made me think of you."

It was a small white bear decked out in the blue and
white Tampa Bay uniform and holding a tiny hockey stick.
It was cute as fuck, though Mitch couldn't guess why something like this would remind Alex of him. Not that he cared.
His hockey crush—who was now his real life crush—had
thought of him while on business, so to speak, in a state
over a thousand miles away.

Was it getting hard to breathe?

Mitch pointed at the jersey number on the back, 25. "It
has your number."

"Yup. You haven't been shy about telling me you want
to sleep with me, so I figure now—" Alex stole the bear
out of Mitch's hands and bopped Mitch on the nose with
it. "—you can."

Swiping his bear back, Mitch laughed and fell backward onto the rear windshield. "I see. This is your way of
getting out of sex with me."

"I'm not getting out of anything, seeing as I never actually said I'd have sex with you." Alex balled the plastic bag,
shoved it in his pocket, then mirrored Mitch's position.

"That's… Well, shit, I guess that's true, isn't it?"

They rested side-by-side, gazing up at the stars. The
temptation to reach out and thread his fingers with Alex's,
or shuffle closer and lay his head on Alex's shoulder, was
so goddamned strong, Mitch almost did it. He wanted to
be wrapped up in Alex's strong arms and he wanted Alex
to want that too. He yearned for it, like he'd never yearned
for anything before. And for once in his life, Mitch wanted

to stop hiding behind his carefully constructed walls and show someone other than his dad and Cody who he really was, even if he didn't quite know how to do that. Although, with the way things were going, Alex would have him figured out before Mitch figured himself out.

Which begged the question: Were Mitch's walls involuntarily coming down, or was Alex that perceptive?

In Mitch's peripheral view, Alex relaxed with a hand on his stomach and one arm behind his head. His chest rose and fell in slow breaths. Had his eyes not been open, Mitch would've thought he was asleep.

"How come you're not in costume?" Mitch asked.

Alex made a rumbly sound in his throat. "Would you believe I forgot it was Halloween?"

Mitch turned his head toward him.

"It's true." Alex scratched his belly. "After my dad left, it was just my mom and me. She sold our house in the suburbs and we lived in this tiny apartment above a Chinese restaurant in Chinatown in Toronto for a few years. We couldn't afford much and Halloween, buying costumes and candy, was an expense we couldn't justify at the time. So, I never really celebrated Halloween after my dad took off on us." A corner of Alex's mouth tilted up in a half smile. "My mom and I had our own tradition. If Halloween fell on a weekday, she'd keep me home from school and we'd watch not-so-scary movies, like *Casper* or *Hocus Pocus* or *Ernest Scared Stupid*."

"That sounds really nice," Mitch whispered into the dark. "There's a party on my street every year for Halloween. I hated going. I was the youngest kid on the block and the older kids would steal my candy. Cody came one year and when some jerk tried to steal my stash, Cody kicked him in the shin." Out of the corner of his eye, he saw Alex turn to him. "My mom never liked Cody. Said he was a bad influence."

"I think he's good for you."

"My dad said that too, not long ago." Mitch squinted against the streetlamp and wished it'd turn itself off so he could see the stars. That'd be way more romantic as he and Alex chatted quietly. "Cody was the best decision I've ever made."

"How so?" Alex's voice was quiet, made deeper by the night.

"He and my dad are the only people who've ever had my back. Cody's been there through everything that happened with my brother—" Mitch sucked in a harsh breath.

"What happened?" Alex asked, as Mitch knew he would.

"I'll tell you sometime." Mitch turned to lie on his side, facing Alex. "I will. But not tonight. Tonight is for…ghost stories!"

Alex jerked back. "Um, what?"

Mitch poked him in the chest. "Tell me a ghost story."

"No."

"Why?" Mitch peered at him, leaned nearer, and whispered, "Are you afraid of ghosts?"

Alex hesitated. "No."

Mitch laughed so hard his tiny Alex Bear almost took a tumble onto the pavement.

NINE

IF MITCH MOVED ONE OF HIS PAWNS FORWARD BY ONE space, it'd leave his knight wide open. But if his opponent made the move Mitch suspected he would, to kill Mitch's knight, it'd leave his opponent's queen unprotected.

Mitch moved his pawn.

"You'll regret that move, young sir," said Mitch's opponent, a gentleman in his eighties with a bald head, eyes the color of the Green Mountains in summer, and wrinkles on top of wrinkles.

The lounge room in Montpelier's long-term care facility was occupied, but not overly so since it was dinnertime and most of the residents were in the dining room. A small group watched a game show on TV on the opposite side of the room, a lady was reading on a couch behind Mitch, and to his left, a woman was visiting either her father or grandfather.

Mitch had been on his way out the door after his shift, and he'd made what he'd intended to be a short pit stop in the lounge to refill his water bottle at the water cooler. Then he'd seen Mr. Baldie von Wrinkleson, whose name he'd yet to learn, sitting all alone in front of a chess set and had offered to play, even though he was supposed to be getting home. He was tutoring in two hours, another soul-crushing session teaching algebra to a couple of freshmen. Fuck his life.

Mr. Baldie von Wrinkleson moved his remaining rook.

"That's cheating!" It had been a while since Mitch played chess, but he remembered the rules, and the rook didn't move diagonally.

Mr. von Wrinkleson harrumphed. "Didn't think you'd notice. Young people these days, they think they're so smart." He killed Mitch's knight with the rook, then Mitch moved his bishop. "Check," Mitch said. "Checkmate, actually."

Mr. von Wrinkleson sat back and gripped the arms of his chair. "Well, I'll be damned. You know, I haven't lost a game since I was a teenager?"

Mitch grinned, unrepentant. "Sorry?"

Mr. von Wrinkleson laughed, apparently delighted that he'd just had his ass kicked by someone six decades younger. The suspicion growing in Mitch since he'd sat across from Mr. von Wrinkleson an hour ago solidified into certainty. His eyes, his laugh, they reminded Mitch of—

"Forest?"

Alex. As if Mitch had conjured him, Alex stood next to their table in dark jeans and a navy pullover, his leather jacket folded over his arm.

"Judd!" said Mr. von Wrinkleson. Or Forest Dean, it appeared. "I didn't know you were stopping by."

Judd was…Alex's dad?

Alex pulled over a chair from a nearby table and sat between Mitch and Forest. "Hey, Mitch." The smile Alex sent Mitch was friendly and warm. Alex raked his gaze over Mitch, lingering longer than usual, and… Was there something in his eyes? Some unnamed emotion that hadn't been there before? Not heat. Not lust. But more than friendship. Want? That was maybe too strong a word, but there was something there.

Whatever it was, it made Mitch's stomach clench.

"Forest, I see you've met my friend Mitch."

"Indeed." Forest crossed his arms and sent Mitch a glare that was more playful than angry. "He just whooped my patooti at chess."

"He—" Alex's head swivelled to Mitch. "Nobody's beat him in years."

"Young sir, I demand a rematch."

"I need to get going soon, but how about next Sunday?" Mitch racked up the game pieces and started putting them to rights on the board. "Same time and place?"

"You're on." Forest turned to Alex. "How's my grandson, Judd? Alex still playing hockey?"

Alex seemed to wither right in front of Mitch. The pained stare Alex sent him, the skin around his eyes bunching, caused a lump to form in Mitch's throat.

"Almost every day," Alex said.

"Of course he is." Forest's booming voice had heads turning their way. "The boy's got more talent in his pinky than you or I will ever have. Now, if you'll excuse me." He stood. "I need to take a leak. Judd, you sticking around?"

"I was going to, yeah." There was something wrong with Alex's voice. It was flat and brittle. He watched his grandpa walk away and once Forest had rounded the corner, his shoulders sagged.

Alex probably didn't realize it, but he flinched every time Forest called him Judd. Mitch had no frame of reference for what Alex was going through, nothing to compare it to. What must it be like to so completely look up to someone, only to have that person forget everything you'd gone through together, everything you'd talked about, everything you'd done and seen, everything you'd meant to each other?

Turning to Mitch, Alex sighed deeply. "He's not going to remember next Sunday that you're supposed to play chess." His eyes were as flat as his voice. "Hell, he won't remember in five minutes."

Mitch swallowed hard and rested a hand on Alex's knee. Alex rested his hand on top of Mitch's and wove their fingers together.

Everything inside Mitch quieted.

In the three plus weeks since Halloween, he and Alex had maybe accidentally, maybe on purpose, stumbled into a routine of sorts. They spent Monday nights playing Mario Kart with Cody. Wednesday morning, after Mitch's practice and before the start of his classes, Alex joined him on the ice for an hour and Mitch taught him the basics of what Alex had dubbed Figure Skating For Dummies (And Hockey). They worked out together at the campus gym on the Thursday mornings Mitch didn't have practice. Alex came to most of Mitch's home games. Mitch emailed Alex all of his creative writing assignments—which, incidentally, were still shit. And in between all of that, they texted like long-lost lovers.

But not once in the six weeks they'd known each other had Alex voluntarily touched him. Alex's personal space bubble was roughly the size of the moon. Yet today, he'd smiled at Mitch with something more than friendship *and* touched him?

You could've knocked Mitch over with a feather.

It was possible that Alex was simply seeking comfort from a friend, but Mitch's hopes nevertheless shot up. Did this mean what Mitch wanted it to mean? Should he ask Alex out on a date, a real one this time? Would Alex reject him again if he did?

Idiot, he's just sad and looking for support.

Yeah. No doubt about it, Mitch was an asshole for thinking about this when Alex was sitting next to him with rounded shoulders, pale skin, and bruises under his eyes. If Mitch was an artist, he'd call it Picture of Dejection.

Mitch propped an elbow on the table and rested his head in his hand. "Doesn't matter. If he's here when my shift ends next week, I'm happy to play a game with him. He makes a worthy opponent."

Alex's laugh was dry. "Yeah. He remembers chess, but he doesn't remember me."

Mitch's hand jerked under Alex's at Alex's broken voice, and his chest burned. His eyes got hot, but he blinked that shit away before Alex noticed.

"Judd!" Back from the bathroom, Forest sat across from Mitch, smile wide. "It's good to see you, son." He turned to Mitch. "Who's your friend?"

Mitch closed his eyes against the spasm that crossed Alex's face and squeezed Alex's knee in silent support.

An hour later, Mitch trudged up the stairs and into his bedroom. He dropped his backpack on the floor, kicked the door closed, and collapsed, face-first, on his bed.

Fuck. Alzheimer's sucked.

It probably wasn't a picnic for the person affected, but for the people left behind, like Alex... God.

The numbers on the alarm clock on his night table read 6:02, bright red in the otherwise dark room. He had an hour to eat before his tutoring session, but the food was downstairs and he was upstairs. Unless it magically floated up to him, dinner wasn't happening. Screw it, he'd make a smoothie before leaving, which was pretty much the only thing he could make with the ingredients in the fridge.

The sun catcher in the window caught his eye, a miniature replica of the one in the living room. It hung motionless, a dark shape against the night. Sitting up, Mitch turned on the lamp on his night table, then reached underneath the bed. His fingers hit something hard and smooth and he felt around until he grasped the metal handle on the side. Dragging the box out, he hauled it up onto the bed.

The box was a wooden treasure chest with a domed lid, about fifteen inches by ten, finished in dark wood with two metal handles and a matching metal latch. His brother had made it for him in shop class in high school what felt like a lifetime ago. There was a skull and crossbones lasered onto the front, except instead of crossbones they were hockey sticks, and the skull was wearing a hockey mask.

There'd once been a time when his brother liked him enough to gift him with the beautiful things he'd made. Mitch played with the latch—open, close, open, close—but instead of lifting the lid, he blew out a breath and hid the box back underneath the bed.

Curling into a ball on top of his comforter, Mitch removed his phone from his pocket, where it'd been digging into his thigh. Thumbing through his contacts, he stopped on the one he didn't use anymore. Dan Greyson.

Six years older than Mitch, his brother had been the one to walk him to school, to nurse the scrape on his arm when he'd fallen out of a tree, who taught him how to tread water and ride a bike with no hands, and who'd willingly driven Mitch to hockey practices and games when their mother wouldn't and their dad was working. Dan used to attend every one of Mitch's hockey games with a sign that read "Mitch the Witch." He used to say that watching Mitch play was like watching magic. Dan thought the nickname was hilarious and they'd never explained its meaning to anyone but Cody, keeping it their little secret.

And then, one day five years ago, all of that had stopped. No warning, no explanation. All he'd got was just "Mitch, I need you to leave it alone for a bit, okay?"

"Leave what alone?" fourteen-year-old Mitch had asked Dan.

"Me."

Despite how hard he'd tried, how hard he'd pleaded, Mitch was still waiting for the answer to his one burning question: Why do you hate me?

Other than the one email he'd sent his brother this past summer, Mitch hadn't bothered trying to get in touch with him again over the past few months. Why would he when every time he tried Dan either ignored him, hung up on him, or told him not to call?

But Alex and Forest were on his mind and Mitch could picture his brother in Forest's place. If something were to happen to Dan, Mitch would have to live with the regret of knowing he'd done nothing to patch their relationship or make amends for…well, for whatever Dan hated him for. The anger he felt toward his brother was never far, but on top of it, and much closer to the surface, was rejection, hurt, and an aching sense of loss that hadn't dulled in five years.

Mitch pressed Call.

It rang, over and over. It rang some more. Dan probably saw his name on the caller ID and pitched his phone against the wall.

But then the call was picked up. "What, Mitch?" Dan's voice was hard. Exasperated and impatient. Unfriendly.

Mitch's heart sank into his stomach and his breathing hitched. "Never mind," he whispered.

And hung up.

TEN

IT WAS ABOUT TWENTY DEGREES TOO WARM IN JAY and Leah's kitchen in Montpelier. Alex removed his pullover, leaving him in a vintage style T-shirt. Returning to his post at the stove to stir the gravy, he caught Mitch eyeing him from across the room. Mitch's cheeks pinked and he looked away, focusing once more on the conversation he was having with Leah and Cody. Something that involved a lot of squealing over turkey necks, from what Alex could tell.

Mitch had been doing that a lot lately, checking Alex out. Not that he hadn't been doing it before, but whereas previously, he'd done it with an air of I'm-checking-you-out-because-you're-hot, now when he sought Alex out, it was with more of an I'm-just-making-sure-you're-still-in-the-room vibe.

Alex stirred the gravy absentmindedly and kept an eye on Mitch while the man was involved in a conversation with Jay about the Mountaineers' win against Connecticut on Tuesday. Dressed in black jeans and one of his many flannel shirts, this one a subdued blue and gray, Mitch's shoulders were back, his smile easy, arms hanging loose at his sides. He was animated and friendly, ready to celebrate Thanksgiving with friends.

But his laugh was too sharp, his hands were balled into fists, his eyes were bloodshot. He faced Jay, and yet his feet pointed toward the back door. Jay spoke with his hands, his words coming fast and loud, and Mitch mirrored his speech patterns and energy in a way that probably didn't look forced to anyone except for Cody and Alex. It was as if Mitch was trying to compensate for… being tired? Sad? Cody stuck close to him and whenever Mitch rambled—which was completely unlike him—Cody jumped in and took the topic in another direction.

Sometimes the dynamic between them was more that of a big brother/little brother than best friends. Cody was Mitch's grounding stone. Yet it seemed even Cody struggled with what to do when Mitch's gaze strayed outside yet again.

"Alex, Jesus." JP moved the gravy off the burner. "Any thicker and it'll be mud."

Oops. "Sorry?"

JP grunted and told Alex to wash the whisk in the sink and snap the ends off the asparagus so JP could steam them. Minutes later, the asparagus were trimmed, the gravy was keeping warm, the mashed potatoes were ready, the stuffing was baking in the extra oven downstairs, the rolls were safely tucked in a bread basket, and the turkey only needed another twenty minutes in the oven. There were also carrots drizzled with maple syrup, green beans, and cucumber salad. It smelled like a five-star restaurant and there was enough food to feed an entire starving NHL team, which was pretty typical of American Thanksgiving, from what Alex had seen in the past few years he'd lived in the States.

Alex had flown home in October to celebrate Canadian Thanksgiving for the first time since his college days. He and his mom had shared a small ham, mashed sweet potatoes, and roasted veggies. The whole going overboard thing that came with American holidays made no sense to him.

"Here." Leah came out of nowhere and handed him the can of cranberry sauce, a can opener, and a blue serving bowl. "Make yourself useful."

"What do you think I've been doing?" he grumbled under his breath.

It wasn't like he'd been slacking off. He'd pulled his weight and had even brought the dessert he'd baked this morning, a French Canadian caramel pudding called *pouding chômeur* his mom had taught him to make when he was—

Where was Mitch?

Distracted, Alex almost upended the can of cranberry sauce onto the counter, but managed to catch himself in time. JP and Jay were conversing over the thermometer stuck in the turkey, and Cody was helping Leah set the table.

Alex caught Cody's eyes. *Mitch?* he mouthed.

Cody tilted his head toward the back door.

Alex finished what he was doing, then went to find his coat.

Outside, the air was still but cold, the first snap of winter hanging in the air. The twilit sky was overcast, casting a gray sheen on a landscape already deadened by fall. Alex found Mitch at the far end of the property, where the yellow grass ended abruptly at a small creek. Mitch sat in one of the two Adirondack chairs, a beer bottle dangling from one hand. Alex took the remaining chair and offered Mitch a roll he'd pilfered before heading out.

Mitch scowled at the roll as if it had personally offended him. "I don't want that."

"Eat it anyway."

Grumbling under his breath, Mitch took the roll and ripped off a small piece. He chewed obnoxiously, as if he was angry with the bread, and turned his scowl on Alex. *Happy now?*

Alex smiled back serenely. *Yes, thanks.*

Mitch ate the roll, one piece at a time, taking small sips of beer in between bites. Other than the occasional voice reaching them from the house, it was quiet. And cold. Alex curled his toes in his boots and sandwiched his hands between his thighs to warm them up.

"When Grandpa Forest would come visit in the winter," Alex said, mostly to distract Mitch from whatever was happening in his head, "he'd take me to this outdoor skating rink. There was a little shack with benches and coat racks and little slots to leave your shoes in. And they sold this truly horrible hot chocolate, more water than chocolate really." Alex smiled at the memory. "Neither one of us liked it, but it was hot, so of course, we always had to have one."

"Why didn't you just bring your own?"

Alex winked at Mitch. "That would've messed with tradition."

Mitch's cheeks were already red from the cold, but Alex could've sworn they colored further under his gaze.

"What's your favorite kind of hot chocolate?" Alex asked.

"The kind with chocolate in it?"

Alex laughed. "Mine's peppermint hot chocolate."

Mitch wrinkled his nose.

"Have you ever tried it?"

"Yes." Mitch wiped crumbs off his pants. "Peppermint and chocolate should never go together."

"What about peanut butter and chocolate?"

"Ew, gross. Even worse."

"It's official," Alex said. "We can no longer be friends."

He counted it a win when Mitch smiled. Mitch set his

half full beer in the grass and went back to gazing at nothing. What was going on in that head of his?

"Want to talk about it?" Alex asked. "Whatever's bothering you?"

Mitch shook his head. "I wouldn't know where to start."

"The beginning?"

Blowing out a hard breath, Mitch tilted his head up to
the sky. "Okay."

Wait, was Alex actually about to get another tiny tid-
bit of personal information from Mitch? Voluntarily? Well,
fuck a duck. Alex stilled. If he moved, Mitch might remember he was here and stop talking.

"Up until, I don't know, five years ago or so, my brother
and I were really close." Mitch picked at a piece of wayward wood in the chair's arm. "He's six years older, but he
was always there for me. Slept in my room during thun-
derstorms, took me to see R-rated movies, bought me my
first condoms. He was always a steady presence. And then
things just…changed. No, that's not right. They stopped. I
still don't understand it. He went off to college, Columbia.
For business and accounting of all things, even though—"
He shook his head again.

"Even though what?"

Mitch turned to Alex. "He wanted to be a woodworker.
Build things. Little things. Like toys for kids, puzzles, other
games." His mouth curved up slightly. "He used to make
these amazing sun catchers, flawless and smooth."

"The one in your living room window?"

"Yeah." The smile fell from Mitch's face. "I don't know
why I keep it. We kept in touch while he was at Columbia,
but then one day, he told me to stop. He wouldn't answer
my calls, my emails. If I was home, he didn't visit." He ran
a hand over his forehead. "Last time I emailed him, he told

me not to. I called him last weekend just to…" He shrugged. "I don't know. Try and make amends? He won't tell me what I did to upset him, so I don't know how to fix things."

"Maybe you didn't do anything."

Mitch scoffed.

"I'm serious." Alex rubbed Mitch's arm through his coat. "Mitch, people don't hold grudges for five years without telling the person who wronged them why they're pissed. And if you can't think of anything you might've done to upset him, I'd bet it has to do with something else."

"My dad said something similar when we had dinner last month." Mitch shifted in his seat and waved a hand. "I don't want to talk about this anymore. Tell me something good."

Something good? Alex said the first thing that popped into his head. "The purple penis comes off on Monday."

Alex expected Mitch to laugh. Instead, Mitch got that faraway look in his eyes again. "That's not something good." His voice was so soft, Alex had to strain to hear him. "It means you're leaving."

"Yeah."

Their Wednesday mornings together on the ice had been fun, and Alex had learned new tricks from Mitch that he couldn't wait to use in a game. Defensemen were supposed to be able to quickly transition from forward to backward and vice versa, and while Alex was good, his new foot skills would no doubt up his game. But skating laps and learning figure skating moves wasn't hockey. They didn't get his adrenaline pumping and his competitiveness revving. But Coach wasn't putting him back in the game until January and as much as he was looking forward to it, part of him wanted to stay right here in Glen Hill, with Mitch.

Over the course of the last few weeks, they'd developed a friendship that, for Alex, was on par with his friendship with JP and Jay. Alex liked the sensible and hardworking yet sensitive and caring guy Mitch became when he dropped his mask. Hell, he even liked the mask because now he saw it for what it was: a defense mechanism. Was Mitch protecting himself from being hurt again?

Underneath Mitch's cultivated veneer of assertiveness and arrogance was a nice guy who just wanted to play hockey and be surrounded by the people he loved.

A knot formed in Alex's belly. He was used to leaving people behind while he played for Tampa. But the thought of getting on the plane on Monday and not knowing when he'd see Mitch again left a sour taste in his mouth.

"When are you coming to visit me?" Alex asked.

Mitch blinked up at a sky that had turned to dusk, turning the clouds an ominous indigo. "You were serious about that?"

"Of course. We'll compare calendars, see what works. I'll come visit you too."

Swallowing roughly, Mitch held out a hand to Alex but aborted the movement halfway and crossed his arms over his chest. Giving in to the powerful need to touch, Alex reached out and took Mitch's cold hand in his. His skin prickled at the feel of skin on skin and his stomach fluttered with the wings of a million tiny butterflies.

Mitch clutched Alex's hand in both of his. "Promise?"

"Promise."

ELEVEN

DECEMBER 2008

Alex: *The purple penis came off today.*

Mitch: *Any problems?*

Alex: *Nope. Don't need rehab. Just strength training.*

Mitch: *Good :) Does it hurt?*

Alex: *No, it's just weak. Also, it looks like an old wrinkly person.*

Mitch: *That's the grossest thing you've ever said to me.*

Alex: *And it's dry...*

Mitch: *Stop it.*

Alex: *My skin's peeling off in four different places.*

Mitch: *Seriously, fuck you.*

Alex: *I'm sending you a picture.*

Mitch: *I'm blocking your phone number.*

Mitch: *I passed creative writing!*

Alex: *Knew you would :)*

Mitch: *Thanks for your help. Couldn't have done that poetry shit without you.*

Alex: *Poetry is not shit and yeah okay, that was a joke. Ha ha.*

Mitch: *Not really. Poetry sucks. Who wants to read between the lines? Not me. You have something to say, just fucking say it.*

Alex: *Hahahahahahahahaha. This from the guy who's so tight-lipped, I didn't even know he had a brother until two weeks ago?*

Mitch: *I don't know what you're talking about.*

Alex: *Did you keep your creative writing elective next semester, or did you drop it for something else?*

Mitch: *Kept it. God forbid my college transcript doesn't portray me as a well-rounded person. Fucking academic advisors.*

Alex: *You'll thank her (him?) later.*

Mitch: *Doubt it.*

Mitch: *Kill me...*

Alex: *What's wrong?*

Mitch: *What's wrong? Where do I start? With the freshmen who don't know how to do long division or the ones who can't solve the simplest of polynomials? Or how about the senior who can't solve a word problem? Fuck my life.*

Alex: *To be fair, I don't remember how to do long division either. Haven't done that since high school.*

Alex: *Also, I don't remember what a polynomial is.*

Mitch: *You weren't a science major.*

Alex: *Oh. OK then, yeah. That's bad. Wait, you're tutoring college seniors in math?*

Mitch: *I'm kinda smart.*

Alex: *I'm playing tonight!*

Mitch: *I thought your coach wasn't putting you in until January. That's still two weeks away.*

Alex: *My arm is mostly back up to strength and Coach is happy with the way I've been performing in practice so... I get to play! On the third line, but I don't care.*

Mitch: *You'll still see ice time.*

Alex: *Exactly.*

Mitch: *Nervous?*

Alex: *Kind of. The last time I was nervous on the ice was in the Frozen Four.*

Mitch: *Yeah, you guys lost in the first round.*

Alex: *Thanks for the reminder, jackass.*

Mitch: *Don't lose this one.*

Alex: *How could we with the fancy new footwork you taught me during our Figure Skating for Dummies (And Hockey) sessions?*

Alex arrived at Amalie Arena half an hour before he was technically due. It wasn't part of his game day routine, but he needed the boost to his psyche that would only come from being alone in the locker room.

He'd already gone through his pre-game rituals: hung his suit jacket on the left hook in his cubby, then on the right; done ten pull-ups in the gym; visited the men's room; located his lucky yellow socks; and eaten a Halloween-sized Kit Kat. Sitting in the locker room in front of his cubby in his base layers, Alex was going through his final pre-game ritual—listening to Third Eye Blind's "Semi-Charmed Life" on repeat on his iPod—when the rest of the team started trickling in.

"Dude!" Yager dropped onto the bench next to him. As big as Alex with hair prematurely gone to gray, Yager was Alex's favorite person on the team. Coach often partnered them together for a game. "Coach has you on a different line than me." A pout on a guy who was six-four and as big as a whale shouldn't have been endearing.

Alex yanked his earbuds out. "Yeah, I think he's trying to assess whether or not I'm really fit to play again."

Yager grunted and stood. "Of course you're fit to play." He removed his jacket and hung it in the cubby next to Alex's. "You don't just forget how to skate. It's like riding a bike."

"Yo, Bomb!" Masterson yelled from across the room.

Yager—whose nickname was Jagerbomb for obvious reasons, though it was more often than not shortened to Bomb—turned at the call.

"Catch!"

Yager caught a small mason jar. "Dean, you weren't here when we picked names for Secret Santa." He handed Alex the jar. Inside was a small folded up piece of paper. "So we picked for you. Here."

Alex unscrewed the lid and fished out the paper. "When's the gift exchange?"

"Tomorrow at the Christmas party at Mr. Awan's. You know about it, right?"

"Yeah, I know about it." Mr. Awan was the team's owner. Last year's Christmas party had devolved into beer pong and karaoke in Mr. Awan's enormous entertainment room right after dinner. His mansion could hold not just the team and associated public relations staff, marketers, trainers, and coaches, but every team in the Eastern Conference and then some. "You couldn't have given me more notice?" Alex grumbled. "Somebody could've looked at the name and texted me."

Jaws dropped all around the room. Yager clutched his chest. "And cheat ourselves out of the yearly tradition? What if you have me and I'd looked, huh? What then? No more surprise for ol' Bomb."

Alex held the paper he'd yet to read between two fingers. "What if it says my name?"

Silence.

"Well, shit," Vidal said from the other side of the room. "It doesn't, does it?"

"It couldn't." Greer's head swivelled, eyes big. "Someone picked his name, right?"

Finally, Alex unfolded the piece of paper while his teammates tried to remember who they'd picked for Secret Santa. *Carlie* was written in messy script. A few cubbies down, Carlie was already dressed in his goalie pads, "Carlson" spelled out on the back of his jersey. All around Alex, men dug through cubbies, bags, and coat pockets, presumably trying to find their own little scraps of paper.

"I think I have Alex."

"You had him last year."

"Doesn't mean I didn't pick his name out of the hat again this year."

"Fuck, I think I have him."

"You don't, idiot. I know who you have and it's not Alex."

Seriously, had nobody bought their gifts yet?

"Guys!" Alex's raised voice cut through the din of chatter. "Crisis averted." He held up the scrap of paper. "I don't have myself."

A collective sigh of relief sounded through the room.

Yager's eyebrows bunched and he faced Alex with his arms crossed over his chest. "You did that on purpose."

Alex tossed him a wide-eyed look of innocence and started pulling on his gear. He was lacing up his skates when he got a text from Mitch. *Remember: don't lose :) Cody and I are watching at home. See you on the ice!*

His limbs tingled with some kind of awareness and nerves hit his belly that had nothing to do with hockey.

Yager punched his shoulder. "What's wrong with you?"

"Huh?"

"What's this?" Yager wiggled his butt on the bench.

Alex pulled on his gloves. "I don't know, what is that?"

"That's what I'm asking you, man. You were the one doing it."

"You're crazy."

The game against Ottawa was ferocious. For both teams, this was the last game before they were off for a few days for Christmas. Tampa had home ice advantage, but that didn't mean anything when Ottawa played as if their lives were on the line.

Coach McNab was usually explicit about how he wanted the lines of offense to work and there were clear delineations between all four. Even though Alex wasn't considered an enforcer, his current line, the third, was typically counted on to check, fight, and generally take up space while the better players took a rest. But this game was so neck-in-neck that Coach switched things up mid-game and sent Alex out on the first line with Yager.

Better. Much better. Alex was an offensive defenseman, not a fighter.

With minutes left in the third period, play stalled in Ottawa's offensive zone for an achingly boring amount of time. Alex followed the puck with his eyes and stayed at the ready at Ottawa's blue line in case play moved toward him, as it likely would. Behind him, Carlie yelled at their forwards from the crease.

Ottawa's defensemen were also offensive defensemen, and once the puck finally crossed into Alex's zone, it was all hands on deck for Ottawa as play moved toward Tampa's net. Alex and Yager kept them from scoring and somehow

Alex ended up with the puck. As he scouted to see who was open, Carlie yelled, "Breakaway!"

Alex didn't hesitate. With his back to Ottawa's offensive zone, he skated backward, fast, using the new moves Mitch had taught him. Both his own teammates and players from the other team followed as if the hounds of hell were chasing them. Heart racing, adrenaline flowing, Alex transitioned to forward seamlessly, crowing in triumph when he managed not to fall on his ass. Ottawa's net came closer and closer and he could hear people catching up to him, but he didn't turn and look.

Don't lose.

Mitch's words played in his head and, as if knowing Mitch was watching gave him an extra burst of energy, Alex surged forward, sent a wrist shot that bounced off the top post of the net and—

The goal horn sounded across the arena.

Whooping loudly, Alex stopped next to the boards where, directly behind the Plexiglass, a TV news camera was mounted. Alex pointed directly into it and almost mouthed *For you*, stopping himself just in time from putting a media bullseye on his back.

The high of scoring his first goal in over two months lasted until they won 4-3, until he'd showered and changed, and until he was once again sitting in front of his cubby in boxer briefs, phone in hand. He had a text from Mitch with an army of smiley faces and thumbs up emoticons, then *You scored that for me, huh?*

Alex was quick to reply back: *You did tell me not to lose.*

"Who you talking to?" Yager leaned over Alex's shoulder.

Alex blanked the screen. "No one."

"Mm hmm. No one makes you smile like that?"

"I'm excited we won the game. I'm not allowed to smile?" Alex dug socks out of his bag and slipped them on.

"Sure you can." Yager checked his teeth in a handheld mirror. "But that smile wasn't a 'we-won' smile. It was a lovesick smile."

"Uh-huh." Alex finished dressing and pocketed his phone. "I don't think you know what that word means."

"I don't think *you* know what that word means. You meet a girl in Vermont while you were there?"

"Hardly."

"What, no girls in Vermont?"

"There's plenty of girls." Alex shouldered his bag and walked out of the locker room, certain Yager was only steps behind him. Sure enough, Yager fell in next to him and they took the maze of hallways toward the exit closest to the parking garage.

"But you weren't 'interested' in any of them?" Yager used actual air quotes around *interested*. Alex was sort of notorious on the team for being the only one who'd never had a girlfriend in the past two years. "People are going to start thinking you're gay."

Alex shrugged. "So?"

"What do you mean *so*?" Yager turned incredulous eyes on him. "You want people thinking you're gay?"

"Being gay's not a bad thing, so why should I care if someone thinks I am?" Alex reached the exit doors and turned to say something to Yager, only to find the man several feet away, where he'd apparently stopped in the middle of the hallway.

"That's a very enlightened way of looking at it," Yager said.

"I guess?" Alex pushed the door open. "Come on, I want to go home and eat."

They made their way to the parking garage and up to their level in silence. The temperature had cooled enough for Alex to be grateful for his suit jacket.

"So…" Yager said when they exited the staircase on level four. "Are you gay?"

Alex's personal life was off limits to most people, the media included, but to teammates he considered actual friends, he might make an exception.

Explaining himself to Yager, however, was about as appealing as pulling on a skate over a broken foot.

Alex leaned against his SUV and crossed his arms. "I'm demisexual."

"Okay?" Yager scratched his head. "What does liking short people have to do with being gay?"

Choking on a laugh, Alex rubbed his hands over his face. "Jesus, Yager, no. Demisexual means I don't get sexually attracted to another person until I've formed an emotional connection with them."

"Oh." Yager dragged the word out to about seven syllables. "Okay. So that means a person's gender doesn't matter, huh?"

"Depends on the person, I guess?" Alex shrugged. "I don't like to generalize. I've always been more attracted to men, so I guess that means I'm gay?"

"Huh. That's why we never see you with anyone," Yager mused. "Not much time to get to know someone when you're constantly on the road." His eyes went big. "Does that mean you could theoretically become sexually attracted to me?" The prospect seemed to delight him, for some reason.

Alex mentally visualized Mitch's unruly curly hair, his brown eyes, his lean build that was more swimmer than hockey player, his penchant for flannel shirts, and addiction to smoothies.

He patted Yager on the shoulder. "You're not my type."

"You did meet someone in Vermont. I knew it! Who is she? He?"

"I'm…" Alex blew out a breath, then loaded his bag into the trunk. His mind had drifted to Mitch more than once during tonight's game, when normally Alex was a master at the art of compartmentalization, of forcing everything else aside, personal or otherwise, in order to focus on the game. "I'm still trying to figure things out there, so, uh…" Did the fact that he missed Mitch, badly, mean anything? Did Alex miss Mitch because Mitch was a friend, or because he was a friend Alex wanted more with?

Months ago, when he'd first met Mitch, the thought of kissing him had been abhorrent. Not because Mitch was ugly or anything, but because the thought of kissing anybody made him want to run away and hide. When he was younger and the other kids in his class had wanted to play seven minutes in heaven or spin the bottle, Alex had always found an excuse to bow out. Who wanted to kiss someone they didn't have feelings for? Not him. Just no.

The thought of kissing Mitch now? Goosebumps broke out over his neck and his stomach fluttered.

Well, shit. Alex wanted to kiss Mitch and it'd taken Yager for him to realize it. There was something seriously fucked up with that scenario.

"I get it." Yager held his hands up. "No pushing." He tilted his head and appeared to think about something. "Do you think being demisexual would make that person more unlikely to cheat?"

Alex's heart clenched in sympathy. Yager had divorced his wife three years ago, after she'd cheated on him.

"I don't know, man," Alex said. "I mean, maybe. It's certainly true for me, but I imagine everyone's different."

Yager grunted. "Where can I find myself one of these demisexuals?"

"Jesus, Yager." Alex pulled his keys out of his pocket and rounded his car. "I'll see you at the party tomorrow."

"Will you have an answer for me then?"

"Bye, Yager."

"It's a valid question."

From inside his car, Alex waved at a scowling Yager, and went home.

TWELVE

CHRISTMAS SUCKED.

Wrapped in a cocoon of blankets, Mitch flopped onto the couch and stared at the lit Christmas tree in front of the bay window in the living room. It was otherwise dark in the room, the tree's tiny white lights casting pinpricks of brightness against the walls and furniture. Almost midnight on Christmas Day and Mitch wanted to be anywhere but here.

Dinner had been, as expected, a study in contrasts. Mitch and his dad having a conversation about hockey, school, and whatever else came to mind. His mother and Dan quietly forking food into their mouths and making occasional small talk about work.

Until his mother butted her head in.

"Mitch, I heard you lost a game recently." She said it all sweet and innocent, as if she was concerned about the team's standing, but Mitch knew his mother and there was a viper underneath the shiny exterior.

Mitch's hand clenched on his fork. "Yeah, you can't win them all, as much as I'd like to. But we've won most of our games this semester."

His mother's mouth pinched into a tight line. "I've left you voicemails over the past couple of months and you haven't returned my calls."

"You mean the voicemails where you quietly rail at me for losing?" *Quietly* because she never yelled. Oh no, she made her feelings clear in a calm and controlled

Mitch-you-have-greatly-disappointed-me voice. Was it any wonder he deleted the messages without listening to them?

His dad's fork fell onto his plate with a clatter, jolting Mitch.

His mother didn't have anything to say to that. Or maybe the glower his dad shot her from across the table was what had her changing tactics.

"You know," she said, cutting delicately into her turkey breast. "Your brother's making excellent strides over at the company."

Mitch stared at his food. From the corner of his eye, he saw Dan shift in his seat. "Good for him," he said between teeth clenched so tight his jaw ticked.

"You could be doing the same."

"Greta," his dad said, voice hard.

His mother pouted prettily and took a tiny sip of wine. "I'm just saying. He could go so far if he applied himself to a business degree."

Mitch started to laugh at the age-old argument. "I'm majoring in kinesiology, and you're just going to have to live with it."

"Sweetheart." Her expression was pitying. "Nobody knows what that is."

Enough. "Fuck this." Mitch pushed away from the table.

"Mitch!"

"And fuck you too."

Knowing what he did about his mother's background might make her more relatable, but that didn't mean he'd sit around and let her badger him all night.

His dad found him in his old room a few minutes later, throwing his clothes into his duffel, ready to buy a bus ticket back to school. Instead of yelling at him for swearing at the dinner table, his dad took Mitch out to dinner at their favorite restaurant and made him talk about what was bothering him.

"Oh, you mean besides Mom being stone cold, and Dan being a Stepford son?" Mitch glanced around the restaurant. It was surprisingly packed for Christmas Day, a mix of old and young and everyone in between. Each table was decorated with a small wreath and candle, pop Christmas music played over the radio, and the servers wore jaunty Santa hats.

"You're moodier than normal, even for you." His dad peered at him over his beer. "What's going on? You and Cody have a fight?"

Which was when Mitch told his dad about Alex, and about how Mitch missed him so much and he wanted to cuddle with him on the couch and watch a movie, and he thought he might be a little in love with Alex even though they hadn't kissed yet, and he was sure Alex felt nothing for him beyond friendship.

Then Mitch proceeded to burst into tears over his manicotti.

"Kiddo." His dad patted his arm awkwardly. "Have you gotten any sleep lately?"

Mitch wiped his face with his sleeve. "Of course I sleep."

His dad made a sound of disbelief. "Have you been eating enough? You've lost weight. You've got to take care of yourself, especially playing a contact sport like you do." He sighed. "No wonder you're more sensitive than normal. You're exhausted. Exams were rough, I take it?"

"I'm not sensitive," Mitch said.

His dad laughed in his face. "Sure." He twisted spaghetti Bolognese onto his fork. "Tell me about Alex. What's he like?"

Mitch blew his nose into his napkin, then played with

his food. He was so fucking tired that he didn't have it in him to be embarrassed over the useless tears. "He's really laid-back. Easygoing. Doesn't sweat the small stuff. He's super competitive, though, even when it's just Mario Kart." He cut off a small bite of cheese-filled pasta and chewed slowly. "He notices everything. Seriously, I can't hide anything from him. If I'm hungry, he knows. If I've got something on my mind, he knows. If I'm worried, he knows. He probably knows how I feel about him even though I just admitted it to myself."

"Sounds like your opposite."

"Hey, I notice things."

"Sometimes." His dad sliced a large meatball in half. "But you're usually focused on what comes next, whatever that happens to be. The next game, the next class, the next exam, the next tuition payment, your next shift at work."

"And that's a bad thing?"

"No, of course not. You're a planner, Mitch. You always have been. Nothing wrong with that. Must be an interesting dynamic between you and Alex."

"I guess?" Mitch kicked the table leg. "He gets me, you know? I don't know how, but he does. He's so chill, so unruffable, so comfortable in who he is and his place in the world. I didn't make the best first impression—" or second or third, "—but for some reason, he still wanted to be friends."

"Sounds like a smart guy," his dad said. "Knows to look past the surface to who a person really is underneath."

Smart, and also incredibly well-adjusted. Alex's dad had left, disappeared from his life, yet Mitch had never gotten the impression that Alex had been badly affected by it. Maybe because he'd had therapy and had worked through it, or perhaps his Grandpa Forest stepping in had filled the hole in his life.

And here Mitch was, hiding from the world because his mom didn't respect him and his brother didn't like him? He was suddenly acutely embarrassed. Tears threatened and he tilted his head, shielding his reddening face with his too-long curls as shame swept through him and prickled his skin. What must Alex think of him, that he couldn't face his problems head-on like an adult?

A couple hours later, they returned home to find Mitch's mother already asleep and Dan's car gone. Mitch's dad headed off to bed and Mitch curled up on the couch, staring at the tree as if it held the answers to all of his questions. Of course, it didn't, but at least the meal and the attention from his dad had made him feel like less of a failure.

Only a few presents remained under the tree, gifts for an aunt in the area and a couple of his dad's colleagues. Mitch and his family had exchanged gifts late this morning in typical Greyson family tradition: fire roaring in the fireplace, classical Christmas music playing in the background. It sounded magical, but the conversation was almost non-existent and the thank-you's were stilted. From his mom, Mitch received a book on how to prepare for the GMAT that he planned on selling as soon as he got back to school. Dan got him a coffee table book with highlights from the past twenty years of hockey. It was a surprisingly thoughtful gift. And his dad gave him a check for two hundred bucks. When he'd found out how broke Mitch was when they'd been out for dinner, he'd taken it back and changed the *2* to a *5*.

Their holidays hadn't always been so terrible. Back before Mitch had told his mom that he wasn't going into the family business, that he wanted to play hockey and study kinesiology, before she'd cut him off, things had been good. Good*ish*, anyway. Although his mom had always been distant and hard, she'd never been mean.

Or had she? Was Mitch looking at his childhood through rose-colored glasses because he wanted it to be better than it had been? It hadn't been *bad*, per se. He'd had Cody, and hockey, and his dad, and Dan—until he didn't have Dan. He'd always had food in his belly and a roof over his head. He hadn't been abused.

Well, except for verbally, by his mother. That was the kicker, the subtle digs and scorn that had become not-so-subtle as he got older.

And his mother wondered why he didn't come home over the summer break. Four months of her bullshit? Hell no. At least all Dan did was ignore him.

Digging his phone out of his pocket, he thumbed through his contacts, but instead of calling Cody, he ended up calling Alex.

"Mitch, hey. Everything okay?" Alex's voice was smooth and warm in Mitch's ear, wrapping itself around him.

Mitch's eyes blurred. "Alex, I'm sorry. I forgot what time it is."

"I was up." Alex paused for a second. "What's wrong?"

His dad was right. Mitch hadn't been sleeping or eating well. Exams hadn't been as rough as his dad thought, though. Mitch had simply gotten into the habit of packing his day with so many activities, he didn't have time to stop and think about…

About how fucking much he missed Alex.

"Mitch?"

"Yeah," Mitch whispered past the knot in his throat.

"Talk to me."

Swallowing roughly, Mitch stared at the tree so hard, his head started to hurt. "It's just been a bad day."

"It's Christmas."

"That doesn't mean much in this house. Not anymore. It's just another day for my mom to pick at me."

"About what? She not like that you're gay?"

Mitch gave a wet laugh. "She couldn't care less about that. It's everything else about me that's an embarrassment to her."

Sound reached Mitch's ears from Alex's end of the line, a kind of shuffling. Was Alex in bed? Naked? Or maybe with tiny briefs that hugged his dick? Was he running his long fingers through his beard?

Stop that.

"I'm sure that's not true," Alex said.

"Oh, it is." Mitch rolled over on his back and stared at the dots of light on the ceiling. "She's obsessed with being proper and constantly worried about what other people think about us. The fact that I won't join the family business? She thinks it looks bad on her. And God forbid the Mountaineers lose a game. I get a you're-embarrassing-me-Mitch voicemail, but if we win? It's like I don't exist."

"Mitch…" Alex sighed. "I don't know what to say besides I'm sorry. What's the family business?"

"Westlake Waterless Printing. My mom is Greta Westlake. Her grandfather started the company years ago. It's the biggest environmentally-friendly print company in the States. Headquarters are in Manhattan, but they've got satellite offices in twenty states. My mom's always wanted me to join the company like my brother, but it's not what I want." A clacking sound reached Mitch's ears. "What are you doing?"

"Googling," Alex said, then more clacking. "Huh. Their motto is 'people first.'"

Mitch laughed, and then he laughed some more.

"What?" Alex chuckled, and the sound reached right into Mitch and warmed his belly.

"Just…the irony." People first. That was fucking hysterical.

"I'm sorry your Christmas sucks. Is your brother there?"

"Yup. Ignoring me like a champ." Mitch kicked the sofa arm and rolled onto his side again. "Even after I gave him his super awesome gift."

"He didn't like the clamp kit?"

"Right?" Mitch still didn't really know what the purpose of a clamp was, or why a woodworker would need one. The tools all looked like torture devices to him, but the guy at the store had said it was a great gift for woodworkers. Dan's hands had shaken when he'd opened his present and he'd paled considerably. His mumbled thank you hadn't exactly been heartfelt.

Whatever. There was a gift receipt taped to the box, so Dan could do whatever he wanted with it. Mitch didn't care.

"His loss then," Alex said. "What've you got planned for the next few days?"

Mitch scratched his cheek on the pillow under his head. "Nothing really. I don't want to be here anymore, so I'll probably buy a bus ticket back to Vermont tomorrow."

"Want to come here instead?"

Mitch stopped breathing. "To…Toronto?"

Alex's chuckle was low and throaty, and there was something underneath the surface that had Mitch's hormones taking notice.

"Yes, to Toronto."

"I…" Sitting up fast, Mitch clutched his head when the movement made him dizzy. The blankets pooled at his waist. "I could do that. I don't know how I'd get there, though. A bus ticket to Vermont isn't that much, but to Canada?"

"Don't you have a car?"

"Cody and I share it. If I take it, he won't have a way back to school. Unless I come back home and get him."

"Where is home? I always assumed you were from Vermont somewhere."

"The Hamptons," Mitch said absentmindedly, drumming his fingers on his chin. "Maybe I can borrow my dad's car? But then I'd still have to come back and drop it off. Fuck." Excitement left him as fast as it'd appeared, leaving Mitch cold and bereft. He fell back onto the couch. "Wait." He popped back up again. "Marco's visiting his parents in Philly. Maybe…" He thought fast, making connections where he could. Alex was silent on the other end of the line, but Mitch could hear him breathing, waiting. "Okay. I think I can make it work. But I have to talk to a couple of people first. Let me call them and I'll get right back to you."

"Maybe wait until tomorrow?" Alex said, a hint of laughter in his voice. "It's almost one in the morning."

"Damn it." Deflating, Mitch rested his forehead against the couch.

"Hey, Mitch?"

"Hmm?"

"Make it work."

He made it work.

It took some bribery on Mitch's part, but he managed to convince Marco to take the tiny detour to the Hamptons to pick up Cody on his way back to school after the holidays. One promise to review Marco's lab reports for their neuromuscular exercise physiology course next semester later, as well as a reassurance from Cody that he was happy for Mitch to take the car for a week and a half, and Mitch was ready to hit the road by lunchtime the next day. Cody had offered to come with him, but Cody's mom had taken time off work over the holidays to spend time with him, and Mitch didn't want to interfere with that.

His mother and Dan were nowhere to be found, and Mitch had already said his goodbyes to his dad, who was the only person he felt bad leaving behind.

"Don't worry about me, kiddo," his dad had said this morning before meeting up with some friends for breakfast. "Go. Have fun. Have Alex take you up the CN Tower and send me a picture from the top."

Mitch wasn't sure how he felt about being up that high, but he hugged his dad goodbye, then finished making himself some snacks for the road—mostly peanut butter and jelly sandwiches, grapes, and protein bars. Google Maps estimated a nine-hour drive, but Mitch budgeted ten for road work traffic, pee breaks, and delays at the border.

Backpack on his shoulders, skates tied together by the laces and hanging around his neck, Mitch picked up his duffel and was halfway out the door for the two-block walk to Cody's to pick up the car when he heard his name shouted from down the hall.

Dan jogged up to him. In pressed khakis and a golf shirt, he looked like he was ready to head out to the country club for a round of scotch on the rocks and gossip. Mitch, in his old jeans, flannel shirt, and scuffed boots, felt like the younger, grubbier brother he was.

"You're leaving already?" Dan stopped a few feet from Mitch. "I thought you were staying until New Year's."

"Change of plans." Mitch transferred the duffel to his other hand. "I'm visiting a friend in Toronto."

"Oh." Dan's eyebrows went up. "Cool. Go visit Kensington Market. You'll love it."

"Um, okay?" When had his brother been in Toronto?

"Got your passport?"

Mitch nodded once. "Yup."

"Good, good. Here." Dan dug into his pocket and came out with some coins. He handed them to Mitch. "Change for the tolls."

Mitch gaped at the coins in his hand for a second. It was a nice gesture from Dan. Completely unexpected, but nice. Mitch already had change for the tolls, but he didn't want to rock this too-nice boat Dan was captaining by giving it back, so he simply pocketed it and said thanks.

"You're welcome." Dan's smile was stiff, but it was there. "Drive safe."

A throat cleared delicately from the landing at the top of the stairs. His mother stood in a knee-length pink dress and matching high heels, her brown hair coiffed in some kind of twist thing. She was as cold as the winter wind seeping into the house from the open door at Mitch's back.

Dan's face blanked and he took a step back from Mitch, then said, "See ya," and disappeared the way he'd come.

What the hell?

His mother cleared her throat again.

Jesus, what? Mitch sent her a mock salute and a cheery smile through clenched teeth. "Merry Christmas," he said, and walked out the door.

THIRTEEN

ALEX DIDN'T ACTUALLY LIVE IN TORONTO LIKE Mitch thought. He lived in Oakville, a suburb west of the city. It was a good thing, according to Alex, because it meant that since Mitch was arriving via Niagara Falls, he wouldn't have to drive as far, thus avoiding traffic through Toronto that was apparently as perpetual as New York City's.

It was dark when Mitch arrived, the sun long set. Alex's mom lived in a townhouse on Robinson Street in what Alex had said was downtown Oakville. There wasn't much to downtown, as far as Mitch could tell, but it was after ten o'clock, and he was tired, so he gave it the benefit of the doubt.

The townhouse was light gray with white trim and had Christmas lights set up along the top of the front door and around the windows on the first floor. It was street parking only and Mitch found a spot directly in front of the house, where there was a parking meter sitting squat between a lamp post and a leafless tree. Fuck his life, he hadn't brought any Canadian money.

Resigned to asking Alex for change, Mitch took a minute to stretch his aching knee next to the car before grabbing his backpack and duffel. The cold was refreshing after being trapped in the car for over ten hours. There hadn't been any snow when he'd left home, but there was a thin layer here. Enough to make a footprint in, but not much else. It was quiet in the neighborhood, kind of like Glen

Hill at night. No passing cars, no din of conversation, no pedestrians. Just a dog barking somewhere nearby. A small, laminated notecard taped to the parking meter caught his eye. *On behalf of the Town of Oakville, enjoy free parking downtown from December 22 to January 5. Happy holidays!*

Sweet.

Ignoring the fluttering in his belly and sweaty palms, Mitch made his way up the steps, but then paused on the landing, his hand poised to knock on the front door.

Fuck, he was shy all of a sudden? With Alex?

That's what happens when you admit you might be in love, dummy. You should've remained ignorant. Nothing good ever comes from self-awareness.

Swallowing hysterical laughter, Mitch knocked.

Alex answered almost before Mitch's knuckles hit the door. Had he been waiting on the other side for Mitch to work up the nerve to knock? Was it possible that he was as excited to see Mitch as Mitch was to see him?

Can anybody say *wishful thinking*?

Alex's smile was wide, crinkling the skin at the corner of his eyes. He opened the door wider and motioned for Mitch to come in. "Hey, Mitch."

Blinking against the bright light of the front hallway, Mitch stepped into the house, letting Alex close the door behind him.

Alex was dressed in black sweats, a loose T-shirt, and white socks with a hole in the right toe. Mitch wiped his palms on his jeans. Had Alex become hotter in the past month? His dark hair was tousled, and—

Mitch's mouth dropped open. "You shaved." And he'd never gotten to run his fingers through the beard! He scowled at the unfairness of it all.

"Yeah." Alex ran a hand over his jaw, where there was

barely a hint of a five o'clock shadow. "I do that every few months and then grow it back."

"So it's not gone for good?"

Alex smirked. "Nope. Come in and say hi to my mom. She's been dying to meet you."

Oh, good. Yet another authority figure Mitch was bound to disappoint. "Lead the way."

Leaving his bags by the front door, Mitch followed Alex down a hallway, tearing his gaze off Alex's spectacular ass only when it finally registered that he was about to meet the man's mother, for the love of God.

The main floor was done in grays and blues, with shots of green and red Christmas decorations. In a large front room connected to the dining room sat a Christmas tree only about as tall as Mitch, with what looked like hand-made ornaments and a popcorn string. The tree's multi-colored lights reflected off a white couch adorned with a cheery throw, a coffee table, and a side table holding no less than two dozen miniature Santa figurines.

Mitch didn't get a good look at the kitchen before he was led into a room at the back of the house.

"Mom." Alex's hand landed on Mitch's lower back, causing Mitch to almost choke. "This is Mitch. Mitch, my mom Antoinette."

"Mitch." Alex's mom muted the TV and rose from the couch. She looked nothing like Alex. Or, rather, Alex looked nothing like her. She was blond and brown-eyed, whereas Alex was dark and green-eyed, and short and slim where Alex was a beast. But her smile was Alex's, identical from the way her cheeks creased to how it made the lines around her eyes deeper. "It's so lovely to meet you."

Mitch held out a hand. "You too, Mrs. Dean. Thank you for having me."

"Oh, it's Toni, please." She ignored his hand and hugged him. At a loss as to what to do, Mitch patted her on the back. "I haven't gone by Dean since Judd and I divorced."

Mitch winced and stepped back. "Sorry."

Toni waved the apology away. "Are you hungry? We have leftover turkey and potatoes from yesterday."

"Um…" Mitch had eaten his snacks hours ago, mostly out of boredom, and was now starving. But should eating their food be the first thing he did as a guest?

Alex took the decision out of his hands. "I'll warm some up for you." He disappeared into the kitchen, leaving Mitch alone with Toni.

"Sit." Toni sat and patted the couch cushion next to her.

"Oh no, that's okay. I've been sitting for hours." Mitch stood with his feet shoulder-length apart and tried to stretch out his hips, but his socks slid on the wooden floor and he almost fell involuntarily into the splits. Once upon a time, he'd done them with ease, but it had been a while. If he did them now, he had a feeling it'd hurt. A lot.

"Here." Toni retrieved a yoga mat from next to the fireplace. "I do yoga in the morning." She pointed to a DVD case on the coffee table. *Yoga for the Over 40.* "Easier to keep it here."

She had an accent, something that indicated English wasn't her first language. Mitch couldn't place it, but the name Antoinette was French, wasn't it?

"Thanks." He spread the yoga mat between the fireplace and the couch, then fell into a lunge. "My best friend, Cody, does yoga in the mornings too."

"It's a good way to wake up."

"I hate it."

Toni laughed at that. "Alex hates it too."

She didn't say *Alex* the way Mitch was used to, either.

She split it into two distinct syllables, added what sounded like a French accent on the *A*, and pronounced the second part *Lex*, like Lex Luthor, so it sounded like A-Lex.

"He says it's boring," she continued. "Gives him too much time to think."

"He's right." Mitch switched legs. "I exercise to keep in shape for hockey, sure. But it's also a good distraction, a way to clear my head. Yoga's so boring, I end up thinking about the things I don't want to be thinking about. And also about how boring yoga is." He stood, widened his stance, then bent at the waist to touch the floor between his feet. "Um, no offense."

"None taken."

Footsteps approached from behind him, then stopped abruptly in the doorway. Alex cleared his throat. "Mitch, here's your food."

His reappearance had the butterflies in Mitch's belly making a comeback, and Mitch almost tripped over his own feet when he stood too fast. *Smooth, real smooth.* "Thanks." Fuck, the food Alex carried smelled amazing. "I can eat in the kitchen."

"Why?" Alex strode around him and placed the plate on the coffee table. Then he grabbed a folding tray table from a stand against the wall and set it up in front of the couch. The plate then went onto the tray table. "I forgot cutlery." He disappeared again.

Mitch rolled up and put away the yoga mat, then made his way slowly to his meal. Nobody would get mad at him if he ate in here? What if he dropped something on the couch? At home, if he ate anywhere other than the kitchen or dining room, his mom had a conniption.

Alex returned and handed Mitch some cutlery. "Here. Sit." He pressed on Mitch's shoulders until Mitch fell onto the couch next to Toni. There was turkey with gravy and cranberry sauce on his plate, as well as diced potatoes, carrots, and onions in some kind of cheesy cream sauce. Mitch didn't know what it was, but it was amazing and he wanted more of it, stat.

"How was the drive?" Alex sat on the loveseat perpendicular to the couch, propped his feet up on the coffee table, and rested his arms behind his head, using them as a pillow.

"Good." Mitch swallowed and looked away from Alex's defined arms, from the vein on the underside that ran along his huge biceps and disappeared into his T-shirt.

"Delays at the border?"

"Only took me twenty minutes."

Alex's head reared back.

"Is that bad?" Mitch asked. It hadn't seemed long to him, but he'd never crossed into Ontario at Niagara Falls before, only into Quebec from Vermont.

"Bad?" Toni scoffed. "One time it took me three hours."

Alex chuckled. "Yeah, and you almost got fined for trying to smuggle Kinder Surprises into the States."

Toni threw up her hands. "I didn't know they're banned in America."

Sitting between them, Mitch swivelled his head from one to the other. "What's a Kinder Surprise?"

"It's a chocolate egg with a toy in the middle." Alex used his hands to form a small oval a bit larger than an egg. "It's a small toy, assembly required."

Nodding, Mitch scraped cheese off his plate, then pushed his empty plate away.

"Want more?" Alex said.

Mitch must've hesitated a second too long, because Alex was gone in the next instant with his plate and a "be right back" before Mitch could tell him he only wanted more of the potato carrot thing.

Alex came back with more potato carrot thing, extra cheesy sauce, hold the turkey.

Jesus, was he able to read Mitch's mind? Seriously, how did he always know?

"Is there anything in particular you want to do while you're here?" Alex asked.

"Not really." Mitch cut a potato in half and drowned it in sauce. "I didn't have much time to research things to do here, so I don't have a list." He maturely ignored Alex's muttered "God forbid" and carried on. "My dad wants a picture from the top of the CN Tower."

"We can do that." Alex pulled his phone out of his pocket. "It's supposed to be overcast the next couple of days, but Monday could work, provided the forecast doesn't change. See?" He turned the phone toward Mitch, where his weather app showed cloudy skies tomorrow and Sunday, and nothing but sun on Monday.

"Monday it is, then." And if Mitch freaked out at the top, he could just hold Alex's hand, right? "I also heard Kensington Market is cool. Can we go there?"

Alex smiled at him and Mitch's belly flipped. "I was going to take you tomorrow, actually. I have a feeling you'll like it."

"It's better in the summer." Toni unfolded a knit throw and spread it over her legs. "But at least it's not supposed to be too cold tomorrow. Alex, I have extra subway tokens if you want them."

Full of carbs, Mitch set his fork down. "Aren't you coming with us?"

"Me? Oh no, you boys have fun."

"You should come with us." Alex had never said it

outright, but Mitch knew he and his mom were close. As much as he hadn't wanted to take Cody away from his mom over the holidays, he now felt the same way about Alex and Toni.

"Yeah, Mom, you should come with us." Alex winked at Mitch. "Told you he wouldn't mind."

"We'll see." Toni took Mitch's plate.

"I can take that." If Mitch could somehow get out from behind this tray table.

"Nonsense. You look so tired. Alex, could you show Mitch to his room?" She brought his plate into the kitchen.

Mitch blinked at Alex. "I'm wide awake."

Making a sound of disbelief, Alex motioned for Mitch to follow him. Alex hefted Mitch's backpack and duffel before Mitch could object and headed upstairs.

At the top of the stairs, a darkened master bedroom was on the right with a bathroom directly across from the stairs. To the left, a short hallway led to two extra rooms. Alex stood in the doorway of the one at the end. The guest room, presumably.

It was small, painted dark blue with a single bed on one wall and a desk on the other. The curtains were drawn on the single window in the middle of the wall, but light still filtered in from the lamp post outside.

"Sorry it's so small." Alex deposited Mitch's bags in front of the closet and turned on the desk lamp.

Mitch sat on the edge of the bed and felt his eyelids droop. "It's perfect." The blue comforter under his palm was feather-soft against his skin. Mitch couldn't wait to wrap himself in it and sleep the past few days away. He glanced up at Alex, slouching against the doorjamb as if he had all the time in the world. He was such a strong and steady presence, Mitch felt his equilibrium balance itself out. "Thank you for inviting me here."

"Seemed like you needed a friend."

Friend. Okay, sure. Mitch could be friends-only. He could ignore his hollowing stomach and the heart that felt like it was shrinking as hope crashed and turned into bitter disappointment that punched a hole into his soul. He'd been so sure he'd heard something more than friendship in Alex's voice over the past few days. Must've been his exhausted mind playing with him.

Alex crossed the room. Standing over Mitch, he placed his hand on the back of Mitch's neck. Mitch broke out in goosebumps.

"I'm glad you came," Alex said, running his thumb up into Mitch's hair.

"You are?" Mitch's voice was little more than a whisper.

"Yeah." Alex's voice was equally as soft, equally as intimate. "I've missed you."

Mitch's nose burned and his throat tightened, but he managed a croaked, "I missed you too."

The corner of Alex's mouth kicked up, and he squeezed Mitch's neck once before letting go and backing away. "I'll see you in the morning. Sleep well."

Mitch fell back on the bed and stared at the ceiling as his mind raced in confusing thoughts. Finally, he fell asleep.

FOURTEEN

ALEX WAS WELL-AWARE THAT HE'D CONFUSED THE hell out of Mitch. It hadn't been on purpose, and truth was, he wasn't even sure how he'd done it. But Mitch kept shooting him confused looks when he thought Alex wasn't paying attention, his eyes all squinty, eyebrows squished together, teeth biting into his bottom lip.

As much as Alex wanted to suck that bottom lip into his mouth, he hesitated. They lived so far away from each other, him in Tampa for most of the year and Mitch in Vermont, that it didn't make any sense to start a relationship. Yet, at the same time, Alex had made a sort of unspoken promise to Mitch months ago, a promise that he'd tell Mitch if he ever developed feelings for him.

Well, the feelings were there, all right. They'd been slowly developing since they met. So damn slowly that Alex hadn't become aware that he had actual romantic feelings for Mitch until his conversation with Yager last month, when he'd realized he wanted to kiss Mitch.

Alex didn't usually want to kiss people he didn't have feelings for. Ergo, he must have feelings for Mitch. Feelings that were confirmed when Alex had opened the door to Mitch's unsure yet relieved smile that had made Alex hurt for him. He'd had to resist the need to pull Mitch close and promise him that every Christmas from now on would be amazing because Mitch would be spending them all with Alex and his mom, who'd spoil him rotten.

Now, two days after Mitch's arrival, Alex *wanted*. He didn't want sex with Mitch, not really. Not yet. But he wanted to kiss Mitch's lips, to trace his eyebrows, run his thumbs over Mitch's cheekbones, caress his skin, lave his nipples, bury his face in Mitch's neck and inhale his scent, his taste. He wanted to hold Mitch in his arms and dance with him, sleep curled around him, hold his hand, cuddle with him, spend hours talking to him late into the night, play hockey with him. Alex often had to stop himself from putting his arm around Mitch's shoulders, or placing a palm at Mitch's lower back, or reaching out to trace Mitch's fingers just to feel his skin.

His experience with relationships was so limited that Alex didn't know how to initiate anything beyond a friendly pat on the back. Hence the hesitation. And he could tell Mitch was getting antsy.

They spent Mitch's first day wandering the shops along Lakeshore Road in downtown Oakville. Mitch slept in late, which gave them a late start to the day, so they pushed Kensington Market to the next day. Alex could walk from one end of downtown Oakville to the other in under twenty minutes. It took four hours with Mitch, because Mitch wanted to see everything and go into every store. His giddiness was fucking adorable, especially with cheeks rosy from the cold and the ends of his curly hair escaping from underneath his toque.

"Can we go in here?" Mitch asked for the sixtieth time. *Here* was a popular bakery that sold everything from cookies to breads and always had something to sample.

Inside, it smelled like yeasty dough and sugar. The entranceway was postage stamp-sized and, as always, it was packed. Alex used his larger size to bully his way to the front, snagged two samples of a cinnamon roll on a toothpick, and made his way back to Mitch.

"Here." He handed Mitch the bigger piece. "If you like these, I'll pick some up for breakfast tomorrow."

"Oh my God." Mitch's eyes rolled back into his head. "Oh my God. So good." He snatched Alex's piece out of his hand while Alex was distracted by Mitch's moan.

"Hey!"

Mitch sent him a cheeky grin and popped the cinnamon roll into his mouth. "I want to see what else they have." They made their way to the front, where Mitch crouched down to peer through the window display. "What's that?"

"Scones." Alex crouched next to him. "You won't like those, though. They have raisins." Mitch made a face. He did not like mushy raisins. "How about this one? Apple cinnamon."

"Ooh, yeah."

The man was easily pleased.

"Tell me something," Mitch said once Alex had purchased their scones and cinnamon rolls and they were back out on the street. "I'm pretty sure I read somewhere that you're from a small town. But when I Googled Oakville before I left yesterday, the website said it has a population of almost two hundred thousand. That's not small."

"No, it's definitely not small." Alex moved out of the way of a lady and her enormous dog. "I don't know, maybe it's considered a small town compared to Toronto?"

"Which has what, two million people?"

"You say 'two million' like it's a small number."

Mitch glanced at him. "It's small compared to New York City, which is where I was born."

"Right. Where there's probably two million people within a city block."

"It's not that bad."

The burger place they were having dinner at with Alex's

mom was predictably busy, but they were early enough to beat the dinner rush, and were seated almost instantly. The restaurant was all exposed beams and rustic tables, antlers on the wall and old black-and-white photos of cottage country.

"Can I get you drinks while you wait?" the hostess asked as she placed cutlery rolled into a napkin on the table.

"Two butterscotch milkshakes, please," Alex said.

"Two what?" Mitch looked up from the menu.

"Trust me, you'll like it."

Mitch eyed his milkshake dubiously when it arrived, stirring the thick drink with his straw. "Butterscotch, you said?"

"Uh-huh."

He took a tentative sip and his eyes popped wide. A couple of heftier sips later, he raised his hands in the air and bent as far as he could over the table. "I bow to you, O Wise One Who Has All Earthly Knowledge of the Good Foods."

Alex laughed and couldn't help being charmed.

Mitch went back to perusing the menu and had finished a third of his milkshake by the time he'd decided on what to order. "There's your mom." He gestured toward the glass window that acted as the restaurant's street-facing wall.

Bundled against the cold, his mom was jaywalking across the street, heading towards them.

Mitch leaned closer. "She knows I don't mind if she hangs out with us, right?" He kept his voice low, as if she could hear him from outside.

"She knows. I think she just wanted to give us the day. Besides, she lives down the street, so she's been to these shops a million times."

Mitch's mouth twisted. "Still, I feel bad. I know you

guys are close and I don't want you to take time away from her to hang out with me."

Alex shrugged. "We are close. But we keep in touch while I'm in Tampa and I'm still here for another week, so it's not like we won't see each other. Besides, you and I are close too, aren't we?"

He'd clearly shocked the shit out of Mitch. His mouth opened and closed, but no sound came out.

"Hi, boys." His mom slid into the booth next to Alex and pointed at Alex's milkshake. "Did you get me one?"

"Not yet," Alex said. "Didn't know how long you'd be."

Mitch paid no attention to them and sucked down his milkshake like a champ. When he noticed Alex watching him, he let the straw pop out of his mouth, licked his lips, and said, "I'm gonna move in with your mom so I can have these every day, m'kay?"

Alex's heart somersaulted and fell at Mitch's feet, right there in a crowded burger joint that smelled like deep fried onion rings.

The server came by to take their orders, and once she left, Alex's mom dug something out of her purse. "Look what I found." She placed two pairs of mittens, both black, on the table. "They're made with alpaca wool. It's supposed to be warmer than sheep's wool. Feel how soft they are?" She ran one mitten over Alex's cheek. Alex sighed and took it as, across from him, Mitch pressed his lips together to keep from laughing. "Here, I got you each a pair." She handed a set to Alex, and one to Mitch.

Mitch's spine went ramrod straight. "These… These are for me?" He picked up the mittens tentatively, and ran a reverent hand over them. "That's… You didn't have to do that."

Alex's mom waved a hand. "Try them on. Do they fit?"

Mitch was quick to comply. Alex followed more slowly, keeping half an eye on Mitch. Mitch grinned ear to ear and, once he had the mittens on, rubbed his hands together gleefully. "These are great! Thank you."

Alex's mom beamed. "You're welcome."

Mitch removed his new mittens and carefully tucked them into the front pocket of his ever-present backpack.

Their meals arrived, and Alex's mouth watered just looking at it.

Mitch's mouth dropped open and he stared in dismay at the burger on his plate. "What the… I can't eat all this. It's as big as my face!"

"I finish mine all the time," Alex's mom said. "If I can finish, you can finish."

"Yeah." Alex sprinkled salt on his French fries. "But he's used to a diet of smoothies and Cheese Whiz-covered celery sticks."

"Oh, Mitch." His mom patted Mitch's hand. "That's not healthy, especially not for an athlete like you. You need nutrients."

Feeling vindicated—Alex had said something similar to Mitch at least five times—Alex sent Mitch a grin. *See? Told ya.*

Mitch sat back in his seat and smirked at Alex like, *You're not the boss of me.* It was oddly endearing.

The next day found all three of them at Kensington Market mid-morning. Alex hid behind a toque and sunglasses, hoping not to be recognized. He almost never was in Tampa, but hockey in the south had a different life force than hockey in Canada.

Ahead of him, his mom and Mitch chatted about something. Had Mitch met Alex's mom three months ago when his walls were still up with Alex, he would've been moody and tight-lipped and conversed only as much as necessary. Now, he was animated and happy and he spoke with enthusiasm. He also kept sneaking glances back at Alex, ostensibly to make sure Alex was still there.

As if Alex was going anywhere.

Kensington Market was much more vibrant in the summer, when it turned into a partial outdoor market. In the winter, vendors didn't hawk their wares in the cold, and there were no artists painting on the sidewalk. But it wasn't Toronto's most unique neighborhood for nothing. Despite the cold and lack of crowds, the vintage clothing shops and eclectic mix of restaurants, cafés, grocers, and bakeries were still covered in cheerful graffiti and colorful awnings. The narrow streets and alleys were lined with bright-colored Victorian homes in every shade of the rainbow, and sidewalk signs advertised everything from sales on T-shirts to drop-in sewing workshops to two-for-one Jamaican patties. And when it started to snow lightly, fresh powder dusting awnings and rooftops and railings, it added an extra dose of charm to the neighborhood.

Inside one of the clothing stores, Mitch found a T-shirt with "What I love most about yoga is the nap at the end" written across the front.

"I need to get this for Cody." Then he found a pair of pink sweatpants with "Yoga" written in white script across the butt. "Toni, look. I'm going to get these for you. What size are you?"

The narrow-eyed glare Alex's mom sent Mitch was unimpressed. "Legging."

Mitch cracked up. In fact, he was still laughing after he'd paid and they'd left the shop.

"I need to find something for Alex," Mitch said to Alex's mom.

"What? Why? I don't need anything."

"Let's try here," his mom said, heading for a store with a blue facade and red shutters around the second floor windows.

"Guys, I don't need anything."

They ignored him and walked into the store. Alex went into the bakery next door and got them each a hot chocolate. By the time he came back out, Mitch and his mom were waiting for him on the sidewalk. Mitch grinned proudly and held up a light gray, vintage T-shirt with a distressed American flag across the chest.

"Get it?" Mitch said. "It's ironic. Because you're Canadian."

It was really very sweet.

FIFTEEN

LATE THE NEXT AFTERNOON, ON WHAT WAS THE first sunny day since Mitch arrived, Alex and Mitch rode up the CN Tower with a dozen other people crowded around them. Mitch, pupils so huge the brown was almost completely obscured, plastered himself against the back of the elevator, his hands fisted so tightly his knuckles were white. Alex bit his cheek and tried not to laugh.

Inching in beside Mitch, Alex slouched next to him and rested his shoulder against Mitch's. "We'll catch the next elevator down once we get to the top."

"No," Mitch said, jaw twitching in a way that told Alex he was clenching his teeth. "It cost thirty-five bucks each to come up here, we're damn well not going right back down." He studiously focused on the floor at his feet and not on any of the elevator's three glass walls as the elevator rose. The trip only took fifty-eight seconds, but they were fifty-eight seconds in which Mitch looked like he was going to hurl.

Finally, they reached the first observation level and as soon as Mitch exited the elevator, he found a couch along a wall, sat, and stuck his head between his legs.

"I'm going to die up here, aren't I?" he wheezed.

Alex chuckled and sat next to him. Opening the backpack on Mitch's back, he dug through and came out with a bottle of ginger ale. He twisted off the top and held the bottle out to Mitch. "Here. Drink some of this."

"I can't move."

Alex snorted. "Now you're just being melodramatic."

"That's a—" Mitch waved a hand out in front of him. "—big window."

Sure enough, dead ahead was a floor-to-ceiling window that overlooked the snow-covered city.

Alex stood and squared himself directly in Mitch's line of sight. "Better?"

Mitch lifted his head tentatively, sat up straight—

And was level with Alex's crotch.

Mitch nodded once. "Yup. Much better." He reached blindly for the ginger ale and took a gulp while staring at Alex's groin area. Not that there was much to see, given his dick was hidden behind underwear, jeans, and a winter coat. Mitch handed the bottle back to Alex, smacking his lips together.

Alex shook his head and recapped the bottle. "What am I going to do with you?"

"Do me?"

Choking on a surprised laugh, Alex leaned over Mitch to put the ginger ale back in his bag. "I was wondering where that guy was," he said. "You've been extremely well-behaved lately."

"It's been hard."

"I bet."

"Like, *real* hard."

"Jesus, you're a brat," Alex said, though his tone didn't match his words. "Come on. Let's walk around and get some pictures for your dad."

"Um, I think maybe I'll stay here."

Alex took one of Mitch's hands and yanked him up. "Here's a tip. If you look out into the distance, instead of straight down, it doesn't feel like you're up so high."

Mitch seemed to contemplate that for a few seconds, his forehead furrowed, then shook his head. "That sounds like bullshit."

"Really, Mr. Science Major? You're not even going to test my theory before rejecting it?"

"Hypothesis," Mitch said.

"Huh?"

"A theory is something that's already been tested and proven, with the scientific evidence to back it up, like the theory of relativity, or heliocentrism, or the Pythagorean theorem. A hypothesis is an idea, a suggested explanation or realistic prediction of an observable phenomenon."

Alex grinned like a dummy. "You're cute when you go all nerd."

That earned an instant scowl from Mitch, but Alex wasn't kidding.

Curiosity eventually sent Mitch to the windows, but he made sure Alex was between him and the glass.

"In case something happens, you'll die protecting me and I'll still have a chance to head for safety," Mitch said with a cheeky grin.

He used Alex's phone to take pictures and send them to his dad, since his own phone was one of those old ones with the keyboard that slid out and didn't take good photos.

"The city looks endless from up here," he said from two feet behind Alex where it was, apparently, relatively safe. "Is that Oakville?"

"No, that's east. Oakville's in the other direction."

"Show me."

Alex took him, but Mitch got distracted halfway there. "I didn't know Toronto had an island."

The windows on this side of the tower faced the Toronto Harbourfront and the chain of small islands just a short thirteen-minute ferry ride away. In the summer, they were lush and green, Lake Ontario a deep blue. Today, the water was murky and uninviting and the islands were covered in a layer of snow that made them look uninhabitable. Beyond was what seemed like an endless expanse of water.

"What's it called?" Mitch asked.

"The Toronto Islands, or usually just the Island."

"Wow," Mitch said blandly. "I wonder how many brain cells it took to come up with that."

"Yeah, yeah, keep moving, smart-ass."

They crossed into an area that was devoid of windows but had a throng of people standing around taking pictures. Alex used his width to create a path for himself and Mitch.

"Hey, where's the glass floor I've heard about?" Mitch asked from behind him.

Alex turned and pointed at his feet. "Look down."

Mitch did…then jerked backward, tripped over nothing, fell onto his ass, and crab-crawled off the glass until his back hit the wall.

Alex laughed so hard, his stomach hurt. A couple of people gawked at them, but other than that, nobody paid them much attention.

"That was… How could… I don't…" Wide-eyed with astonishment and a healthy dose of fear, Mitch's mouth opened and closed, but no sound came out.

Alex kept laughing.

Mitch was slowly getting his color back, so he must not've been too traumatized.

"Come on." Alex held out a hand to help Mitch up.

Mitch ignored it and pressed further into the wall. "I'm not going anywhere with you, you traitor."

Alex didn't quite abort a laugh fast enough for Mitch not to hear it. "It was an accident, I swear. I was just trying to cut us a path through the crowd. I didn't realize the floor was there."

Mitch's eyes narrowed suspiciously and his lips pursed.

Alex wiggled his fingers and sent him what he hoped was a charmingly apologetic grin. "Please?"

Right in front of Alex's eyes, Mitch's whole body unclenched and he reached for Alex's hand.

God, the trust implicit in that action… It made Alex's chest tighten. Fuck, he hoped he didn't screw this up.

A few minutes later, Alex led them to the restaurant, where, unbeknownst to Mitch, Alex had made them early dinner reservations.

"Can we get a table away from the window?" Alex asked the hostess.

"Uh, sure." She turned and motioned for them to follow. "I think you're the first person who's ever asked me for a non-window table."

They were seated far enough away from the glass that Mitch didn't panic, yet close enough to watch the sunset paint hues of pink and purple across the sky, and witness the first streetlights coming on in the city. The restaurant was fairly quiet, the hum of conversation around them nicely muted. Candles flickered on the tables, and the lights were dim.

"Alex, what are we doing here?"

"Having dinner."

Mitch stared at him dispassionately. "Yeah, thanks, genius. I mean, why here? Jesus!" He gaped at something on the menu. "The lobster is ninety-five fucking dollars," he said in a hoarse whisper.

"Then don't have the lobster," Alex said reasonably.

"Don't have the—" Mitch rolled his eyes. "And you say I'm impossible. Seriously, Alex, this is too much. Let's just go to McDonald's or something." His head swivelled around the restaurant as if the ninety-five-dollar lobster was about to cut him for defamation.

"You're not coming to my city for McDonald's. You can have McDonald's anywhere. Besides, I still owe you a second date."

Mitch's head swung toward him, cheeks pink. He stayed quiet for so long that Alex's stomach cramped, heart sinking as reality hit. Fuck, he'd read Mitch wrong, hadn't he? Alex had waited too long, squandered Mitch's feelings. Mitch had probably given up on him a long time ago. Not that Alex blamed him. Who wanted to wait around for a *maybe* like Alex?

"I'm sorry," Alex said, grimacing. "I shouldn't have assumed—"

"No!" Mitch winced and lowered his voice. "No, I—I'm just…surprised. I didn't think… I mean, I know you said it might happen, but I guess I didn't expect…." He blew out a breathy laugh and the corners of his lips tilted upward cautiously. "This is actually a date?" He waved a finger between the two of them. "You and me?"

Alex smiled back at him, hope returning and backing the breath in his lungs. "If you want."

"I want. But what do I do now?"

"What do you mean?"

Mitch played with his cutlery. "I don't know what to do. I've never been on a date before."

"Me neither."

"Oh." Mitch sat up straighter. "I guess we wing it, then?"

"I guess."

Mitch didn't look too thrilled at the idea. "I'm not much of a winger."

"You're a left winger."

"Oh my God." Mitch buried his face in his hands. "That was so bad."

Mildly insulted, Alex said, "What? No, that was clever. Laugh, damn it. It was funny."

Mitch laughed, but Alex had a feeling it was at him and not at his joke. Still, the sense of rightness that hit Alex at making Mitch laugh made him feel like a fucking superhero.

Lame, but true.

"Sorry for the delay, folks." The server, a gentleman in his fifties with gray hair and a cropped goatee, stopped at their table and filled their glasses with ice water. "Can I start you off with a drink?"

Alex ordered them each a local beer and when the server asked for their IDs, Alex reached into his pocket while Mitch pondered the menu. Alex poked him in the foot under the table and, when Mitch looked up, jerked his head at the server. "You too. I'm not drinking both beers."

Bewildered for a second, Mitch simply frowned at Alex as Alex handed his ID to the server. "Oh!" Mitch said, finally catching on. "Shit, I'm legal here, aren't I?"

The server took a quick but thorough glance at their IDs, handed them back, said, "I'll be right back with your drinks," and left.

"You did say you'd buy me a beer when I was legal," Mitch said. He twisted his water glass on the table, the condensation leaving a trail of circles behind. "Should you be drinking, though? You're the one driving back home."

"I'm only having one," Alex countered. "Besides, we're not going straight back after dinner."

"We're not? Where are we going, then?"

"Didn't you wonder why we brought our skates today?"

"Honestly, I kind of hoped you have friends who play

for Toronto and were taking me to meet them," Mitch said, all cautiously optimistic.

"No," Alex replied, laughing. "That's not it at all. Toronto's not even your team, anyway."

Mitch shrugged. "So? It'd still be cool to meet the players."

The server returned and placed their beers on the table. "Ready to order, or do you need another few minutes?"

They ordered, and before the server could leave, Alex said, "Actually, can you bring us the poached lobster too?" The server didn't even blink at their meal-for-three-for-two.

Mitch's mouth fell open. "Are you crazy? It's ninety-five dollars," he whispered harshly over the table, as if Alex could forget.

Unconcerned, Alex lifted an uncaring shoulder. "I wanted to try it. I'll share."

"What if we don't like it? That's ninety-five bucks down the drain."

"Mitch." Alex resisted the need to reach out and put his hand over Mitch's. Had they been in private, he wouldn't have hesitated. But in public, where anyone here might've already recognized him? Wasn't happening. Alex leaned closer and lowered his voice. "I play for the NHL. I can afford to eat fancy once in a while."

Mitch glanced away. "Still."

"You know," Alex said, contemplating Mitch, "for someone from the Hamptons, you're awfully stingy about money."

It was the wrong thing to say.

"Seriously?" If Mitch's eyes could shoot sparks, Alex would be a flaming ball of hurt. "You think I'm rich, just because I live in the Hamptons?"

"Aren't you?"

Mitch shook his head, his fingers flexing around his beer glass.

"Tell me," Alex pleaded. *Please don't revert back to the scared guy who never talked about anything important.*

Mitch turned his head away, gazing either at the couple dining next to them or the city beyond the window, awash in hundreds of lights as the sky turned to dusk. Or maybe he wasn't seeing anything but the thoughts circling in his head.

"I'm sorry, I—"

"No." Mitch rolled his eyes—at himself or at Alex, Alex couldn't tell. "No, I'm sorry. Everybody assumes that, but for some reason, it always gets my back up. Okay, first of all—" He held up his index finger. "—not everybody who lives in the Hamptons is rich. I mean, sure, you've got your socialites who get thousand-dollar haircuts or five-hundred-dollar manicures and men who pay a shit-ton of money to play golf at the clubs. But the people who give the haircuts or manicures or drive golf carts? They're just ordinary people who wouldn't be able to make a living without their jobs."

"You're right," Alex said, suitably chastised. "I never considered it that way." And given that he hadn't grown up the richest of kids, who was he to judge?

"And second." Mitch blew out a long breath and rested his forearms on the table. "My mom's rich. The printing business."

"I remember."

"So yeah, her family's loaded. And the money was always there for me when I was growing up. I even had an account with money deposited into it every month. But then a few years ago, when I told my mom I wasn't going into the family business, that I wanted to play hockey and study kinesiology instead, she cut me off. My brother got a full ride to Columbia, but I didn't see a penny of tuition money." The skin around Mitch's eyes pinched, making him seem older than his nineteen years.

Alex had known Mitch worked two jobs, but it hadn't occurred to him that Mitch's financial situation was quite that bad.

Mitch's closed-off personality made so much more sense now. A brother who ignored him, a mother who'd cut him off. Alex would be afraid to show his true colors too, if the people who were supposed to love him had so callously tossed him aside.

Underneath the table, he pressed his knee against Mitch's. "So you've got the partial hockey scholarship and the rest is covered by financial aid?"

Mitch's incredulous chuckle scraped Alex's nerves raw. "You're kidding, right? Financial aid is based on parental income. I would've been laughed out of the office. The rest I pay out of pocket."

"Your dad doesn't help?"

"I'm sure he would if he, uh, knew."

"Mitch—"

Mitch raised his hand in the universal motion for *stop*. "Don't, okay? I know what you're going to say, and it's not happening." He must've accurately read the unimpressed expression on Alex's face because he said, "Look, my parents' marriage has been strained since I was a kid. I'm not going to be the one who gives them something else to fight about."

"I can understand that." *Let me help you.* What not to say to a guy who was determined to go through life on his own. Talk about being laughed out of the office—or the restaurant, in this case.

Alex had money. Lots of money. Not veteran player money, but it was still two years with the NHL money. And it was just sitting there, helping no one. Sure, he donated to his favorite charities, but if he could help a friend who needed it, why wouldn't he?

But he didn't offer. Mitch really would laugh his way all the way down the CN Tower, then avoid the topic until Alex forgot about it or they were several states apart from each other, whichever came first.

Everything about Mitch made Alex want to bundle him up in bubble wrap and keep him safe. He kept that thought to himself too. Mitch would probably throw his knife at him for that one.

"Mitch…" It was now or never. This was the first time Alex had considered asking for Mitch's help with the book where he didn't fear getting shot down. Alex had interviewed eleven hockey players as well as some of their close friends and family—mostly spouses and parents, along with a couple of siblings. He'd also interviewed Chris Blair, as well as his team's nutritionist, psychologist, and physician. He didn't *need* Mitch's perspective. But he wanted it. Mitch's background, his struggles, his dedication, his total focus on getting to where he wanted to be, no matter the cost… It would add an additional layer of realism to the book. "Do you think I could use your story in the book I'm writing?"

"Oh. Um…"

"I don't have to," Alex said, backpedaling. "And if you want, I can change your name to protect your privacy. In fact, I already have a pseudonym picked out."

Mitch blinked at him. "You do? What is it?"

"Adrian."

"I look like an Adrian?" He looked adorably insulted for some reason.

"No. But your hair reminds me of Adrian Grenier's in *The Devil Wears Prada*."

"Oh." Mitch ran a hand through his too-long curls. They tumbled over his forehead and his ears, perfect little chocolate-colored corkscrews Alex wanted to touch. Mitch could probably pull it into a man bun, if he wanted. "Except mine's better."

"Undoubtedly."

He beamed at Alex. "You can use my story. I don't mind being an Adrian."

"Yeah?"

Mitch shrugged. "Of course."

Of course. Like it was no big deal. And maybe, at this point in their relationship, it wasn't.

Their meal came. Mitch's chicken stuffed with cheese and spinach smelled way better than Alex's prime rib in that someone-else's-food-always-looks-better-than-mine kind of way. They maneuvered the poached lobster into the middle of the small table.

And stared at it once the server left.

Mitch leaned toward it and sniffed. "Smells okay."

The lobster was a light pink in the middle of the plate, sitting in a pool of tarragon butter sauce. Steamed asparagus, spiced fingerling potatoes, and glazed carrots finished off the presentation.

Alex poked the lobster with his fork. A small piece flaked off. "You go first," he said to Mitch.

Mitch sat back fast. "Hell, no. You ordered it, you go first."

That was fair. Alex forked a small bite, chewed slowly. Ninety-five dollars was not indicative of a good meal, but in this case Alex could cede that although it wasn't worth ninety-five dollars, it wasn't as bad as he'd feared. "It's good. Tastes like fish in a tarragon butter sauce."

Mitch eyed him distrustfully.

"Here." Alex cut off another small piece, dipped it in the sauce thoroughly, and held it out to Mitch.

"Huh," Mitch said as he chewed. "It is pretty good. Maybe not ninety-five bucks worth of good, but I don't hate it."

It so accurately reflected what Alex had been thinking that he smiled at Mitch with what he was sure was a dopey smile on his face.

"Um…" Mitch's cheeks pinked and he smiled back just as dopily. "Did you know lobsters are either right-handed or left-handed, like humans?" He made a snapping motion with his hands.

Fuck, he was cute. "You would know something like that."

"I almost majored in marine biology instead of kinesi-ology," Mitch said, slicing into his chicken.

Alex paused with his fork halfway to his mouth to peer at Mitch, skeptical. "Are you making that up?"

Mitch grinned at him and kept eating.

Alex wanted him.

The victory dance going on in Mitch's head looked like a combination of the Carlton and the moonwalk.

It wasn't just that Alex had all but told him he wanted him by taking him out on a date. It was also in the way Alex's gaze slipped to Mitch's mouth every so often, how he reached out to touch Mitch but aborted the movement before he made contact. It was in the underlying tension between them, the way their eyes snagged and held.

Alex didn't, however, want sex. Mitch was sure of it. He knew what someone who wanted sex looked like, and it wasn't evident in the long, searching looks Alex sent him, or the way Alex took care of him. Which meant he had no idea what Alex wanted and it was making Mitch crazy, even though he was one hundred percent certain that whatever it was, he'd be happy to give it. More than happy.

It was almost like Alex wanted, but didn't want to want. Like Mitch three months ago, when he'd wanted to be friends with Alex but had been afraid to be himself.

Conclusion?

Relationships were complicated as fuck.

After dinner, they walked to where they'd parked the car, grabbed their skates, then headed north, away from the lake. Alex carried Mitch's skates. It was so cute, it gave Mitch butterflies. Like this was a real date or something.

Which it was. Jesus.

Alex took him to an outdoor ice rink at Nathan Phillips Square, right next to City Hall. It was beautiful, with the lights from the surrounding skyscrapers and the red and green spotlights on Old City Hall, a Romanesque building now used as a courthouse, illuminating the area. Its clock tower read eight p.m. The curved giants that were New City Hall were dark slashes against the night. There was a twenty-foot tall Christmas tree lit in red and white on one side of the ice rink. The three arches spanning the rink were covered in tiny white lights, with golden stars hanging from the highest part of the arches, where they spun lazily in the wind.

It was packed. Apparently, everybody in Toronto had decided to cram themselves onto a piece of ice that, from this angle, didn't look much bigger than an NHL-sized hockey rink. Regardless, they left their shoes and Mitch's backpack in the coin-operated lockers in the locker room and headed onto the ice.

Most people either stood in clumps next to the elevated

concrete walkway around the perimeter of the rink or skated in laps. Mitch and Alex joined the skaters, but they skated nearer to the center of the rink where it wasn't as crowded.

The good news was that since it was dark, and with Alex's hat over his head and scarf up to his chin, he was unrecognizable as Tampa Bay's D-man, Alex Dean. Which meant they could hold hands without anyone knowing any better.

Yeah, that's right. They were holding hands. Alex had instigated it. Mitch was just along for the ride, since he had no idea what the fuck was happening.

"This place reminds me of Rockefeller Center," he said on one of their many laps around the ice.

"I've never been." Alex's hand tightened on his and Mitch wished it wasn't cold enough to require mittens. Not that his new alpaca mitts weren't as soft as Toni said, just that he'd rather feel Alex's bare skin against his.

"I love New York at Christmas," Mitch said. "Toronto reminds me of New York, actually. Lots of people, lots of congestion, lots of skyscrapers. What's your favorite city that you've travelled to with the team?"

"It's hard to say," Alex said, pulling Mitch out of the way of a group of teenagers who appeared to be doing nothing but taking up space. "I don't often get to see the city I'm in. I do like Boston and Denver."

Mitch rubbed his cold nose with his free hand. "We used to go skiing in Denver when I was a kid."

"I've never skied," Alex said. "I've always wanted to try snowboarding, but when I was young, there wasn't enough money for two expensive sports. Hell, sometimes we didn't have the money for one."

"Yet, here you are."

"Yeah. My mom gave up a lot so I could play."

"Is that why you came home for Christmas?"

Alex chuckled, the sound low and rumbly among kids squealing and people laughing and talking. "No, I come home because I want to. My mom and I are close, but if I didn't come home for a holiday, she wouldn't hold it against me. That's not how she is. And besides, she has her own life."

They'd somehow ended up on the edge of the rink, and Alex gave a couple and their dog sitting on the elevated walkway a wide berth.

"Tell me you're not afraid of dogs," Mitch said. He was mostly kidding, but the look on Alex's face said it all. "You are! But dogs are man's best friend."

"I'm not *afraid* of them," Alex said in what sounded like a token protest. "I just have a healthy respect for the damage they can cause."

Mitch chanced a glance over his shoulder at the tiny terrier wearing purple booties and a matching purple coat. It couldn't have weighed more than thirty pounds. "Uh-huh, lots of damage. I see exactly what you mean."

"Also, animals wearing clothes is just creepy," Alex said, ignoring Mitch completely.

"No, it's cute."

"I read an article once that said clothes are bad for dogs because it creates chafing, and unlike humans they can't scratch an itch or adjust their clothes. Would you want chafing in your private parts that you couldn't get rid of? Doubt it."

Mitch burst out laughing.

Peripherally he was aware of a few onlookers, but beyond a brief moment of oh-shit-I'm-holding-hands-with-a-dude-in-public, he quickly forgot about them. He might not be out to most of his friends and teammates, but here, where nobody knew him, he could be. He wasn't particularly worried about getting his ass kicked by some douchebag homophobe. First, Alex had told him Toronto was a pretty progressive city. And second, Alex was a six-foot-four defenseman with the biggest shoulders Mitch had ever seen. Whoever picked on him and, by association, Mitch, was just asking for an ass kicking.

Abruptly, Alex turned to skate backward facing Mitch, and took Mitch's hands in his.

"What are you doing?" Mitch asked as they continued to skate laps, but slower now, almost as if they were dancing.

"I wanted to look at you."

"Aww." Mitch's fingertips tingled inside his mitts where they rested in Alex's mittened palms. "You're a sap."

Alex's scowl was glorious. "No, that was romantic."

"Sappy."

Alex sighed sullenly. "I'm trying to woo you."

Total sap. "I see." Mitch stuck his tongue in his cheek to hide his smile. "Well then, by all means. Carry on. Woo me."

"I can't now," Alex said, huffing. "You threw me off my game."

"Is that all it takes to throw you off your game?" Mitch shook his head in mock pity. "It's a wonder you ever made it to the pros."

Alex slowed down so much that he might as well have stopped moving. Mitch didn't see it coming and skated right into him. With an apology on the tip of his tongue, he glanced up at Alex, only to find Alex's gaze on his mouth.

Mitch's throat went dry and his body heated underneath his winter clothing as Alex snaked an arm around him and brought him in even closer. He had to consciously prevent his skates from tangling with Alex's, but given they were now merely coasting, it didn't take much concentration. Which was good because his concentration really needed to be on Alex and how Alex breathed softly against Mitch's face and how safe Mitch felt in the cocoon of Alex's arms and how Alex was going to kiss him. Right? Please?

"How's my game now?" Alex's whisper ghosted across Mitch's lips.

"Um…" Mitch gripped Alex's bicep. "What?"

Alex's arm around him tightened. His gaze went from Mitch's mouth to his eyes, where he seemed to search for— well, Mitch didn't know what for, but whatever it was Alex must've found it. He leaned down and Mitch tilted his head up in anticipation, breath faltering and the world falling away and—

"Yo, dudes! Watch it."

A teenager, obviously new on skates, bumped into them, knocking them off balance. They hit the ice hard, Alex on his back, Mitch sprawled on top of him, legs tangled.

Alex groaned underneath him. "Ow, fuck." He probed the back of his head.

Mitch pushed himself off Alex's chest with a hand and grinned down at him. "This is so not how I imagined getting you under me."

Alex cracked up and let his head thunk back onto the ice.

Alex led the way into the house a couple hours later, quietly, in case his mom had gone to bed. But it turned out he needn't have worried. She was coming down the hallway, a mug of tea in hand, when they walked in.

"Hi, boys."

"Hey, Mom. How was work?"

"Busy." She paused in front of the stairs. "How was your day? What did you guys get up to?"

"It was good," Mitch said as he dropped his backpack and skates on the front carpet and took off his coat and shoes. "We went up the CN Tower."

"Ooh, did you love it?"

"It was horrifying," Mitch said with perfect truthfulness, his eyes big in his face.

Alex's mom laughed and patted Mitch on the arm. "Stick closer to the ground from now on. Have Alex take you to the Hockey Hall of Fame."

Shit, how come Alex hadn't thought of that?

If it was possible, Mitch's eyes went even bigger. "I can't believe I forgot that it's here," he said almost reverently. He turned to Alex. "Can we go tomorrow?"

"Sure. Mom, want to come?"

"Oh no. I've got the early shift tomorrow. Which is why I'm off to bed." She gave them both a kiss on the cheek and headed upstairs.

Alex turned off the light in the front hallway. Alone with Mitch in the small entranceway, it felt like they were the only two people in the universe. The questions lurking in Mitch's eyes were expected, given they'd continued to skate for another hour after they'd fallen yet Alex hadn't initiated another kiss.

"Come on." Alex headed for the living room and plugged in the Christmas tree, the dozens of multicolored lights creating an appropriately intimate atmosphere in the otherwise dark room.

Mitch perched on the edge of the couch and Alex felt his gaze following him like a touch as he grabbed the throw and spread it out over Mitch's lap.

"I'm going to make us some hot chocolate," Alex said. "I'll be right back." Leaving a bewildered Mitch behind, he headed for the kitchen.

His hands shook slightly as he prepared the hot chocolate on the stove. Nerves and a severe case of what-the-fuck-is-wrong-with-you. He'd almost kissed Mitch right there, in public, in the middle of what felt like the entire fucking world. What if someone had recognized him? It wouldn't just fuck up his own career, but Mitch's future prospects, as well. He'd been so caught up in the moment, he hadn't thought past the need to have his lips on Mitch's. It was stupid and reckless and impulsive.

But it had also felt extremely right. Not the part where he'd almost kissed a guy in public, but the part where he'd held Mitch in his arms and breathed him in, where he'd held Mitch's hand, where he'd carried Mitch's skates to the rink and Mitch had blinked at him with baffled surprise.

The rightness of it all, of *them*, settled in his heart, and he walked back into the living room carrying two mugs with steady hands.

Mitch stood next to a side table. He jumped when Alex walked in and guiltily placed a small wooden Christmas figurine back on the table among the others. "Sorry. I'm sorry. I didn't mean to touch." He sounded like a child apologizing for breaking his mother's fancy china.

"It's fine," Alex said, setting the mugs on the coffee table. "Here." He held the figurine out to Mitch, then placed the fat Santa in Mitch's palm when he hesitated. "It even opens. See?" Alex showed him where to twist and let him do the rest.

Mitch sat on the floor in front of the coffee table and opened all of the little Russian dolls, lining them up in a neat row, from tallest to shortest, on the table. Fat Santa,

Mrs. Claus, a snowman, a penguin, a gingerbread man, a nutcracker, and a tiny Christmas tree. His lopsided smile tugged at Alex's heartstrings.

"We were never allowed to touch the decorations at my house," Mitch said, changing up the order of his line so that the dolls sat in a row of alternating heights. "My mom has the house professionally decorated every year. For Thanksgiving and Halloween too. It's always beautifully done, but Dan and I were never allowed to touch anything. We even had a huge sleigh in the front yard one year, a real one with a bag of fake gifts in the back, and when I asked my mom if I could sit in it, she slapped me."

He said it all so benignly, as if he was talking about the weather. *We're expecting an uncommon cold front with a side of frigid bitch.* His panic when Alex had walked in made more sense now, if he expected to get in trouble for touching something he wasn't allowed to. Alex wanted to wrap him up and tell him that he could touch whatever he wanted in this house, nothing was off-limits. Hell, if he wanted to pluck popcorn off the popcorn string on the tree and eat it, no one was going to stop him. Except Alex might, since the popcorn was almost a week old and probably stale and gross.

"I remember one time I came home from school with an ornament we made in class," Mitch continued. Now he was rearranging the dolls into teams, as though he was setting them up for a scrimmage. "It was just a Styrofoam ball with a bunch of marshmallows pinned to it, nothing fancy. When I asked my mom if I could put it on the tree, she said 'Mitch, dear, we don't want anybody seeing *that* on the tree, do we?'"

Alex sat on the couch and rested his elbows on his knees. "What did you do?"

"I threw it away," Mitch said, all *what else was I supposed to do?* "It was ugly. Why would I keep it?"

Alex dug his nails into his palms and clamped his jaw shut on the words that wanted to escape. Insulting someone else's mother was not cool, and although he suspected Mitch wouldn't care, Alex refused to sink to that level. But he could think it.

And you might also see periods of scattered showers made up of Greta Westlake's victims' tears during the cold front.

Alex pushed Mitch's hot chocolate in his direction. "Drink this," he growled. "I'll be right back."

He was barely gone two minutes, and in that time Mitch had put the Russian dolls away, drank half his hot chocolate, and was still sitting on the floor, eyeing the doorway. He tracked Alex as Alex set a large plastic box on the floor next to him.

"What's that?" Mitch sat up on his knees.

"This," Alex said, removing the lid, "is my mom's craft box."

"Okay." Mitch paused for a second. "Why is it here?"

Alex took out scissors, felt material and construction paper in a rainbow of colors, a glue gun, a glue stick, rhinestones, sparkles, googly eyes, pipe cleaners, pinecones, Styrofoam balls of all sizes, clothes hangers, popsicle sticks, three dozen markers in an old Le Kit pencil box, a mini paint kit, and a bag of small pompoms. "We're going to make Christmas decorations."

Mitch's mouth twisted. "Is this because you feel sorry for me because I never had a handmade ornament on the tree?"

"No. This is because everyone deserves their own ornament on the tree." Alex had a feeling Mitch didn't even have one of those "Baby's first Christmas" ornaments. Or maybe he did, because his dad seemed cool. "So, go crazy. Craft away."

Mitch looked at him morosely. "You're never going to try and kiss me again, are you?"

"Oh, honey," Alex said, staring pointedly at Mitch's pink mouth. "You don't need to worry about that. But first, crafts. Then kissing."

Mitch crafted.

Alex created his own ornament too, but he kept a close eye on Mitch, who inventoried everything in the box before deciding what to make, then set aside the specific materials he'd need for whatever he was making before he started. Then he took a scrap piece of paper, sketched his design on it, and once he seemed happy with it, he started putting everything together. Alex was exhausted just watching him.

"Do you ever do puzzles?" Alex asked.

"Sure," Mitch said, carefully cutting into red felt. "I'm doing a twenty-four piece one right now called Why Are We Doing Crafts When We Could Be Making Out Instead?"

Alex chuckled and traced the outline of his hand on a piece of construction paper. "Why twenty-four?"

Mitch merely raised an imperious eyebrow. "You're twenty-four, aren't you?"

They worked in silence for a few minutes, until Mitch looked over and said, "Are you making a Christmas octopus?"

"Hey!" It wasn't a work of art, but it certainly wasn't a goddamn octopus. Alex gathered his materials and shuffled to the other end of the coffee table. "You just worry about your own ornaments."

"Sure, sure."

Alex took a sip of his now lukewarm hot chocolate

and went back to work. He cut out the trace he'd made of his hand, added white felt to the fingers, glued googly eyes to the palm, used a pipe cleaner for the mouth, and added small red pompoms to the bottom of each finger-tip-turned-beard, just because he could. Finally, he cut out a red felt Santa hat, superglued it to Santa's head and called it a day.

Mitch, on the other hand, had taken a couple of pine-cones and painted the ends white before sprinkling them in green glitter. Then he superglued a small Styrofoam ball onto the top of each pinecone, used a marker to dot a couple of eyes, glued a small felt hat on its head…and had himself a little elf duo. Alex contemplated hiding his Santa octopus before Mitch saw it for the abomination it was.

"I take it back," Mitch said when he got a look at it. "That's not an octopus. That's a zombie octopus."

"No, it's Santa." Alex held it up.

"If you say so."

"Do you think zombies believe in Santa?" Alex asked.

"I think zombies would eat Santa. All that meat on his bones? He'd be the first to go."

"Poor Santa. Guess Mrs. Claus wouldn't stand a chance either."

Mitch snorted and held up one of his elves. "What do we do with these now?"

Alex handed him a black marker. "First we put the date on the back."

"Why?"

Alex blinked at him. "Because we do."

"Uh-huh. Should I add my name and age too?"

"That's a good idea, actually, yes."

Mitch huffed, but did as told. He made a small hole at the top of his elves' hats and looped a string through it. Alex did the same for his zombie Santa octopus and then they were hanging their new ornaments on the tree.

"Are you sure your mom won't mind?" Mitch's voice was small, but his lips were titled upward when he gave his elves a little push to make them sway.

"Yeah," Alex said, voice gruff. "I'm sure."

Mitch gave some of the other ornaments a push. Alex left him to it and sat on the couch, admiring Mitch's lean frame and how he stood with feet slightly further than shoulder-width apart. Mitch was probably used to a Christmas tree that had a new color theme every year. What must he think of Alex's tree, with its eclectic mix of candy cane reindeer, cookie ornaments, and popcorn string?

"You made all these?" Mitch asked.

"My mom and me, yeah." Alex tucked a leg underneath himself on the couch and twisted sideways, elbow on the back of the couch, head resting on his hand. "Some I made at school when I was a kid. Others, my mom and I made over the years. It was tradition every year to make a few new ornaments. We couldn't afford to buy any, so we used what we could."

"Like this?" Mitch gestured at an empty tin can covered in Christmas stickers. A piece of frayed red felt was glued to opposite ends and looped over a tree branch. Inside the can was a small stuffed cardinal that had somehow appeared among their Christmas decorations years ago.

"Yeah. Old cans, broken down cardboard, hangers, construction paper I'd steal from school. Whatever we had. They got a bit more sophisticated as I got older and we could afford to buy stuff."

Mitch walked around to the other side of the tree where Alex had hung his zombie Santa octopus and pointed at it. "If you think this is sophisticated, you're seriously demented."

"Yeah, okay, fair point," Alex conceded.

Mitch took his time, admiring every ornament, grimacing at some, laughing at others, asking for the story behind certain ones. Alex sat and let him talk out his nerves. For his part, Alex's nerves had solidified into certainty. He'd been nervous before because of his lack of experience, but if the past few days had told him anything, it was that he wanted Mitch to be his. Badly.

Eventually, Mitch sat next to Alex and mirrored his position so that they faced each other on the couch. Mitch's gaze dipped to Alex's mouth, but as much as Alex wanted to, he didn't respond to the clear invitation.

He did, however, place a hand on Mitch's knee because he was *dying* to touch him. "I want to talk to you about something."

"No."

Alex jerked back. "No?"

Mitch shook his head, curly hair falling over his forehead. "Nope. You said crafts then kissing. We've done the crafts, so it's on to part two of tonight's festivities."

Amused by him, Alex said, "That so?"

"Mm hmm." Mitch shifted nearer, just a little.

Yearning gnawing at his stomach, Alex yanked on a lock of Mitch's hair. "But I need to talk to you about—oh! It does spring right back."

"What did you expect? It's hair, not a pipe cleaner."

Somehow they'd shifted closer when Alex wasn't paying attention. Mitch ran his fingers over Alex's stubble. "You need to grow this out," he whispered.

"I will." *Anything. Anything for you.*

Mitch's breath warmed his lips. Wanting him even closer, Alex moved his hand from Mitch's knee and palmed Mitch's lower back, drawing him closer. Startled, Mitch's breathing hitched and his hand landed on Alex's neck, warm and firm. They were almost chest to chest, and Mitch's breathing sped up. Alex was hyperaware of him, of how close they were, and every coherent thought flew out of his head.

Light-headed, limbs tingling, Alex closed the last inch of distance between them. He wanted to savor this moment, commit it to memory, so he took his time. He kissed the corner of Mitch's mouth, a barely there kiss that had Mitch sucking in oxygen. Then he kissed the other corner, and Mitch's hand tightened in Alex's hair, making him groan.

"Fuck, Alex," Mitch whispered hoarsely.

Alex kissed Mitch's eyebrow, the skin beneath his eyes, his cheekbone, tasting Mitch, memorizing him. Mitch's free hand snuck under Alex's T-shirt, and when Alex froze at the foreign sensation of someone else's hands on his skin, Mitch pulled back enough to meet Alex's eyes. "Okay?"

Alex expected the touch to feel unfamiliar and uncomfortable, but it didn't. Not at all. He nodded once, definitively. "Okay."

Mitch's fingers were at once firm and sure, and soft and tentative. Alex's skin broke out in goosebumps and he shivered involuntarily. Tilting Mitch's head back, Alex placed tiny kisses on the underside of his jaw, painting a trail down his neck to his collarbone. Mitch mumbled something and hung on to him, breathing hard, fingernails digging into Alex's back.

And then, as if a switch had been flipped or they'd telepathically mutually decided, their lips finally met.

They didn't inhale each other—but it was close.

Alex had kissed all of three people in his life, including Mitch. The first had been a girl he'd sort-of-but-not-really dated for a couple of months in his freshman year, back when he'd been trying to pretend that he was a normal, horny teenage boy. The second was a guy he'd made out with at a club in Rome on his graduation trip with JP and Jay. He'd been drunk enough not to care that he was kissing a total stranger, and that said stranger kissed with too much tongue and not enough finesse.

Neither of those people had done anything for him. In fact, until right this moment, Alex had hated kissing.

The craving that hit him as he kissed Mitch floored him. He wanted to leave fingerprints on Mitch's skin, to run his fingers through Mitch's hair, to hold him close and assure himself that Mitch was real and his.

They were all legs and arms as they clutched at each other, tangled up on the couch. Mitch tasted like hot chocolate and he licked his way into Alex's mouth with a level of skill that had Alex tightening his hold on him. To Alex's surprise and pleasure, Mitch wasn't all tongue. In fact, his tongue was a secondary character in this book called Kiss Alex's Brains Away.

Alex tore his mouth away for a much-needed breath of air. Mitch's lips travelled down the side of Alex's neck, up the other. He nuzzled his cheek against Alex's, making Alex groan.

"I like your beard," Mitch muttered.

"I noticed."

Mitch pulled back minutely and opened his mouth to speak, but a yawn big enough to crack his jaw seemed to take him by surprise.

Alex patted his butt. "Come on." He placed a small kiss on Mitch's jaw. "Let's go to bed."

Instead of getting up, Mitch snuggled into Alex, his head tucked into Alex's neck. "But I want to stay right here."

"Okay." Alex fell back on the couch with Mitch lying

half on top of him. There really wasn't enough room, but he covered them with the throw and tucked Mitch into his side. "Better?"

"Perfect," Mitch said into Alex's neck.

With arts and crafts supplies still scattered on the table and the Christmas tree lights shining cheerily, they fell asleep curled into each other and only woke briefly in the middle of the night to crawl into Alex's bed, where they promptly went back to sleep with Mitch in Alex's arms.

SIXTEEN

ALEX'S TEAM ONLY HAD ONE GAME SCHEDULED between Christmas and New Year's and, coincidentally, it was against Toronto, which was how Mitch found himself sitting next to Toni at the Air Canada Centre at six thirty on New Year's Eve.

The rule, according to Alex, was that each team had to make two tickets available for purchase to each player on the visiting team, up to a certain amount of tickets. Or something like that. Mitch wasn't sure about that last part. He'd been too busy ogling Alex's huge biceps as the man bench-pressed Mitch's weight and change in the small workout room in his mom's basement.

"Think you could bench-press me?" Mitch had asked from his position at Alex's head where he was acting as Alex's spotter.

Alex had eyed him, assessing. "Let's try it."

Except as soon as Alex had repositioned himself onto the mat on the floor, Mitch had straddled him, hauled him up, and kissed him, successfully distracting Alex from the rest of his workout.

There was never any heat in Alex's gaze when he looked at Mitch. His looks said *I'm glad you're here* and *I want to cuddle with you* and *You make me happy,* not *I want to jump you* or *You make me so hot, bow-chicka-bow-wow.* Really, it was very strange. Mitch knew some of his own looks said *Do me right now!,* but he tried to hide them so he didn't scare Alex away with sex, didn't push for something Alex wasn't ready for. If he was ever ready for it. What if he wasn't? Mitch would've sworn an oath that he was hard and horny all the time. And as much as he wanted sex, needed relief, he only wanted it with Alex. Yet he knew from Cody and from Google that some demisexuals identified closer to asexual on the spectrum and weren't interested in sex at all. Would Alex be one of those people? What was Mitch supposed to do if he was? At this point, Alex would probably rather bake a cake with Mitch than have sex with him.

Great, now he was sitting next to Alex's mom with a semi and a raging case of confusion, in seats that probably cost over three hundred bucks each. In typical Alex fashion, he hadn't let Mitch pay for his own ticket—not that Mitch could've afforded it, and Alex knew that—just like he hadn't let Mitch pay for anything on this trip except parking on the days they'd come into Toronto to play tourist, which amounted to roughly thirty dollars total. Big whoop. Mitch was both annoyed and grateful. He was annoyful.

"I think everyone forgot to show up today," Toni said. She held her popcorn bag out to Mitch.

"Yeah, there's not much happening, is there?" The game was about as interesting as watching a curling match. It was as though the players were still in holiday mode, lethargic and overstuffed on food and needing a nap. Alex had been excited for tonight's game, but his teammates' lifelessness must've rubbed off on him, because as the game went into the third period, he played about as enthusiastically as the rest of the team. So not at all.

Mitch hadn't seen him since late this morning, when he'd left for team practice at the ACC right after his workout turned make-out session, leaving Mitch alone with Toni for most of the day. A day alone with his, um, boyfriend's mom? Good friend's mom? Guy he was seeing's mom? Yeah, they still had to talk about that. Anyway, it would've been daunting, had he and Toni not gotten along so well. They went to the movies right after lunch, and they got in for free because Toni was one of the managers at the movie theater. Then they'd taken the train into the city so they could drive back home with Alex after the game. And since they'd arrived two hours early for the game, they'd killed time window shopping at the Eaton Centre, which was a truly terrifying place. All those *people!*

Toni, it turned out, was French Canadian, from a small town in Quebec Mitch couldn't remember the name of. Despite the fact she'd lived in Ontario for thirty years, French was still her first language and sometimes English colloquialisms still eluded her. Like f-bomb.

"Isn't that a fart?" she'd asked.

Mitch had laughed his ass off. "Yes, a fart. That's exactly what it is." He couldn't wait to tell Alex.

"I've watched golf games that were more interesting than this," Toni said now, taking the popcorn bag back from Mitch.

"Do you think maybe we're biased?" Mitch asked. The rest of the crowd was screaming and hollering and waving hats and jerseys and signs as if this game wasn't putting them to sleep. It was possible that Mitch and Toni were so entrenched in hockey life, they could tell when players were making a lackluster effort.

"You might be right."

Still, they didn't leave, not when Alex had spent so much on their tickets.

"Tell me something." Toni wiped her hands on a napkin and shifted closer. "Alex… Is he okay? I know he spent a lot of time with his grandpa when he was in Vermont and Forest isn't doing well. How is Alex taking it?"

Alex was on Tampa's first line tonight and, to watch him play, nobody would know that he had anything on his mind besides hockey. "I think he's preparing himself for the worst," Mitch said. "I think he's been visiting Forest as much as he can because he knows Forest doesn't have a lot of time left."

In the loud crowd, Mitch didn't hear, so much as feel, Toni sigh.

"Did Alex tell you that I work in the same facility where Forest lives?" When Toni shook her head, Mitch continued. "I work in the admin offices on Sundays, and on my last shift before the holiday break, I went into the lounge to see Forest. We play chess together sometimes after my shift. Anyway, he was…not having a good day. The nurses actually sent me away because they thought Forest might get violent. He was angry and confusing his words and refusing to eat or bathe."

Toni glanced away and blinked wildly.

"I haven't told Alex yet," Mitch admitted. "Don't know if I should."

Toni squeezed his hand. "He would want to know."

Mitch nodded. "Maybe I'll wait until it's not New Year's Eve to tell him."

"I don't think it'll make a difference."

Tampa lost 1-0, but it wasn't much of a surprise to Mitch and Toni.

A couple of hours later, Mitch and Alex lay on Alex's bed after a drive home where Toni recounted everything Alex had done wrong during the game and Alex rolled his eyes at Mitch in a way that was more fond than annoyed. For her part, Toni scolded Alex with maternal affection, much swearing at the other team, many imaginary exclamation points, and hand gestures. It was a far cry from Mitch's own mother's cold you-have-disappointed-me-child voice.

It was thirty minutes to midnight and Toni had already left for a party at her girlfriend's place.

"You were going to leave me alone on New Year's Eve?" Alex had pouted as Toni put on her boots.

She patted his cheek. "I would've stayed had you been alone, but now Mitch is here." She hugged them both, called a "Happy New Year's!" over her shoulder, and left.

Lying face-to-face in front of Alex, both of them in boxer briefs and T-shirts, Mitch poked him in the forehead and chuckled when Alex jerked back.

"What was that for?" Alex grumbled.

"Just making sure you're not asleep like you were on the ice."

"Ha ha," Alex said blandly. "You're hilarious."

"I'm also right."

"I blame the holidays."

"Me too."

Mitch ran his fingers over Alex's eyebrows, his cheekbones, his six-day old scruff, committing his face to memory, every freckle, every expression, every almost imperceptible blemish. They had three more days together here, and then on Sunday, they were leaving early for the drive back to Vermont. Alex would visit with Grandpa Forest Sunday evening, then jump on a plane to Tampa on Monday morning, leaving Mitch alone in Glen Hill to resume his normal routine, which would now include missing Alex like a missing limb, and counting down the days until he saw Alex again. Which would be…when?

"What's on your mind?" Alex asked.

"I guess I'm just wondering how we're going to make this work. The long-distance thing."

"Guess we should've talked about that before I kissed you, huh?"

"Doesn't matter." Mitch lifted a shoulder in a half-shrug. "I just…"

Alex smiled at him, soft and full of affection. "You just like having things in neat little boxes. I know."

"That's not true."

"Really?" Alex tangled their legs together, his own hairier ones rubbing against Mitch's. "So if I said, 'I don't know how we're going to make this work, Mitch. I guess we'll just have to wing it,' that'd be okay?"

Mitch tried not to let the panic show.

"Uh-huh," Alex said, smug. "Thought so."

"Sometimes I hate how well you know me."

"If I didn't know you so well, we wouldn't be here, would we?"

Mitch grunted and tucked his face in Alex's neck. "Stupid demisexuality."

"I'm offended on behalf of demisexuals everywhere."

"No, you're not," Mitch countered. "You think I'm charming."

"I also think pandas are charming."

Mitch reared back. "Pandas? They're the most useless animals on the planet."

"But aren't they super endangered or something?"

"Doesn't make them any less useless. And we're spending so much time and effort and money on protecting their habitat when there are other ecosystems that are more important and support a higher diversity of species."

Alex was grinning at him, amusement written all over his face.

Mitch scowled. "What?"

Alex nuzzled Mitch's cheek and Mitch felt his annoyance cool. "I like when you talk nerd to me," Alex said. "Keep going. Talk nerdy to me. Please?"

Laughing, Mitch pushed him away.

Alex kissed him, rolling on top of him, pushing Mitch into the mattress with his weight. It was glorious and fun and Mitch's dick stiffened in his boxers. Surely Alex noticed, since Mitch had nowhere to go to hide it, but he didn't mention it, didn't react in any way.

He nipped Mitch's lips, then pulled back to rest his head on his hand and stare down at Mitch. "You know, I never liked kissing before you."

Mitch sputtered for a second. "You… What? Who doesn't like kissing?"

"A lot of people, I assure you. It's messy and gross and… It's always felt like a chore to me. But don't worry." He gave Mitch a smacking kiss. "I like kissing you."

"I wasn't worried until now, you asshole." In retaliation for the messy and gross comment, he pushed Alex off him. Alex fell onto the bed with a laugh. He tugged Mitch close with an arm around his shoulders.

"Here's how it's going to work, to answer your question," Alex said. "We're going to compare calendars and pick weekends for me to visit you or for you to visit me when they make the most sense, like when we'll actually have time to spend together instead of running around to practice or games or work or school or whatever."

Mitch nodded, following along.

"And we'll do that for however long we have to."

Mitch's sigh was miserable to his own ears. "Could be a while."

"It could, yeah. The next two and a half years for sure, while you're still at GH."

"And if I get drafted…"

"*When* you get drafted," Alex corrected, his lips twitching into a lopsided smile. "We'll make it work then too. Plus, we'll have the summers, starting with this one."

Mitch would finish finals in early May, and he wouldn't need to be back for the new semester until early September. He'd spent last summer working full-time at a café in Montpelier, earning next year's tuition. There was no reason he couldn't do the same thing this year, but in Florida. They had cafés in Tampa, right? He'd get to spend every day with Alex as a bonus.

"You talk about our future as if it's a given," Mitch said. "That we'll still be together in a year, two years, more."

"Yeah, and we might not be, I know that." Alex ran the back of his hand over Mitch's cheek. "But I have a feeling that since we were friends first, it'll make our relationship stronger. The long-distance thing will suck at times, but I think we can make it work as long as we want it to."

"I want it to. Work, I mean."

"Me too." Alex's lips were soft on Mitch's skin when he kissed the corner of his mouth. Mitch smiled because it was already a favorite spot of Alex's and it made Mitch feel treasured.

"Does this mean I can call you my boyfriend?" Mitch asked the question with a teasing lilt to his voice, but he was dead serious.

Alex hugged him closer and kissed his temple. "Yes. Except, ah…" The arms around Mitch went taut. "Fuck, we definitely should've talked about this earlier."

"What?" Mitch scooted backward an inch, anxiety snaking through him, causing his voice to shake. He'd fucked things up already, hadn't he?

Alex rubbed his jaw, the sound of skin on beard *scritch*

scritch scritching through the room. "I was never going to… No, wait, let me back up." He cleared his throat. "Even though I've always been more attracted to men, I thought that being demi in the kind of life I have meant that I wouldn't have this—" He waved a hand between the two of them. "—until after I retired, when I'd have time to get to know someone. There's less than ten people who know about me—about me liking men, I mean, not the demi thing 'cause that's a pain in the ass to explain. My mom, some close friends, one of the PR people who works for the team that I trust, and…" He flopped onto his back, an arm over his eyes, frustration evident in the hard lines of his body. "Fuck, I'm not explaining this properly."

Mitch had a feeling he knew where Alex was going with this. He straddled Alex's hips and took one of his hands. "I think what you're trying to say is that you don't want me to feel offended when you tell me that you have no intention of coming out to the world."

"Mitch—"

"No, Alex, it's fine. I'm not coming out either. The only people who know about me are my family, Cody, Yano, and you. You don't come out in pro sports. It's just not done. Maybe in ten years, but now? Yeah, no. It's career suicide."

Alex's body deflated under Mitch, and he let out a relieved laugh. "You get it. I don't know why I thought you wouldn't."

"I don't know either. Give me some credit, would you?" Mitch teased. He leaned down for a quick kiss. "Besides, if you did come out, the press would be all up in your business, and I know how private you are about your personal life. I mean, do you know how much information there is about you online? Hardly anything."

"You looked me up?"

Mitch chuckled and sank back onto Alex, his head on Alex's shoulder. "No."

"Liar." Alex kissed the top of his head.

"Is that what you wanted to talk about the other day?"

"What? When?"

"Before you kissed me." Mitch prodded him in the side. "You said you wanted to talk about something, but I wouldn't let you because—"

"First crafts, then kissing," Alex finished for him. "I remember. And no, that's not what I wanted to talk about, although I think I might want to talk about that even less than the coming out thing."

"Now you have to tell me."

"It's about sex."

"Um, okay?" Shit, was this where Alex told him it was never going to happen?

"I know you want it."

Mitch glanced down at himself, where his semi was surely poking Alex in the hip. "Well, my boners aren't exactly subtle, so…"

"There's nothing subtle about you."

"I can be subtle."

"You're as subtle as an elephant."

"Rude," Mitch said. "Elephants are smart, though. And even the lions get out of the way of an elephant stampede. Talk about a charming animal. You know what, I take it back. It's not rude. I'm flattered. Elephants are fierce."

Alex's laugh did something funny to Mitch's stomach, and he propped himself up on an elbow to peer down at him. "What were you saying about sex?"

"I was saying," Alex said, "that I don't want it. Not yet," he added when he caught the wince Mitch couldn't hide. "Mitch, I'm attracted to you." He took Mitch's hand and kissed his palm. Mitch's breath caught. "Not your outside, but your inside. Who you are at the core, the person you are. You could gain two hundred pounds and go bald and I'd still be attracted to you. So I can't imagine that I won't ever want to have sex with you, can't imagine that I'll never want to experience that kind of intimacy with you. Just not yet. And it has nothing to do with you, or me. It has to do with us mostly. I think I need us to be more solid first, as a couple. Does that make sense?"

Mitch ran his hand over Alex's chest, his fingers catching in the material of Alex's T-shirt. "Yeah. Thanks for telling me. I won't push you. Much. Okay, I probably will, but feel free to tell me to fuck off."

Alex's laugh vibrated through his chest and into Mitch's hand. He shifted onto his side so they were once again face-to-face and kissed Mitch's nose. "I'm not going to tell you to fuck off. Besides, I'm not afraid of your boners. Please."

"M'kay. Are we done with the serious talk now?" Mitch asked. "Is it almost countdown time?"

Grunting, Alex rolled over to reach for his phone on the nightstand, then turned the lit face toward Mitch. "Twelve-oh-six. We missed it."

"Man, talking about serious stuff takes forever."

Alex put his phone away, and yanked Mitch on top of him with one arm. Fuck, he was strong! It was seriously hot that he could maneuver Mitch around without effort.

"Give me a New Year's kiss," Alex said.

So Mitch did.

SEVENTEEN

JANUARY 2009

Mitch: *You left your sweater in my car.*

Alex: *Which one?*

Mitch: *The blue hoodie. It's mine forever now. You also left your last bag of ketchup chips.*

Alex: *Damn. I was wondering where that was. All yours, I guess.*

Mitch: *Ew. No. They're already in the garbage.*

Alex: *That's no way to treat ketchup chips. You're cut off forever!*

Mitch: *Fine by me. They're truly the worst things I've ever eaten.*

Alex: *They're an acquired taste.*

Mitch: *If by acquired you mean tastes like BBQ'd feet, then yes, I agree.*

Alex: *Happy birthday :)*

Mitch: *How'd you know?*

Alex: *Cody texted me. Question is, why didn't you?*

Mitch: *Meh. It's not a big deal for me. Just another day.*

Alex: *Mitch.*

Mitch: *Is it weird that I can totally hear your Mitch-I-am-annoyed-and-exasperated-yet-charmed-by-you tone even through text?*

Alex: *No. Because I can hear your just-another-day-but-really-I'm-kinda-sad-nobody-makes-a-big-deal-out-of-it tone through text.*

Mitch: *Cody makes a big deal out of it. And my dad.*

Alex: *Sorry I couldn't be there to celebrate with you.*

Mitch: *No big. I'll see you in two weeks anyway! Hey, when's your birthday?*

Mitch: *Never mind. Found it.*

Alex: *Did you Google me?*

Mitch: *September 12.*

Alex: *Stop that. It's weird.*

Mitch: *:)*

Alex: *Talk nerdy to me.*

Mitch: *What, now? It's almost midnight. Why are you awake?*

Alex: *Can't sleep. I spent all day working on the book and now my thoughts won't settle.*

Mitch: *How'd you know I'd still be awake?*

Alex: *You're always awake. Do you ever sleep? Never mind, don't answer that. I already know you don't.*

Mitch: *I sleep.*

Alex: *More than four hours a night?*

Mitch: *…I'm busy.*

Alex: *Don't think I won't sic my mom on you if you don't start taking care of yourself.*

Mitch: *I take care of myself.*

Alex: *Not according to Cody.*

Mitch: *Cody's a snitch and we're no longer friends.*

Mitch: *I saw Forest after my shift today. First time since before the holidays.*

Alex: *How was he? Better than the last time you saw him?*

Mitch: *Alex…*

Alex: *Shit, what?*

Mitch: *He has pneumonia.*

Instead of visiting Mitch the last weekend in January, when Tampa had no scheduled games and Mitch only had one on Friday evening, Alex arrived a week early so he could be there in case his grandpa got worse. Thankfully, Forest had started getting better before Alex even landed in Vermont, but Mitch had a feeling Alex wouldn't take the doctor at his word until he'd seen Forest for himself.

"I'm sorry I won't be at your game tonight," Alex said over the phone. He sounded exhausted, his voice like gravel.

Mitch stuck his phone between his shoulder and his ear and threw fruit into the blender. "Don't apologize. There'll be other hockey games. Your grandpa…"

Alex's sigh was heavy, loaded with grief. "Won't be around forever."

Mitch abandoned his smoothie and rested his forehead against the cabinet. "I'm sorry, Alex. You're at the hospital now? Have you seen him?"

"Yeah, he's…pretty unaware of his surroundings. He called me Alex when I got here—" Alex's voice wobbled. "—but then he got confused and I was Judd again. Now he's unresponsive, and…"

"Fuck this. I'm coming over there."

"No," Alex said, and he chuckled, but it was sad. "No, you're going to play, Mitch, okay? I'm going to put your game on here, and hopefully it'll jar something in Grandpa. Text me when you get home after your game and I'll come over."

"You're still staying with me, right?"

"Nowhere else I'd rather be," Alex whispered.

"Alex…" *I love you.*

"Did you eat?"

Mitch turned his back on his half-made smoothie, as if Alex could see his so-called dinner through the phone. "Yeah."

"Good." It was a testament to the mood Alex was in that he didn't catch Mitch in the lie. "You should probably leave now so you're not late. I'll see you on the ice."

Mitch finished making his smoothie and got ready to leave for the game, but he wasn't happy about it. As much as he loved hockey, he'd rather be with his boyfriend right now.

The Mountaineers were playing against Merrimack who, so far this semester, had a much better track record than GH, who'd lost their first four games and then barely eked out wins in their last two. For some reason, the team had lost its cohesiveness after returning from the Christmas break. Even Alex noticed, though he hadn't been able to watch as many of Mitch's games on TV since he'd been back on Tampa's roster. Coach Spinney had taken Mitch and a couple other guys aside after they lost their third game in a row to let them know that he was proud of them for keeping their game playing top notch and hanging on to their mojo. (He used the word "mojo." Mitch had never been more de-lighted with him.)

Nonetheless, the success of a team couldn't be carried on the backs of three men alone, so now the team had an additional morning of practice on Tuesdays for the foresee-able future. Given that they'd won their last two games, the strategy seemed to be working.

Yano scored twice in the first period, giving them a lead of 2-0. The game was scoreless in the second period, but in the third, one of Merrimack's guys set up a pass for his teammate in front of the crease, scoring their first goal of the game and bringing the score to 2-1.

But then Coach Bedley challenged the play, bringing the game to a halt for seven excruciating minutes.

Mitch skated up to the GH bench. "What's going on?"

Craig "Goldie" Golding tipped his stick to where Bedley was conferring with Assistant Coach Spinney and one of the refs. "Coach thinks Baedeker was inside the blue line before Offill brought the puck in."

Jesus, they could be here forever waiting while officials watched and re-watched the same twenty seconds of tape. Fuck.

Mitch nodded his thanks to Goldie. He skated over to Yano, who was deep in conversation with the possibly offending Baedeker from Merrimack.

"Definitely Mama Jean's, man," Yano was saying. "The Green Onion's good, but it's small and they're more… What's the word I'm looking for, Grey?"

"Uptight?" Mitch said, coming to a stop next to them. "They're anal about how much noise you can make and will kick you out if they find you offensive. But Mama Jean doesn't care. You can get as rowdy as you want, as long as you clean up after yourself."

"Yeah." Yano clapped Mitch on the back. "Besides, you can't beat Mama Jean's pizza."

"Mama Jean's it is, then." Baedeker fist bumped first Yano, then Mitch. "Thanks for the tip. Maybe we'll see you guys there after the game." He skated off to join his teammates at the visitor's bench.

"You coming to Mama Jean's tonight?" Yano asked Mitch.

"No, I've got a friend visiting from out of town."

"Bring him. Or her, whatever."

Mitch shook his head. "His grandpa's in the hospital. Don't think he'll be in the mood for a loud crowd of assholes like us."

"Mm hmm."

"What?"

"I'm just wondering what you've been up to lately." Yano skated circles around Mitch. "We haven't seen much of you outside of games and practice."

"I've been busy with school and work."

"Creative writing kicking your ass again?"

Mitch sighed. "Yeah." He'd told Alex he'd kept it because of his academic advisor and the whole well-rounded student bullshit, but at the time, all he'd really wanted was an excuse to stay in touch with Alex once Alex went back to Florida. Now that they were together, he didn't need that excuse, but he'd kept this semester's creative writing class because…he was a sucker for punishment?

Of course, he was, once again, failing. JP took pity on him and set him up with a new tutor who was nowhere near as hot as Alex. But Mitch had to pay for this one. He'd asked the long-term care facility for extra shifts but they didn't need him more than once a week, which meant he had to tutor more math students to make the cash that would pay for his own tutor. The cycle was exhausting. Hell, he was exhausted just thinking about it. And more tutoring equalled less time for homework and course readings. Alex hadn't been wrong in his estimate that Mitch was only getting four hours of sleep each night. Mitch was fucking tired and there was no relief in sight until the end of the semester.

Plus, he was supposed to visit Alex in Florida over the President's Day long weekend in three weeks—which also happened to be Valentine's Day weekend—but Mitch had yet to figure out how to do that, short of asking his dad or Alex for cash for the flight. Not happening. Hence even *more* tutoring, less time for schoolwork, and even less sleep. Somebody kill him.

Play finally resumed, and the score was brought back to 2-0 after the officials verified that Baedeker had, in fact, been over the blue line. With their goal nullified, Merrimack came back with a vengeance, determination stamped all over their pissed off faces, but the third period ended scoreless for them.

It was fucking loud in the GH locker room after the game. Fatigue weighed Mitch's muscles down and it took him twice as long as usual to shower. Knowing Alex was only twenty minutes away at the hospital in Montpelier was the only thing that got him moving. He didn't take part in any of the locker room trash talk, and he could practically feel Yano and Marco eyeballing each other over his head. The silent conversation probably went something like this:

Yano: You talk to him.

Marco: No, you.

Yano: I tried already. Your turn.

Marco: You're his bestie on the team. Clearly you didn't try hard enough.

Yano (scowling): Fuck you.

Marco (cheerily): No, fuck you!

"What is it, guys?" Mitch eyed them both as a group of their teammates exited the locker room chanting "Mama Jean's! Mama Jean's!" Because hockey players were children.

Yano and Marco had another silent conversation, then tried to egg the other on by elbowing each other in the ribs. Fuck, Mitch wanted to go home. He slipped into his boots and winter coat, grabbed his equipment bag, and headed out.

He was halfway down the hallway when Yano and Marco caught up to him.

"Yo, Grey! Wait up." Yano caught his elbow, bringing him to a halt.

Mitch swallowed an angry retort. He turned to his friends. "What? I have somewhere I need to be."

Yano cleared his throat. "We just wanted to, ah, invite you and your, um…" He scratched his head.

"Friend," Marco piped in.

"Yes, friend. To, ah, have a late dinner with us at Mama Jean's. Or wherever."

The fuck were they on about? "My…friend?"

They jostled each other again, whispering under their breaths. Mitch dropped his bag and crossed his arms. "Spit it out already. I'm tired and I want to go home."

"Right, right. Uh…" Yano scuffed his boot against the tiled floor.

"Jesus." Marco rolled his eyes and faced Mitch head-on. "What our inept friend here—"

"Hey!"

"—is trying to say is, we'd like to treat you and your…" He glanced around them, but there was no one else in the hallway. "…boyfriend," he whispered before resuming in a normal voice, "to dinner sometime."

"My…" Heat flushed through Mitch's body and he jerked his head toward Yano. "You told him?" he growled.

"I guessed," Marco said. "I'm not stupid."

"He's not stupid," Yano repeated.

"And you're kind of obvious," Marco continued.

Yano slapped Marco's chest with the back of his hand. "That's what I told him."

Marco squinted at Yano, sighed at Yano's obliviousness, and raised his eyes to the ceiling. Yano had known Mitch was gay because his high school best friend was gay and Yano knew what to look for. Mitch had a feeling such was not the case for Marco. Man, Mitch's gaydar was for shit.

He sent his friends a grateful smile and picked up his

bag. "I appreciate it. Really. But at the moment we're kind of laying low." He held up a hand before they could protest. "He also lives out of state and he's here this weekend mostly so he can visit his sick grandpa. So, another time?"

"You probably also want your alone time too, huh?" Yano waggled his eyebrows. "To…" He pumped a fist and made a sound not unlike a broken chainsaw.

"Man, you're so crass." Marco put a hand on Mitch and Yano's shoulders and steered them all outside, where the cold slapped Mitch in the face and stole his breath. He tugged his scarf up over his nose and pulled his alpaca mittens out of his pocket. "Seriously," Marco said when they reached Mitch's car. "Next time he's here, we'd love to treat you guys."

Touched, Mitch could only nod. "Thanks, guys. I'll let you know. See you later."

He texted Alex before driving home. Once he got there, he paced a five-foot trail in the tiny space between the living room and kitchen.

"What's wrong with you?" Cody asked from his perch on the couch where he was playing Super Mario Galaxy on the Wii.

"I'm nervous."

"It's just Alex."

"Just Alex, who I haven't seen in almost three weeks."

"Aww." Cody paused the game to grin at him. "I knew you were smitten."

"Fuck you," Mitch grumbled, and promptly stubbed his toe on the leg of one of the island barstools. "Fuck!"

Cody laughed at him and kept playing.

When the doorbell finally rang what felt like five years later, Mitch had worked himself into a bundle of nervous tension. His toe throbbed, his hands were knotted, and he felt like he was going to throw up what little he'd eaten today.

But the smile on Alex's face, an impossible combination of misery, relief, and happiness, had concern and pleasure replacing Mitch's nerves, and he was on Alex before Alex could say hi.

Alex squeezed Mitch just as hard, his arms steel bands around Mitch's waist. Mitch used his grip around Alex's neck to haul him inside. Alex kicked the door closed behind him, shutting out the dark and the cold, dropped his bag to the floor, and stuck his frigid nose in Mitch's neck.

"God, I've missed you," Alex mumbled, pressing a small kiss to the skin between Mitch's neck and shoulder, and that was all it took for Mitch's eyes to water.

He'd joked with himself that he'd miss Alex like a limb. Truth was, Alex had stolen a piece of his heart that he didn't want back. It was Alex's, for better or worse. And sure, doubt might've crept in now and then over the past few weeks they'd been apart, dangerous thoughts slithering into his brain when he wasn't paying attention, telling him Alex was going to change his mind and dump him any second. Those thoughts might scare Mitch shitless, especially in the middle of the night when he couldn't sleep, but he'd rather be scared than be without Alex, no matter how difficult things might get.

"I missed you too." Mitch kissed Alex's ear, his cheek, his mouth, keeping his movements slow and soothing.

A sound behind Mitch had him pulling away and glancing over his shoulder to where Cody was walking toward them.

"Hey, Cody," Alex said.

"Hey, man." Cody clapped Alex on the shoulder. "How's your grandpa?"

"Better. Relatively speaking, anyway." Alex hung his coat on the wall hook and untied his boots. "He's kicked the pneumonia, so…" His shoulder twitched in a half-shrug. Mitch took his hand and linked their fingers.

"That's good." Cody seemed at a loss for what more to say. He jerked his head in the direction of the stairs. "I'm heading to bed. See you guys in the morning."

Mitch moved right into Alex's personal space again. Alex wrapped his arms around Mitch's shoulders and cuddled him close.

"What do you need?" Mitch asked, tracing tiny circles on Alex's lower back.

Alex exhaled a long breath, ruffling the hair on top of Mitch's head. "Just this."

"Okay. Come on."

Upstairs, in Mitch's bedroom, they undressed to their underwear. Crawling into bed, they fell asleep with Alex's big body firm behind Mitch.

EIGHTEEN

AT EIGHT THIRTY THE NEXT MORNING, MITCH blearily followed his nose to the kitchen. It smelled like…bacon? The house never smelled like anything other than used sports equipment and laundry detergent.

An equally bleary-eyed Cody was sitting at the island, one foot dangling off the stool, watching Alex do something at the stove.

Mitch took the stool next to Cody, rubbed grit out of his eyes, admired Alex's enormously broad back, and croaked, "What's he doing?"

Cody pillowed his head in his hand. "I think it's called cooking."

Alex spun to face them, one hand on his hip, the other wielding a spatula he pointed at them both. "Man cannot live on Cheese Whiz and smoothies alone."

"Actually, I think we can," Cody said.

Mitch nodded his agreement.

The spatula pointed at Cody. "You, maybe." Then at Mitch. "But not an athlete. You've lost weight since I last saw you."

Insulted in the way of the sleep-deprived everywhere, Mitch rebutted with, "No."

Cody plucked the T-shirt away from Mitch's chest. "He's right, you know."

Mitch turned his frown on his best friend. "You're supposed to be on my side."

"I'm always on your side, dummy."

Alex deposited bacon, pancakes, scrambled eggs, sliced fruit, and little individual containers of yogurt on the island in front of them.

Mitch gaped at it all. "Since when do we have ingredients to make pancakes?"

"I went shopping this morning," Alex said, placing plates and cutlery on the table. "Eat."

Yeah, okay.

"Mitch, you'll want to balance it out, but with more protein than carbs."

Mitch nodded to show he'd heard and stuffed his face with a crispy piece of bacon.

"You remember when I said you and I could eat Mitch for breakfast?" Cody said to Alex. "This is what I meant."

On the other side of the island, Alex poured maple syrup onto his pancakes, bacon, eggs, and fruit. Mitch eyed his own plate and the food that must've been lonely without all that maple syrup.

"You mean," Alex said, "that we can tell him what to do and he'll do it?"

Mitch was drowning his food in syrup when he finally tuned into the conversation.

"Yup!" Cody said cheerfully.

"Hey!" Mitch scowled at his so-called best friend. "Seriously, whose side are you on?"

"Not yours, if you're going to waste the maple syrup. Jesus, enough." Cody wrenched the jar out of Mitch's hands. "This shit's expensive."

Mitch's food was swimming in a pool of syrup. "I need more," he said.

"You've got enough," Alex said mildly, forking a bite of pancake.

"Yeah, okay."

Cody grinned at Alex. "See?"

Mitch threw a syrup-drenched slice of bacon at him.

Visiting Grandpa Forest in the hospital was about as depressing as Mitch expected. Forest was asleep when they got there, a good thing according to the nurses. He'd apparently awoken this morning confused, belligerent, and bullying the nurses into letting him see Joanie.

Joanie, it turned out, was his wife, who'd passed away before Alex was born.

"He didn't talk about her much," Alex said. They sat in a pair of chairs next to Forest's bed. "I think it was too hard for him. Once, he called her his light. 'Alex, my boy,' he said, 'she was my light, your grandmother. You woulda loved her.'" His voice bottomed out and his head drooped.

A weight settled in Mitch's heart, one that told him Forest would never be the same person Mitch had played chess with last month. He scooted his chair closer to Alex's and, hidden by Forest's hospital bed, he took Alex's hand. As much as he wanted to lay his head on Alex's shoulder, there were too many eyes here.

Alex squeezed his hand tight.

"We can stay as long as you need," Mitch reassured him.

"Actually, can we go?" Alex ran his free hand through his hair, his movements jerky. "Sorry, I know we just got here, but... The nurses said they had to sedate him, so he'll be out for hours. I'll come back tomorrow morning on my way to the airport in Burlington."

"Whatever you want." Mitch squeezed his thigh and stood. "Come on."

Alex placed his hand over Forest's and whispered, "See you tomorrow, Grandpa."

It wasn't until they were back in Alex's rental car that Mitch asked, "Where to?"

They went to Stowe, where they parked on a side street, then wandered the snow-covered streets and eclectic shops. Alex even bought him an ice cream at a tiny ice cream parlor that hadn't closed down for the winter.

"Ice cream in January?" Mitch asked.

"I'm Canadian," Alex said with a shrug. "If I can't eat ice cream in winter, there's something wrong with me."

They talked about everything and nothing. Their favorite foods, their favorite movies, what country they most wanted to visit, their favorite spots in Vermont, if they had pets growing up.

"Are you kidding?" Mitch asked. "I've told you about my mom, right?"

Alex winced. "Good point."

Mitch kept half an eye on Alex as they walked and talked. His mood improved as the day wore on. That evening, as the sun set, they ate at a restaurant in Stowe that didn't serve anything that cost anywhere close to ninety-five dollars.

When they got home hours after they'd left, the house was dark, but there was music coming from Cody's room upstairs. They left their boots, coats, and hoodies by the front door, and when Mitch turned to say something to Alex, he found Alex's eyes already trained on him.

Was his fly open? Nope. No food stains on his T-shirt or jeans either. "What?" he finally asked.

Alex was giving him that you're-so-adorable grin. One of these days, Mitch would argue that he was most definitely not adorable. He was a tough, badass hockey player, thank you very much.

"What?" Mitch asked again.

Alex cupped Mitch's neck, tilted his head back, and kissed him. It was the first time Alex had kissed him with passion and sensuality, and all Mitch could do was hold on for dear life as his toes curled. Alex walked him backward until he was up against the wall, and Mitch used it as leverage to try and climb Alex's body like a goddamn tree.

Laughing into Mitch's mouth, Alex palmed Mitch's ass and hoisted. Mitch hopped, wrapping his legs around Alex's waist. Jesus fuck, he was being hauled up the stairs by a giant, as if he weighed nothing at all, and it was all kinds of awesome. His cock took notice. Alex took notice that his cock took notice, but just like he'd promised on New Year's Eve, Mitch's boner didn't scare him away. In fact, he palmed it, right after he dropped Mitch onto the bed.

"Fuck, Alex," Mitch screeched, his hips lifting off the bed, seeking more friction for his desperate dick.

"Did I do it wrong?"

Mitch's laugh was desperate. "No. Fuck, no. But—"

"Okay, then." Alex straddled Mitch's thighs and unzipped Mitch's jeans.

"Um," Mitch squeaked. "Not that I want you to stop—because I don't. But, uh, what happened to waiting?"

"I did wait." Alex pulled Mitch's jeans off, his grin gone from you're-so-adorable to let's-have-some-fun. Fuck. "I waited almost four weeks." He ran the tips of his fingers along Mitch's painfully erect dick, clearly outlined behind his boxer briefs.

Mitch's eyes rolled back into his head. "But it was four weeks where—" He groaned when Alex pressed his fingertips in harder. "—we didn't, um…" He lost his train of thought when Alex peeled his underwear off and his cock sprang out, ready for business.

"We didn't see each other, you mean?" Alex said, with all the patience of a saint. Mitch wanted to kill him. And tell him to do something with his dick instead of sitting there atop Mitch's thighs staring at it as if it were a foreign object. "That's true," Alex continued. "But you know what I realized?"

"I don't care anymore," Mitch said. "Take your shirt off."

Alex did. Wow, score one for Mitch.

"I realized," Alex said, dragging those damnable fingertips up and down Mitch's bared erection, "that we're already pretty solid." There was something else that was solid in this room, and it wasn't their relationship. "We actually talk to each other. Do you know how many couples talk to each other?"

"Um, all of them?"

Alex snorted, then closed his hand around Mitch. Mitch hissed in a breath through his teeth.

"Too tight?" Alex asked, relaxing his grip.

Mitch shook his head against the pillow. "Not tight enough."

Alex squeezed and *Oh fuck, please!* Mitch couldn't even move his hips, since Alex was still on his thighs and he was too consumed with lust to tell Alex what to do.

"I've never done this before," Alex muttered under his breath in a whisper Mitch wasn't sure he was supposed to hear.

Alex's artlessness was obvious in his tentative touches, but at the same time, it was juxtaposed with the fact that Alex had been the one to kiss Mitch, to carry him upstairs, to toss him on the bed and undress him. His confidence in the face of his uncertainty was fucking hot. Everything about Alex was hot.

Especially that thing he was doing with his thumb on the tip of Mitch's cock.

"Does this mean—" *Gulp.* "—um, that..." His cock dripped pre-come and he clutched Alex's strong thigh.

"Sorry, I didn't catch that," Alex said, his voice teasing.

"I hate you so much right now."

"Hmm." Alex glanced down at Mitch's hard dick in his hand. "Do you?" He spread Mitch's pre-come over his cock head.

Fuck, Mitch was so hard, harder than he'd ever been. "Alex, please."

"Please, what?"

"I don't…" Alex was going to kill him. Mitch wasn't usually on such a hair-trigger, but it had been *months* since his dick had seen any action other than his own hand. At least, since before he'd met Alex. He was going to die if he didn't come soon. That it was Alex giving him a hand job, the guy he'd wanted since they'd met? Fuck. "I don't know."

Alex shifted off his thighs to lie next to Mitch, his jean-clad legs rubbing against Mitch's bare ones. He never took his hand off Mitch's dick, thank God.

He placed a kiss on Mitch's temple. "What do you need?"

Mitch cupped Alex's neck and brought him in for a kiss that was far dirtier and messier than any they'd shared so far. Alex went with it. In fact, Alex took it further, forcing Mitch's mouth open wider, slipping his tongue inside. Mitch was going to have serious beard burn in the morning and he didn't even care.

"What do you need?" Alex asked again, green eyes gone dark, face flushed.

"I need to come." The unrelenting circle of Alex's thumb on the head of his cock was making him crazy, but it wasn't quite enough.

"'Kay. Tell me how to do that."

"I can't… I don't…" Alex's hand moved off his cock

and he wanted to cry until he felt those fingers ghosting over his sac. "Alex, please."

"Tell me," Alex ordered, and *fuck* his confidence just turned Mitch on that much more. "Assume I'm game for anything."

Mitch waved a hand at the nightstand. "Lube."

Alex left him for a second as he grabbed the lube and coated one hand with it. He lay back down next to Mitch, his head propped on his clean hand.

"What…?"

Alex smiled that let's-have-some-fun grin again. "I want to watch your face."

Mitch had never, ever, had anyone who cared what he looked like when he came. Men before Alex had knelt between Mitch's knees and either jacked him or blown him without care about whether or not he enjoyed one thing over another. That Alex was eager for his orgasm face was mildly embarrassing, yet also—

His dick twitched. Yeah, that.

Alex noticed and closed his hand around it again.

Mitch's hips lifted off the bed and heat pooled in his balls, ready to explode. "Harder."

Alex tightened his hold. Then he started to jack Mitch, slowly at first, gaining momentum, avoiding touching the underside of his tip, as if he knew Mitch was hypersensitive there.

Skin heating to a boiling point, Mitch clutched at Alex with one hand and held onto the bedcovers with the other. "I need… I need you to…" He sobbed, unable to finish as Alex tightened his hold on him further.

"What do you need?" Alex asked. He was breathing as hard as Mitch, sweat dripping down his temple.

"My balls."

Mitch parted his legs and Alex kneeled between them. Alex kept jacking him, keeping up his steady pace. He didn't seem to know what to do with Mitch's balls, and then, to Mitch's complete and utter shock, he bent and swirled the tip of his tongue around Mitch's scrotum.

Mitch stopped breathing.

Alex licked Mitch's balls with the flat of his tongue in long, wet strokes, as if they were as delicious as this afternoon's ice cream cone. Then he flicked his tongue endlessly against the skin between his testicles and, combined with the nail Alex ran underneath Mitch's ridge, the fire blazing through him converged at the base of his dick and Mitch went rigid and came with a loud groan.

When awareness returned, Alex was still lying between his legs, half off the bed, and the heat in his eyes was impossible to look away from.

"You're fucking gorgeous," Alex said.

Mitch made grabby hands. "I want to do you now."

"No need." Alex suckled the inside of Mitch's thigh, making Mitch moan. "I came when you did."

"Fuck, that's hot."

Alex still held Mitch's dick in one hand. He used the other to trace a path through the come on Mitch's belly.

Mitch's legs were still twitching from his orgasm. Hell, his dick was still twitching as it sort of half-softened. Minutes later, when he'd finally gotten his breathing under control, Alex was still lying between his legs, his hand still on Mitch.

"You barely softened," Alex said, wonder clear in his voice.

"Alex," Mitch said with an embarrassed laugh, covering his face with his hands. "It's been a really fucking long time."

Alex grunted. "Okay."

He still didn't move.

"What are you doing?" Mitch's thighs were starting to cramp.

"I'm going to wait for you to get hard again," Alex said seriously. "And then I'm going to blow you."

"Oh God." Mitch went fully hard instantly, thigh cramps forgotten, and covered his eyes with an arm. It was the only reason he was surprised when Alex's tongue replaced his hand on Mitch's dick. Mitch shivered uncontrollably as Alex's tongue explored him. When he eventually took Mitch into his mouth, he wasn't able to take him very far. But combined with the testicle massage he was giving Mitch, it felt like only four seconds later that Mitch was coming for a second time, swearing under his breath.

"This is so not how I saw this evening going," Mitch said to the ceiling.

Alex's voice was hoarse when he said, "I think I could become addicted to this."

Mitch could only laugh.

NINETEEN

ALEX RESURFACED FROM HIS WRITING SPRINT AND read the passage he'd just written. He was done— officially done—with the first draft of his book, and two weeks ahead of time too. He'd spend the next two weeks self-editing and polishing before sending it to his editor, but the bones were there.

He sat back in his office chair and released a breath. He'd been writing for as long as he could remember, but this was the first project he'd ever finished that he felt good about. Better than good. His book dug into the nuts and bolts of professional sports and into how the high expectations of friends and family, coaches, scouts, and the athletes themselves, affect a player's decisions.

Now all he needed was a title. His editor had already nixed "The Dark Side of Sports," claiming it was too doom and gloom. He'd think of something.

But after his weekend with Mitch.

Saving his work, he checked the time, grabbed his keys, and headed out. Mitch's flight was landing in less than half an hour and it'd probably take Alex that much time to get to the airport.

Mitch had bitched and groaned when Alex had told him that he'd gone ahead and purchased Mitch's ticket to Tampa for him to visit over the President's Day long weekend, but Alex wasn't about to let him pay when the man could barely afford food.

"You did what?" Mitch had been sexily rumpled, bed-covers pulled up to his mouth to ward off the early morning Vermont cold the day after their visit to Stowe.

"I bought your ticket," Alex repeated, knowing full well that Mitch had heard him and was simply having trouble processing. He pulled a hoodie on over his T-shirt and waited for the inevitable protests.

"You can't do that," Mitch said. He sat up in bed, shivered, and hunkered down again, covers up to his nose.

Alex stuffed dirty underwear into his duffel. "I already did."

"Alex." Mitch rubbed his forehead hard. "You can't just buy stuff for me."

"Sure, I can."

Huffing, Mitch rolled out of bed and struggled into the closest items of clothing he could find, which happened to be yesterday's boxer briefs and the blue hoodie Alex had left in his car on the road trip to Vermont after New Year's. Standing in the middle of his bedroom with his arms crossed over his chest in nothing but morning stubble, underwear, and an oversized sweatshirt, hair all over the place, he made Alex want to simultaneously give him a noogie and tumble him back into bed.

Last night had been completely unexpected. He hadn't set out to seduce Mitch, as much as it might seem like it. He'd been dying to see Mitch, to hold him, to talk to him, to sleep curled around him, to kiss him until his lips went puffy and red. But then Mitch had been so attentive to him, asking Alex what he needed and making sure he had it, visiting Grandpa Forest with him and then spending all day distracting him when it turned out Alex couldn't handle seeing his grandpa broken and sick in the hospital. It'd hit Alex that they were already solid. And the way Mitch took care of him, the way he was as attuned to Alex as Alex was to him? It solidified something in Alex, something that had him seeing Mitch in a new light. In a way that said *life partner*, rather than merely *boyfriend*.

And that was a damn sexy image that made Mitch even more attractive to him, which, of course, had led to last night's double orgasms.

Fuck, he wanted to do that again.

"I can pay for my own ticket," Mitch said.

Alex cleared the want from his throat and zipped his duffel. "You're just mad I stepped on your pride by getting it without asking first."

Mitch growled at him like an angry fox.

"Yeah, yeah, you hate how much I know you. Look." Alex cupped his face and kissed his unsmiling mouth. "First, I have the money. Second, it's just sitting there, so if I want to use it so that my boyfriend can come visit me without putting a dent in his own wallet, I'm going to. And third, if our situations were reversed, wouldn't you do the same?"

Mitch softened and wrapped his arms around Alex's waist. "That's different."

"Why?"

"Because it is," Mitch said in Alex's neck.

Alex chuckled and hugged him close. "If you say so." There was a lonely three weeks coming up. Sure he'd be busy, but that wouldn't stop him from missing Mitch, from wishing he could reach out and touch him whenever he wanted. He stuck his nose in Mitch's hair and inhaled deeply. Mitch smelled like come and sweat and a little bit like laundry detergent.

With a heaviness in his stomach, Alex kissed Mitch's forehead, and pulled away. "I need to go."

Mitch's sigh was sad, his eyes downcast. "Yeah, I know."

Alex kissed him once, twice, and before he knew it, they were wrapped around each other tightly, breathing hard, one of Alex's hands down the back of Mitch's underwear. Mitch's nails dug into his lower back and heat like Alex had never felt before last night pooled in his belly. He wrenched his mouth away even as his hips sought Mitch's, making Mitch laugh and kiss his neck once before stepping completely out of his arms.

"Come on." He picked up Alex's duffel and headed for the door. "I know you need to leave."

Reluctantly, Alex followed him down the stairs. "I'll make you dinner on Valentine's Day."

"For the love of God, nothing that costs ninety-five dollars," Mitch said, dropping Alex's bag on the bench by the front door.

Alex sat to put on his boots. "How about fettuccine Alfredo with chicken?" he suggested, knowing how much Mitch loved cheesy things.

"Yeah?" Mitch grinned. "Can I have beer too?"

Alex finished tying his laces and stood to put on his coat. "It really goes better with wine."

Mitch wrinkled his nose.

"Beer it is." He held a hand out to Mitch. "Come here."

And with his arms around Mitch for what was going to be the last time for almost three weeks, Alex almost said the words, the ones he'd been thinking since Christmas. But it didn't seem right to say them when he was about to walk out the door, so he swallowed them, squeezed Mitch tight, gave him a last thorough kiss, and left.

Three weeks later, Mitch was taking his own personal tour of Alex's apartment while Alex fixed them each a chicken salad sandwich as a late dinner in the kitchen. He also chopped up some raw vegetables and put them on Mitch's plate, since the man's daily veggie intake was somewhere between nil and Mama Jean's pizza sauce.

"Have you really read all these books?" Mitch called from the second-floor loft.

"Yup," Alex called back, licking mayo off his thumb.

Mitch's footsteps sounded on the stairs. Seconds later, he padded into the kitchen on bare feet. He'd fallen asleep almost instantly on the drive here, but now he was wide awake, eyes trying to take in everything at once. Sometime since Alex had last seen him, Mitch had gotten a haircut. His hair was still longer than most men tended to wear it, but those perfect curls no longer fell every which way over his forehead and ears. Instead, they curled upwards into a fluffy, mini afro, which made him look delightfully mussed at all times.

"This isn't what I expected your place to look like." He hopped up to sit on the island.

"What'd you expect?"

"Less space. Less...personality."

Alex's seventeen-hundred square feet condo in the Channel District wasn't huge, but it was stylish, with low-ceilings, exposed brick, blackened steel, and wood finishing. He had an open living room/kitchen with floor-to-ceiling windows along one wall, a bedroom and bathroom on each floor, office space in the loft, and a small patio he was never around to use.

"I guess I expected it to look like an interior decorator put it together."

"Nope." Alex passed Mitch his plate. "All me. Why are you making that face?"

"Why is my sandwich on a croissant?"

Alex bit into his own sandwich. "Why wouldn't it be on a croissant?"

Mitch blinked at him. "Yeah, okay, I guess that's as good an answer as any." He popped a piece of carrot in his mouth. "What are we doing tonight?"

It was past nine-thirty. What could he possibly want to do? And shit, when had Alex gotten old? "What do you want to do tonight?"

Mitch shrugged and ate his sandwich. "Nothing. Just didn't know if you had anything planned."

"Well, first I'm going to feed you. Then I'm going to put you to bed."

"And then?" Mitch asked, sitting up straight.

"And then you'll probably fall asleep in about point two seconds."

His shoulders slumped. "I slept on the plane. I'll be up for hours."

"It took you four minutes to fall asleep in my car."

Mitch grumbled something Alex didn't catch and polished off his sandwich.

"Cheer up." Alex nudged his knee. "We'll fool around tomorrow. I even bought condoms."

Mitch choked on his food. "You…what? Well damn, I'm wide awake now if you feel like putting them to use."

"Tomorrow."

"But why?"

"Because it's Valentine's Day."

Mitch's grin started slow, the corners of his mouth twitching as his eyes lit up. "Aww. You're such a sap."

Alex crossed his arms over his chest. "I prefer the term 'romantic.'"

"Sap." Mitch ate another carrot. "How's the book coming? Is Mitch slash Adrian having lots of adventures?"

Alex leaned a hip on the island next to him. "It's not that kind of book." He stretched a kink out of his neck. "Actually, I finished the first draft today."

"Holy shit." Mitch's mouth fell open. "Alex, that's awesome! Can I read it?"

"You want to?"

"Of course. You wrote it."

Touched beyond words, Alex loaded their plates into the dishwasher. He could feel Mitch's eyes on his back. The man might as well have been touching Alex for how fast he broke out in goosebumps. Shutting the dishwasher, he turned and leaned against the counter, facing Mitch, who kicked his legs against the island like a little kid.

It had been barely twenty minutes and already Mitch had taken over Alex's apartment. His duffel was in Alex's bedroom down the hall, his running shoes by the front door, backpack next to the couch, discarded socks dropped onto the living room rug, flannel shirt draped over one of the island barstools, and his cell phone sitting on the island. Less than forty-eight hours from now, he'd take everything with him when he left, leaving Alex alone again and his apartment feeling less like a home and more like a stopover onto something else.

Mitch reached out with a foot and poked Alex in the thigh. "What are you thinking about?"

That I miss you already and you're not even gone yet. "I like having you here."

Mitch's mouth quirked, his smile tentative yet quietly pleased. "Yeah?"

"Yeah," Alex said, voice gruff. He walked into the space between Mitch's legs and ran his hands up Mitch's sides, nuzzling Mitch's throat. "I've missed you."

Tilting his head back, Mitch sighed softly and clamped

his legs around Alex's hips. "I've missed you too. Being here is…"

Alex kissed him gently. "It makes us feel more real."

"Yeah." Mitch's eyebrows pulled together in that way he had that told Alex he was surprised Alex understood him so easily. "I don't know why, though."

"Maybe because," Alex said, kissing the fingertips of one hand, "it's just us here. No parents, no roommates. And we can just…"

"Be."

"Yeah." Alex brushed his thumb over Mitch's lips. "We can just be."

TWENTY

THEY WOKE LATE THE NEXT MORNING AND LAZED in bed, cuddling and quietly chatting and exchanging lazy blow jobs, before getting up to start their day. After breakfast, they went to the aquarium because apparently Mitch hadn't been kidding about the marine biology thing. They stayed for hours. Mitch wanted to go to all the shows and talks, including the African penguin meet and greet that wasn't until mid-afternoon. He took everything in like a sponge, memorizing details, talking about sea level rise and coral bleaching, and the many species of sharks—apparently there were over four hundred—and the weird mating habits of deep-sea fish.

"Like some anglerfishes," Mitch said as he read an information panel on seahorses at the same time. "Some of them reproduce via symbiosis."

Alex had no idea what that meant, but he liked listening to Mitch blather on. "Science makes no sense sometimes."

That pulled Mitch's attention away from the seahorses. His mouth worked soundlessly and he eyeballed Alex, brow furrowed. "Science is, like, the only thing that makes sense."

"Not really. Take rainbows."

"What about them?"

"They don't make sense."

Mitch stared at him with an expression that clearly said *Buddy, you don't make sense.* "Rainbows are formed by sunlight passing through water droplets. How does that not make sense?"

"Okay. I'll give you that." Alex snapped his fingers. "Dark matter. Dark matter makes no sense. I mean, it's supposed to make up most of the universe, like ninety percent or something, yet nobody knows what it is?"

Mitch didn't have anything to say to that except a mumbled, "Astronomy is for wusses." Then he wandered off to look at something else.

Alex counted it as a win.

When Mitch had finally seen and done everything there was to see and do at the aquarium, they walked back to Alex's apartment for his car and drove to Pass-a-Grille. Alex bought them each an ice cream cone in the Historic District before they headed for the beach.

It was getting late in the day, so there weren't many other people there—just a couple on a colorful picnic blanket, a jogger, and a woman and her dog. Mitch left his shoes behind and dug his toes into the sand. He went right up to the water line and let the waves wash over his feet, not seeming to care about how cold the water must be.

Alex left his shoes with Mitch's and stuck one foot in the sand, letting the warm grains squelch between his toes, and stayed far, far away from the water. Popping the last of his ice cream cone into his mouth, he fell into step next to Mitch as they strolled along the beach, their fingers occasionally brushing. The sun was warm, but the wind was cool, and Alex was grateful for the long-sleeved T-shirt he'd pulled on over his shorts.

A woman passed them going in the other direction, holding the hand of a little boy who couldn't have been more than five. Mitch watched them go, then turned to Alex. "She's wearing boots."

"So?"

"It's Florida."

Alex chuckled. "Yeah, the natives bring out the coats and boots when the temperature dips below twenty."

Mitch's brow furrowed and he cocked his head. "Twenty? Oh, you mean sixty-eight. You still use Celsius, even though you've lived in the States for six years?"

"Habit," Alex said, sticking his hands in his pockets. "Also familiarity. If someone told me sixty-eight, I'd have no idea what the fuck that means. Shorts or jeans?"

"It's easy. You just deduct thirty-two, multiply by five, then divide by nine. So sixty-eight Fahrenheit is twenty Celsius, and seventy-five is twenty-three point eight, and eighty-six is thirty."

"Yeah, you lost me at deduct thirty-two," Alex said, mind reeling at how Mitch did the math without even pausing. "You're the only person I know who thinks math is fun."

"Math *is* fun. It's, it's, it's…"

"Don't say the bomb diggety."

"Oh God." Mitch stopped walking and hung his head. "I can't believe I ever said that. I was hoping you wouldn't remember."

"It was adorkable."

He pointed a finger at Alex. "I know you just said I'm handsome and tough."

Laughing, Alex pulled him along by the arm. "Sure, that's exactly what I said."

The gulf stretched out to their right, as far as the eye could see. The setting sun threw golds and peaches across the sky, reflecting off Mitch's sunglasses. He eventually took them off, setting them on top of his head when the sun dipped behind the clouds, casting bright yellows, or-angey-reds, and deep blues into the sky. It was as though someone had lit a bonfire and threw it into the air. Alex might not like the ocean, but the sunsets were spectacular here. That he got to share one of the only things he liked about living in Florida with Mitch was surreal.

They walked in companionable silence, the waves crashing, the seagulls crying, the occasional conversation reaching them from the street. The air held a faintly salty taste to it, a taste he couldn't wait to lick off Mitch's body later.

"We should probably turn back," he said. "Otherwise we'll be eating a really late dinner."

They headed back to where they'd left their shoes, their quickened steps affirming an eagerness to be home alone. Once Mitch had his shoes on, he nudged Alex moving again. The too-short, small touch sent tingles through Alex's body and he had a brief vision of the brand-spanking-new box of condoms he'd bought expressly for Mitch's visit sitting lonely and abandoned in his nightstand drawer.

Alex had never wanted anybody as badly as he wanted Mitch's hands on him. For years, he'd thought he wouldn't find the level of comfort and trust he needed with someone to reach a place where he could want to have sex with that person. And as much as he'd wanted to be friends with Mitch when they'd first met, he'd never expected this connection between them. But as he'd gotten to know Mitch, and as Mitch had finally opened up and Alex had connected with him emotionally, the deeper Alex had fallen for him. The physical attraction had developed alongside those emotions.

He'd always known Mitch was good looking, but it hadn't hit him on a visceral level. Now Alex found himself noticing everything about Mitch, all of the tiny quirks that made Mitch, *Mitch*. The way his eyes crinkled when he was confused or surprised, the furrow in his brow that told

Alex he had something on his mind, the way his eyelashes swept across his cheeks when he blinked, how he bit his lip when he was happy, as if to contain the emotion for fear that it wouldn't last.

Before he knew it, they were back in the car and Mitch was snapping his fingers in Alex's face since Alex wasn't doing anything but sitting there grinning.

"What's this?" Mitch asked, waving a hand at Alex.

"What's what?"

"This look. You've been looking at me like that since I got here."

Because Mitch was funny and smart and sweet and way out of Alex's league. But here he was anyway, all in, just like Alex.

"I love you," Alex said.

Mitch stilled. Alex would've bet he stopped breathing. His fingers clutched the door handle, his knuckles turning white. "Don't say that unless you mean it," he whispered.

Alex briefly thanked God and shady mechanics for illegally tinted windows, and leaned over the center console to hold Mitch's face in his hands. "I love you," he said firmly. "I love you." He kissed the corner of Mitch's mouth. "I love you." Kissed the other corner.

Slowly, Mitch started to smile. "You mean it."

Alex gave him a loud, smacking kiss, shocking Mitch into silence. "Of course I mean it. Now let's go home so I can make you dinner then take you to bed."

"Is there any flexibility on the order of those two scheduled events?"

Alex laughed and pulled out of the parking spot.

It wasn't until they were almost home, stopped at a red light, that Mitch reached over and took his hand. "I love you too, you know."

Heart melting, Alex squeezed his hand. "Yeah? I thought you might."

"How'd you figure?" Mitch blinked at Alex from the passenger seat, his elbow propped on the door and head resting on his fist.

"You showed yourself to me, Mitch." The words to explain were nowhere to be found, so in the end, Alex jerked a shoulder and repeated, "You showed yourself to me."

"Guess that means I do have substance, then?" Mitch asked after Alex had parked.

"Oh Jesus." Alex rubbed his hands over his face. "Mitch, I'm sorry I ever said that. It was so, so mean."

"Hey." Mitch yanked on Alex's wrist, pulling his hands away. "I'm kidding. I know you don't think that, not anymore."

"I never did," Alex swore. "Really, I didn't. I'm sorry I ever said it."

"I know." Mitch kissed him, a quick, barely there peck. "I know. Stop worrying." He got out of the car.

But Alex worried. They'd barely known each other when he'd said the words, but they still must've cut deep, must've made Mitch think Alex would never want anything to do with him.

"I'm surprised you wanted anything to do with me after that," Alex said, letting them in to his apartment.

Mitch led the way into the kitchen. "You can thank Cody for that."

Alex's eyebrows shot up. "Really?"

"Yup. He told me to give you a chance. That you'd never want me unless I was real with you."

"He was right."

Mitch hopped up onto the island. "He also said you'd be good for me."

"He was right about that too."

Alex started putting together dinner while Mitch munched on pre-cut veggies from a container Alex handed him.

"Got Cheese Whiz?" Mitch asked.

Alex tossed him a look he hoped conveyed how unimpressed he was. "No."

A knock at the door had them eyeing each other, the time—almost seven thirty—each other again, and finally the front door.

Huffing, Alex set down the cheese grater and stalked down the hall. Whoever was interrupting his Valentine's Day with Mitch was about to get his ass kicked.

Alex checked the peephole before opening the door. "Yager. What are you doing here?"

Hands on his hips, eyebrows pulled together, huge shoulders outlined by the porch light, Yager would be scary standing there on Alex's doorstep in the dark if Alex didn't know him.

"Hello to you too," Yager said, sarcasm dripping off his tongue. "Would it kill you to check your text messages? When you said your boyfriend was coming to visit, I didn't think that meant you'd cut off contact with the rest of humanity."

There was a squeak from the kitchen. Mitch better not have burned himself on something.

"Is there an emergency?" Alex dug his phone out of his pocket to find that yes, he did have a dozen missed texts from Yager, all of them of the dude-where-the-fuck-are-you variety.

"Are you going to let me in? It's cold."

Alex rolled his eyes but opened the door wider and moved out of the way. The Canadian and the native

Floridian had vastly different opinions about what *cold* meant.

"You remember that bookshelf I bought at Walmart?" Yager said. "It's too big. Doesn't fit in the corner I wanted to put it in. You want it?"

"Seriously, this is your emergency?"

Yager's face took on the expression of a kicked puppy. "Today's the last day to return it."

"Of course it is. Yeah, I'll take it."

"Awesome. It's in the truck. Come help me—oh. Hey, you must be Mitch." He stuck his big hand out to Mitch, who was hovering a foot behind Alex. "Good to meet you. I'm Ashton Yager."

"I…know," Mitch said in awe, shaking Yager's hand.

Yager whacked Alex on the chest with the back of his hand. "Come help me get the shelf." He turned and headed for his truck parked on the street.

Mitch grabbed Alex's wrist. "You didn't tell me you're friends with pro players."

Alex peered at Mitch in confusion. "Honey, I *am* a pro player."

"You go make dinner." Mitch turned Alex around and gave him a slight smack on the butt. "I'll go help your friend."

Shaking his head at the absurdity of the situation, Alex went back to the kitchen. The Alfredo sauce was simmering, the pasta was cooking, and the sliced chicken breast was browning by the time Mitch and Yager had not only lugged the box upstairs to the loft, but unpacked it and assembled the shelf. When they came down, Alex had a beer for each of them waiting on the island. They sat on the L-shaped couch perpendicular to each other while Alex set the table for two, letting them get to know each other. If

Mitch was going to be in his life, he should get to know his friends, even the ones Alex wanted to bean with a hockey stick for interrupting their night.

"What's it like to have sex with a dude?" Yager asked.

Mitch kicked his feet onto the coffee table. "What's it like to have sex with a girl?" he countered.

Yager scratched the scruff on his chin. "Huh. You know, I thought I was bi once."

"You…" Mitch met Alex's eyes over Yager's head. Alex shrugged.

"Yeah, there was a maybe guy once," Yager said.

"A maybe guy?"

Yager grunted his affirmative. "Guy I could've had something with but it didn't work out. Because reasons. It was a long time ago, before I met my now ex-wife, when I spent a summer working in New York. He kind of looked like you, actually." Yager gestured at Mitch with his beer. "Hair all curly and cute and soft." He tugged a lock of Mitch's hair.

Scowling at the back of Yager's head, Alex considered pouring the pot of boiling water on it. But that'd be mean, right? He had to hand it to Mitch, though. The man didn't appear phased at all by the conversation as he swatted Yager's hand away.

"And no one since then?" he asked.

"Nope. Must mean I'm straight, right?"

Mitch shrugged. "Only you can answer that."

"Hmm. I'll think on it some more." Yager leaned back, one arm across the back of the couch, and sipped his beer. "Hey, Dean," he called over his shoulder. "What are you making? Can I stay for dinner?"

The dual chorus of "No!" was enough to convince Yager to beat it.

Staring into the fridge after dinner cleanup, Alex considered the pros and cons of strawberry cheesecake for dessert, right after a filling cheesy dinner. He let the door slam shut. Probably not a good idea.

He took his shirt off instead.

"What…are you doing?" Mitch asked, standing on the other side of the island, his glass of water halfway to his mouth, forgotten. His eyes roamed Alex's chest, catching on his nipples, his belly button.

Alex undid his belt, nerves kicking a path from his stomach all the way into his throat. "Getting naked."

Mitch set his glass down, slowly, as if he thought Alex would run away—or put his clothes back on—if he moved too fast. "Not that I'm opposed, but…why?"

"Because I want to have sex now." Alex stepped out of his shorts. "But I don't know how to initiate it, so I figured if I got naked, you'd get the picture."

Mitch swallowed hard, Adam's apple bobbing. "That's…not a bad strategy. One problem." He came around the island and stood less than a foot from Alex. "You're not hard."

Alex erased the distance between them and ran his fingertips over Mitch's unshaven jaw. "That's because I'm not the type of guy who only has to think about dick and ass to get hard."

"Uh-huh." Mitch ran his hands up Alex's sides, sending shots of pleasure rushing through Alex's veins.

"The only dick and ass that get me hard," Alex said against Mitch's mouth, "are yours." He kissed Mitch, and he didn't take the time to tease or play. Instead, he swept right in, forcing Mitch's mouth open, taking Mitch's tongue, tilting Mitch's head to get a better angle.

Mitch moaned and clutched at Alex's back, fingernails surely leaving scratches.

Alex wrenched his mouth away and walked Mitch backward toward the bedroom. "But it's not just your dick and ass," Alex said as they walked. "It's this." He kissed Mitch's temple. "Your smarts, your intuitiveness, your brain that never stops working. It's this." He traced a heart with a fingertip over the left side of Mitch's chest. "Your heart, your soul, who you are at the core. Insecure yet confident, sensitive, determined, fiercely loyal, kind. That's what turns me on. Not the way you look." Mitch lay on the bed and Alex straddled his thighs. "But I'm not going to lie. Your body—" He lifted off Mitch's T-shirt. "—is a nice perk."

"Alex." Mitch's whisper was ragged, and he fought with the zipper on his shorts. "Off."

Alex helped, stripping Mitch of his shorts and underwear in one shot. He took in Mitch's lightly haired, muscular thighs, his defined chest, the erection curving up toward his belly, hot and hard, the swollen purple head already leaking pre-come.

Gut clenching with desire, Alex took off his own underwear, freeing his now hard dick from its confines. Mitch whimpered and reached out a hand. "Gimme."

Alex gave. One leg on either side of Mitch's body, Alex made his way up Mitch's chest and fed Mitch his dick. From this vantage point, sitting atop Mitch, his forehead resting on the arm positioned on the back of the headboard, Alex could watch Mitch's eyes go hot, watch his cock disappear into the perfect O of Mitch's mouth.

Mitch's tongue laved his head, probed his slit. Alex's thighs clenched and he swore under his breath.

"Stop." He ran a hand through Mitch's hair. "I want to be in you when I come."

Mitch gave one last suck, making Alex see stars, before letting him go with a grin. "You taste good."

"Jesus." Alex slid down Mitch's body, tangling their legs. Their mouths met, open, wet, demanding, not giving an inch. Alex's skin heated everywhere they touched, electricity sending shocks through him.

He got the lube, condoms, and a thin, nitrile glove out of the nightstand. He'd done a lot of research and watched a lot of porn and was confident he knew how to prep Mitch so that he didn't hurt him. Truthfully, the research had been much more informative. In fact, the porn had been completely useless except in serving to convince Alex that it was completely unsexy.

The glove made a *snap* when he slipped it over his hand.

Mitch's eyes went wide and he grinned. "Are we playing Naughty Doctor? Kinky."

Alex snorted a laugh. He hadn't expected to laugh during sex, but he should've anticipated it. This was Mitch, after all.

"I've heard," Alex said, coating the fingers of his gloved hand in lube, "that there are a lot of nerves… right…here." He traced Mitch's hole, feeling it flutter under his thumb.

Mitch's hips left the bed and he swore under his breath, all traces of mirth gone from his face. Alex used a hand on Mitch's lower belly to keep him still, and let his thumb breach Mitch's hole.

Mitch growled something under his breath that sounded like "Fucking finally," then said, "Alex. Fuck, you're taking forever."

"Don't want to hurt you," Alex said. And because Mitch's dick was right there, neglected, Alex bent his head and licked the underside, bottom to top.

Mitch threw his head back and moaned at the contact. Fuck, he was beautiful, stretched out on the bed, flushed, eyes squeezed tight, legs wide, hands fisted in the bedcovers. By the time Alex had inserted three fingers into him and was massaging the little nub of his prostate, Mitch was incoherent and chanting "Please, please, please," over and over.

Alex had done that. He'd reduced Mitch to sobbing breaths and a one-word vocabulary. Mitch didn't even seem to care that Alex was making shit up as he went— with pointers from Google—and Alex gave him all the goddamn brownie points in the world for not teasing Alex about his inexperience, especially since Alex was five years older than him and should, theoretically, know what the fuck he was doing.

Alex was a quick learner. And he knew that if he ran his thumbnail along the underside of Mitch's cockhead just so, Mitch would unravel in his arms.

"Oh fuck, oh shit, Alex." Mitch practically flew off the bed. His heels dug into the mattress and he moaned loud and long.

"Fuck." Alex hissed out a breath and rested his forehead on Mitch's thigh, taking a minute to regroup. Mitch was so hypersensitive, so responsive. That he was so turned on turned Alex on, and he needed a fucking minute to breathe.

"Inside me," Mitch said, tugging on Alex's hair. "Now."

Condom in place, lubed up, Alex flipped off the glove and dropped it to the floor before lining himself up with Mitch's stretched hole. He pushed. There was a bit of resistance and his eyes flew to Mitch's, but Mitch simply nodded and said, "Keep going." So Alex kept going, sweat dripping down his back, legs shaking. Once his head was past the ring of muscle, Mitch sucked the rest of him in with little resistance. Alex clenched his teeth against the sensation of his cock rubbing against the walls of Mitch's channel.

Heart hammering, extremities tingling with pleasure, he pumped once, twice, slowly, watching Mitch for any discomfort. Mitch's pupils were blown and he grinned wildly, meeting Alex's thrusts. Alex sped up in increments until Mitch's body tensed. Then he went to town, jacking into Mitch fast, leaving barely half a second between thrusts. Alex wasn't going to last, not with the sight of Mitch's open mouth as he sucked in air and of his own cock stretching Mitch open seared into his retinas.

Mitch jacked himself frantically. Alex's limbs went heavy when Mitch yelled and came, sending ropy white streaks across his stomach and onto the bed. His clenching ass clasped Alex tight, tighter than anything he'd ever felt before, and Alex lost it, coming into the condom, body shaking uncontrollably.

Breathing hard, Mitch's entire body went lax and he wiped sweat off his face with the edge of the bedcover. "Holy fuck."

Alex propped himself up with one hand on the bed so he didn't fall onto Mitch and squish him. "Happy Valentine's Day?"

Mitch started to laugh.

The boxed books in Alex's office space in the loft were in no order whatsoever. Mitch found titles by John Grisham and Stephen King spread among four different boxes, interspersed with other mysteries and thrillers he'd never heard of, a few YA novels, school textbooks, and what looked like four different editions of *Les Misérables*.

It made no sense. None.

Mitch did Alex a favor—unasked, but whatever—and sorted them all alphabetically by author while Alex made breakfast. Then he started placing them on Alex's new bookshelf. He didn't know if any of these were series, though, so he jogged downstairs, borrowed Alex's phone so he could Google whatever he needed, and departed again with a kiss to Alex's cheek and a pat on the butt.

Mitch's own butt was sore this morning, but it was a good kind of sore, the best kind. The kind where he'd be walking funny for hours and perching on an asscheek in his seat on the flight back to Vermont this afternoon.

Last night had been amazing. Mitch grinned and did a happy dance wiggle while placing books on the shelves. It wasn't even that he'd had sex last night. Okay, it wasn't *only* that he'd had sex last night. It was that he'd had sex with the person he loved, who, for some reason, loved him back. It was this morning's repeat after the best sleep of his life, a lazy consummation when the sun had barely been up, throwing muted sunbeams across the walls, Alex spooned around him and taking him from behind. It was last night's strawberry cheesecake in bed. It was this morning's yet-to-be-made breakfast.

It was this entire weekend. Alex had even indulged him by spending almost four *hours* with him at the aquarium yesterday. Really, who did that?

A man in love, that's who.

Mitch was standing there smiling at nothing when Alex called out, "Mitch, breakfast is ready." Mmm, it smelled like bacon and something doughy. Pancakes maybe, or—Whoops. He'd missed a box. It was tucked under the desk, half hidden by the desk chair. He dragged it out, careful not to bump it into anything and topple the picture frame on the desk. In the delicate, silver frame was a five-by-seven photo of Alex's Grandpa Forest and a kid who wasn't a day past ten—Alex presumably. Alex wore a hockey uniform, stick in one hand, and Forest was bent over halfway, bringing him to Alex's height. They were both grinning.

Lifting the box onto the table, Mitch removed the lid to see what titles were in it and how much rearranging he'd have to do on Alex's shelf. But they weren't books. They were journals, ten of them, all filled from the first page to the last.

August 27, 2005

It's the first week of senior year. I should be thrilled— or sad, I don't really know. But all I can think about is that Grandpa Forest's Alzheimer's is getting worse. I still can't believe he has Alzheimer's of all things. The man who can tell you what he had for breakfast five fucking years ago...

Mitch flipped forward a few pages.

October 4, 2006

Played my first NHL game today, on the third line. It was exhilarating, like nothing I've ever felt before. This is what I've worked toward my whole life. Mom came. Grandpa Forest... Grandpa Forest doesn't remember who I am anymore. Thinks I'm Dad. All the support he's given me, all the times he was there for me after Dad left, the money he sent Mom to help pay for hockey...he's never going to see the result of all that. Never see me play in the NHL.

Mitch put the journal away and chose another at random.

March 10, 2008
The spring breakers have descended on Florida. Kill me.

Chuckling, Mitch closed the journal.

"Mitch."

"Jesus!" Heart jumping into his throat, Mitch swallowed guilty laughter and sent a small wave Alex's way. "Um, hi."

Alex leaned a hip against the wall. "What'cha doin'?"

"Um." Mitch hid the journal behind his back. "Organizing?" Shit, Alex was going to be so mad that Mitch had snooped through his personal stuff. Well, they had to have their first fight sometime, right?

"Try again."

Mitch's shoulders slumped. "Fine, I was looking at your journals. But I didn't read them. Okay, maybe I read a couple," he said when Alex kept staring at him.

But Alex just shrugged. "It's fine."

"It's...fine? What's fine?"

"That you're reading it." Alex took the journal out of Mitch's hands and flipped through it.

"Seriously? If I had a journal and someone read it without my permission, I'd be fucking pissed."

Alex chuckled and sat on the desk. "But you're not just someone. You're you. And I trust you."

The simple statement had Mitch swallowing past a lump in his throat made up of all the mushy feelings he had for Alex.

"If you want to read them, go right ahead, but they're probably really boring," Alex said.

"You have a lot of them."

"Yeah." Alex glanced at the box. "I started them when Grandpa Forest was diagnosed with Alzheimer's. It was a way to cope, a way to talk about it without actually having to talk to someone. But I also didn't want to forget anything, you know? Depending on what research you believe, Alzheimer's either is or isn't inherited, and if I ever get it…" He shrugged, sheepish. "I'll have these as a way to remember. I try and record the important stuff, so I never forget, but also the mundane to remind me that life isn't always about ups and downs. Sometimes it's just a steady journey, and that's okay too."

There was no swallowing past this lump. Eyes burning, Mitch moved between Alex's legs, threw his arms around him, and held him tight. "I'm sorry. I'm so sorry."

"Hey, it's okay." Alex's arms were iron bands around Mitch's waist.

Mitch kissed Alex's neck and drew back. He wiped his eyes and nodded at the box of journals. "Am I in there?" he asked, hoping to inject some levity into a morning that had turned blue.

"Yeah. Want to see?"

Did he? Did he want to know what Alex had written about him? "No," he said before he could cave.

"Really?"

Mitch rubbed Alex's thighs. "I already know how you feel about me."

"Yes. You do."

"I trust you too. You know." Mitch's shoulders twitched. "In case you were wondering."

"Yeah?"

"Yeah." Mitch ran his thumb over Alex's nose, his cheekbone, through his beard. "I was so lost before I met you."

"No—"

"I was. I didn't know who I was or who I wanted to be. Cody said he knew, but I didn't believe it. And then you came, and you insisted that I be myself if I wanted anything to do with you. I didn't know how to do that and I was afraid you wouldn't like me." Mitch played with Alex's sleeve. "But you make me feel safe. And just by being you, by being patient and kind and nonjudgmental and basically the most reliable and steady person I've ever met, you let me be me. Let me find myself. And it turns out, you do like who I am," he finished in a whisper.

"I love who you are." Alex grasped Mitch's chin and forced him to look at him. Alex's gaze was a combination of fierce and gentle, and his eyes begged Mitch to take him at his word.

Mitch kissed him high up on his cheekbone and laid his head on his shoulder. "I know. I love who you are too. That's what's going to make it so hard to leave later."

"I know," Alex said, wrapping those huge arms around him again. "I know."

TWENTY-ONE

MARCH 2009

Alex: *I have an idea.*

Mitch: *Does it involve phone sex?*

Alex: *No. I mean, now it does but… No. Listen. There's a café in the Channel District that's looking to hire full-time employees for the summer. I know the owner. I could put in a good word for you? It's minimum wage, but it's full-time plus tips.*

Mitch: *Is this your way of asking me to move in with you?*

Alex: *I'm going to take that as a yes.*

Mitch: *How far of a drive is it?*

Alex: *It's a five-minute walk. I live in the Channel District.*

Mitch: *Don't be mad but…can I talk to Cody first?*

Alex: *Why would I be mad? I can put in a good word for him too.*

Mitch: *Huh?*

Alex: *He can have the guest room in the loft. It means you and I won't have much privacy, but…*

Mitch: *Are you for real?*

Alex: *You think I don't know that you come as a package deal?*

Mitch: *Cody's in!*

Alex: *That was fast. Did you even ask him?*

Mitch: *Yeah. He's right here. He's texting you now.*

Alex: *What's YTFBE?*

Mitch: *Cody-speak for you're the fucking best ever.*

Despite the team finally coming together over the last month and a half after a dismal start to the second semester, the Glen Hill College Mountaineers were officially done for the season as of the first weekend in March. They didn't make it to the Frozen Four. Hell, they didn't make it to the Hockey East Quarterfinals. They played in the Hockey East Opening Round and lost twice against Providence. It was a bitter end to the season, especially for the graduating seniors.

Mitch, however, still had two years of college left, which meant two more tries for the championship.

He dragged his feet into the house on Saturday night after losing Game Two and stood in the kitchen, staring aimlessly at the island counter. Cody had dropped him off before leaving again to pick up their to-go pizza at Mama Jean's, but in the meantime Mitch had reading to catch up on, a creative writing assignment to start, and three—count 'em, *three*—lab reports due next week.

All he wanted to do was to pass out on the couch. It looked so inviting with all those couch pillows. He could sink into it and be asleep in less than a minute.

Stomach gnawing at him, he dropped his equipment bag right there in the middle of the kitchen and sank onto one of the barstools before he swayed off his feet. He was running on maybe twenty hours of sleep this week total, and had eaten nothing but protein bars and smoothies. Alex would be appalled.

Speaking of Alex... Mitch got his phone out of his pocket, ignored the message from his mom, and gave Alex a call, but it went right to voicemail. Right. Alex was playing in a different time zone tonight. Dallas? Or was tonight the night of Alex's team's annual end of season charity game? Fuck, Mitch couldn't remember and was too tired to care. All he knew was that he wanted Alex here.

He missed sex with Alex, sure, but more than that, he missed talking to him, cuddling with him. He missed being able to reach out and touch him or kiss him whenever he wanted. He missed Alex's strong arms and steady, calming eyes. Alex propped him up. And right now, Mitch felt like he was falling.

Shit, he really was falling. Off the barstool, that was. Had he fallen asleep sitting up? He was so damn hungry, and his hands trembled from lack of food. He'd eaten today, hadn't he?

His vision darkened when he got up for a glass of water to wet his dry mouth. Any second now, his stomach was going to claw its way out of his body in search of food. Limbs heavy, he walked back to his stool with his water. Jesus, had he played like this? Lightheaded and nauseated? No, he'd been alert for the game, he was sure. It had been afterward that the exhaustion had hit, with the loss hanging heavy over his head, and the too-busy last three weeks catching up with him. Three weeks since Valentine's Day and his weekend at Alex's. They talked every day and although it wasn't the same, it made Mitch feel closer to him.

He missed the counter trying to set his water down, and the glass fell to the floor, shattering into tiny shards against the ceramic tile. The sound was loud in the otherwise quiet house, maximized by the throb already pounding behind Mitch's eyes. He sighed miserably and considered leaving it there, but he didn't want Cody to come home and step in it. He got the broom and dustpan from the closet and the garbage can from underneath the sink. But when he bent over to sweep the glass, his vision grayed and went dark.

The lights were too bright when he woke up on an uncomfortable bed that was barely wide enough to hold him and there were people in his room. His dad, sitting on the windowsill and plugging away at his iPhone. Cody, lounging in a chair with his head tilted back, mouth open in sleep. And Alex, pacing a path from one end of the tiny room to the other. Mitch must've made a sound because all three heads turned to him at once.

"What?" he croaked.

"Hey, kiddo." His dad came over to him and took his hand. "How're you feeling?"

"I..." How had he ended up in the hospital? Last thing he remembered was coming home from the game. Cody dropped him off and he went inside and... What?

In his confusion, he said, "Where's the pizza? And how did you get here so fast?"

"Took the first flight out," his dad said, patting his hand.

"No, I mean…" He looked at Alex.

"My answer's the same as your dad's," Alex said, a growl to his voice, the anger underlying his movements palpable. He continued to pace, barely glancing in Mitch's direction.

Something was wrong. What had he done to make Alex so angry with him? Nothing made sense. Had he gotten in an accident? "Did I hurt someone?"

"Just yourself," Alex snapped.

"I… What?"

"Kiddo. You fainted. Do you remember?" His dad gestured to Cody. "Cody found you and called nine-one-one."

Their conversation had woken Cody and he stood at the foot of the bed, arms crossed, his glower making his eyes burn. He was clearly as pissed as Alex.

"I thought you were dead, you asshole," Cody growled. "I even stabbed you with your damn EpiPen."

That was probably why his thigh hurt. "Did I get stung?"

"No. But I thought you might've."

"In March?"

Cody threw up his hands. "What else was I supposed to think with you lying facedown in the kitchen in a pool of broken glass with a cut on your forehead? I didn't know you'd passed out from fucking exhaustion."

Is that what had happened?

"Wait." Alex finally stopped moving. "You're allergic to…bees?"

"Yeah," Mitch said. "There's an EpiPen in my backpack." He looked around for his backpack, but it wasn't anywhere in sight. "Or there was." Fuck, he was so confused.

Alex stared at him head-on. "You didn't think that's

something I should know? God, your short story makes so much more sense now."

Had Mitch written a short story before passing out? It didn't seem likely, but his brain was fuzzy.

Alex released a long sigh and headed for the door. "I'm going to get the nurse." He was gone a second later.

"He's so mad at me," Mitch said. And burst into tears.

He was tired, he was confused, and combined with Alex's abandonment, Mitch was just done. But Alex was back less than a minute later, a tall nurse in turquoise scrubs in tow. Alex took one look at Mitch's face and his eyes widened in absolute horror. It would've been funny under different circumstances.

Cody patted Mitch's leg through the thin hospital blanket. "Don't worry," he said to Alex. "He only gets overly emotional when he's exhausted."

"How are you feeling?" the nurse asked as she fiddled with the baggie attached to his IV.

Mitch blew his nose with the tissue his dad passed him and nodded at his hand. "My hand is throbbing. Whoever put the IV in is incompetent. My thigh hurts, but I figure that's where Cody stabbed me with the EpiPen. My forehead itches—" He probed it with his non-IV hand, only to find a small butterfly bandage over a cut. "—but it's not going to kill me. I have a headache that's about a seven, a desire to nap for a year, and confusion that's the size of the state."

The nurse blinked at him. "That was, uh, very thorough."

His dad, Alex, and Cody all snorted in unison. It made Mitch give a watery giggle even though he had no idea what was so funny.

"The doctor will be in to speak with you in a few minutes," the nurse said and left.

Mitch struggled to sit up, but his body wouldn't cooperate. His dad took pity on him and lifted the bed. Once Mitch was semi-vertical, he said, "Can someone please tell me what's going on?"

"You fainted from exhaustion last night after the game," his dad said, taking Cody's vacated seat. "Cody found you and called nine-one-one. You woke up a few times since then, but this is the first time you've been aware."

"I don't remember that." Mitch rubbed his forehead. "Wait. Last night? How long have I been out?"

"Almost seven hours. It's six in the morning."

Mitch shifted, wincing when his IV pulled. His dad and Alex must've taken the red-eye. He clenched his jaw and tried to find a comfortable position in the lumpy bed. Punched his pillow a few times to fluff it up. Kicked his blanket off. His hospital gown was bunched around his thighs, and they'd even removed his briefs for fuck's sake, leaving his dick bobbing in the air, all do-si-do. If waking up in the hospital wasn't bad enough, he'd just flashed his entire family.

"I—"

"I see my patient's awake," the doctor said, coming through the door and interrupting what would've been a truly petulant *I wanna go home*. "How are you feeling?"

Pissed. Embarrassed. Overwhelmed. And frankly, a little scared.

The doctor, a tall, thin lady with brown hair going to gray tucked back into a ponytail, didn't give him a chance to respond. "I'm Doctor Pariselli. You've given your family here quite a scare, Mr. Greyson. I assume they told you what happened?"

"I passed out from exhaustion," Mitch said woodenly,

resting his head against the pillow and closing his eyes against his family's haunted and haggard expressions.

"You were dehydrated and had low blood sugar. Have you been ill recently or were you on any medications?"

Mitch shook his head.

"We've got you on some nutrients here, and once that's done—" Mitch opened his eyes to find her checking how much liquid remained in the IV bag. "—which should be any minute now, you're free to go. Assuming you have someone to take care of you."

"I can take care of myself."

Silence.

"Yeah, okay."

"I'll be right back with your discharge papers and instructions for the next few days." The doctor left, leaving him with an angry giant of a boyfriend, an unimpressed best friend, and a concerned father.

"Could you two give us a second?" his dad said to Alex and Cody.

"Sure." Cody patted Mitch's foot and followed a tense Alex out the door.

"I'm sorry, Dad."

His dad took his hand. "Cody says you've been taking on extra kids to tutor, leaving you less time for schoolwork and other important things like eating and sleeping. Why didn't you tell me money was so tight?"

Damn Cody and his big mouth. Mitch shrugged and picked at a thread in the bedding.

"More importantly," his dad said, squeezing his hand to get his attention, "why didn't you tell me your mom took your tuition money away?"

His dad was hurt. Realization came so fast, Mitch's eyes burned. His dad was hurt that Mitch hadn't confided in him. "I didn't want to cause any more strain between you and Mom."

"Kiddo, your mom and I have been sleeping in separate rooms since you moved out for college. Except for Christmas, when we put up a pretense, but… We're meeting with our lawyers in a couple weeks to sign the divorce papers."

"You—" Heart jackhammering, Mitch sat up, the lumpy pillow falling off the bed. "I did this." His dad deserved better than his mom, but that didn't mean Mitch wanted his parents to divorce, even though it was probably best for both of them. Fuck, he was so conflicted.

"No." His dad actually chuckled. "No, none of this is your fault. The divorce has been in process for a long time now. I tried to make it work with your mom, but… She turned into someone I don't recognize anymore. I've spent years trying to bring out the part of her that I fell in love with, but…" He smiled thinly and patted Mitch's hand. "Anyway, we'll talk more later. I'll be around for the next few days and we'll discuss the money thing and the divorce and anything else you need to talk about, okay? Right now, I'm going to let Alex in here before he blows a blood vessel."

"He's so mad at me." Mitch's eyes burned again and he wiped them using the collar of his hospital gown, pissed at himself, at the situation, at the fear he'd put in everyone. And oddly scared that this was what was going to do it for Alex and have him running in the other direction as fast as he could, leaving a trail of heartbroken Mitch-dust behind. Ever since Alex had caught Mitch snooping through his journals last month and hadn't blinked twice at the intrusion of privacy, Mitch had wondered what it would take to make him angry.

Looked like he'd found it.

Out in the hallway, Alex kicked the wall and stared at a smudge in the white paint.

"Stop doing that," Cody said, leaning against the wall. "It's annoying."

Alex swallowed his retort. *Don't yell at Cody.* The self-loathing practically dripped off Cody's stiff shoulders and tight fists, and Alex wasn't a big enough jerk to add to it. He might be pissed at Cody for not realizing sooner that Mitch was in danger, but Cody was clearly already beating himself up over it. He didn't need Alex's censure too.

Besides, Alex was equally, if not more, pissed at Mitch's dad. How could the man not know that his own wife had withheld his son's tuition?

To top it off, Alex was also equally pissed at himself, and even more so with the person sitting in the hospital bed in the room across the hall.

It was quiet in the hallway, still too early in the day for visitors. The hospital didn't have official visiting hours, but it had quiet hours between ten p.m. and eight a.m. Murmuring voices reached them from the nurse's station further down, a beeping machine from someone's room, the hum of the fluorescent lights.

Geoff Greyson came out of Mitch's room, hollow-eyed and weary, bags beneath his eyes, lines of stress and concern etched into his face aging him ten years. He nodded at Alex. "Go on in. I'll go see about those discharge papers." He clasped Alex's shoulder. "Don't be too hard on him, okay?"

Oh, Alex wouldn't be *too* hard. No, he was going to be

very hard. Someone as smart as Mitch should've known better than to push himself to the edge.

But the sight of Mitch sitting on the hospital bed, his shoulders slumped, lip caught between his teeth, a butterfly bandage on his forehead where he'd landed on glass, had Alex's ire turning to relief and affection.

He sat on the edge of the bed and ducked down to catch Mitch's gaze. Mitch's eyes were wet and he gave a surreptitious sniffle. Alex pulled on his arm. "Come here."

Mitch scrambled onto Alex's lap, careful of his IV, and tucked his nose into Alex's neck. Alex held him close and sighed into Mitch's messy hair, touching him everywhere, inhaling his scent, reassuring himself that Mitch was in one piece.

"You scared me," he whispered. Cody's phone call had scared the absolute shit out of him, despite the other man's reassurances that the doctors were sure Mitch had only fainted from exhaustion and not something else— not something deadly—and that he'd be fine with rest and nutrients.

"I'm sorry." Mitch slumped into Alex, as though it was too much effort to hold himself up. The doctor had warned them that Mitch would be lethargic for the next few days.

"You know things need to change, right?" Alex said.

Mitch's body went rigid and he sat up, climbing off Alex's lap with movements mired in molasses. He didn't meet Alex's eyes when he said, with no expression whatsoever, "You're breaking up with me, aren't you?"

"What?" Alex's heart broke for him, and he cursed Mitch's mom and brother, who'd made Mitch so wary and distrustful. "Mitch, no. Of course not."

Mitch's brow furrowed. "But I made you so mad."

"Yeah. Yeah, you did. But I'm also really fucking relieved

290 | AMY AISLIN

that you're okay." He pressed a kiss to Mitch's cheek, and his throat went thick when Mitch nuzzled into him like a puppy seeking comfort. "But things do have to change. You have to ask for help when you need it."

"My dad said we're going to talk about the money. He's going to help me with tuition, I think."

"Good." Alex pulled back to meet Mitch's contrite gaze. "But it's not just about the money, okay? You have to take better care of yourself. Better time management and a better diet. And you're going to let me help too, in any way I can."

Mitch nodded, half-reluctant, half-accepting.

"You're not going to fight me on it?"

"No." Mitch wiped his nose with the back of his hand. "This scared me too. It scared me to wake up here, not knowing what was happening. A true come-to-Jesus moment." He ran his fingers over Alex's jaw. "I'm sorry I scared you. And I'm sorry you had to take a flight all the way here. You must be so tired."

"We'll take a nap when we get back to your place. How's that?"

Mitch's sad eyes brightened. "You're staying?"

"I've got a flight out Tuesday morning. Game Tuesday night."

"If it helps," Mitch whispered, his voice choked, "it's really damn good to see you."

Alex pulled Mitch into his arms again, and Mitch sank into him, laying his head on Alex's shoulder. "I miss you." Alex kissed Mitch's temple next to the butterfly bandage. "I miss you so much. It's like I can't breathe when you're not there."

"Yes." Mitch kissed Alex's neck. "Yes, exactly." He sniffled once and relaxed against Alex. "This is going to end up in your book, isn't it?"

"Not if you don't want it to."

It was quiet as Mitch seemed to ponder that for a minute. "I think it should," he eventually said. "Chapter Seven: The Dangers of Spreading Yourself Too Thin, Mitch slash Adrian-style."

Alex released a puff of relieved laughter into Mitch's hair.

Cody and Geoff found them like that a few minutes later, tangled together on the bed. Cody's face was drawn and sallow, and Mitch took one look at him, extricated himself from Alex, and threw himself at his best friend, letting one arm dangle where the IV wasn't long enough.

"I'm sorry, Cody."

Cody stood limp for a second, his arms hanging at his sides. Then he clasped them around Mitch and squeezed his eyes tight. "Asshole. Don't ever do that again."

Alex couldn't imagine what it must've been like for Cody to come home and find Mitch passed out on the floor, not knowing if Mitch was dead or alive. He shuddered hard and ran his hands over his face.

Geoff cleared his throat. "Kiddo, there's someone outside who wants to talk to you."

"Coach Bedley?" Mitch asked. He sat on the bed and Alex stood to give Cody his spot next to Mitch since Cody looked like he needed the assurance of being close to his best friend right now.

"No. But I did speak with your coach and he wants to see you as soon as you're up for it," Geoff said. Mitch winced. "No, this is someone named Jenny Lynn?"

"Okay?"

"Says she's a writer with the Mountain Chronicle?"

Shit, the Glen Hill College student newspaper hadn't wasted any time in sending someone for an exclusive, had they? Barely seven on Sunday morning. That was ambitious for a tiny college like GH. Probably Coach Bedley had something to do with it. But why would he send someone to interview a hockey player about something that had nothing to do with hockey?

When Mitch gave his okay and Geoff let Jenny Lynn into the room, he got his answer.

"Coach Bedley wanted an exclusive on a student athlete's perspective on mental and physical health," she explained.

That didn't make any sense. Alex distinctly remembered Coach Bedley telling him that they tried not to put Mitch in front of reporters because he tended to speak before thinking.

However, it turned out that Jenny wasn't a sports writer. She wrote for the Issues & Ideas section of the newspaper, and Coach Bedley had requested her, not only because her pieces were thoughtful, but because he didn't want the article run in the sports section, which only sports enthusiasts read. He wanted it somewhere that would gain the most attention.

Jenny told them all this as she settled into the only chair in the room with her notepad and a small recorder. Cody didn't leave Mitch's side and Alex leaned against the wall next to Geoff and rested his eyes. He didn't pay much attention to the interview, but he heard enough to be proud of Mitch, at his smart and concise answers, despite how tired he must be.

Until it all fell apart.

"Just one last question," Jenny said half an hour later. "I did some research on you before coming." If that was true, she must've been up for hours. "And I understand you're part of the Westlake family? Your mother is a Westlake?"

Next to Alex, Geoff tensed.

Mitch crossed his arms over his chest. "So?"

Jenny faltered briefly at the flash of temper on Mitch's face, but managed to carry on. "From what I can tell, the Westlakes own Westlake Waterless Printing, a family business started by your mother's grandfather, yes? Correct me if I'm wrong, but I assume that, since you're majoring in kinesiology, you don't intend to go into the business?"

Mitch nodded once.

"Despite being in the hospital, things seem to be going well for you. You're the Mountaineers' top scorer with a current GPA of three-point-eight."

Mitch grumbled something.

"Sorry?"

"I said, it used to be four-point-oh," he said. "Stupid creative writing brought me down."

Alex couldn't help an amused snort. As if three-point-eight was anything to sneeze at. Jesus, his boyfriend wasn't just smart, he was *smart*.

"Oh." Jenny wrote something down. "Anyway, I was wondering how the support of your mother has affected your studies. She must be so proud." She smiled wide, as if she thought this was going to be an easy answer. *Yup. My mom couldn't be more proud of me. End of story*.

Instead, she got a scoff from Mitch. "Support? I haven't seen any support from my mother, emotional or otherwise, since I told her I wanted to play hockey and study kinesiology. The reason I work so hard for my GPA is that if it slips below a three-point-two, I lose my partial hockey scholarship. And since I don't get tuition money from my mom, losing the scholarship would mean no more school and no more hockey."

Jenny's mouth fell open. Then she shut off the recorder, thanked Mitch, and left.

Geoff sighed deeply and his head thunked back against the wall.

"That, uh…" Alex scratched his head. "Could've gone better," he said diplomatically.

Cody slapped the back of Mitch's head. "You're an idiot."

Geoff grunted, apparently agreeing with both of them.

Mitch rolled his eyes and asked if he could go home.

TWENTY-TWO

THE ARTICLE WOULDN'T APPEAR IN THE MOUNTAIN Chronicle until Wednesday, but it went up on the Chronicle's website first thing Monday morning. It didn't mention the Westlakes, Westlake Waterless Printing, or Greta Westlake. However, weaved into the body of the story was a subtle mention that Mitch didn't see much support from his mom, and that he was dependent on the partial hockey scholarship, like many other GH hockey players.

Geoff wasn't worried. He didn't anticipate an article from a small student newspaper to affect the Westlake business, especially since the Westlakes weren't mentioned by name. Coach Bedley had been right in selecting Jenny Lynn to write the article. It was thought-provoking, while questioning how much was too much for a student athlete. Had Alex not already sent the first draft of his book to his editor, he would've used Jenny Lynn's article as a reference. Hell, he still might.

For reasons Alex didn't understand, Geoff intended to stay with Westlake Waterless Printing, despite his impending divorce from Mitch's mom. The man either loved his job or was too dedicated to leave. But he was, he'd told Alex, Mitch, and Cody this morning over a breakfast of bacon and French toast, transferring from the head office in Manhattan to the smaller satellite office in Burlington to be closer to Mitch. As the Account Director for the East Coast, his job involved a lot of travelling and he could technically work from anywhere.

It was early evening on Monday and Alex and Cody were watching some kind of dance competition marathon on TV, while Mitch napped with his head in Alex's lap. Mitch and Cody weren't on spring break until next week, but they'd skipped classes today, given the weekend's activities, to stay home and rest, and would get notes from their classmates. Geoff was cooking them dinner in the kitchen, something that smelled like garlic and onions and sautéing chicken.

Feet propped up on the table next to a wooden treasure box with a skull and crossbones etched into the front—except the crossbones were hockey sticks and the skull was wearing a mask—Alex responded to text messages from Yager, JP, and Jay. Fed up with answering the same questions three times, he created a group chat and texted them all an update at the same time along with brief introductions to each other.

Dudes! Yager texted. *You're the fuckers who played with Dean in college?*

Alex smiled at Yager's manners and put his phone away. He nudged the box to the side a bit so he could stretch without knocking it off the table.

"Hey, Mitch?" he'd asked this morning when Mitch had come back into his bedroom after his shower. "What's this?"

Mitch took one look at the box in Alex's hands and narrowed his eyes on Alex. "Were you snooping?"

"Maybe."

"Under the bed?"

"I'm a good snooper?"

Mitch snorted and sat on the bed next to Alex. "Guess I can't get too mad, since I snooped through your journals." He took the box from Alex and set it on his lap, then opened it.

Inside were a dozen wooden sun catchers. A sun, a moon, a couple of stars, a 3D box, a heart, a distended oval. All with an inset piece of glass, or a circle of glass hanging by a thread, to reflect the sun.

"These are beautiful." Alex picked up a sun made of the same wood as the small sun catcher that hung in Mitch's bedroom window. "Why don't you hang them up?"

"My brother made these," Mitch said.

"You said once he's a woodworker?"

"He was. Before he went to work with my mom. Sun catchers were his niche, and I thought for sure he'd open up a small studio someday." Mitch's mouth kicked up. "He used to try out new shapes and give me one once he'd perfected it. He made this box too. But when he—" Mitch lost his smile and pressed his lips into a tight line.

"When things changed?" Alex prompted.

Mitch shrugged. "I took them all down from where they hung in my window at home. They were a reminder of what we used to have, and it hurt to look at them. Honestly, I don't know why I kept them."

"Hope." Alex placed the sun back in the box. "Hope that things might get better between you someday?"

Mitch rested his head on Alex's shoulder. "Maybe."

"Did he make this one too?" Alex gestured at the sun catcher in the window. "And the one in the living room downstairs?"

"Yeah. Maybe it's time I put a couple back up?" Mitch yawned and settled back into Alex. Within seconds, he was asleep.

"You know," Cody said now from the loveseat perpendicular to Alex, "it wasn't just the money thing."

"Huh?" Alex shook his head. "Sorry, what?"

Cody jerked his chin at a sleeping Mitch. "The reason

he's so tired? It's not just because he took on extra students to make money. He misses you, so he's been keeping himself busy to distract himself."

Alex ran his hand through Mitch's hair and watched his chest rise and fall. The right thing to do would be for Alex and Mitch to take a breather from each other, let Mitch get himself back on track. But just the thought of that made the back of Alex's neck break out in a cold sweat. Mitch trusted him. Trusted him not to play with his heart that way, not to make relationship decisions without talking to him first. And frankly, despite what had happened, Alex firmly believed they were stronger together. They just had to figure out how to make their relationship work without Mitch going into a frenzy over it.

Besides, Alex had already told Mitch he wasn't breaking up with him over this, and he intended to keep his word. They were stuck with each other until one of them called it quits for reasons that didn't equal letting the other go for their own good.

As far as Alex was concerned, they were stuck with each other forever.

"He needs a better coping mechanism," Alex said to Cody.

"No doubt. Dance classes, maybe?"

"Hmm. Something he could practice at home a couple hours a week might work better. What about music lessons?"

"He'd probably like that." Cody gave Mitch a fond look. "Piano or something."

Alex tugged a lock of Mitch's hair and grinned down at him, feeling his heart clench in affection for him. "He'd be a maestro before the end of the year, wouldn't he?"

"Probably. Overachiever."

The doorbell rang, startling Mitch into wakefulness.

Geoff turned from the stove and raised an eyebrow at Alex and Cody. It was Cody who went to answer since Mitch was still occupying Alex's lap.

"Hey," Alex said as Mitch's eyes opened.

Mitch reached up and ran a hand over Alex's jaw. "Hi," he whispered, voice sleep-rough.

There was a commotion from the front of the house. An unfamiliar voice told Cody to get the fuck out of the way. Cody responded with a snapped "You can't just barge in here, douchebag!" and two pairs of feet clomped down the hallway. And then a stranger strode purposefully into the room, followed by a furious Cody.

The stranger was about six feet tall with a swimmer's build. Dressed in pressed dark slacks and an open wool coat that reached his knees, he was GQ in the flesh: only a hint of five o'clock shadow, hair slicked back, tie perfectly tied, suit coat buttoned. He had Mitch's chocolate brown eyes and the same curly hair, although where Mitch's hair was brown, the stranger's was ash blond.

Alex knew the stranger's identity immediately. This was Dan, Mitch's brother.

Mitch sat up and stared, first at his perfectly put together brother, then at his fuming best friend, who stood glaring metaphorical daggers at Dan—seriously, if looks could kill—then at his dad, who looked just as surprised as Mitch felt, then at his boyfriend, who wasn't any more pleased than Cody. His scowl was ferocious. And kind of hot. And with his arms crossed over his chest that way, huge biceps hugged by his tight-fitting T-shirt? Under different circumstances, Mitch would've dragged him upstairs.

Instead, he turned back to his brother and the mess his life had suddenly become. "Did you get lost on your way somewhere?"

Dan slung his fancy overcoat over the back of one of the island barstools. "Don't be a smart-ass. Hi, Dad."

"Son. What are you doing here?"

"Don't sit down," Cody snapped at Dan. "You're not staying."

Dan huffed and leaned against the island, crossing his feet at the ankles.

Mitch looked around him to his dad. "Did you know he was coming?"

"He asked me for your address," his dad said, moving the pan off the burner. "But he didn't tell me why."

"Can you please stop talking about me like I'm not here?" Dan snapped.

"This from the guy who's ignored me for the past few years?" Mitch said, at the same time as Cody said, "You're not here. You're leaving," and thrust Dan's coat into his arms.

Dan ignored Cody and addressed Mitch. "I wouldn't have had to come all this way, had someone told me you'd passed out and been taken to the hospital. Instead, I had to find out from some fucking amateur newspaper article."

"I didn't know you cared."

Dan had the grace to flush. "I deserve that. Look, can we talk. Please?"

Mitch got comfortable on the couch, propped his feet on the coffee table, and waved a hand at Dan. "Talk."

Dan glanced from their dad, to Cody, to Alex—who he squinted at, as if he recognized him, but eventually dismissed him. "Alone?"

"Why should I?" And yes, Mitch was aware he sounded like a petulant five-year-old.

Alex bumped their shoulders. "Go."

"Fine. But I'm not happy about it."

Alex grinned at him and rubbed Mitch's back as he got up. "Noted."

"Come on, then," Mitch said to Dan, who was eyeing Mitch's treasure box on the coffee table as if he'd never seen it before.

Mitch led Dan into his bedroom, slamming the door behind them. Because he could.

He took a seat on his bed while Dan wandered the room. Dan picked up a textbook, then set it back down again. Peered at a photo of Mitch and Cody tacked to the wall. Shoved a dirty sock into a corner with his foot. Played with the ear of the little Alex Bear Alex had gifted him on Halloween.

He was nervous.

Well, Mitch didn't get nervous. Okay, that was a lie. Alex made him nervous all the time just by breathing.

"How did you know about the article?" Mitch hugged a pillow to his chest. "Did Dad tell you?"

Dan cleared his throat and muttered, in a very quiet voice, "Google Alerts."

Mitch stared at him. "That's weird and vaguely stalkerish."

This was so bizarre. Mitch had lived here almost two years and he could count on one hand the number of conversations he and Dan had had in that time. And he wouldn't need every finger. Not to mention that Dan had barely spoken to him over Christmas. So how did one trip to the hospital change things?

"Yeah, well." Dan sat on the window seat. "It's the only way I can keep up with you."

"Why would you want to?"

Dan leaned his head back against the window and closed his eyes. "I have quite the story to tell you." And then he did.

The story went something like this: Once upon a time, there was a boy who wanted to build things, and he took all sorts of classes after school to become better at working with wood, eventually becoming quite the skilled wood-worker. But the evil witch—AKA, his mother—somehow convinced him that there was no money to be made, no recognition to be had, in that type of career. So he caved and went into the family business instead, putting all of his aspirations aside.

But, midway through college, he had a change of heart. "No more business degree!" he decried. The evil witch, however, threatened to withhold the boy's younger brother's college tuition, if the boy didn't finish his studies and come work for her.

"I'm sorry, she did *what*?" Mitch's screech echoed around the room and he winced when it aggravated the headache that hadn't quite abated.

"It's the only reason I stayed at Columbia." Dan's voice was flat, dead. "I didn't want to be the reason she took your tuition away."

"She did that anyway when I told her I wanted to play hockey and didn't want anything to do with the family business."

"Yeah. The article mentioned the hockey scholarship and I asked Dad about it, and…" Dan leaned his elbows on his knees and dropped his face into his hands, pressing his palms against his eyelids.

"I'm sorry," Mitch whispered. "It must've been horrible to have that hanging over your head." A heaviness expanded from his core, leaving him cold. Swallowing past a bitter taste in his mouth, he fell sideways onto the bed. "Does Dad know about this?"

"No."

His mom had always been distant, but this…this was… He didn't have the words to express how awful it made him feel, knowing that she'd dangled this over Dan's head for years. As if they were pawns in her game of manipulation.

"They're getting a divorce," he said.

"Yeah."

Mitch buried his nose in his pillow and muttered, "This doesn't explain why you've been so mean to me." The five-year-old was back, less petulant, more hurt.

Dan's hands fell away and he looked at Mitch head-on. "At first, I was pissed. At you too, even though you had nothing to do with it. Misguided, I know. And then I got scared that if Mom saw us together, she'd think I told you about the arrangement we had and take your tuition away, anyway. Stupid, but…" His shoulder twitched. "And then I really *was* pissed when I found out you were going to a non-Ivy League school for freakin' kinesiology of all things. I couldn't believe she put her support behind that, except it turns out she didn't, so…"

"And you found out the truth, and came here to…what, exactly?"

"Apologize," Dan said, and Mitch almost fell off the bed. "And explain. But mostly apologize. I should've talked to you about this a long time ago. Instead, I let her manipulate me. Let her dictate my life. You were brave, Mitch." He smiled at Mitch and it was his old smile, his Dan-the-proud-older-brother smile. "You stood up to her and did what you wanted, damn the consequences. I took the coward's way out."

"No." Mitch joined him on the window seat. The window

was cold at his back, matching the feeling spreading through his limbs. "No, you were trying to protect me. I get it. I don't like it, but I get it. Maybe if you'd talked to me about it, we could've come up with a solution together, one that didn't have you doing a degree you hated and treating me like dirt."

Dan grimaced. "I'm sorry," he said, dejection rounding his shoulders. "I'm so sorry."

He was only a year older than Alex, but he looked a lot older, as if life had aged him prematurely. Still handsome, but the lines around his mouth and eyes were deeper than they had been at Christmas. Mitch wanted to stay mad. He had over five years of anger built inside him, anger and confusion and an aching sense of loss.

Mitch rubbed a palm with his thumb. "I thought it was my fault. That I did something to make you hate me."

Dan's breathing stuttered and he ran a hand over his chest. "No. God, no. I'm so sorry you ever felt that way."

Enough. That was enough. Dan was wrecked: voice hoarse, eyes watery. Even his suit seemed to droop. As much as Mitch wanted to stay mad, he also desperately wanted his brother back. If Dan could come here and eat crow, then Mitch could meet him halfway.

"I forgive you," he said.

The breath Dan sucked in was unsteady and wet, and he turned his face, presumably to wipe his eyes. Mitch did the same and then chuckled at the absurdity of the situation. Two grown men trying unsuccessfully to hide the fact that they were crying from each other.

Dan rubbed his hands on his slacks. "Thank you."

"You're welcome."

"Are you okay? The whole passing out thing," Dan tacked on when Mitch looked at him with a question on his face.

"Yeah, I'm fine. It's been a hectic year. I guess it caught up with me."

"I'd like to hear about it."

"Yeah?" Mitch smiled at the floor. "Maybe you could stick around for a few days?"

"I can do that."

"Cool." Mitch tried not to blush like a younger brother whose older brother had just bestowed him with praise for a job well done. And failed.

"Cody's going to be mad at me forever, isn't he?"

"Yup."

Dan grunted. "Who's the jacked guy downstairs?"

"Alex. My boyfriend."

"Why does he look familiar?"

"He plays defense for Tampa."

"Holy shit, Alex Dean?" Dan goggled at him. "I didn't know he's gay."

"He's not. He's demi." Shit, he shouldn't have said that. It wasn't Dan's business and it wasn't Mitch's secret to tell. Although knowing Alex, he'd probably shrug and tell Mitch it was no big. He'd told his brother, not the world.

"Demi what?" Dan asked.

"Sexual."

"The hell is that?"

Mitch explained, watching Dan's forehead furrow as he did so.

"That's a thing?"

"Yup. You can't tell anyone."

"Goes without saying." Dan nudged Mitch. "Alex must really like you then, huh?"

Mitch grinned wide, happiness making him feel weightless. "Yeah."

TWENTY-THREE

MAY 2009

THE HUM OF THE HOSPITAL'S TRACK LIGHTING WAS the only sound Alex registered. He was sure there were others. Nurses conversing down the hall, the squeak of shoes on tile, the rattle of a cart rolling by, the drone of the newscaster on the TV in the waiting room. He heard none of it.

He'd arrived an hour ago, less than eight hours after the phone call informing him that Grandpa Forest was in the hospital again with pneumonia. He'd come to visit, only to be sat in a chair in a corner of the waiting room and handed a bag of Grandpa Forest's things… The clothes he'd worn into the hospital. His ugly brown loafers. His wallet. The wedding ring he never took off, even though Joanie Dean had been gone for almost thirty years now.

Grandpa Forest had passed away while Alex was somewhere over North Carolina. But it didn't make sense. Alex had visited him last week at the long-term care facility and he'd been fine. Unresponsive, but alive. Someone had made a mistake. Alex needed to find a doctor and explain that they had it wrong, but the only other people in the waiting room were a couple who must've been waiting for word on a loved one's surgery, and the volunteer who directed visitors.

Alex blinked, and there he was, nine years old again, days after his dad left. Grandpa Forest came to stay with them for four months to make sure Alex and his mom were okay. Blink, and Grandpa Forest was taking Alex through the sports store and buying him a pair of rollerblades so he could play street hockey in the alley with the neighborhood kids during the summer. Blink, and Grandpa Forest was helping Alex wrap a Christmas present for his mom. Blink, and Grandpa Forest was showing him how to do a mean cannonball into the community pool. Blink, and he was talking to Grandpa Forest on the phone about a game gone wrong. Blink, and he was waving to Grandpa Forest and his mom in the stands at the first game he'd played as a Glen Hill College Mountaineer. Blink, and he and Grandpa Forest were making faces at his mom behind the camera on college graduation day.

An elephant was sitting on his chest, pressing into him until he couldn't breathe, until he thought he might die too. He couldn't stay here, couldn't stay in this place of death anymore, but he couldn't move. Couldn't think. Couldn't do anything but stare at the wall and hold tight onto Grandpa Forest's possessions—all he had left of him.

"Sweetie, is there somebody I can call for you?" the volunteer asked.

He must've answered, because what felt like thirty seconds later, but was probably closer to thirty minutes, JP and Jay were suddenly there. They sat on either side of him. JP placed a hand on his knee, and Jay, one on his shoulder.

"Hey, man." JP rubbed Alex's knee. "Mitch called us. He was about to walk into an exam when the nurse or whoever called, so he sent us."

JP's mouth continued to move, but the frantic hum of the lights was back, and Alex couldn't hear past it. The world continued on, but for Alex, it had stopped hours ago when the person who'd been his rock for most of his life had died.

Somehow, he didn't know how, he ended up curled up on Jay's couch. In a fog, the world dimmed and incomplete, he hugged Grandpa Forest's bag of belongings to his chest like a beloved childhood teddy bear, and slept.

Mitch was there when Alex woke up.

For one aching minute, he was so damn glad to see Mitch that his heart soared and his pulse thrummed. But then he remembered why he was here, where he'd spent his morning, and his heart dropped into his stomach, leaving him trying to breathe through the pain.

Crouched next to the couch by Alex's head, Mitch reached out and pulled an unresisting Alex in. "Alex. God, I'm so sorry."

Alex's soul was being torn apart by angry claws, and he stuck his face in Mitch's neck. Every part of him ached, the hurt in his heart spreading outward and taking over his body. Mitch's arms were tight around him, taking some of the pain away, but he still felt like he was going to disintegrate into nothing and float away.

"He's gone," he croaked into Mitch's shoulder, chest squeezing.

"I know, babe." Mitch's own tears wet Alex's neck. "I know. I'm so sorry."

Mitch moved Grandpa Forest's bag of personal things onto the coffee table and climbed onto the couch. It was barely big enough for Alex, let alone both of them, but they made it work, Alex's back wedged into the couch, Mitch half on top of him so he didn't fall onto the floor. Mitch kissed Alex's forehead, his wet eyelids, his hot cheeks. Something moved through Alex that wasn't grief. Something closer to peace. Mitch did that.

"He's with your Grandma Joanie now," Mitch said.

Alex's eyes burned again and his throat went thick. He couldn't do anything but nod. When people left, it was always hardest on those left behind. When Alex's dad had left, his mom had been a rock but Alex had heard her crying in her room at night and caught her staring into space in the middle of conversations. Judd Dean hadn't been a bad dad. He didn't hit them, didn't drink excessively, didn't talk down to them. He just didn't care. It was as if he was simply going through the motions of being married and having a kid because it was what was expected of him. The last time Alex had heard of him was when he'd been in high school, when his mom and Judd had officially divorced. But he hadn't seen him since the day he left. It had been over fifteen years and Alex hadn't heard a peep from him. He must have loved Alex's mom at some point, right? To marry her?

Alex tried to picture himself leaving Mitch for any reason, and his eyes watered again. "I didn't get to say goodbye."

"I know." Mitch ran his hand over Alex's chest. "People aren't always lucky enough to say goodbye before someone dies."

"No, I mean… When my dad left. I never got to say goodbye." Alex stared at the popcorn ceiling. A tear escaped and trailed down his temple toward his ear. "He was there when I went to school in the morning, then gone when I came home. All my mom said for a long time was 'He had to go.' I never knew what that meant. How could you have to leave someone you love? But I don't think he loved us, not really. I think he was waiting for something better to come along. And when it didn't, he went out to find it."

"And did he?" Mitch asked. "Find it, I mean?"

Jay poked his head into the room. He left just as quickly.

"I don't know," Alex said. "I never spoke with him again. A few years ago, I thought about trying to track him down, but why bother? He would've gotten in touch if he'd wanted to see me. And now Grandpa Forest is gone too."

"He loved you." Mitch propped himself on an elbow and caught Alex's gaze. "He loved you so much."

"I know, but…" Alex wiped his eyes. "I thought I wanted him to remember me so he could see me play in the NHL. But I realize now that I just wanted—" His breathing hiccupped and he had to force the words out past a too-tight throat. "—I just wanted to say goodbye."

Mitch sighed and rested his forehead against Alex's. "Like you didn't get to say goodbye to your dad. Is that why you text me goodnight every night?"

"And to tell you I love you. So you know. In case something happens. It's important."

"God." Mitch wiped his face on Alex's T-shirt. "Stop talking. You're breaking my heart."

Miraculously, it made Alex chuckle. It was watery and constricted, but it was there. "How did your exam go?" he asked, just to think of something else for a bit.

"Please. Neuromuscular exercise physiology? I killed it."

"And creative writing? How'd that one go?"

"I didn't have one, remember? Just the final portfolio assignment that was due last week."

"Right." Alex lifted his head in search of tissues, and flopped back down when he didn't spot a box within arm's reach.

"Thanks for your help with that, by the way."

Jay poked his head in again.

"Jay," Alex said before he could leave. "What's up?"

"Sorry." Jay held up Alex's phone. "I've been fielding your phone calls. Your grandpa's lawyer called earlier. She's coming by to talk to you about the will."

Mitch sat up. "That's fast."

Jay shrugged. "She didn't know how long Alex would be in town."

"How did she know, though?" Alex asked. He sat up and scrubbed his face with his hands. "I haven't called anyone."

"I guess the hospital called your grandpa's facility, and they called his lawyer. They've been trying to reach you too."

Fuck, there were things to do when someone died and Alex was ignoring it all, but he didn't know where to start. His mom might know. Or Google. *What to do when someone dies.* He'd probably get over a million hits, but at least it'd be a start. First he had to call his mom, though. Shit. He so didn't want to be the bearer of bad news.

Grandpa Forest's lawyer was a tiny Italian woman with a booming voice and a slick cap of dark hair. Okay fine, she was only a couple inches shorter than Mitch, who was five-foot-nine, but for Alex, who was six-foot-four, anyone below six feet was short.

Alex sat next to Mitch at the kitchen table, across from Benedetta Onetti. Jay was chopping something at the kitchen counter, presumably for dinner, although Alex suspected it was for show and that he was not-so-subtly eavesdropping.

Benedetta was apparently a huge hockey fan, and she started off saying how it was too bad Tampa hadn't made it to the playoffs. Then she asked Alex for his autograph while Mitch stared on in wide-eyed fascination, before seeming to remember why she was there and getting down to business.

"Your grandfather left you everything. The money in his accounts, his possessions, his house," she said.

Mitch turned to Alex. "I didn't know he had a house."

"Oh, it's all paid off," Benedetta said. "And it has been for years. But he never had the heart to sell it. It's where he lived with his wife before she passed. It's being rented by a young couple at the moment, but the lease is up in about eight months. We can re-visit what you'd like to do with it in a couple of months, Alex." She pulled an envelope out of her briefcase and handed it to Alex. "He left this for you."

The envelope had the firm's address in the top left corner, and Alex's name written in the middle in Grandpa Forest's neat handwriting. Alex swallowed hard and traced the lettering. Part of him wanted to tear into the envelope, desperate for any last word from Grandpa Forest. The other part of him didn't want to acknowledge that this would be it, the final time he'd ever hear from the person who'd been his sounding board for so long. He wanted to tuck the letter away, keep it someplace safe with the knowledge that Grandpa Forest wasn't too far away if he ever needed him.

"You don't have to open it now," Mitch told him.

Ignoring the three sets of eyes on him, Alex carefully opened the envelope and pulled out the single sheaf of paper.

Alex, my boy,

Once I pass on and join your grandma, I need you to do two things for me. First, take some of the money I've left you and donate it to a charity, anything that'll help kids play sports. You and I both know that sometimes a kid needs a helping hand once in a while. Second, save yourself the hassle and skip the funeral. I don't need a priest to send me off to my maker. Grandma Joanie will be there to show me the way, so don't worry about that. Cremate my old bones and bury them next to your grandma, but then have a party. A big one. Invite everyone you know. (And there better be ketchup chips.)

Be happy, Alex, my boy. Be smart. Be brave. And play as much hockey as you can (and kick some butt while you're doing it).

All my love,
Your Grandpa Forest

Alex laughed and cried at the same time and the words on the page blurred even as the elephant finally stepped off his chest. He wiped his nose with the back of his hand, feeling lighter than he had all day.

"What's so funny?" Mitch asked. His smile for Alex was inquisitive and soft.

Alex handed him the letter. "It's just Grandpa Forest. Saying goodbye."

TWENTY-FOUR

AUGUST 2009

ALEX WAS NERVOUS. AND IT WAS FREAKIN'
adorable.

The bookstore at Bay and Richmond, in downtown Toronto, had been turned into a mock event venue for Alex's book launch and signing. Display tables and stands had been moved aside or relocated to make room for a folding table draped with a white tablecloth and topped with a dozen copies of Alex's new book. Next to the table was a thirty-six by twenty-four-inch poster with an image of the book cover, short quotes praising the book from review sites, newspapers, and other authors, and a picture of Alex's handsome face.

People browsed the bookstore, yet four dozen more stood in line, waiting for the man of the hour, who should've been sitting behind the table, ready to sign copies of his book for his fans.

But instead, he was hiding in the employee lunchroom, tugging at his tie. "I changed my mind."

"About the book launch?" Mitch peered out the lunchroom door's glass window. The line extended from the table, around displays, to the front of the store, out the door, and onto the street. Wow. "Because I'm pretty sure it's too late for that."

"About the signing," Alex corrected. He finally managed to get his tie off and paced a path between the refrigerator and the little round table. "I should've done it in Tampa."

The NHL preseason started in less than two weeks and Alex was needed in Tampa for team practices, which was why he'd pitched it as the book launch location. His editor, Kate Harvey, had ixnayed that idea. Alex's publishers wanted a huge turnout and big name bloggers and journalists. They wouldn't get that in Tampa, where hockey just wasn't as popular as it was in the north. So here they were, at the end of August at the height of a scorching hot summer in Toronto, on the second of Alex's three days off and four days before Mitch needed to head back to GH for his junior year.

Yet Alex wasn't having it.

Out in the bookstore, Toni met his eyes through the door's window. She tapped her watch.

Alex was officially ten minutes late to the start of his own book launch.

The publicist who'd organized the event appeared from behind a long display of magazines, where she'd hidden half a dozen boxes filled with additional copies of Alex's book. Upon spotting the table with the empty chair where her author should've been sitting, her jaw clenched and she headed for the lunchroom Alex and Mitch were currently occupying.

Mel Hassler was cute and perky, all blond and blue-eyed, with a smile a mile wide. But holy crap, she was scary. Mitch exited the room, giving Alex a minute alone, and blocked her entrance.

"I just need five more minutes," he said.

Her eyes narrowed. "You have two."

"I can work with two."

She crossed her arms over her chest. Mitch palmed the

handle behind him and opened the door, slipping back into the lunchroom while keeping an eye on the scary dragon lady. She didn't move, even when he closed the door and held up two fingers to indicate he had two minutes.

She scowled at him through the glass.

All right, then.

Mitch hustled Alex to a corner of the kitchen, out of Mel's direct line of sight, and gave him a hard, fast kiss.

"Cody's going to meet us out back with the car," he lied. "You ready to go?"

"Go?" Alex stared at him blankly. "I can't leave. All these people are here and most of the team came out to support me. I can't let Kate and the publisher down, and oh my God, I can't believe your reverse psychology just worked on me."

"Me neither," Mitch said, ridiculously proud of himself.

"Ugh." Alex leaned against the counter and scrubbed his hands over his face.

Mitch grabbed Alex's tie off the counter and ran the silk through his fingers. His man looked especially dashing today in fitted black suit pants and a light blue shirt. The forest green tie Mitch held would make Alex's eyes pop. Alex was tense as hell, the prospect of being on display in front of all the people here intimidating the crap out of him. It was kind of funny, given that he played hockey in arenas that held thousands.

Moving Alex's arms out of the way, Mitch slipped the tie around his neck. "You're going to be awesome out there."

"You think?"

"Uh-huh." Finished knotting the tie, Mitch took a step back and ran his hands down Alex's arms. "Besides, those people out there are probably way more nervous about meeting you than you are about meeting them."

"If you say so."

"I don't get it." Mitch eyed Alex curiously. "Remember when you were a guest panelist at the kinesiology lecture? The day we met? You didn't seem nervous at all."

Alex shook his head. "That was different. I wasn't promoting myself. This is… This is way more personal."

Mitch put his arms around him and held him close, but pulled back abruptly. "Holy shit balls!"

"What?" Alex pulled back, panicked eyes huge in his face. "What's wrong?"

"You never answered my question." Mitch fisted a hand in his hair. "I can't believe I forgot."

"What question?"

"About why the NHL is and isn't what you expected."

It took Alex a second, but when he finally figured it out, he threw his head back and laughed, long and loud. The sound never failed to make Mitch grin like a dummy.

Alex brought Mitch's hand up to his lips and kissed the back. "God, I love you. I'll tell you later. Promise."

"I'll hold you to that."

There was a hard knock at the door. Mitch tugged on Alex's hand to get him moving. "My two minutes are up. That's how long I had to get you out there."

"Wait, come back here." Alex reeled Mitch in and kissed him softly, making Mitch's belly flip. They shouldn't be kissing where anyone could walk in on them, but with Mel watching the door, Mitch didn't worry. She knew about them and wouldn't let anyone barge in.

Two days from now, they'd fly back to Tampa. And then two days after that, Mitch and Cody would fly to Vermont for school, leaving their perfect Florida summer behind. Mitch had gotten used to seeing Alex every day, but he'd have to get used to seeing him once a month until next summer.

When he looked at it that way, the school year seemed endless.

He held on to Alex tighter and nuzzled Alex's throat. Alex's hold was just as strong, unbending, as though his thoughts had gone in the same direction as Mitch's.

A second knock at the door.

"Okay," Alex said into Mitch's neck. "I'm ready."

Mitch wasn't. Not if he ever had to let Alex go.

Alex pulled back and placed a chaste kiss on Mitch's lips. "Thank you."

"For what? I didn't do anything."

Alex just smiled at him and kissed him once more before heading for the door. Mitch followed.

Because he'd follow Alex anywhere.

The roar that greeted Alex when he finally exited the bookstore's employee lunchroom was so loud, he took an instinctive step back, bumping into Mitch. Mitch's hand at his back steadied him, grounded him.

There was a line of people out the door waiting to meet him, but the group that snagged his attention was huddled together just a few feet away, carrying a huge banner that read "Congrats, Alex!" The group was made up of half his team, including Ashton Yager, plus JP and Jay, as well as his mom, Cody, and Geoff and Dan Greyson.

Alex glanced back at Mitch, who grinned merrily and joined in the cheering.

Overwhelmed, and touched beyond words, Alex's nerves finally subsided in the face of the support from his friends and family. There was only one person missing.

At the back of the group stood a tall, thin man in his eighties with a bald head and wrinkles on top of wrinkles, grinning a toothy grin from ear to ear. His green eyes, the same color as Alex's, shone with love and pride.

Alex's heart soared. Grandpa Forest?

But when he looked again, there was no one there.

Mitch's hand on his elbow dragged him back to the present. Mitch led him to the table with the empty chair behind it where he'd be signing books for the next few hours.

"Wait." Alex reversed course, taking Mitch with him to a hidden corner of the fantasy section, away from prying eyes. "Wait here a sec."

"What?"

He left a sputtering Mitch behind and went back to the table. Or, more specifically, to his messenger bag hidden underneath the table.

Mel tapped her foot impatiently. "Are you ready?"

"Two minutes."

He ignored her frustrated sigh and pulled a copy of his own book out of his bag, one he'd saved especially for Mitch. He'd gone full sixth grade and drawn a heart under the dedication, with a personal note to Mitch written in pink marker.

The dust jacket of "No Guts, No Glory" was shiny, with raised lettering and an attractive cover that depicted an action shot of a player in full gear, stick in hand, chasing after the puck. Alex's headshot was on the inside back flap, right beneath his author bio. It was all so surreal.

He headed back to Mitch. Evidently, Mitch had spent the minute Alex had been gone perusing the novels on the shelves—he now had a small stack at his feet. He turned at Alex's approach and grinned at him. Mitch had foregone his penchant for flannel for this event, instead opting for fitted charcoal pants and a light purple shirt. His curly hair flopped everywhere and he only had eyes for Alex.

God, Alex would miss the shit out of him when he headed back to Glen Hill College in a few days. He'd gotten used to having Mitch in his space. Sharing a bed, sharing meals, folding Mitch's laundry on laundry day, coordinating who got the bathroom first. Alex never thought he'd have the kind of relationship he did with Mitch, but now that he did, he wasn't ready to give it up, even if only for the school year.

Living together hadn't always been easy, especially at the beginning as they got used to each other. Not to mention that having Cody underfoot, whose bedroom was a door-less loft, had severely impacted their sex life. But they'd made it work and four months had flown by faster than either of them expected.

Mitch now had full monetary support from his dad so that he wouldn't have to work as much while at school, as well as a tidy sum from his full-time work at the café in the Channel District that he'd put into a savings account. He'd also grudgingly agreed to let Alex pay for his flights to Florida so he could visit without straining his financials. And instead of working himself to the bone in an effort to distract himself from how much he missed Alex, Mitch had signed up for piano lessons. Alex had secretly bought him a grand piano as a gift that was scheduled to be delivered the day after Mitch arrived back in Glen Hill. They didn't have much space for it in the house, but Cody said that if they stored the dining room table they never used in the basement, they could put it there.

Alex handed Mitch the book.

Mitch grasped it gingerly in both hands. "For me?"

He hadn't yet seen the finished product. The advance reading copy Alex had been sent over the summer hadn't had the dedication.

"Alex," a voice growled. Alex turned and there was an annoyed Mel, glaring at him and pointing at the table. Alex touched Mitch's hand briefly before following her and finally taking his seat.

Mitch appeared from the fantasy section seconds later and tucked himself in next to his dad and Dan against a wall of sci-fi novels. He ran his hands over the front cover of Alex's book reverently, then flipped the book over and did the same to the back. Alex's gut clenched as he waited for Mitch to open the cover and flip through the first few pages. Would he think it was lame?

Mel led the first person in line over to him, which was, of course, when Mitch landed on the dedication page.

His breathing hitched. His eyes went wet. His chin trembled. He glanced at Alex with red eyes, an expression of utter devastation and profound love on his face. Alex's heart clenched so tight, he thought he could die happy right here, right now, with everything he'd ever wanted right in front of him.

He winked at Mitch, who gave him a watery smile and hugged the book to his chest.

For Grandpa Forest. I miss you every day.
For Mom, for your unwavering love and support.
And for my own real-life Adrian. Thank you for bringing love and laughter into my life when I needed it most.

A + M
Forever
I love you

EPILOGUE

THE LOCKER ROOM AT THE STAPLES CENTER IN Los Angeles was loud. They'd just won their sixth game in a row and Mitch had scored three out of tonight's four goals, thank you very much.

He put his suit on after his shower, because playing in the NHL meant you had to be fancy. The chain with the ring hanging off it that he only took off for games went around his neck, tucked under his shirt.

There were only about a dozen people who knew about the ring. His dad and Dan. Cody. Yano and Marco. Alex's mom. JP, Jay and Leah. Ashton Yager. A couple of Alex's teammates. People they trusted with their secret. If anybody else asked about it, Mitch said it was a family heirloom. It wasn't exactly a lie. Alex had given him Grandpa Forest's wedding ring. Sometimes Mitch still couldn't believe that he'd been wearing it for almost four years.

He and Alex had talked about it at New Year's all those years ago—a guy didn't come out in pro sports. Even when they marry the love of their life. If that had made the past few years a little more difficult than they'd expected, they dealt with it as a couple.

"Yo, Grey." Fraser clapped him on the shoulder. "Coach wants to talk to you."

Dread pooled in Mitch's belly. Dread and irritation.

With the trade deadline only four days away, Coach could only want to see him about one thing.

He was being traded. Again. A season and a half with Boston, two with L.A., and now he was, once again, being shipped elsewhere. He was a goddamn good player, so why did nobody want to keep him?

Did it have something to do with what he'd said to the reporter the other day? It wasn't his fault that professional reporters asked the same stupid questions as college ones.

Still, this sucked. It was like being picked last in gym class. Not that Mitch had ever been picked last, but he imagined this is what it would've felt like. Shitty. Demoralizing. Embarrassing.

And just as he was starting to get used to L.A. too. Not that he considered it home, because he didn't. L.A. sucked. But he'd made friends on the team, the coaches liked him—he was pretty sure, anyway—and he could now manage L.A. traffic like a fucking native.

Not to mention, he and Alex would have to re-jig their schedules. They had their entire hockey seasons planned out: when Mitch would visit Alex, when Alex would visit him, and when it was simply easier for them to meet in the middle, in Denver where they had an apartment on retainer.

Trudging his way to Coach Perrault's office, he sent a message to anyone who was listening, that if he could please be traded to a team closer to Toronto, where Alex had been playing for the past four years, then he'd stop being mean to reporters. Okay, he'd *try* to stop being mean to reporters. That had to count for something, right?

He walked out of Coach's office ten minutes later. In a daze, he headed back to the empty locker room where he found his phone to FaceTime his husband.

"Hey!" Alex said when he answered. "Nice hat trick tonight." He was lying on the couch in the living room of their townhome in Toronto's Annex neighborhood, with his laptop on the coffee table next to him. He was probably working on the new romance novel he'd been writing for the past few months. The one he wouldn't let Mitch read, the jerk.

Fuck, Mitch missed Alex's face. Alex was thirty now and the laugh lines around his eyes and mouth were more pronounced, but he was no less gorgeous. Mitch took in his thick eyebrows, his green eyes, his ever-present beard. The two-year-old scar bisecting his eyebrow, the outcome of a fight that had resulted in the visor on Alex's helmet breaking and embedding itself into his face. Mitch had watched in horror from his hotel room in whatever city he'd been in at the time, as the announcers speculated on whether or not Alex was going to lose an eye.

Thankfully, the glass has pierced the skin above his eye, not his eyeball. But God, Mitch had been frantic. He still remembered sitting in that hotel room, desperately calling Alex and everyone he could think of on Alex's team until someone finally picked up.

"Alex…" Mitch ran a hand through his hair and dug his nails into his scalp.

"What's wrong?" Alex lost his smile and the picture on Mitch's screen wobbled for a second as Alex sat up. "What happened?"

"I got traded."

"Again? I'm sorry, Mitch. I know you were just starting to not hate L.A. so much." Alex's eyebrow quirked. "On the plus side, you couldn't possibly get sent any further from Toronto. Except maybe if you're going to Texas. Or Arizona. Tell me that's not where you're going."

Mitch pointed at his screen. "To you."

Alex blinked at him for a second before comprehension dawned. Excitement lit up his face, but then suspicion clouded his features. "Are you fucking with me?"

"No." Mitch shook his head for emphasis.

"If that's true, then what the hell are you still doing over there?"

Mitch couldn't help but laugh. "I just found out. I called you right away."

"Mitch." Alex brought the phone right to his face. All Mitch could see was his eyes and nose. "Go back to your apartment, pack your shit, and get your ass over here."

Mitch laughed again and it was free and happy. He couldn't stop smiling and he kept leaning into his phone, as though he could touch Alex just by being closer to the damn thing.

"I will," he said, feeling weightless with glee. He was going to play with Alex on the same team, instead of always against him. They were going to play together, live together, make a home together. Not that they hadn't done the latter two, off and on, for the past six years during the off season, but this was official. No more flying back and forth, no more syncing schedules. Just them, making a life together. "My flight's in the morning. I guess…I have a game tomorrow?"

"Yeah, you do." Alex's grin was all teeth. "Holy shit, I really will see you on the ice now."

Mitch leaned his forehead against his cubby and laughed under his breath.

"Mitch."

He brought the phone up again and if there were tears of happiness in his eyes, Alex wouldn't mention it.

"I'll see you tomorrow," Alex said.

"Yeah."

"Love you."

Mitch swallowed roughly. "Love you too."

They disconnected and Mitch left the arena, a bounce in his step. He was going home. To his husband.

Did you enjoy *On the Ice?* Check out the rest of the Stick Side series:

The Nature of the Game

Shots on Goal

Risking the Shot

AUTHOR'S NOTE II: DEMISEXUALITY

As far as I can tell, the term "demisexual" was first coined in 2006 but didn't start seeing traction until early 2008. It's entirely possible that, in 2008, most people hadn't heard of the term yet. I certainly hadn't. In fact, the first time I heard it was in late 2016. But I wanted my characters in *On the Ice* to be familiar with what demisexuality means, and since this is fiction, I took creative liberties.

Alex's experience with demisexuality closely mirrors my own, so while his journey is accurate based on my own experiences, it's important to remember that everyone's sexuality is unique.

I hope you enjoyed Mitch and Alex's story as much as I enjoyed writing it!

ACKNOWLEDGEMENTS

On the Ice would not have been the novel it is today without the help of several key people:

Shayan, who willingly read every one of my hockey scenes to make sure I got things right, and who answered numerous texts about hockey lingo. Thank you! This book would've been a hot mess without you. (Any errors or inconsistencies that remain are entirely my own.)

Foster, J.V., and John-Michael, who beta read my original draft and have been so supportive of this story ever since. You guys are awesome!

Many thanks to Gene, who willingly gave this a read when I said, "Hey, I could use another perspective." You're the best!

Thank you, Leslie at LesCourt Author Services, and Clare at Meroda UK Editing, for a beta read/content edit of my first, unpolished draft. And to Lee Hyatt for tirelessly sticking with me when I couldn't decide what the heck I wanted as cover art. Your patience is endless!

Brenda Chin, who took the time to read the manuscript of a virtually unknown author. Your intuitiveness and feedback were invaluable in making *On the Ice* as strong as it could be.

Huge thanks to Kiki at LesCourt Author Services for proof-reading and making sure everything was perfect before *On the Ice* went out to the public. I wouldn't have spotted those continuity issues without you!

To each and every one of you, you have my sincere and endless thanks!

ABOUT THE AUTHOR

Amy's lived with her head in the clouds since she first picked up a book as a child, and being fluent in two languages means she's read *a lot* of books! She first picked up a pen on a rainy day in fourth grade when her class had to stay inside for recess. Tales of treasure hunts with her classmates eventually morphed into love stories between men, and she›s been writing ever since. She writes evenings and weekends—or whenever she isn›t at her full-time day job saving the planet at Canada›s largest environmental non-profit.

An unapologetic introvert, Amy reads too much and socializes too little, with no regrets. She loves connecting with readers. Join her Facebook Group to stay up-to-date on upcoming releases and for access to early teasers, find her on Instagram and Twitter, or sign up for her infrequent newsletter.

Website: amyaislin.com

Newsletter: bit.ly/AmysNewsletter

Instagram: www.instagram.com/amyaislin

Facebook group: www.facebook.com/groups/amyaislin

Facebook page: www.facebook.com/AmyAislinAuthor

Facebook: www.facebook.com/amy.aislin

Bookbub: www.bookbub.com/profile/amy-aislin

Twitter: twitter.com/amy_aislin

Pinterest: www.pinterest.ca/amyaislinauthor

Goodreads: www.goodreads.com/author/show/16693566.
Amy_Aislin

QueeRomance Ink: www.queeromanceink.com/mbm-
book-author/amy-aislin

Made in the USA
Monee, IL
12 November 2020